MORE *than* ENOUGH

MORE *than* ENOUGH

MORE THAN SERIES | BOOK FIVE

JAY McLEAN

MORE THAN ENOUGH
Copyright © 2015 Jay Mclean
Print Edition

Published by Jay McLean
www.facebook.com/jaymcleanauthor
www.jaymcleanauthor.com

Published: Jay McLean November 2015

Cover Design: Ari at Cover it! Designs
Edited by: Vanessa Bridges at Prema Romance

Dedication

To those who struggle to find peace amongst the chaos of your silence.
May your voices be heard.

Note to Readers

Please note than More Than Enough (More Than #5) is part #5 in the More Than Series and should not be read prior to reading More Than This (More Than #1), More Than Her (More Than #2), More Than Him (More Than #3) and More Than Forever (More Than #5)

MORE than THIS

MORE than HER

MORE than HIM

MORE than FOREVER

Part I
The Falling

Prologue
Riley

HE SMILES THAT half smile I love so much. "You're kind of beautiful."

I drop my gaze, waiting for the seconds to pass before the butterflies in my stomach settle. I wait and I wait, but it doesn't seem to fade. It never does when I'm with him.

"Riley," he says, and I can hear his smile through his words. "You're blushing."

I look up, ready for the onslaught on my heart that only he can create. He's chewing his lip, his green eyes dancing with amusement. He shakes his head, then laughs and moves next to me. The warmth of his bare arm wraps around my shoulders. "You know how I feel about you but you still look surprised when I tell you. Why?"

"Because it still is a surprise to me—that you chose me over—"

He laughs again and settles a hand on my bare leg. "I had no choice," he cuts in. "I've always wanted you. I'm just lucky you let me have you." He runs his lips across my jaw, his hand drifting higher until his fingers reach my bikini bottom. "How long until the others get here?"

Wanting to feel more of him, I turn my head to the side, welcoming him. He doesn't falter, not for a second. His lips part as they move to mine and I get lost in the familiarity of his kiss. Over two years we've kissed like this and it only gets better. He lies down on the rocky embankment and pulls me with him until I'm on top and his arms are around me. His hands drift lower down my back, lightly skimming my butt. He laughs into my mouth when I moan. I pull back, a glare already in place. His eyes are shut tight, his lips pursed, trying to hold in his laughter.

"You're a tease," I tell him, sitting back down next to him.

He shoves his hand down his shorts and adjusts himself. "It's not like we can do much here." He points to our surroundings. "People can come by at any time."

I raise an eyebrow. "So?"

"Riley, you talk a lot of talk but you'd die if anyone caught us in the slightest of compromising positions."

I roll my eyes, but we both know he's right.

He waits for my laughter to settle. "Last thing off the bucket list, right?"

I follow where he's pointing, to the top of the cliff edge twenty feet above the lake we just swam in. The grin on my face can't be contained. Yesterday, there were two things left on that list. Making love for the first time was one of them. "Take The Leap," I muse.

"The Leap" is what kids around here call it. Most seniors do it during the summer right before they leave for college and Jeremy and I are no exception. It's almost like a rite of passage out of our childhoods and into the big, wide world.

Into reality.

"You ready?" he asks, standing up and throwing a hand out for me.

I take it, nodding as I do.

We walk up the path, made clear by the few hundred if not thousands of kids who have walked there before us.

"Holy shit!" he breathes out once we're at the top. His eyes move quickly from the drop to me. He takes a couple steps backward, moving further away from the edge. His brows bunch, his bare chest heaving frantically. He looks like he's in pain and I don't know why. "I think I'm afraid of heights," he murmurs.

I look over the edge, and then back at him. Then I laugh. "How can you be afraid of heights? Or better yet, how did you not know you were until this point?"

He shakes his head with so much force that beads of water fly off his shaggy, dirty blond hair, some sticking to the tips of the strands. "I don't know, Ry, but this is bad. This is really fucking bad."

For a split second I think it's a joke, but his face has paled and his breaths have become more erratic.

I step to him, taking his hands in mine. He doesn't take his eyes off me. "Jer, if you're really that afraid you don't have to do it."

His forceful breath hits my forehead. "Are you still going to?"

I nod. "Yeah, I think I am. Bucket list isn't complete if I don't. We can lie; tell people you did it too. No one will have to know."

He pulls his hands out of mine and runs them through his hair. "I don't care about that. I just..." he trails off and slowly walks closer to the edge. "Holy fucking shit," he mumbles when he looks down the drop. His voice shakes. At first I think he's laughing, but looking at him now, laughing doesn't even come close. He walks past me, moving further away from the edge and starts pacing, his hands behind his head, his fingers linked, and his head tilted back eyeing the sky. "Okay," he says, and then repeats it a few more times. He squares his shoulders and shakes out his hands. "We can do this," he says, but there's not a single hint of belief in his words. "Yeah," he nods, "I can totally do this."

He's adorable. Beyond adorable. His six-foot frame and the manly muscles that take residence there seem so out of place with his current demeanor. He's like a kid, afraid to jump off a four-foot-high diving board.

"Babe," I say through a laugh, even though I know I shouldn't. "It'll be fine. I'll hold your hand," I assure. "We can run up, jump together. You'll never even see the drop until we're falling."

He chews his thumb, his eyes boring into mine. I want him to laugh with me, as if he finally realizes how ridiculous this entire thing is. Especially for him. *I guess even big, macho jocks get afraid sometimes.* He steps toward me, his fingers linking with mine. Dropping his mouth to my ear, he whispers, "You gotta hold my hand, okay? And don't let go." He ends on a laugh, but it's not from humor. It's from nerves.

I pull back so I can see his face. There's a shadow of doubt covering all of his features. His eyebrows pinch and his teeth clamp harshly around his bottom lip.

I kiss his cheek and start pulling him away, just enough so we can get a decent run up.

I stop at a suitable spot and turn to him. "You good?"

He nods, releasing my hand so that he can shake his out—once, twice, and then a third time for good measure. He tilts his neck to either side a couple times, relaxing the muscles I can see pressing out of his tanned skin. "I love you," he says, as if it's the last time we'll ever see each other.

I laugh, not at him, but at the situation. Taking his hand and gripping it tight, I face the edge. "Ready?"

Not a second passes before I start running, holding his hand tight, not letting go—just like he asked me. It's a ten-foot run up, nothing huge, but it's enough so that he can't see the drop beyond the edge. Three more steps and we'll be airborne. One. Two. Th—

"NO!" he shouts, his hand gripping mine tighter.

I jump.

Resistance.

A resonating thud fills my ears.

Loose gravel hits my shoulders.

And I fall.

Dylan

A year and a half later.

"DOES THE AIR feel thicker here?" Dave mumbles, half turning to me with a lit cigarette in his mouth. With the kid's fiery red hair and freckles all over his face—it's pretty clear why the other boys in the unit have dubbed him "Irish."

I kick the back of his boot, urging him to keep walking. "Not that I can tell. Maybe your lungs are dying. Quit smoking."

He stops suddenly. "I'll quit smokin' when you quit preachin'." He jerks his head, suggesting I walk ahead of him.

Our shoulders bump as I take his place in the line so his smoke won't get to me. Not that I mind, but that's all Dave. He's always looking to take care of other people—something I worked out since I roomed with him during basic. See, Dave, unlike me—never wanted to be a marine, but when your old man's the type with the heavy hand and an even heavier drinking problem and your mom's left to take care of your three younger brothers, you hit a turning point. Dave's point was when he walked in on his dad using his youngest brother in place of himself or his mom. Dave chose to turn the tables that night…

So, with Drunk Dad now in lock up it was on Dave (or Davey, as his mom calls him) to take care of shit. At barely eighteen, he found himself stuck with me twenty-four seven. He soon learned I didn't have much to say, so he says enough for both of us.

He asked once why I chose this life. I told him a half-truth. I said I was avoiding. He said he was doing the same. I was too much of a pussy to admit that his version of avoiding and mine were on completely different spectrums.

Now here we are: kicking dry dirt in fuck-knows-where, Afghanistan.

"It's bullshit they make us do this," he says, and I can hear the frustration in his voice. Hell, we're all frustrated, but only he has the balls to speak it.

"It's our job," I tell him.

"You think we trained all that time to be knocking door to door looking for threats?"

I ignore him and keep my eyes on my surroundings, bringing my weapon closer to my chest.

"D?"

"What?"

"Are you happy?"

With a sigh, I mumble, "Quit with this bullshit already."

"D?"

My shoulders drop. "I'm happy enough, okay?"

"That's a fucking lie if ever I heard one," Leroy chimes in from in front of me.

"Who's talking to you?" Dave responds.

Leroy shakes his head, never once looking back. "Anyone who says they're happy in this shithole is a fucking liar."

Dave steps up next to me. "Who the fuck are you to tell him he can't be happy? Maybe D's the kind to get off on being miserable."

"Shut the fuck up, assholes," First Sergeant Fulton whisper-yells from the front of the line. He places his weapon in position, eyeing the rest of us before knocking on what feels like the hundredth door of the same old dilapidated house we've seen every day for the last few weeks.

"Yo," Dave whispers, coming up so close behind me I can feel the metal of his gun against my back. "How many more of these you think we got?"

"How the fuck am I supposed to know?"

We enter the house and go through every room, every crawl space. We open every door, flip over every piece of furniture. It's a routine check, or at least it was. It's not until I hear screaming coming from a far room that my pulse begins to pound and the adrenaline spikes.

"Put your weapon down!" someone yells.

Dave and I eye each other in the small, dark kitchen—the only source of light coming from a crack in the pieces of wood nailed over the window. Dust particles fill the air and now it's silent again, all but for the beating of my heart.

"What the fuck we do, D?" Dave whispers. Gone is the frustration in his words, now replaced with something no one should hear, let alone show. Especially here. Amidst a fucking war.

I walk past him, nudging his elbow with mine as I do. I assure him that he'll be okay even though I have no idea. But he's young, and the fear in his eyes is something I'm sure he's had to hold back in his past life.

We walk side by side through the narrow hallway, our weapons drawn, until we get to the other side of the house. The yelling starts again, only this time it's louder and more than just one voice. "Put it down!" I hear over and over.

Then another voice.

A different one.

One of a kid.

He's yelling back, his volume matching that of my unit's. He's screaming; muffled words in a different language and my feet, though they feel heavy, find a way to keep moving forward.

"Don't fucking do it!" Leroy yells.

I round the corner first, Dave behind me, to a room I'm sure was once a bedroom. Five of my brothers cramp in the space, all facing the corner just to my left, their weapons aimed, fingers on their triggers.

My gaze quickly moves to their target—to a boy no more than twelve holding a semi-automatic, his eyes frantic as his weapon moves from my brothers to me.

I was wrong. The air *is* thicker here.

"Put your weapon down!" Leroy screams, splatters of spit leaving his mouth and joining the dust flying through the dead air.

"Jesus Christ," Dave says, stepping to my right. "He's just a fucking kid." He loosens his hold on his gun, one hand in front of him—a peace offering to a kid he's never met who's aiming a gun at us. Only *here* would this situation make any fucking sense.

I try to stop him from whatever he's about to do but my feet are stuck to the floor, my hands glued to my gun, my finger on the trigger. Ready. Waiting.

No amount of training can prepare you for this. *None.* Not even in my nightmares, in the intense heat of the days or the shivering colds of the nights did I ever think I'd have to blink back the sweat falling from my brow while my finger shook—my weapon aimed at a *kid*—his life in our hands.

One wrong word is all it'd take.

One sound.

Or in Dave's case, one move.

From the corner of my eye, I see him reach into his pocket. The pocket I know carries a picture of his family. But to this boy—this scared shitless little kid—whatever's in there could be the end of him.

He screams, a sound so deafening it rings in my ears. But it's nothing compared to the sound of his gun shot, or ten, as he raises his semi above his head, screaming, chanting the words of Allah.

More gun shots, familiar ones.

Not from him, but from us.

He falls to the floor.

More screams.

Davey's in my ear now, yelling for it to stop.

It does.

I don't know how long or after how many rounds, but eventually it does.

And then it's silent again.

The smell and sight of gunpowder fills the air along with the dust and the harshness of all our breaths.

"Is he dead?" someone asks, but no one moves.

Breathe.

Blood pools around the kid's limp frame, now leaning against the wall behind him. I wipe my eyes. It's not sweat anymore. It's something no one wants to admit.

"Is he dead?" Same voice. Different tone. *Fear.*

My shoes make a squishing sound as I step forward and for a moment I think it's blood. It's not. It's clear and it trails back to the bottom of Dave's pants.

I pretend not to notice as I take another step, then another, until my ears fill with nothing but the constant roar of my heart.

Thud. Thud.

Thud. Thud.

I reach for the kid's hand to look for a pulse but his eyes snap open, stopping me.

He takes a final breath.

A final attempt.

A single, final shot.

More screams.

Then I feel the pain.

And I fall.

One
Dylan

MEDICS.

Helicopters.

Doctors.

That's pretty much all I remember after the kid let off his final round. That and an indescribable pain in my right shoulder.

Then there was the flight back home. The stares and the proud smiles as I hopped off the plane. The unwarranted attention and the nods of acknowledgment from random strangers and finally, an eerily silent cab ride home. Which is where I am now, standing on the sidewalk in front of a house I haven't been to since I left for basic. The house hasn't changed. Still the same single story, timber cladded, tiny home surrounded by a chain-link fence. It's a different color now, I notice, which means Dad finally got around to repainting it like he'd been meaning to do since we moved in eight years ago.

The TV inside is loud—louder than necessary, like it always has been. The flickering of the screen illuminates the front window of the living room, causing a light display on the front lawn.

I exhale loudly, my left hand going to my pocket and fingering my set of keys. It feels wrong to use them. Almost as wrong as it feels to knock on the door.

With another sigh, I turn my back on the house and everything it represents. Just for a moment. Because I need the time to settle down, to think, to breathe. Tilting my head, eyes narrowed, I stare at the horizon, completely fascinated by it. Strange, I know, but it seems off—the way the sun sets over the earth. It feels calm. And that calmness makes me want to run. Fast. So does thinking about Dad's reaction to seeing me. The pride in his eyes—pride greater than the smiles from everyone when

I landed on home soil. Sure it was meant to be comforting, but it wasn't. It just made me mad—because while I was here with an injured shoulder, my brothers were there. And the threats we were all searching for—they were everywhere... even in the hands and eyes of a scared shitless little boy.

I BLINK HARD, trying to push back the memories but the pain in my shoulder reminds me of the truth. It always does. Frustrated, I remove my hat and pick up my bag, then ignore the thumping of my heart as I kick open the metal gate and make my way up the uneven pavers of the path toward my home.

Home.

Like that's supposed to mean something.

I take one more look over my shoulder at the horizon, hoping the calmness it emits will somehow make its way to me. It doesn't. And without another thought, I drop my bag and raise my fist.

Knock knock.

Nothing.

I knock again. Stronger and harder so it can be heard over the television.

Silence.

He's muted the TV. I know that much. The screen still flickers but besides that, nothing.

A light shines on the side of the house from the neighbor's car as they pull into the driveway. I peel my eyes away from the lady stepping out and raise my fist again, but before I can knock, the sound of the TV starts again. Laughter, both from the TV and from the man watching it—a deep roar of a chuckle that flips my insides.

I smile.

For the first time since before the "incident," I smile. And that smile, that emotion, that sense of home is enough to make me reach into my pocket and pull out my keys. I unlock the door and with the key still in the lock, I grab my bag and push open the front door. The smell of gravy fills my nostrils and has my stomach turning.

Two steps.

That's all it takes for me to move from the front door, through the hallway, and into the doorway of the living room. I ignore the loudness of the television and look at my dad sitting in his recliner, a frozen dinner tray on his lap, his eyes on the screen and his fork halfway to his mouth.

He's aged more than I expected, but besides that, he's still my old man. Still the man who raised me. His dark beard is longer than I ever remember seeing it and for a moment I try to recall if I've ever seen him without one. I don't think I have. Through all twenty-three years of my existence he's had the same beard. Same huge towering frame. Same gentle tone and blank expression.

I clear my throat, preparing my voice so he can hear me. "Dad."

He freezes, everything but his eyes. They drift shut. And I know what he's doing because it's exactly what I'd be doing too. He's waiting. Making sure he's not dreaming… like the countless times I'd try to hear his voice *over there* during the times I'd needed to find it within myself to help me get through it all.

"Dad," I repeat, louder, because I want him to hear me. I want him to feel the same way I felt when I'd heard his voice.

His eyes snap open, his head shifting to the side and when he sees me, his eyes widen quickly. About as quickly as he stands, dropping his food onto the worn carpeted floor. He doesn't speak. Neither do I. We've never been much for talking. But he runs. Okay, maybe not runs… but that's what it seems like. At least to me. And before I can tell him to slow down because I know he's about to hurt me, I'm in his arms, held tight, and sure it fucking hurts… the sharp pain runs from my shoulder and down my back, but I ignore it. Just like I ignore the shaking of his shoulders as he holds me to him, gripping the back of my shirt in his fists. I ignore time. I ignore the way he wipes his eyes as he finally releases me and stands back, his gaze taking me in from head to toe. Then he smiles.

So do I.

And then I hear the sound that gave me the calm I needed to walk through the door. He laughs, deep and gruff. "Jesus Christ, son. You are a sight for sore eyes."

"You too, old man."

"You on R&R?"

I shake my head. "Medical."

His eyes widen, just slightly. Then he looks me over again. "Where?" he asks.

"Shoulder." I point to it.

"Fuck."

"Yeah."

"Bullet?"

I press my lips together and nod.

"Ah, shit! I probably just made it worse," he mumbles, shaking his head, his hands on his hips.

"Nah. You're good."

He rubs his hands together, his smile back in place and his gaze still on me. "Well." He claps once. "You hungry?"

"Yeah," I say through a smile wider than his.

"Why don't you go shower and I'll heat you up some food."

"Sounds great." I take a few steps down the hall toward my old room before he curses behind me.

"Your brother's taken over your room for his computer gear. If I'd known—"

"It's fine," I tell him, cutting him off. "I'll make it..." My words die in the air when I open my bedroom door, or at least what used to be a bedroom. Now it's just a room with no bed filled with more metal junk than I'd know what do with. "I can't even see the floor."

"Yeah," Dad says with a sigh. "He's been into all that shit since he got home from his deployment. He calls it work. I don't even know what the hell he does with it all."

"Where is Eric anyway?"

"I don't know. He sleeps all day, 'works' or is out all night. I don't ask questions."

"And he's still livin' at home?"

Dad chuckles. "It's been way too long since I've had both my boys home. He was already gone six years before you left for college. It'll be good."

"Or awkward," I mumble. Because it will be. It's been a long time since I'd seen him. Who knows who he is now... time + deployment can change people.

It sure as shit has changed me.

✧ ✧ ✧

I TAKE THE longest shower in the history of the world and change the bandage on my shoulder, then I eat five different versions of the same frozen, processed meat and veg—the best meals I've had in months.

Dad makes a bed for me on the floor of Eric's room. Dad did offer me his bed, but I refused. I told him I'd take the couch, but considering we didn't have a couch anymore—just two recliners—didn't help my cause.

It's comfortable though—especially considering my old sleeping quarters. Soon enough, the travel, along with the painkiller I popped with dinner catches up with me. My eyes drift shut and I welcome the calm that comes with the silence. The sweet, sweet, silence.

It doesn't last long before the bedroom door slams open, hitting the wall behind it. I jerk awake and for a moment, I forget where I am and reach for my weapon… the weapon that isn't there.

"I can't believe you live at home," a girl whispers, before the door closes and I'm surrounded by darkness again. Eric mumbles something completely incoherent and I lay frozen, unable to move or speak because right now, I don't know what the proper protocol is.

The bedsprings squeak and the girl laughs, then silence again.

Followed by moans.

Then clothes being removed.

More moans.

Springs again.

"Ouch," the girl whispers. "Wrong fucking hole, you drunk asshole."

"Okay, STOP!" I shout.

The girl squeals.

So does Eric.

So do I when a lamp falls on my head.

More shuffling.

Springs squeaking.

Then a light so bright it causes me to squint.

"D?" Eric says, standing by the light switch, shoe in his hand, naked as the day he was fucking born. He's changed. A lot. I was thirteen when he enlisted and we hadn't seen much of each other since. The occasional holiday here and there. But now he's twenty-eight and bigger than I remember. Not as big as me, though. Fuck, that would annoy him. He adds, "What the hell are you doing here?"

Removing the lamp from my face, I lean up on my elbow. I glance over at him, and then at the blonde sitting in his bed, her knees raised, gripping the blanket tight to her chest. Then I look back at my brother and smirk. "So this is why you left me stranded in San Antonio? For a girl?"

"What the fuck?" he mumbles, his eyes wide.

The girl says, "Who the fuck is this, Derek?"

"It's Eric," he says, and I stifle my laugh just long enough to say, "I'm his lover. Who the fuck are you?"

"Shut up, D!" he shouts, dropping the shoe and covering his junk. "He's my brother," he tells the girl.

"That's the story you're going with?" I shake my head. "Your dad didn't even know who I was when I showed up, *Baby*."

"Eric, what the hell's going on?" his girl fumes, her body shaking with anger.

I look over at her. "He tried to shove it in your ass, didn't he? That's how he got me."

"Dylan," Eric warns, his jaw tense and his eyes thinned to slits.

I sit all the way up, letting the blanket fall to my waist. His eyes zone in on my shoulder and the bandage that surrounds it. Then his breath and his anger seem to leave him at once. "You on medical?" The seriousness of his tone causes me to cut the bullshit and face reality.

I rub my jaw and nod at the same time.

"When did you get home?"

"A few hours ago."

"Via Germany?"

I nod again.

He returns it, his gaze moving from me to the girl in his bed.

"Should I go?" she asks, her voice calmer than before.

Eric opens his mouth, but before he can respond, I say, "It's fine." I get up and bring the blanket with me. "You guys finish what you started."

"So you're really his brother?" she asks, looking between us.

"Yeah," Eric answers for me. "This is my baby bro, Dylan."

I give her a two-finger salute as I make my way toward the door. Eric steps to the side and opens it for me. He waits until I'm in the hallway, my back to him, before he calls my name. I pause, but I don't face him. I don't want to. I know what's coming. "It's good to have you home, bro."

Two
Riley

I HEAR THE sounds outside my room, the standard morning routine of my mom getting ready for work. Normally, I count down the seconds in my head until she's gone… listening to the clicking of her heels against the hardwood floors as she makes her way to the front door, and I can be alone again. Not that her physical presence makes me less lonely. It just means I don't have to hide out in my room, away from the scrutinizing stares that follow my every step, every move, every muttered sentence that escapes unfiltered from my lips.

THE DOOR NEXT to mine, her bedroom, slams shut.

She's in a rush.

Click click click, go her heels, the sound fading as she moves further away.

She picks up her keys from the table by the front door, and for the first time ever, I actually wish time would slow because surely she's not just going to leave.

Not today.

Without a thought, I jump up from my bed and open my bedroom door, bottle still in my hand, my head spinning and feet swaying from the amount of wine I've already consumed.

She doesn't notice me standing in the hallway, watching her check her face and hair in the mirror by the front door one last time before her hand covers the handle.

I watch and, as if in slow motion, she pushes down on it. My heart hammers and breaks all at once.

"Bye Riley," she calls over her shoulder, opening the door wider.

"M-mom," I stammer, but it's a barely whisper. I try again, louder, stronger, my shoulders squared. "Mom!"

She turns around, her eyes already mid-roll. "What is it, Riley?"

I clear my throat so she can't hear the sob fighting to escape. "It's my birthday."

Her eyes narrow, just for a moment, before she says, "Shit. It is too."

I lean against the wall because standing seems impossible. Not because I'm drunk—if you can even call it that—but because her admission to forgetting my existence has made me weak.

"There's probably a cupcake in the fridge." She forces a smile so pathetic even *I* feel sorry for me. "I know how much you love to make wishes," she says, throwing in a full-blown eye roll just for extra emphasis.

Great.

She's forgotten me *and* she's mocking me.

Sighing, she closes the door and then walks with rushed steps toward the kitchen. "We have to be quick. I have a client at the salon first thing." I follow behind her, my palm against my temple to stop the pounding.

I wait for her to go through the contents of the fridge and once it's closed, I lean against it. Hastily, she opens and closes the drawers looking for what she needs and when she pulls out a packet of candles and a lighter, I almost smile. *Almost.* Because I used to believe in the power of wishes.

Unlike the other kids I knew, my mother wasn't into birthday parties, which is probably why I didn't care too much about parties, guests, balloons, games, or even cake. It was the moment my cheeks would warm from the heat of the candles. I'd close my eyes, suck in a breath, and then I'd release it with the strength of my one and only wish.

Today, there are no gifts, no guests, none of it.

Mom forces a lonely cupcake under my nose.

A single candle.

And I can see it in her eyes… they used to be filled with sadness, the same as mine. Then the sadness turned to frustration, even anger at one point. Now, they're back to matching mine. They're consumed with loss. It's a justified emotion because she has lost me.

And me? Well, I'm just lost.

She just doesn't know how much.

"Make a wish, Riley," she says through a smile faker than the eyelashes she's currently batting.

I return her smile, just as fake. "Go on," she says, and I sense her patience fading.

Another justified emotion.

I blow out the candle just to make her happy—but I don't give up my wish. Not yet.

"I'll be home late." Mom eyes me one last time, from head to toe, her gaze pausing for a beat on the bottle of Boones Farm wine still in my hand—the one she supplied me with. "You got everything you need, right?"

I roll my head against the fridge and face her, returning her pathetic smile from earlier. Then I grip the neck of the bottle tighter and lift it to my heart. "I got everything I need right here."

For a second, her features drop and her eyes seem to soften. Like she sees the girl I used to be, the girl she loved, the girl who loved her back. Her posture stoops. Her chest rises. Her breath releases. But her feet stay put. "I'll see you tonight," she says, and then moves to place a kiss on my forehead.

My eyes drift shut at the only piece of affection she's shown me in over a year. "Bye, Mom," I whisper.

And then she's gone, exiting the kitchen and slamming the front door shut behind her.

I bring the bottle to my mouth and take swig after swig until there's nothing left, all while I listen to her car start and then reverse out of the driveway.

Stupid, I tell myself, rolling my eyes and pushing off the fridge. For a second, I thought she'd come to me. Notice me. See my pain. Try to remove it like other mothers would. But she didn't. It's fair, I convince myself, because it's been over a year since the "accident." And while the sun rises and falls and the world moves on, I'm still there—stuck in my endless goddamn nightmare.

I pick up the discarded cupcake from the counter and relight the candle.

Then I close my eyes and finally let the tears fall. I inhale a breath, hold it for as long as my lungs can handle, and then I let it go.

My wish?

I wished I'd never lived to see my twentieth birthday.

Three
Dylan

I DIDN'T BOTHER trying to get back to sleep. I knew I couldn't. Instead, I went out to the garage, praying it was the one room in the house Dad and Eric had left untouched. It was exactly how I'd left it before I moved away to college. My truck was there, covered with a huge cloth shielding it from the dust. So was the engine Dad had bought me for my sixteenth birthday—something we'd worked on together.

I flicked on all the lights and removed the cover, then sat in the driver's seat and got reacquainted with my one true love. I ran my hand across the dash and rested my cheek on the steering wheel. "I missed ya, girl," I whispered, then laughed at myself because I might possibly be insane.

When the sun started to rise I stepped out of the garage and brought the smaller engine parts with me, tinkering away in the semi-light of a new day. I'd spent months doing that exact thing, only now I didn't have to keep looking over my shoulder, jumping at every sound.

The sun came up, the birds chirped, neighbors woke, and slowly, people's lives started over again.

Mine didn't.

There were no distinctions between the days. Just an endless fucking cycle of barely-awake semi-consciousness.

✧ ✧ ✧

DAD STEPS OUT from the back door, his eyes on the parts in my hand. "You been here all night?" he asks, walking toward me.

I squint from the sun when I look up at him. "Yep."

He nods once and glances at the garage. "I kept her clean for you.

Made sure to keep her runnin' while you were gone. Had to hide the keys from Eric."

"I appreciate it."

"Was that you and him yelling last night?"

"Sorry."

"He got a girl in there?"

"Yeah," I say, focusing on my half-ass job of cleaning the piston ring in my hand.

After a few seconds of silence, Dad sighs. "Listen, I'm supposed to work today, but I can call in—we can spend the day together."

"It's fine," I say, a yawn taking over my entire body. "I'm probably just gonna sleep anyway."

"Okay, son. You'll be here when I get back?"

I shrug, or at least attempt to. "I don't plan on going anywhere."

Without another word, he goes back into the house and I sit, my shoulder aching and my mind going places I don't want it to go.

My eyelids become heavy. So does everything else. I go in the house, grab the blanket from the recliner where I'd left it the night before and ignore the banging and moaning sounds coming from Eric's room. Then I head back out to the garage, throw the blanket in the back of the truck and make a new temporary bed for myself. I pop another painkiller and I lie down, my eyes focused on the metal beams making up the roof of the garage. The sounds outside are loud, or maybe I'm focusing too much on trying to hear them.

Old habits.

My phone sounds and I reach into the pocket of my discarded pants and retrieve it, swiping my finger across the screen to read the text.

Dave: *Fucking sucks here without you, my friend. Take all the time you need. I'll just cry myself to sleep at night missing your gigantic arms around my frail tiny body. I miss you, big spoon. Seriously though, make the most of it. Get money. Fuck bitches. All that shit.*

Dylan: *I'm sure you canxfindxsomeonexelse to offer your catina to.*
Dylan: *Catina.*
Dylan: *Vagina.*

Dave: *Dude. Do you even technology?*

I drop the phone and lie back down, feeling the effects of the pill as well as no sleep for the past forty-eight hours completely take over. But just as I'm about to pass out, loud music blares, rattling everything inside the garage, including my fucking truck.

I kick the blanket off me, reaching a new level of frustration, and jump down from my truck. My fists ball at my sides as I listen for the source. It's not in my house so I press down on the button for the garage door, shielding my eyes from the sun when the door lifts high enough for it to get to me. I march, in nothing but my boxer shorts, down the driveway and search up and down the street, looking for the car causing the disruption. I imagine walking up to it, pulling the driver out, and then beating his face in because fuck—I'm beyond tired, beyond exhausted, beyond giving a shit. Time + deployment + getting shot + lack of sleep = not caring + murder. Or at least in my case.

I pace the sidewalk, focused on finding the source of the music. But it's not a car. It's a house. My next-door neighbor's house. The same neighbors who shined their headlights on *my* house on *my* return home from *my* fucking war.

And now I'm back to insanity.

My strides are long, bare feet stomping through the grass of my neighbor's front yard, my anger rising with every step. I bang on the door, not caring how I look or who I upset.

Bang. Bang. Bang.

Nothing.

I knock harder.

Still nothing.

I peer through the window next to the door, feeling it shake from the base against my hands.

I knock again.

Louder.

Stronger.

Whatever the fuck the song is, it sounds like a drowning cat, clawing its way out of a chalkboard bathtub.

Insanity is an asshole.

"Yo," I shout, along with more banging.

Finally, the door swings open, the volume doubling.

There's a girl who I kind of recognize. Her feet are bare, just like mine. So are her legs—long and lean and pasty white. Her dark blonde hair's a complete mess. So is everything about her. She's wearing an over-sized shirt that goes past her hips and nothing else. She's holding a bottle in one hand, a cupcake in the other. She's older than I remember, not that I had a lot of interaction with her before. "Riley?"

She pulls a phone from somewhere inside her shirt and taps it a few times. The music stops. "What?" she snaps, dropping the phone onto the hardwood floors. She takes a sip from the bottle and cocks her hip to the side, her eyes on mine the entire time.

It's barely nine in the morning and the girl's drunk off her tits.

And it just makes me pissed. Or pissder. More pissed? What the fuck ever. "Turn the music down. Or *off*. Preferably."

She takes one final swallow before pulling the bottle away and holding it to her chest, her eyes unfocused, lids heavy. "Can you go away? Or *fuck off*. Preferably." She slams the door in my face.

"What the fuck?" I whisper, banging on the door again.

The music returns, louder than it was, and I've fucking had enough. I kick the shit out of her door. And I'll keep kicking the shit out of it until the music is off and I can finally sleep.

The door opens again. "What?!" she shouts, spitting food out of her mouth. Half the cupcake is gone. Half the icing is smeared on her lips. "Who the fuck do you think you are?"

I ignore her question and step into the house, pushing her to the side as I search for the source of the sound. It doesn't take long. A few steps down the hallway, second door on the left and I'm in a bedroom. *Her* bedroom. Whoever is singing now sounds like she's drowning while strangling the clawing fucking cat. I find the speakers set up on her nightstand and try to switch it off but I can't fucking find the power button. Now Riley's yelling from behind me, asking me what the hell I'm doing. I find the cord, follow it to the outlet and yank until the music dies.

Silence.

Sweet, sweet, silence.

"What the fuck are you doing?" she yells.

I pick up the speaker, lift her window, and throw the source of my insanity outside.

"You can't do that!"

I slam the window shut and finally face her.

Her eyes are wide. So is her stance as she glares up at me, her nostrils flared, her lips pursed. "I hope you die a rotten death and go to hell for all of eternity."

As weird as a time to think it—she's real pretty. Not that it's relevant. In fact, the irrelevance of it makes me even angrier. Because pretty girls have ugly hearts, and I've had enough of both. "I asked you to turn it down," I seethe, towering over her.

"You didn't *ask* me, asshole. You *told* me. And no. Fuck off. It's my house. My rules. Now get out!"

"My pleasure," I yell back, walking around her toward her door.

"Wait!"

I don't.

"Fucking wait!" she yells again.

I still don't.

Then something soft hits my back.

I turn swiftly. "What the hell is wrong with you?"

The cupcake's gone now, but she's still gripping that bottle like it's somehow saving her life. "You better get my speaker and bring it back to me."

Now I lose it. Beyond lose it. And I don't even care if she knows. "Look. I just got home last night. My room is gone. The couch is gone. I couldn't even sleep on the floor of my own fucking house. I tried. Oh, how I fucking tried. But everything's fucking changed since I've been gone. I can't fucking sleep at night because I hate the dark. I hate the sounds. Every fucking sound. And the only way I can sleep is with the help of the fucking meds they got me on to somehow deal with being shot in the goddamn shoulder. But that doesn't change the fact that I close my eyes and I'm fucking back there again, listening to the gunshots going off around me." Pause. *Breathe.* "I don't care who you are or what your problem is that has you drunk off your ass at nine in the goddamn morning because right now I've got a bed waiting for me in the back of my truck, and it's the best I can do, and I need to sleep because if I don't I'll probably end up killing somebody so please, please, for the love of God—" Pause. Breathe. *Calm.* "Please, just let me sleep."

She hasn't moved.

Hasn't said a word.

Hasn't even blinked.

I doubt she's even taken a breath.

But her eyes are wide and on mine and for a moment it's like she can see right through me—through the bullshit anger I've just shown and she can see the fear because I couldn't restrain it like I did with Dad and with Eric. Quickly, her chest rises with her intake of breath, as if she's coming up for air after being left to drown.

She takes a step back, and then another, away from my form of crazy. The back of her knees hit the side of her bed and I think she's about to sit down… about to let me walk away with a win. But she doesn't. She turns around and pushes her covers aside. Then she faces me. "Take my bed. I'll wake you in a few hours."

"What?"

She's staring at my bandaged shoulder. "You won't even know I'm here," she says, moving around her room, only half closing the blinds and the door to her bathroom. "You're Dylan, right?"

I nod once. "I don't need your pity. I just needed some quiet," I tell her, sighing as the reality of what I've just done sets in. "I'm sorry about—"

"It's not pity," she says, pointing to her bed. "It's understanding." She takes another swig from the bottle then offers it to me. "It helps take the edge off… keeps the nightmares away."

I take the bottle from her and take a few sips, ignoring the foul taste as it goes down my throat. Then I take her offered bed, watching her watching me with a frown on her face—but something tells me it isn't pity. It's exactly what she said. It's understanding.

She sets herself up in the corner of her room where cushions are scattered along with jars filled with pieces of paper. Then she starts silently writing in a notebook.

I turn to my side and face her, watching without really watching, feeling the exhaustion start to take over again. "Riley?"

She looks up.

And though barely awake, I ask, "What was with the cupcake?"

It takes a few seconds for her to answer. "It's my birthday today."

"Is that why you're drinking?"

"No." She goes back to writing. "My alcohol is like your medicine. It dulls the pain."

Four
Riley

I WAKE UP the next morning to Mom's standard routine: the shower switching off, her movements in the next room, and then the clicking of her heels as she leaves for the day. I sit on the edge of the bed and stare at the full bottle of wine sitting on my dresser, wondering why it is I didn't feel like drowning myself in it last night. I mean, a part of me knew. Of course I knew, but I didn't really know *why*. I was only awake a couple hours after Dylan—the boy (or more like man, now) next door had fallen asleep. I got comfortable on the floor, surrounded by cushions and an empty bottle of wine. I'm not sure what time he woke himself up, but when I finally came to, my speaker was back on my nightstand and the empty bottle I fell asleep with was next to it, two small flowers placed inside and a note that read:

> ***Thanks for letting me use your bed. I promise I'm not crazy. Just tired. And happy birthday, by the way. It's not much of a gift, but I thought you should know... you look real pretty when you sleep.***
>
> ***That was a whole lot less creepy in my head.***

I pick up the note and read it for what feels like the hundredth time and each time leaves me with the same feelings. Butterflies first, then emptiness, and then guilt. The guilt is the worst. The guilt is what has me putting the note back down. But the butterflies—they're what have me picking it up again. Over and over. Like the stupid song I have on repeat from the moment Mom leaves to the moment she returns. The same song I had playing when he showed up at my door wearing nothing but boxers and an anger in his eyes that I only ever show myself.

And it's because of that anger, I'm positive of one thing: *he doesn't know.*

That fact alone gives me the courage to do what I do next.

I turn on the speaker, switch the volume to as loud as it will go, and use the Bluetooth on my phone to start the song, filling my ears with the words of weep-inducing lyrics.

Then I pick up the bottle, take the first sip of the morning, sit down on my bed and I wait.

The song plays once.

Twice.

And by the third time, half the bottle is gone and so is my confidence and once bright mood because I'm *dumb*. Dumb dumb dumb. And seriously, by the way, why the hell would I even think he'd show up? *Here, Riley,* says dumb brain, *play that shitty music that got him so mad he basically kicked down your door and told you you were the Worst Human Alive* and holy shit I'm drunk already.

I SCOFF AT myself and stand quickly, swaying on my feet while I take another sip. I tilt the bottle too far and it pours out of my mouth and onto my chin… *drip drip drip* down my neck onto my shirt. I laugh. Because in times like these, there's no other cure but laughter, and more alcohol—which I'm now out of.

The song ends and then starts again. I drop the bottle to the floor and shuffle my feet across the carpet toward my door. I step out and start for the kitchen where Mom keeps the wine and before I've made it two steps… *knock knock.*

I stand in the hallway facing the door… looking at it—no, *glaring* at it… waiting to hear the sound again.

Knock knock.

My one sock covered foot glides across the floorboards, moving closer to the door.

"Riley!" *Bang bang bang.*

I open the door, my head lowered, eyes squinted at my one bare foot. "Where did you go?" I ask it.

"Home," Dylan shouts, and I look up at him. He looks nice. Not as nice as he looks almost naked but still… he looks nice. His dark buzz-cut hair—I assume mandatory for whatever military branch he's part of—does nothing to lessen his general good looks.

"My sock is at your house?"

"What?"

"Huh?"

His eyes are tired, which takes nothing away from the blueness of them. But he's tall. So tall I have to crane my neck to look at him. He still wears the same clothes I'd seen him in through the years he lived next door. White tank, often grease stained from working on his or his friend's car, and a flannel shirt over it. It's the same way his dad dresses, and even his brother. I guess that's what happens when you don't have a woman living with you. You dress in whatever you can buy in bulk for cheap and move on.

He rubs the few days' growth on his jaw while he watches me look him over. "Your what is where?" he shouts, then rolls his eyes and steps inside, carefully placing me to the side so he can march to my room. I follow behind him and watch as he unplugs the speaker from the socket. *Why doesn't he just turn it off?*

He spins around, his eyes immediately locked on the empty bottle on my floor. "How drunk are you right now?" he huffs. "And where is your other sock?"

I scoff, a little confused. "You said it was at your house."

He lifts his gaze. "What?"

"Huh?"

He shakes his head. "You're a hot mess, Riley."

I shrug. "Thank you for my flowers."

He looks from me, to the flowers, then to his note sitting on my bed. He huffs out another breath, his shoulders dropping with the force of it. "So listen," he says, sitting on the bed and moving the note to my nightstand. "I know it was probably a once off for you but can I crash for a few hours in here? My brother—"

"Yes."

His smile is instant. It's also hot. I'm pretty sure I hate his smile. And I'm definitely sure I hate him—or, at least, how he makes me feel.

He kicks the bottle on the floor and watches it roll away from him and toward me. "I take it you had a good time last night… celebrating your birthday and all."

"No."

"No?"

I shake my head.

He looks around the room. I stand with my hands at my sides, pressing one foot on top of the other, willing myself to stay put and not run to the fridge for the other bottle like I really want to do. "So I tried to sleep last night and when I couldn't I started thinking about you," he says.

"Oh?" *Fuck you, butterflies.*

He shakes his head quickly. "Not like that… not like, in a creepy way."

"Oh." The first "Oh" was a question. This one was a semi-disappointed, semi-guilty statement.

"So I think I have you worked out."

"You do?" I ask, clearly surprised.

"Well," he says, eying the corner of my room where I ended up sleeping last night. "From what I know about you, which isn't much… and the facts that I've accumulated from the small amount of conversing we've done… I think I've come to the conclusion about who you are. Well, not so much *who* you are… but what you do…"

"You talk a lot," I blurt out.

He laughs, this deep, gruff, warm chuckle that emits from his mouth and floats to my ears, then races down to my stomach and again… *Fuck you, butterflies.* "You're the first person who's ever said that," he says.

"I am?"

He nods slowly. "So… you're drunk at nine a.m.… not once, but twice now, and you seem to be tired during the day, which means you don't sleep at night, and whatever has you drinking is something you're more than likely ashamed of…" He points down my body, past the oversized shirt I'm wearing, pausing for a moment on my bare legs, and then he looks away. "So you work nights, sleep days, and you're ridiculously drunk in the morning, which I guess is your night… and I don't think you're a hooker, so—"

"What the fuck?" I spit.

"And you have a mouth on you, which yeah… I gotta admit… kind of hot."

"No!"

"No?"

"I'm not a hooker and you can get out now!"

He raises his hands in surrender, then winces and rubs his right shoulder. "Hooker wasn't my first guess, anyway."

"I'm scared to ask."

Cringing slightly, he says, "Stripper?"

"Seriously. Get out." I point to the door, but he just chuckles, releasing another set of butterflies inside me. Yeah. I *definitely* hate the way he makes me feel.

He crosses his legs at his ankles and makes himself comfortable on my bed. "I think I'll stay."

I pick up a cushion off the floor and throw it at him. He blocks it quickly but then grunts, his hand on his shoulder again.

"Get out!"

"Riley," he says, all amusement gone. "I was kidding."

"No you weren't!"

"You're right. I wasn't. But it's good to know you're neither of those classy professions."

I leave him in my room and grab the wine from the fridge, ignoring the judgment in his eyes when I walk in, unscrewing the cap and taking the first sip. He lies down on top of the covers while I half close the blinds, hoping he takes it as a message to shut the hell up and go to sleep. I like him better when he's not talking. I like to just look at him. And Hello, *Guilt*.

"So yesterday..." he says.

I sit down on the cushions and grab the pen and paper.

"I was kind of an asshole and I apologize..."

He's ending his sentences with an open invitation for me to finish them for him but I can't. And I won't. He wants to talk, I'll listen. Apart from that, he's on his own. In fact, I don't even *want* to listen.

After a sigh, he adds, "But I kind of bared my soul to you a little bit. You don't think you owe me anything in return?"

And now he's just annoying me. "I'm giving you my bed. I don't think I owe you shit, Banks." I throw the paper and pen down and focus on the bottle in my hand. And by focus, I mean focus on emptying it.

"You know my last name?"

I roll my eyes. "We went to the same high school."

"I know that, Riley, don't patronize me. It's fucking annoying."

I ignore his anger… or welcome it… I'm not sure. "Of course I know your name," I tell him, my voice softer. "You're *the* Dylan Banks. Mr. Popular. Half of the 'It' couple."

"The 'It' couple?"

"Yeah… you and Heidi, right? I assume you aren't together anymore…"

"What makes you say that?" he asks, his voice so low it's almost a whisper.

"Because if I were your girlfriend, I would've been waiting for you at home, counting down the seconds until you showed up. I wouldn't be letting you sleep in the back of your truck and I sure as hell wouldn't be letting you sleep in another girl's bed."

He's silent for a long time. So am I. But I know he's awake because I can see and hear his breathing get faster, heavier… and then stop. "Good night, Hudson."

"You know my name?"

"Of course I know your name, Riley. You're the girl next door…"

Five
Dylan

I COULD COME up with a hundred different excuses as to why I'm lying in a random girl's bed while she sits on the floor watching me, not bothering to hide that she knows I'm watching her, too.

I could say I was tired because I didn't get to sleep last night, or that I wanted to get out of the garage, or the house—where Eric was once again entertaining the same girl. I could say that I was bored, or lonely even, and that I just wanted to be around someone. Even if it meant being in the same darkened room not speaking or even acknowledging each other. But like I said, they'd just be excuses because the truth? The truth is that I'd waited up all night, almost on the edge of impatience, anxious for the loud music to sound so I had a reason to knock on the door. See, I had it all planned. Music would play, I'd get mad, then come marching over here hoping for the same outcome as yesterday. I'd yell, she'd offer me her bed, and the rest didn't really matter.

When the music started, I smiled… then I panicked. Because I had no idea why I was smiling.

I listened as the song ended, then started again, all while I stood in the garage fucking around with the engine and trying to convince myself that whatever curiosity I had about her… that's all it was: *curiosity*. And by the third replay that curiosity was enough to have me dropping my tools and walking over to her house. I was nervous, to be honest, because unlike yesterday, I wasn't running on exhaustion or annoyance. Though, I wouldn't tell her that.

She opened the door, looking worse than she did the day before, but that's not what caught me by surprise. It was the fact that she *wasn't* surprised.

I span some bullshit about not being able to sleep but before I could finish, she'd already offered me her bed. I told her I thought she was a hooker, and then a stripper… which got the reaction any sane person would expect. What can I say? It'd been a long time since I'd had a one-on-one conversation with an attractive girl. Not that I was trying to impress her, but I wasn't trying to unimpress her either. That's not even a word. Heidi—she would've called me out on that in the most patronizing way. Riley, though—she'd probably laugh at me, call me an idiot, but do it in a way that had me laughing with her. Maybe. Or maybe she'd throw something at me. Either way, I'd take it.

And now I was comparing them like it somehow mattered. It didn't. But it mattered that Riley liked me, at least enough to tolerate me, because as strange as it seems, I enjoy the semi-darkness and the silence we share. But most of all, I enjoy the unspoken understanding between us, the one that says "Hey, we're fucked up. One gets drunk. One gets mad. And we don't even care why or how we got to be like that but it doesn't matter. We don't want to know. Let's just be fucked up together but apart."

So.

Maybe I've thought about her way too much.

Maybe I haven't stopped thinking about her since I wrote her that stupid note.

And, maybe, going by the way she keeps looking at me from whatever she's scribbling in her notebook, she's thought about me, too.

✧ ✧ ✧

I DON'T KNOW how long I've been lying here watching her. An hour, maybe two.

She has this routine, I've worked out, where she takes a sip of her God-awful wine, looks up, and then smiles. After a moment, she'll scribble something down, tear out the page, fold it, then place it in one of the many jars that line her wall. She does this a few times before looking over at me. There's no smile when she does. It's the opposite. And just like the reasons of our fucked-up-ness, I don't want to know why. The longer I watch, the less she smiles, the less she writes, the more she drinks, and the more she looks over at me. After a while, there are no more smiles, no more writing, just silent tears streaming down her face—tears that reflect the sunlight.

Everything in me stills—everything but my fingers itching to reach out and touch her.

Fuck.

It's selfish—I know—but I don't want to speak. I don't want to ask. At least not yet. Because I know what will happen if I do. She'll tell me the truth and will want the same from me. I'll give it to her. Floodgates open. Snowball effect. And the next thing we know we're in deep. Too deep.

I don't want deep.

I want the horizon.

I want the calm.

SHE DOWNS THE rest of the wine between breaks of her sobbing, gripping the bottle to her chest. She doesn't even care that I see it. Maybe because she's seen me at my worst and left it alone, she expects the same from me.

She falls asleep, or passes out, which in her case could be either. Her body lays still, curled in a ball, her breaths shallow, and maybe it's messed up for me to feel grateful that she's out. Not because I don't have to deal with it, but because I have a feeling this is her way of searching and finding the same thing I'm looking for: *The Calm*.

QUIETLY, I GET out of her bed, grab the blanket by her feet and place it over her. She exhales loudly, almost like a sigh and I stare at her sleeping form, just for a moment.

I try to remember the color of her eyes, and the only thing I can come up with is *sad*.

Her eyes are the color of *sadness*.

MY GAZE CATCHES on the notebook placed next to her head, and even though it might be wrong, I still find myself giving in to the curiosity and reading the words that caused her tears to fall.

> ***If I told you to jump, would you ask how high? Or would you just jump? If there were no reason behind it, would you still take the leap? What if I told you that at the end, there would be nothing? What if you made a splash on the world and***

lived in an eternal state of floating? Would you make waves? What if you couldn't float? What if air lost the battle, and you lost the war? Would you want to know what was on the other side? Would you care? Or would you just jump... because I was the one who asked you?

Six
Dylan

IT ALMOST BECOMES a joke, I convince myself, waiting until I hear the music playing so I can knock on her door and pretend to be pissed while she pretends to be irritated I'm there.

It's a *game*. Because I'm not mad and she's not annoyed. I know this because she's never surprised to see me show up at her door.

Over the next few days, we set a routine.

Me knocking. Her opening. Us in her room. Me in her bed. Her in her corner.

I sleep. She writes. I watch. She cries.

We never ask why.

Sometimes we'll talk, which always ends in a bunch of humorous insults and the occasional throwing of a cushion. Two days ago, she kicked me out by saying her mom was coming home soon. I hadn't even realized how long I'd spent there. She didn't seem to mind.

Then, yesterday, there was no obnoxious music/invitation.

Yesterday fucking sucked.

Riley

DYLAN KNOCKS ON my door halfway through the first play of the song. He doesn't bother with any pleasantries, just pushes on the door, steps around me and marches up to my room where he unplugs the speaker and then turns to me, his hands on his hips. "You left me hanging yesterday," he says.

I try to remember what all happened the day before but the morning booze already in my system has my memory a little hazy. "My mom was home," I tell him.

He nods and rubs the back of his head while his gaze wanders around my room. Finally, he sighs, his head jerking toward the bed. "Can I?"

I shrug. "You still having trouble sleeping?"

He makes his way over to the bed and sits on the edge to remove his shoes. "A little." He climbs under the covers and pulls the blankets to his chin. "Why are you home during the day, anyway? You're not in college or something?"

"No," I answer, taking up my spot on the cushions.

"You don't work?"

"No." I pick up the notepad and start to write.

Why is he here?

"So you're what? Taking some time off?"

Why do I like that he's here?

I shrug in response.

He shifts in the bed until he's facing me. "How drunk are you right now?"

~~***Why do I like that he's here?***~~

I hate that he's here.

"I like you better when you don't talk."

He stifles a laugh into the pillow and I narrow my eyes at him. I don't know why he thinks it's funny. It's not. If he keeps talking, keeps asking questions, I'll revoke the privileges of my bed which I've so kindly offered for the last week and he can get the hell out. I'm grumpy. Not because I'm drunk, but because he's not the only one who's been losing sleep. Guilt can do that—make you lose sleep, I mean.

"Hey, Riley."

I roll my eyes at him, trying to make it as obvious as possible that I wasn't kidding. I really do like him better when he shuts the hell up.

He laughs again, then quickly recovers. "Can you adjust the blinds? I'm already in bed and it's so warm and cozy."

I get up and do what he asks because the quicker he's asleep, the sooner I can go back to drinking. When I'm done, I sit back down in my spot, grab the bottle and take a long, well-earned swig.

"Hey, Riley."

"Jesus Christ! What?"

"God, you're feisty."

"I'm sorry." My words come out in a clipped tone. "This isn't part of the deal."

"The deal?" he asks incredulously.

"Yeah. You. Here. Talking and asking questions. It's not part of the deal."

He's silent a long time before he shifts again, putting his left hand behind his head now, his face toward the ceiling. With his voice low, he says, "I was just going to say, after I crash for a couple hours, I'd like to take you out to lunch or something. Just to say thank you, I guess." He clears his throat. "I've never once seen you eat while I'm here. I thought it would be fun. Maybe get some cake to celebrate your birthday…"

I take my time trying to form an appropriate response. I take too long.

"So?" he asks.

"So… I can't."

He sighs. Long and loud and with obvious disappointment. Not at my answer, but at me. It should hurt. It should make me feel something, but it doesn't. Maybe because I've done nothing but disappoint people for the past year and a half.

"I'm actually sleeping okay," he admits out of nowhere. "My brother moved some shit around in my old room and put a mattress on the floor. I don't come here to sleep, although it helps. I come here because you don't ask questions and being at home… I guess I get scared that my dad or brother are going to ask me something I don't want to answer and it becomes a bigger deal than it is. They were both Marines so it's like… the thing that connects us all together. My brother and I don't have much else in common. In fact, I don't think we really know each other at all. So I'm here hiding out because I don't want to risk it."

I take another sip. Write another sentence.

~~I hate that he's here.~~

I like that he's here.

He continues, "None of my friends know I'm home. I haven't told them. So, I guess you're the only person I have right now—which is dumb—because up until a week ago, I didn't even really know you. So I'm sorry if I'm asking the wrong questions. Pushing the wrong buttons. Because I completely get why you're pissed—"

"I'm not pissed," I cut in, my voice barely a whisper. His words hit me hard—right in the feels—I *totally* get it. "I'm not used to having anyone around," I continue. "And it's been a while since I've had to talk to anyone besides my mom so—"

"Does your mom know you drink?" he interrupts.

I scoff and bring the bottle to my lips. "Who do you think supplies me with it?"

"You do realize how fucked up that is, right?"

"Says the guy sleeping in his neighbor's bed because he can't deal with reality."

"We're such a fucking mess," he says, and I can hear the humor in his voice.

"That's because you're pushing the wrong buttons," I joke.

"It's like the worst form of slow dance."

"A horrible act of foreplay," I add. Then choke on my own breath.

He laughs. "Foreplay, Hudson? Really? Are you planning on this leading to sex? Because it's been a while and I'm down for whatever."

"Shut up." I throw a cushion at him. I was going to throw the bottle of wine but I like it too much.

"Quit throwing shit at me."

"Quit making me want to."

"So what do we do now? Make out?"

"Shut up!" I tell him, but I'm laughing.

I add another note to my stream of thoughts.

He makes me laugh.

He chuckles with me, low and deep.

"Dylan?"

"Yeah, Riley?"

"The lunch thing…"

"Mm?"

"I'm not really up for leaving the house..." I admit.

"I can bring us something back?"

"And the cake..."

"How many candles?"

Butterflies.

FOR THE NEXT ten minutes, he tosses and turns in bed while I try to concentrate on anything but him. Then he huffs out a breath and says, "I skipped breakfast. I could eat now. You?"

"Okay."

He rushes to his feet and opens the blinds fully. "You got a preference?" he asks, turning to me with a smile on his face—a smile that matches mine.

"Bacon."

"Just bacon?"

I laugh. "Anything with bacon."

"And the cake?" he asks, grabbing his phone, keys and wallet from my nightstand.

"Anything. Just don't forget the candles."

He nods. "Yes, Ma'am."

I stay in my spot and watch him slip on his shoes, trying to hide my excitement.

His eyes stay on mine as he starts to leave. Stopping at my doorway, he says, "Riley?"

My grin gets wider.

"Please don't pass out while I'm gone." He eyes the bottle in my hand.

I shake my head. "I wouldn't dream of it."

With a chuckle, he mumbles, "Wow. You must really like bacon."

And then he's gone.

"It's not the bacon," I whisper to myself, my smile wiped as I write:

He's giving me a wish.

I like wishes, Jeremy.

That's all it is.

Please don't be mad.

Seven
Dylan

I RUSH TO three different places before I find the one I need. Then I speed back home, park in my garage and carefully bring the bags with me. I place them against the wall of her house, hidden from her view and then I knock on her door.

My eyes widen when she answers. She'd changed while I was gone. Maybe even showered going by the dampness of her hair. Her eyes are still a little faded but besides that, she looks completely different. She's wearing a plain white dress—a dress that shows off the curves she'd been hiding behind the oversized T-shirts she normally wears.

"That was quick," she says, the same time I say, "You look nice."

We both laugh, but the kind of nervous laugh I hadn't felt since I was fifteen and Heidi started talking to me.

I clear my throat and pull my eyes away from her. "I need you to hide out in your room."

Her eyes narrow. "Why?"

"Surprise." I try to smile but my lack of breath makes it a struggle.

She purses her lips. "I don't like surprises."

I shrug. "Suck it up. It's only your birthday once a year."

She smiles at that, before walking backward and into her room, closing the door behind her.

When I know she can't see me, I take a calming breath. And then another. And another, wondering the entire time why it is she has my heart racing and my palms sweating when we can't even hold a decent conversation.

"Can I come out now?" she yells.

How the hell long have I been standing here? "No!" I grab the bags and bring them inside and toward where I assume is her kitchen. "I'll tell you when you can! Just don't come out and don't peek."

"Dylan!" she yells, and I picture her nose scrunched in annoyance like I'd seen so many times before. She's fucking cute when she gets like that. Cuter than she is when she's passed out drunk or throwing shit at me.

"I'll be two minutes!"

I empty the contents of the bag, set it all out on her kitchen counter, light the candles and rush over to her room before they begin to melt. "Okay," I say, opening the door.

She's standing in front of her dresser with her hands on her boobs. She drops her arms to her side and turns to me, her face fifty different shades of red. "Heard of knocking?" she snaps, raising her hands.

I cower beneath my arms.

"What the hell are you doing, Banks?"

I chance a peek at her and when I see her walking toward me, her hands free of anything she could possibly throw, I relax my arms and tell her, "I thought you were going to throw something at me. *Again*."

She rolls her eyes and gives me that same annoyed look I've just deemed cute. Cute doesn't do it justice. *Hot*. Definitely hot.

"I told you I'd be quick."

"You said you were going to call out, not barge into my room!"

"I didn't know you were going to be fondling yourself," I tell her, waiting until she's walked past me before covering her eyes. She stops in her tracks causing me to bump into the back of her. "It's a surprise, remember? Just go with it, Riley."

"Fine." She starts to walk forward, her hands out in front of her.

I bend down, my lips to her ear. "I'm not going to crash you into a wall, Hudson. Relax."

She brings her arms in and grasps my wrists. "I'm also a little tipsy," she reminds me. Then she mumbles something about not being able to smell anything, but I don't really know what she's saying because all my other senses have been drowned out by her touch on my arm. Her back on my chest. Her breath on my cheek as she turns to me. "Are we there?" she whispers, her lips an inch away from mine. I realize we've stopped moving, though I don't know when. I blink twice, forcing my eyes away from her lips—her wet, slightly parted lips and her mint/wine breath brushing against mine. "Dylan?"

Fuck, I want to kiss her. "Huh?"

"Can I open my eyes?"

"Shit."

"What?" she says, her grip getting tighter. "Did you do something? Is the house burning down? What?"

I shake my head to clear my thoughts and start moving again. I try not to focus on the heat of her body against mine when I stop in front of the counter, the glow of the candles setting off patterns of flickering light against the walls of the dark room. "Ready?" I ask.

Her grip tightens again. "No."

I lower my hands. "Happy birthday."

Her intake of breath matches mine when I realize she hasn't let go of my wrists. Now I'm standing behind her, my arms around her waist.

She releases a chuckle, or at least I think that's what it is, but when she turns to me, still in my arms and her eyes instantly on mine, I can see her tears. "You got me bacon cupcakes?"

I nod. "Bacon and maple."

"They each have a candle," she whispers, but she's not looking at the cupcakes, she's looking at me.

"All twenty of them."

She takes a huge breath, causing her chest to rise, and then fall as she lets out a tiny laugh. "You gave me twenty wishes."

I SPEND THE next half hour watching her blow out each individual candle. She asked that I blow them all out first, and then she'd do them individually. I didn't ask why. If I've learned one thing from today, it's to not ask questions.

She takes her time, her gaze lifting before each blow, as if she's really thinking hard about her wishes. I guess they mean something to her—these wishes she makes. And it's good, I decide, because it means she has something to look forward to which before today, I would have never guessed.

Her reaction after each wish is different. Sometimes she smiles. Sometimes she frowns. Sometimes she moves right on to the next, and others, she just stares as the smoke rises from the freshly put out candle. But on her last one she looks at me standing right next to her. Right into my eyes. I swallow loudly, my nerves on show, hoping she doesn't see the real me. That behind the bullshit front I show her and the small details of my current existence I've admitted to her, I hope to God she doesn't see that maybe I'm just as fucked up as she is. That while she uses alcohol to hide the mayhem inside her, I'm using *her*.

Her eyes are gray—one hidden behind a strand of hair fallen from the loose knot on her head. I run my finger across her forehead, her lids slowly dropping. Her lips are wet again, parted slightly allowing her shaky inhales, followed by even shakier exhales. My finger's behind her ear now, my palm on her jaw.

Her head tilts back.

I lick my lips.

And then I do something I've wanted to do since I saw her in that dress. I lean down, close my eyes, and press my lips to hers, and I kiss her. I ignore her loud intake of breath, her palms as they flatten on my stomach and I kiss her some more. I kiss her until her lips part against mine and her tongue slides across my bottom lip and then I do the same, and with both hands on her face, I use my lips to memorize every single thing about this moment.

It's the slowest form of slow dance.

The most passionate act of foreplay.

It's not until she moans into my mouth, her arm curled around my neck as she drops down to her feet that I realize she was as desperate for the kiss as I was. I remove my left hand from her face and wrap my arm around her waist, pulling her into me. Then I push us back until her back hits the counter. I swipe my arm along the counter, discarding the once moment-defining cupcakes and I lift her onto it, standing between her legs as they wrap around me. We break the kiss, just long enough for her to remove my shirt and for me to do the same with her dress and fuck—she's not wearing a bra. I blink hard, staring at the perfect pink of her nipples contrast against her pale skin and lower my gaze to her white panties. I run my hands up her bare thighs as I take one of her nipples in my mouth. She arches her back and releases a moan so fucking sexy, it takes everything in me not to rip off her panties and dive right in. Her hands are on the back of my head now, my thumb running across the dampness between her legs. She reaches for the band of my sweats as I move to the other breast; paying it the same attention I did the other. I circle my tongue around her nipple, flick it, then suck it into my mouth while I push her panties to the side and now my thumb can feel the full effect I've had on her. *She's wet.* Soaking fucking wet. So wet it drives me to the brink of explosion. I moan, releasing her nipple and move back up to her mouth. She bites on my bottom lip as she takes my cock in her hand, slowly stroking it, and if she keeps it up, it won't be long. Before she can push my sweats down with her free hand, I reach into my pocket and pull out my wallet, then dump it on the counter and blindly retrieve a condom. My sweats drop to my ankles while I insert a finger into her pussy, my eyes drifting shut when she runs her thumb across the head of my dick. I pull away from the kiss, place the condom packet between my teeth and open my eyes but she's already watching me, her breaths heavy, her cheeks flushed.

With my eyes, I ask a silent question—but then I realize… we don't ask questions.

I tear the packet with my teeth and roll on the condom at the same time she removes the only piece of clothing that's stopping us from going all the way.

I have to ask. I can't not. I don't want her to regret it. "Riley," I breathe out.

She responds by pressing her lips to mine, her hand around my neck, bringing me down until her entire back is lying on the counter. I grasp her thighs as best I can and pull until her ass is on the edge. Then I reach up, groping her breasts in both my hands, watching and listening to the results of her pleasure. In a single thrust, I'm inside her. She's warm. And so fucking tight. Her back lifts off the counter, her quiet scream of pleasure and pain mixes with mine and we start to move. Slow at first, and then as one, we speed up. Her hands are on my waist as I lean up, watching her tits bounce with each thrust. My gaze moves lower, my cock getting harder as I watch it slide in and out of her perfect fucking body. She's fucking ridiculous. Every move. Every sound. Every touch from her pushes me closer to the edge. Then she tightens around me, her body heated and covered in sweat as her stomach contracts, her release as close as mine. I hold out, just long enough for her to finish and when the shaking stops and her breaths seem to settle, I go off, releasing a grunt into her neck while her fingers curl into my back.

And then… silence.

I've never hated silence as much as I do right now.

Because reality hits.

And reality's a bitch.

She's drunk.

Beyond drunk.

And now I'm regretful.

She breaks the silence.

I wish she didn't.

Because she's crying, pushing away from her.

I lean back. "Riley, it's—"

She pushes until I'm completely off her, wiping her tears and covering her mouth like she's about to puke.

I make her sick.

We make her sick.

She rushes to the sink and empties the content of her stomach. Then grips the edge of the counter, her shoulders heaving with every breath.

I discard the condom in the trash and pull up my pants before going to her. Placing my hand on her shoulder, I say, "Riley, it doesn't—"

"Mean anything," she cuts in.

"*—change* anything," I finish.

Slowly, she turns to me, using her arms to cover her most private parts—parts I was drowning in only minutes ago. "Dylan," she cries. "It changes *everything*."

Eight
Dylan

SHE ASKS ME to leave.

I do because it's not one of those times where she's joking around or pretending she hates me. The look she gives me mixed with the regret in her eyes is proof of that.

And as much as I don't want to admit it, she was right. It changes *everything.*

Because now I'm in deep. Too fucking deep.

So I do the only thing I know when nothing in the entire world seems to make sense.

I drive.

And then I drive some more.

And when the sight of the sun dipping down on the horizon doesn't give me the calm I was hoping for, I head home and face reality.

ERIC'S STANDING IN the garage as I pull into our driveway, *my* tools and *my* engine parts in his hands. "Do you even know what you're doing?" I yell out, getting out of my truck and making my way to him.

"Nope," he says, popping the *P*. "This car stuff has always been you and Dad's thing. Kind of pissed me off, to be honest."

I stop in my tracks. "What's with you?"

"Where have you been, Dylan?" he says, facing me.

"What are you talking about?"

He places his hands on his hips and widens his stance. Fuck, he looks like Dad. Acts like him, too. "You've been home over a week, and I've barely seen you." His eyes narrow, as he cups my chin. He tilts my head from side to side while he steps closer, his eyes right on mine.

"Dylan?"

"Uh...what?"

"Are you on The Drug?"

I swat his hand away. "Fuck off."

"Dylan." He stifles his laugh. "I'm being serious. Are you, or are you not, on The Drug?"

"Oh my God, Eric." I push him aside and start replacing the tools back where they belong. "I'm not on The Drug... whatever the hell that means."

"Good." He leans back on the workbench and crosses his arms again. "I just feel like I should be looking out for my kid brother, you know?"

"I'm not a kid anymore, E. I can take care of myself."

He points to my shoulder. "Clearly."

I freeze. So does Eric when he realizes what he's just said. "I didn't mean that, man. I overstepped."

"Yeah, you did." I shut the lid on the toolbox and face him, matching his stance, waiting for him to leave.

He doesn't. Instead, he says, "Did you... want to talk about it or something? About what happened?"

"Not really."

"Okay." He takes a breath. "Well, if you do—"

"I don't. *Ever.*"

"Right." He nods but doesn't look away. "Your friends know your back?"

I shake my head and drop my shoulders.

"Why not?"

"Not ready," I rush out, and when I realize this is the most we've had to say to each other in ten years, I ask, "What's with the twenty questions? Dad ask you to talk to me or something?"

"What? A brother can't talk to his brother to see if he's okay?"

With a sigh, I reply, "I'm fine, Eric."

"Cut the shit, okay? None of us are *fine*. You, me, Dad—we've all been there, but you're the only one who's come back with a scar to remind us of it. If '*fine*' is the story you want to spread for everyone else, then good for you. But don't use it on us. We're your goddamn family, Dylan."

I turn away because if I look at him any longer I'll probably punch him. "You're right. It happened to *me*. Not you. And if I say I'm fine, I'm fucking fine. Leave it alone." I walk to my truck and pop the hood, then spend the next few minutes ignoring his presence, pretending to fix something that isn't broken. Which, I guess, is exactly what he's doing… trying to fix me. I'm not broken. Or at least I wasn't. Not until I decided to take advantage of the drunk and damaged girl next door.

"You want to know why I came home?"

I roll my eyes even though he can't see me. "I'm sure you're going to tell me anyway."

My truck sways when he leans against it. "For Dad."

My hands freeze mid-movement. "He asked you to come home?"

"No. You know Dad, he'd never ask. But think about it… the man lost his wife, raised two boys on his own. Then I go and enlist, deploy, and eight years later you do the same and he has no one. We're all he has—just us and the constant thoughts of where we are and what we're doing and if we're even fucking alive."

I drop my gaze, my grip loosening around the wrench in my hand.

He adds, "So if I ask you if you're okay or if you want to talk about shit, I'm not doing it to set you off or because I feel like I need to. I'm doing it because I fucking love you. And I love Dad. And if me coming home and giving up on early retirement means Dad will at least have one of his family members alive and standing next to him until the day he dies then that's what I'll do."

I release my anger with a shaky breath and blink. Once. Twice. Then over and over until the dryness returns. Then I swallow loudly, pushing down the lump in my throat.

"Dylan?" he asks, his voice softer, and I'd give just about anything to be in Riley's room again. Away from everything… away from what he's making me feel and making me think and making me remember.

"Look at me, Dylan."

I inhale deeply and prepare myself. Then lift my head from under the hood.

He asks, "Are you okay?"

With my eyes on his, I slowly shake my head. "Not yet," I tell him, my voice strained.

He nods in understanding. "But you will be?"

I raise my chin. "Yes."

"You want to go back?"

I don't hesitate. Not for a second. "Yes."

He motions to my shoulder. "When's your next checkup?"

"Tomorrow."

"VA?"

"Yes."

"You want me to go with you?"

"No, Eric. I'm good."

He takes a step back, his features relaxing a little. "So," he says, hands in his pockets. "Who's the girl?"

I shift my gaze. "What girl?"

"You're such a shitty liar."

"Am not."

"Okay Mr. *I wasn't playing basketball in the house, Grandma's spirit broke her own urn*!"

A chuckle bubbles out of me. "Shut up. Totally happened."

"Sure." He starts to leave, but stops just beside me. "Call your friend… the one who was over a lot when we first moved here."

"Why?"

"To thank him for dropping by and visiting with Dad whenever he was in town."

"He did?"

Eric shrugs. "People do that, you know? Join forces when they miss or worry about the same person. Makes it easier to deal with, I guess."

Riley

I CAN'T TELL if it's the tears building or the water I'm drowning in causing the sharp ache pricking my eyes.

I welcome the pain—the burn in my lungs, my throat, my lips as I press them tight—holding my breath… keeping the bubbles from forming.

There's pressure forcing its way into my eardrums…

…the water's winning.

For now.

But in the end, my body will give in.

It always does.

It's just a matter of time.

Tick. Tock.

My mouth fills with water first, then my throat, then my lungs. And finally my eyes as they snap open—my surroundings a blur. My fingers dig into my palms when my hands form fists. My legs kick. My body shakes. A single muffled sound escapes me.

One bubble. Two. Then many more.

I choke on a gasp when I quickly sit up, the water cascading down my naked body. It's cold—the water, the air, it's so cold.

And so damn perfect.

Bringing my knees to my chest, I breathe through my nose. A regular routine I use to keep my desperation for air almost silent. My gaze shifts to the floor of the bathroom where water's spilled over the edge of the tub. *At least it's just water*, I tell myself. The pain, physical and emotional, now all-consuming.

Because I don't want to forget…

…and he's making me forget you, Jeremy.

Nine
Dylan

"SO YOU KNOW how long it's going to take to heal?" I ask Dr. Garvis—the doc assigned my case at the VA hospital. I could have easily opted to use someone in town and, honestly, I'd thought for a second about asking Dr. Matthews, Logan's dad. But that would mean betraying Logan in a way. And betraying seemed a lot worse than just not telling him at all.

He looks up from his clipboard and taps the pen against it. "I'm going to be honest with you, Lance Corporal Banks. It's different for everyone, but you're doing everything you can. I know you want to get back, but doing more than you should and forcing it might make it worse. It's still early. It's been less than three weeks."

"You can call me Dylan," I tell him, rubbing my neck in frustration.

He runs his hand through his salt and pepper hair, then adjusts the glasses sitting on the edge of his nose. I kind of hoped for someone younger, maybe someone with a history of active duty so he'd understand me a little more. I'm not a hundred percent sure Doc hasn't but if I had to put my money on it, I doubt he'd ever set foot in a warzone. "Are you okay, Dylan? I don't just mean your shoulder. I mean mentally? Are you getting enough sleep?"

"I'm fine," I tell him, even though I hadn't slept a wink the night before. I'll give you two guesses why, even though you'd only need one. Her name rhymes with slimy and I'm pretty sure that's the exact word she'd used to describe me.

Fuck, I need sleep.

He sighs at my response. "Dylan, I get it. Trust me. I see hundreds of guys just like you—frustrated that they're here while their unit's there but there's nothing you can do. Take the time. Relax. Go spend it with your family, your friends, your girl. Whatever. Make it count, you know?"

Yeah.

He has no fucking clue.

✧ ✧ ✧

I SIT IN my truck, banging my head against the steering wheel trying to calm down, but I'm angry. I'm frustrated. I'm everything I shouldn't be and the fact that some doctor thinks his advice of "Relax and make it count" is somehow plausible in my situation or any other situation where a single gunshot keeps a man from doing his duty is bullshit. Sure, it was supposed to help me but it just made shit worse and now all I can think about is the comfortable fucked-up silence of Riley's bedroom which I'm sure I'll never get to experience again.

I DECIDE IT'S a bad idea to go there, where she's more than likely drunk and angry and I'm whatever the hell I am. So, I dig deep, deeper than I want to. I pick up my phone and scroll through the few contacts I have and I send a text.

Dylan: *You around?*

I don't bother waiting for a reply. I simply start my truck and begin the two-hour drive to UNC, my old college, and the place where I know I can find the only person I can stand to be around right now.

✧ ✧ ✧

HE SHAKES HIS head, his eyes as wide as his smile when he makes his way toward me. "Swear, I thought this was one of your fucked up Operation Mayhems."

I push off my truck and glance behind him at Bryson Field. "No mayhem, Jake." I look back at him and shrug. "I'm home."

"It's good to see you, man."

He approaches and with each step closer, my anger and frustration begin to fade. "Likewise."

He drops his gear and stops in front of me. "So are you back for good? What's the deal? You were home a few months ago at Cam and Lucy's wedding..."

Nodding slowly, I tear my gaze away from him. "Medical leave."

"No shit?"

"Shit."

"Bad?"

"Depends."

"On what?"

"On how quickly a bullet through a shoulder heals."

"Fuck."

I throw my keys at him. "She missed you, man."

His eyes light up. "Oh, Bessie."

"Don't call my truck Bessie," I say over my shoulder, moving to the passenger seat.

He's already seated when I get in the truck, his hands gliding across the dash. "Time hasn't changed her. Your old man take care of her while you were gone?" He starts the engine, then rubs his hands together.

"About as much as you took care of him while I was gone."

He shrugs. "I like your dad. It's no big deal."

It is a big deal. It's a big deal to me and to my dad, but that's just Jake. Senior year of college and the MLB chasing him and he hasn't let any of that change him. He's still the guy I met in high school with the weird accent who took in a kid who wasn't really going out of his way to make friends. Up until Heidi came along, he was pretty much the only friend I had.

His phone sounds and he shifts to the side to pull it from his pocket. "It's Kayla. We were supposed to be going to look at new bedspreads or some shit. I'll just cancel."

"Oh, man. It's cool. You don't—"

"Dude," he says, raising his phone between us, his thumbs sliding across the screen. "I can go out with Kayla whenever. Bessie though...."

I can't help but laugh. "Quit calling her Bessie."

He kisses the steering wheel, his smirk in place and his eyes on mine. "She likes Bessie." His smile falls when he goes back to his phone. "Yo. You don't want people knowing you're back, right?"

I shake my head. "I'm not going to ask you to lie to your girl."

Jake shrugs. "I'll tell her training went overtime. Besides, I think she's with Luce and you know Luce." He taps the phone one last time before switching it off and shoving it back in his pocket. "Shall we?"

"Whenever you're ready."

I grip my seat belt when he slams the brakes and the accelerator at the same time, causing the wheels to spin and screech against the concrete of the parking lot. Then he releases the brakes, allowing the truck to jerk forward and speed out of the lot, his shout of "Bessssssyyyyy!" causing a fit of laughter I haven't had since the time Dave was caught jerking off to a picture of the cast of *The Desperate Housewives*.

Maybe the doc and Dave were right.

Maybe I should make the most of it. Maybe I should make it count.

Get money: *Not yet.*

Fuck bitches: *Tick.*

And now I just feel like shit again.

JAKE DRIVES. I sit. He talks. I listen. This goes on for hours—something we'd done plenty of times before. He tells me about baseball, about his family and Micky and what his plans are after college. He talks about the other guys and what they're up to. He keeps me entertained, especially with Cameron and Lucy's marriage shenanigans. He leaves out the parts about Heidi, though I catch him a couple times cutting himself off.

We drive around, stopping at a few abandoned parking lots to do donuts or burnouts or anything else his truck (and Micky) won't allow him to do. He loves it. Always has. And me? I just enjoy his company.

He doesn't ask about my injury. He doesn't ask about my time away. He doesn't ask anything of me and that's why we work, because he knows me better than anyone. Even Heidi.

"How long have we been gone?" he asks.

"Three hours and fifteen minutes."

He's silent for a while as he drives the familiar streets back to the field. Finally, he says, "So what's her name?"

"Anything but Bessie."

He slows down as he pulls into the stadium parking lot and looks over at me. He's wearing a shit-eating grin and I know why. I just don't know *how* he knows. "What?" I ask.

"You've been looking at the clock every few minutes. I ask you how long we've been gone for and you don't skip a beat. You want to be somewhere else—"

"That's not true." *It's a little true.*

"So what's her name?"

I drop my gaze to the phone in my hand wishing I'd gotten her number. "Riley."

"Riley?"

"Yeah."

"And?"

I shrug, a smile pulling at the corner of my lips. "And I don't know what to say. She's got me checking the time, I guess."

"She in your unit or something?"

"Nah. I've only really started talking to her… or not even really talking… for, like, a week."

"How did you meet?"

"She's my neighbor."

He parks next to his truck and puts mine in gear but he's looking out the window, his mind elsewhere.

"What's up?" I ask.

"What's her last name?"

"Hudson. Why?"

"Riley Hudson," he murmurs, her name rolling of his tongue. He repeats it again. "Why does that sound familiar?"

"She went to our school. She's a few years younger so I don't know if that's how you'd know her."

"Maybe." He shrugs, then faces me and smirks again. "Either way, dude. She's got you checking the time."

✧ ✧ ✧

IT'S DARK BY the time I get home and my house is the same as it was the first night I got here. The TV's on too loud, the lights from the screen flicker out the window and onto the front lawn. I have the same nerves too, same anticipation, but for a completely different reason. Because I'm not standing outside my front door. I'm standing outside *hers.*

I START TO smile when the door swings open after my first knock, then stop when a woman appears. She doesn't look like Riley at all, besides her eyes. Her hair's bleached blonde, her lashes fake, and her make-up flawless. Rewind twenty something years and she's Heidi. "Good evening, Ma'am. I was hoping to see Riley."

Her eyes narrow, first at me, and then over her shoulder. She takes a step forward, closing the door quietly behind her. "You're the youngest Banks, right?"

"Yes, Ma'am. I'm Dylan." I throw my hand out for her.

She looks down, ignores it, then lifts her gaze again. "And you know Riley how?"

"We're neighbors," I tell her. *Obviously.* I check her eyes, because maybe she's as drunk as her daughter gets. Or maybe she's the one on The Drug.

After a sigh, she tells me, "Riley's sick. She's not up for guests."

"Is she okay?" I ask, looking at the closed door. "Is there anything I can get her or..."

"No." Another sigh. "She just needs to rest and sleep it off."

"Okay. Well, can you tell her I dropped by?"

She doesn't respond, just turns her back on me and goes back in the house. For a few minutes I just stand there, waiting for any sign of Riley's existence. When enough time passes and the only sound I hear is Dad's television, I leave and make my way back to the garage... my *room*... where I know I'll spend the entire night with thoughts too loud to silence and questions too complicated to answer.

Ten
Dylan

"SO I WAS thinking..." Dad says, pouring the rest of his coffee into the sink.

I finish my mouthful of cereal and say, "This can't be good."

He turns to me and leans back on the counter, his arms crossed and his brow bunched. "I see Afghanistan gave you a sense of humor."

Eric walks into the kitchen, butt naked, and sits opposite me at the table. "Gave him balls, too," he quips.

"Do you mind? I'm trying to fucking eat here."

"Don't swear at the table," Dad says.

Eric points at me. "Yeah, asshole."

Dad sighs. "When are you two going to grow up?"

"I don't know," I answer. "Why don't you ask the naked thirty-year-old still living at home?"

Eric sticks his tongue out.

I roll my eyes.

Dad laughs.

"So you were thinking..." I say to him.

"Are we ever going to actually rebuild that engine?"

"What engine?" Eric asks.

I get up and take my bowl with me to the sink. "The engine I got for my sixteenth."

"That's still the same one you're fucking around with?"

Dad ignores him. "I was looking at a few shells for it. What do you think?"

"Sounds good." I check the time. 8:56. Four minutes. "I'll catch up with you guys at dinner," I tell them, walking out of the kitchen and toward the bathroom.

"Friday night football!" Eric shouts, which makes absolutely no sense because it's the end of February.

"It's not even football season," I hear Dad tell him.

"Friday night *insert random sport here*," Eric yells.

I laugh when I open the bathroom door, then cringe when the same girl from the first night squeals from her seat on the toilet. "Go away!"

"Sorry!" I shut the door quickly.

"Oh, yeah," Eric shouts. "Cindy's using the bathroom."

"Sydney!" the girl yells.

Jesus.

Eric approaches, his junk on full display. He pushes me to the side and starts to open the bathroom door. "How the fuck is this your life, man?" I ask him.

He chuckles and closes the door again. "How the fuck is it *not* yours is the real question."

"Dad!" I shout, smirking at Eric. "Eric's hiding a girl in the bathroom!"

Dad laughs. "Morning, Sydney!"

"Morning, Mal!" she yells back.

I shake my head. "What the hell?"

Eric scoffs. "Maybe you'd know what goes on in here if you weren't out all day on The Drug."

Dad walks over to us. "Dylan, are you on drugs?" He cups my chin and looks in my eyes just like Eric did.

I swat his hands away the same way I did with my brother. "No, I'm not on drugs. What the hell?"

"I found weed in his footlocker, Pops!"

I shove his chest. "You did not."

"Dylan?" Dad asks.

"Swear it, Dad. Eric's talking shit."

"Am not!" He stands behind Dad, smirking while giving me the finger. "Go check it, Dad."

The bathroom door opens and we all freeze, our words left hanging in the air.

"What's going on?" Sydney asks.

"Nothing, babe," Eric answers.

I lift my chin and look at Eric. "You know Dad and I will support you no matter what, E. You're making it a bigger deal than it is," I tell him, placing my hand on his shoulder. "Besides, the pamphlet said there was a high chance it could be sexually transmitted from dogs. Not that it *definitely* was. And that case against you when you were seventeen was dropped because you were a minor, right? Plus, the zoo had no *real* evidence."

The windows of the house rattle and the familiar song filters through, saving me from Eric's response. I pat his arm twice, basking in the glory of his completely shocked face. He shakes his head slowly, as if accepting defeat.

"I'll see you later, bro." Then I look over at Sydney and point to her neck. "You got a little rash…"

Riley

I DON'T KNOW why Dylan's standing at my door, his hands in the pockets of his sweats, his shoulders square, and his ridiculously gorgeous smile beaming down at me. Even in my drunken haze, I've concluded that he gets better looking every time I see him. Not that it matters.

"What's up," I mumble.

He steps back slightly and looks down on me. "Regret does *not* look good on you."

Regret doesn't *feel* good, either. "What?" I squeak, then shake my head to clear my thoughts but it just makes the pounding worse. "Were you as drunk as I was when you fucked me in my kitchen that you've somehow forgotten about it? Because now you're standing here ignoring the fact that we did, actually, fuck in my kitchen."

"Riley, come on."

"And now you think it's okay to show up, looking like you do and smiling like you are after leaving me hanging the day after your so-called 'regret' and—"

"Riley, I don't regret it," he interrupts.

"Bullshit, Banks. It was the first word you said when I opened the door. And it's cool if that's how you feel because I regret it too." I take a moment to catch my breath. "It's probably a good idea if you don't come around anymore." Maybe my anger is unjustified. Actually, I'm sure it is because regardless of how I try to spin the events of two days ago, I didn't push him away. I did absolutely nothing to stop it from happening. In fact, I encouraged it. And even though I know all this, it didn't stop me from drinking enough alcohol to cause me to puke in the bathtub. Twice. Then pass out in it while I tried to clean it... and that's exactly how Mom found me. So while my hurt might be uncalled for, Mom's reaction to Dylan at the door yesterday wasn't. She knew he had something to do with my actions. *He had to have.*

"Is that what you want?" he asks, dropping his gaze and pulling me from my thoughts.

It takes a few seconds for me to remember what we were talking about and when I do, I nod.

His eyes narrow. "I'm sorry if what we did hurt you. I regret you were drunk. I regret that I may have unintentionally taken advantage of that. But I don't regret *it*." He starts to turn away, but stops suddenly. "I hope you find whatever it is you're looking for in life..." He points at the wine gripped tightly in my hand. "I just don't think you're going to find it at the bottom of a bottle. And just so you know, I *do* like you, Riley. A lot." He steps forward, but I push him away.

I *have* to.

Because the butterflies are already starting. But, after the butterflies come the emptiness, and then the guilt. And the guilt is what has me closing the door on him and whatever feelings I might have had for him.

I GO BACK to my room, my solitude, and I play the song—the song that brings me closer to *him*. Then I grab my wine, sit in the corner with the pen and paper in my hand, and I remember him.

> ***It was sophomore year. You knew I was a nervous wreck. You knew I hated the attention. So it made absolutely no sense to me why you showed up at my swim meet with half the JV basketball team holding up signs and chanting my name in the stands. I paced the side of the pool glaring at all of you. Every time you started to chant I'd tell you to shut up. You kept going, your big goofy smile getting wider every time. Then they announced my name and I removed my towel, slowly walking to my block as your cheers just got louder.***
>
> ***I was so angry.***
>
> ***So livid.***

I stood there and tried to ignore your chants and cheers and shouts but it was so deafening. Everyone was looking at you. Everyone was looking at me. I swore to myself I'd fly through the freestyle as fast as I could just so I could get out and kick your ass.

I came in first and before they could even announce it, I stormed up to the bleachers, my wet feet thumping against the floor. You were three rows up. I remember because I could see all the eyes of the crowd move from me to you, and back again. You were smiling. "Why would you do this!" I shouted, stomping my foot. I was so, so mad. And when your grin got wider I wanted nothing more than to climb the three rows—people and all—and smack you on the back of the head.

But then you said, "Because I know you, Riley Hudson. You swim best on adrenaline. And nothing gets your blood pumping like being mad."

I was confused. "What?"

"I did it for you!" you shouted.

I wanted to smile, but I wanted more to keep being mad at you. "You didn't do it for me!"

You nodded. "I did so!" And I don't know if it actually happened, or if it was just like that in my head, but everything went quiet. Everything went still. You smiled wider. "And I did it because I'm in love with you, stupid!"

We were sixteen, me in my swim gear, dripping wet, surrounded by your friends and two hundred strangers… and you told me you loved me for the very first time.

I stopped being angry. I stopped caring about the stupid signs and the stupid chants and everyone around us. I ran up to you, through the people in those front three rows and wrapped my wet arms around you. And then I kissed you. And you kissed me back. And the world stopped and my heart grew and when my coach called out and said I had to prepare for the next round, you told me I sucked and that my suit made my ass look fat.

I told you I loved you too—more than everything and anyone in the history of forever.

And I meant it, Jeremy.

More than anything.

Eleven
Dylan

I HAVEN'T SLEPT.

Not since I left her house two days ago.

I can't fucking focus on the stupid engine in front of me. Maybe because all my focus is on the pathetic music streaming from her house. I wonder how long it's been going on and why everyone else lets her get away with it. I chuck the screwdriver on the workbench and grasp my right shoulder with my left hand, then I begin to do the stupid exercises the doc instructed me to do. Move it in slow circles until the pain becomes too much.

The pain is already too much.

Dave: *No one's told me to fuck off in three days. I miss you, you giant ogre of a man.*

With a halfhearted smile, I respond:

Dylan: *Duck off, asshole. Better?*
Dylan: **Fuck.*

Dave: *You're the worst.*

Dylan: *Notwgat your mom said last beige.*

Dave: *What?*

Dylan: **Norway*
Dylan: **Not.*
Dylan: **What.*

Dave: *What?!?!*

Dylan: **Night.*

Dave: *Good night, bro.*

Dylan: *No.*

Dave: *No?*

Dylan: *Your mom's far.*
Dylan: **Gay.*
Dylan: **FAT.*
Dylan: *FUCK.*

Dave: *What are you typing with? A potato?*

Dylan: *Duck you.*

"Hey, Dylan?" Sydney says, her head poking through the garage door. She's wearing one of Eric's shirts and nothing else. "Do you have a second?" I don't know why it bothers me that she's standing there—a girl I barely know—in the only bit of personal space I own.

I shut my eyes and nod, giving up on my so-called physical therapy for the moment.

She steps inside, one bare leg after the other and I look away because she's not mine to look at. "Sorry," she says, walking over to me. "I probably should have put some clothes on but I was in a rush."

"It's fine," I tell her, picking up the screwdriver again. I grip it in my right hand and squeeze a few times, feeling the dull ache filter down my arm. "Did you need something?"

She stands close to me and leans against the bench. Then she opens her mouth, shuts it, and then does it again. "I feel kind of strange now," she says, pulling her top down a little. "I just didn't know what else to do."

There's a desperation in her voice that's enough to make me look away from my hand and up at her. "What's up?"

"Do you… I mean, do you have nightmares… about—" She shakes her head. "Never mind."

She starts to leave but I stop her. "About what?"

She looks at the door and then back to me. "Eric—he's been having these nightmares, I guess. He tosses and turns and kicks in his sleep. I don't know what to do. He says he's fine afterward, but he doesn't get back to sleep, he just holds me. I don't know if I should ask him about it or just let him be and I just thought because you and he… I mean, you've both been there and you're his brother so if anyone knows—"

"I don't know," I interrupt. Truth is, I have no idea what he'd want.

Her gaze drops. "Oh."

"It's not like Eric and I are close, you know?" I say, trying to justify my response. "So I can't really tell you much about him."

"But you've been there, right?" She shakes her head again. "I'm sorry. This is probably inappropriate and bad for you to think about."

"It's fine."

"I just worry about him. Whatever's making him wake up in a pool of sweat can't be good."

"You worry about him?" I ask incredulously.

She tilts her head, her brow bunched in confusion. "Of course I do," she replies, as if I'm the dumbest person in the world. She rolls her eyes. "Dylan, your brother and I are really good at faking our feelings. I mean, look at us. We've known each other a couple weeks and we've spent practically every second together. We could be out having sex with different people every night but we choose to have sex with each other." She laughs a little when I scrunch my face in disgust. "A little too much information?"

"A little."

"I don't know," she sings, a slight smile pulling on her lips. "He says I keep him sane and he makes me happy, so why not? Yolo, right?"

"What the hell is a Yolo?"

She eyes me sideways. "You Only Live Once. How long were you deployed?"

I can't help but laugh. "I've always been out of touch, I guess."

"So no advice?"

I look down at the screwdriver in my hand, squeeze it once, and look back at her, thinking about what Eric would say if the roles were reversed. "Just keep letting him hold you when he needs to."

She smiles again, her hand soft as she squeezes my arm. "That's perfect advice, Dylan." Then she gazes toward the garage window that faces Riley's house. "Are you going to go over there and tell her to turn off that God-awful music again?"

"How do you—"

"I'm here every day, D. I'm not stupid. I see things."

"Nah. Pretty sure she hates me."

"Doubt it," Sydney says, her smile still in place. "Maybe you guys are just like Eric and I—really good at faking it. Besides, you could be out seeing other people, but you choose to see each other."

Riley

"GO AWAY," I mumble, my face smeared into a cushion. I can feel the dried drool on my cheek and smell the wine that must've spilled onto the floor while I was sleeping. Not passed out. I've lived through both enough times to know the difference. Last I remember, the bottle was half full. *Great.* I just wasted half my portion of alcohol for the day.

The knocking sounds again and I mumble another, "Go away," a little louder than before but not by much.

Another knock.

"Jesus! Okay!" I take my time getting up, not because I'm drunk, but because I hope whoever the hell is knocking gives up by the time I get there.

MY STOMACH DROPS to the floor when I open the door to Dylan standing there, his hands in the pockets of his sweats, his lips pressed tight while he looks down at me. Then he smiles and rocks on his heels. "You look *beautiful*, Riley."

I eye him sideways while I bring the bottle to my lips and take another dose of *my* painkiller.

He clears his throat before saying, "Look. I get it. You're mad. You have every right to be. But I'm not going to stand here and act like what we did was wrong because at the time, we both wanted it, and you can't deny that. Do I wish it'd gone down differently? Of course. Regardless of what you might think about me, I've never done anything like that before. With anyone. Ever." He takes a deep breath and squares his shoulders. "I have feelings for you, Riley. Feelings I can't ignore. Sure, I would've liked for us to take our time and to get to know each other a little… maybe convince you to actually enjoy the time we spend together, like I do, instead of…" He shakes his head. "…whatever it is you feel when you're with me."

My heart aches. For *him* and for me. He has no idea that I feel exactly the same way, and that it's those feelings that causes the guilt that's slowly eating away at me. "Dylan…"

"Just give me a chance to explain."

I push back the tears burning behind my eyes. "You don't need to—"

"I do, Ry. You need to hear it."

I nod slowly, opening the door wider.

"You ever feel stuck, Riley?" he says, but it's not really a question because he doesn't wait for my response. "I don't mean in your house or anything like that. I mean in time. Or in your head. I feel like I am. I feel like I'm stuck in a dust-filled room with gunshots going off around me, staring into the eyes of the kid who shot me. I feel like I'm there and I can't shake it, and even though so much has happened since that day, and time has passed, and I've moved more times than I can count, I'm still there. Sometimes, I close my eyes and it's all I can see." He takes a breath. "But being with you—being in your room—it's the only place I feel free from it all. I can't explain it. I'm not even sure I want an explanation for it. All I know is that I want *it*. Because even though, technically, time itself is the same for everybody—every second, every minute, every hour—it's not when I'm with you. It's like it doesn't exist. Or I don't care that it does." He pauses, his jaw tense and his lips thinned to a line, then he curses under his breath and shakes his head. "I'm not good with words," he mumbles. "Am I making sense?"

He makes more sense than anyone has before and if I could've found the words to articulate my exact feelings since the day of the "accident," he's just used them all. Every single one.

He takes another long breath, speaking before I can answer him. "When I was about fifteen, I think, my buddy Jake and I went to this party and got hammered."

I start to speak because I have a feeling he's about to ramble and go off track but he raises his hand between us to stop me. "Just let me get it out."

I nod once.

"We got home at God knows what time and my dad was up waiting for us and he was so mad and we were both so drunk that we couldn't even register what was happening. My dad said something like 'Do you boys know what time it is?' and I kept my mouth shut but Jake, he just started laughing. And then he said—God, it's so stupid—" He rolls his eyes. "—He said, 'Nope. Time flies when you're having fun.' And we all burst out laughing, even Dad. So, it became this dumb joke between Jake and I—like, whenever we hung out we never looked at the time because we always deemed that we were having fun or whatever, and the other day, after my first check up for my shoulder, I went to UNC to see him—that's why I didn't come over. I would've, Riley. I wasn't avoiding you because of what happened with us. Even though you asked me to leave that day, it didn't change anything for me. I still wanted to see you." He shakes his head, as if trying to refocus. "Anyway, Jake—he called me out. He asked who the girl was that my mind was obviously preoccupied with and I told him about you, and when I asked how he knew, he said I kept looking at the clock." He inhales another breath, taking mine with it. "So I guess what I'm trying to say is that even though I feel stuck there, in the middle of a warzone, trapped in the mayhem of my mind, and feeling like time isn't moving at all—you had me wanting more. You had me wanting *you*. You had me checking the time, Riley."

I wipe the tears off my cheek, but they do nothing to stop the million emotions flowing through me. Maybe it wouldn't be so bad. Maybe I'd been looking at it all wrong. It's not the chaos we created in the four walls of my room that had me fearful. It's the comfort he provided. And I think, deep down, I want that comfort as much as he does. I've just never been willing to admit it.

Until now.

A slow smile pulls on my lips as I tug on his shirt and bring him closer. "You need to quit talking so much, Dylan."

ONCE WE'RE IN my room, he admits he hasn't slept since I saw him two days ago. I offer him my bed, which he accepts without hesitation. I'm adjusting the blinds when he mumbles, his mouth pressed against the pillow as he laughs to himself, "I'm twenty-three and afraid of the dark which is stupid, because you close your eyes and it's all the same darkness, right?"

I don't respond, just sit on the cushions and pull out a notebook.

It's not the same. The nightmares you fear when you're awake are worse than the ones you can't control in your sleep. That's why I write it all down. Why I try so hard to remember. Because lately the nightmares are clearer than the memories and I don't want to forget. I won't ever forget you, Jeremy.

Twelve
Riley

DYLAN KNOCKS ON my door for the second time the next day, looking the same as he did a few hours ago. Same clothes. Same squared shoulders, same hand in his pocket... but now the other's holding a few plastic bags. He must see the confusion on my face when I look up at him because he says, "What? You didn't expect me to come back?"

"After I told you I felt like shit because I'm on my period and that I was really grumpy and I'd probably end up throwing something at you? No. I didn't think you'd come back."

He holds up the bags in his hands. "Well, first, I wasn't sure if it was the booze talking."

"I haven't had *that* much to drink."

"Second. I wasn't just going to leave knowing you were cranky..." He waits for my response. I don't give him one. "I just got you some stuff that I've heard helps with the..." he points to my vagina. "The lady business."

"Are you seriously pointing at my vagina right now?"

He looks at where he's pointing.

"And now you're looking at it?"

His eyes snap to mine, his lips pressed tight to stop his smile from forming.

I sigh, half amused, half still confused. "What are you doing, Dylan?"

"I told you," he says, lifting the bags again. "I got you chocolate, chips, Gatorade, some girly books and DVDs... I wasn't sure what you'd prefer, and I even got you some stuff to take care of..." he points to my vagina again. "...that."

"Stop pointing at my vagina."

"Stop calling it a vagina."

I cover my mouth to stifle my laugh.

"I guess I'm hoping that by buying your friendship it would help get me back in your bed." His eyes widen. "Room. *Bedroom.* I meant bedroom. Not, like—so anyway…" He rocks on his heels and glances up at the sky. "It's a nice day out. Weatherman says it's going to be warm but I don't know. It's a little chilly at the moment. Kind of wish I had somewhere warm and cozy to hide out." He looks back at me. "Do you like turtles, Riley? I like turtles. Not the ninja type ones, but the real ones. They're so slow. So cute. They're like—"

"What the hell are you talking about?" I burst out laughing. I can't help it.

Then he smiles and I curse the damn butterflies for defying me.

I grasp his shirt and pull him inside, taking the bags from him at the same time. His smile remains as he walks backward down the hallway toward my room, watching me pull out the block of chocolate from the bag. "Riley?"

"Yeah?"

He stops in my doorway, blocking me from going in. "Are we going to ignore what happened the other day?"

I stop in front of him. "I don't think I'm ready to deal with it yet. Can we just…" I motion to my room. "…be?"

His smile reaches his eyes. "We can *be* whatever you want, Hudson. As long as I'm with you."

I SWITCH ON the TV and tell him to pick one of the DVDs he bought while I jump in the shower. When I return, he's sitting on the edge of my bed, facing the TV. He smiles when he looks over at me.

"I was thinking…" I tell him, unwrapping the towel from my head. I sit down next to him and start drying my hair.

"You were thinking what?" he asks, turning to me with his leg up, knee bent, on the bed.

His knee brushes against mine and I pull away. Having him here is one thing, having him touch me is another. "How long were you in the navy for?"

"Riley," he deadpans.

"What?" I ask, flipping my hair back and facing him.

"That's not hot at all," he mumbles. Then stands up and moves to the corner of the room. Not *my* corner, but the one where my bookshelf is. He picks up the books he'd bought and places them next to my other ones. "And you smell."

"I smell?" I drop the towel and sniff my armpits. "I just showered."

"Not in a bad way." He shakes his head and turns back to me, but doesn't close the gap between us. "And *Marines*, by the way. Not Navy."

"Oh. Sorry. So how long?"

"Just over two years including basic. Why?"

"Why'd you enlist?"

He stares at me a moment, as if trying to decide what version of a lie he wants to tell me.

I know that look.

I *live* that look.

He doesn't respond, just turns back to the shelf and runs his finger across the spines of the books. He stops at a set of blue books. My yearbooks. Then he pulls out the one from my freshman year. When he turns around, he holds it up as if asking for permission. He waits a few seconds for me to answer and when I don't, he grabs the other three off the shelf and brings them with him back to the bed. He sits down next to me, further than he was before but still close enough that I can feel his warmth against my skin. He starts to flip the pages of my freshman year yearbook, starting at the back. "So when you were a freshman, I was—"

"Junior," I cut him off. The response is quick. *Too quick.* Clearly, it's not the first time I've thought about it. I drop my chin to my chest and hope he can't see my blush. Or worse, call me out on it.

He points to my picture in the book.

"Oh God," I cover my face to hide my embarrassment.

"You're prettier now than you were then."

I scoff and smack his leg. "Thanks, jerk!"

He bursts out laughing. "I didn't mean it like that. Swear it."

I take the book from him and flip to the junior pictures. "Let's see *you* back in high school."

He groans and fakes a shiver. "Maybe this was a bad idea."

I find his profile picture and spend a few seconds taking him in. He hasn't changed much. His hair's shorter and his face is a little more masculine now but besides that, he's still the same Dylan in the picture. We go through the next book, me as a sophomore and him as a senior. I flip to his picture and read his caption out loud. "A man of many words."

"What?" He leans over me and looks to where I'm pointing on the page. "I didn't tell them to write that."

"What did you tell them to write?"

"I don't recall telling them anything."

"Maybe they just improvised?"

"I guess."

"What does it even mean?"

He shrugs. "No idea," he says, then quickly looks away.

I don't press on. I just flip the pages, ignoring the turning of my stomach when he moves closer again, his arm touching my back as he leans into me. I stop at the pictures of his senior prom and search the pages for any sign of him. There's none of him. But there's one of Heidi—his ex—with a crown on her head next to a guy who isn't Dylan. "You didn't win prom king?" I ask, eyeing him sideways.

"Nah." He shakes his head slowly. "I think that was the year I put my foot down and told Heidi I didn't care much for any of that shit."

"That *shit*?"

"Yeah. You know… the whole arm candy thing and trying to get votes and making posters and pins and whatever."

"So you just let another guy stand next to her, get these pictures, wear matching crowns and hold the title of king and queen on a night that was probably important to her?"

He leans back a little. "You make me sound like an asshole."

"I'm sorry," I say. "I guess I just see it differently."

"How do you see it?"

"It's just a night of memories, you know? High school isn't forever." I pause a moment and swallow the lump in my throat, the memories I speak of flooding my mind. My voice drops to a whisper. "Sometimes high school is as good as it gets."

He takes the book from me and throws it behind us, then grabs the one from junior year. "I don't know," he says, flipping through the pages, most likely looking for me again. "I guess we had different experiences."

"Oh, I'm sure we did," I tell him, moving his hand away so I can flip to the page I know is mine. I point to my picture and add, "You and your circle of friends owned the school."

"We did?" he asks, clearly surprised.

"Don't act like you didn't know that."

"I mean, I guess. It was more my friends and Heidi, though. It wasn't really me."

I shrug. "Then you were popular by association. Still valid."

"Maybe," he mumbles, his mind elsewhere. "How do you even remember this?"

I roll my eyes. "Please. You and those guys you hung out with. All the girls knew you."

He tears his gaze away from my picture and slowly looks up at me. "What?" he says, a half smirk pulling his lips. "Did you crush on Jake or something?"

"No. Not Jake. Logan though...."

He pushes on my arm until I fall to my side, losing it in a fit of laughter. "What? Are you offended?" I joke.

"Offended? No." He drops his gaze back to my picture. "Jealous? Maybe."

Butterflies are stupid.

He taps on the book. "You were on the swim team?"

"Yeah. All four years."

He starts flipping the pages again. "Is there a picture of you in your swim gear?" His hand stops mid-movement as he looks from the book and straight ahead. "Wait. This is a little skeezy." He throws the book over his shoulder and picks up the one from senior year. "You were eighteen at some point in this one, right?"

I try to take it from him but he won't let go. His finger skims across the page of H's until he comes across my picture. Then he stops. I watch his face as his eyes narrow and he chews the corner of his lip, just for a moment before he faces me. His throat bobs with his swallow. "Future Mrs. Walters," he murmurs. It's neither a statement nor a question and I don't know how to respond so I don't. I just keep looking at him. And when his body tenses and his eyes drift shut, I know he's found it. "You were prom queen?" he whispers.

"Yes."

"Now I *really* feel like an asshole."

"It's fine."

He's silent a moment before tapping the book and saying, "And this Jeremy guy… he's…"

"My boyfriend," I whisper.

He drops the yearbook onto the floor and slowly stands up. Facing me, he rubs the back of his neck. "*Was* your boyfriend? Or *is*?"

"It's irrelevant."

He shakes his head. "How is it—"

"Because he's dead, Dylan," I cut in. I ignore the dropping of his jaw when I pick up the yearbook from the floor, along with the others on the bed and place them back in their spot on the shelf. "He died the summer after senior year, the day before we were meant to leave for college together." I feel the lump rise to my throat, feel my heart drop to my stomach, killing the butterflies that were once so prominent. My eyes fill with tears—tears that I let slide across my cheek and over my jaw. Then I face him, giving him everything I am. Because what's a little truth amongst the chaos we've created? "He's dead, and that's why it's irrelevant."

He licks his lips—his sad, dry eyes on my wet ones. "I'm sorry," he says, taking a step forward, and I take a step back because I hate that look in his eyes—the one that warns me of what's coming next.

So I beat him to it. "I don't want to talk about it."

"Okay."

"Okay? Just *okay*?"

He shrugs and sits back down on the bed, his head lowered. Then, after a long moment of silence, he speaks. "I enlisted because I wanted more out of my life. I followed a girl I loved, who I thought loved me back, all the way to college because it's what she wanted. I wanted her. And there was no either/or for us. Then things started to fall apart, things she was oblivious to—which I guess is a sign of what our relationship was like. I wasn't happy. Not happy *enough*, anyway. I wanted to make a difference, serve a purpose, you know?" He looks up and my legs lead me—as if on their own—until I'm standing in front of him. "I ran away. I ran because I wanted to avoid the truth, and you—you're doing the opposite. You're facing it head on. Every day. And if drinking is how you do that, then I can't tell you it's wrong, or that you shouldn't be doing it." He tugs on my hand until I'm standing between his legs. "I got shot by a kid, Riley. A kid no more than twelve. And now he's dead because of it. He'll never go to high school, never dance with a girl he thinks he's in love with, never follow his heart and learn from the mistakes of doing so." Then he looks up, his eyes right on mine, and he says something that brings a sense of peace to my once fear-filled chaos. "You got to stand with a boy you love on a night you'll never forget. You were his queen and he was your king and no one can take that away from you."

I wipe my eyes, my tears flowing faster and freer than ever.

"But it is relevant. Because *is* and *was* is the difference between time standing still, and time moving forward."

Thirteen
Riley

I CAN FEEL his eyes on me. Not that he's trying to hide it, though I really wish he would. I look up from my blank page and glare at him. "What?"

"Nothing," he says, sitting on the edge of my bed with his elbows on his knees. Days have passed since I've told him about Jeremy and he hasn't brought it up since. He shifts in his spot. "Do you always drink the same stuff?"

I pick up the bottle sitting next to me and take a sip, cringing slightly when the foul taste of it hits my tongue. "It's the cheapest stuff they have that'll give me a buzz," I tell him.

"A buzz? You're more than buzzed."

"Not yet."

He shrugs. "It's early."

I pick up a cushion and threaten to throw it. "You can leave if you plan on judging me some more."

He laughs and sits down next to me. "Give me some."

"No." I hold the bottle to my chest.

"Dependent much?"

I roll the back of my head against the wall and turn to him. "The door's right there."

"You're so cranky when you're on your lady business." He starts to get up but I stop him.

"Where are you going?"

"Liquor store."

"Why?"

"To buy my own shit."

"Don't," I tell him, the plea in my voice evident.

"Don't what?"

"Drink."

He chuckles from deep in his throat. "Seriously?"

"It's not good for you," I tell him, my gaze dropping as soon as the words leave my mouth and I realize how pathetic I sound.

"That's a little rich coming from you."

"I know," I say through a sigh. "I just don't want you to drop down to my level."

"You're so cute when you're pouty and needy."

"Shut up." I scribble across the page and tilt it so Dylan can't see.

He's just kidding, Jeremy.

Then I close the notebook and face him.

"Hi," he says.

I laugh. "Hi."

"You're real pretty, Riley."

I hide my smile. "Shut up, Dylan."

He rolls his eyes and scoots closer to me, his arm against mine. "Tell me something, Riley."

"Like what?"

He runs his hand over the top of his head, his short hair shifting beneath his touch. "Anything you feel comfortable telling me. Like..."

I hold my breath, waiting for him to continue.

"...Where's your dad?"

I can *totally* answer that. "My mom and him split when I was super young. Like, three or something. I don't really know much about him and I guess he doesn't care to know much about me."

"Yeah?" he asks after a moment. "You think maybe your mom has something to do with that?"

"What do you mean?"

"I think I hate your mom."

I don't respond.

"I'm sorry if that's out of line but what kind of mom supplies their underage daughter with enough alcohol to keep her in a permanent stage of semi-awareness and thinks it's okay."

"It is out of line," I tell him. "There's a lot of shit you don't know about, Dylan, and she does it because she cares. Because she doesn't know any other way to show me that and because it's what we both want so—"

"If you want to believe that bullshit lie she feeds you then you're weaker than I thought."

"Fuck you." He's so fucking good at pushing the wrong buttons. "And where the hell's your mom, by the way?"

"Dead."

I drop my head in my hands. "I'm so sorry."

"It's okay," he tells me, rubbing my back. "She died during childbirth... with me, obviously."

"Jesus Christ, Dylan..."

He laughs, which is such a strange reaction given the conversation. "We suck at talking."

"I know."

"Want to make out instead?"

I pause a beat, either from shock or... no. Just shock. "No."

"It was a joke, Riley. Relax."

Relieved, I try to come up with something lighter to talk about. "I was looking through the yearbooks after you left last night."

"Yeah?" He shifts next to me until he's lying across the floor, his head on my lap. "Find anything interesting?" He looks up, the blue of his eyes brighter than I'd seen them.

I lose my breath, along with my train of thought. And as much as I'd like to blame it on the alcohol, my mind is clear when my hand reaches out, my fingers brushing his hair. "Kind of."

His eyes drift shut, his hands resting on his stomach as he releases one long, drawn out breath. "What did you find?" he murmurs.

I pull my hand away.

"Don't stop," he pleads, his eyes open and on mine. "It's nice. You touching me like that."

I continue to stroke his hair, even though it's wrong, and I glance at the notebook quickly before pushing down the guilt. I grab the bottle and drink as if my life depended on it. "You and Jeremy," I begin, my stomach turning at the mention of their names together. I fight through it, just enough to say, "You guys played a few games together."

"Really?" he tilts his head up, as if getting more comfortable, but his eyes don't leave mine. "*Walters,* right?"

I nod.

"I remember him. He was a good ball player. He filled in for varsity a few times. Holy shit…" He rolls his head to the side and faces my stomach, grabbing my hand to make sure I don't stop stroking his hair. "I totally remember him now. He was a good kid."

"Don't do that," I mumble.

"Do what?" he asks, his eyebrows raised.

"It's just annoying for me to have to listen to people who didn't really know him talk as if they do and drop lines like, '*he was a good kid*' and '*he was gone way too soon*' and '*he was really going places.*'"

"I didn't mean to—"

"I know," I cut in. "It's nothing personal against you. It's just annoying, you know? Like you didn't know him, would've probably never thought about him again if it weren't for me and now you remember him but your memories are generic and mine aren't and it's just frustrating. That's all."

He rolls onto his back again. "That's completely valid, Riley."

"Thank you."

"Why are you thanking me?"

"Because you understand my frustration. My mom says—"

"Do me a favor. Don't talk to me about your mom anymore."

I press my lips tight.

He sighs and places his hands on his chest. "What else did you see?"

"Just your caption. I can't stop thinking about it. It's confusing."

"What was it again?"

"'*A man of many words.*' It just doesn't make sense."

He smiles. Not out of humor, but the kind of childish innocent smile his mother would've loved had she been around to see it. It's a side of him I hadn't seen before now and something I'm completely fascinated with. Something I'm drawn to. Like the flashes of color in his eyes after every blink. The way his nostrils flare with each exhale. The way his lip curves slightly higher on the right than the left. I want to ask him what he's thinking—what it is about this moment that has him smiling the way he is. But I don't. I stay silent. So silent I can hear every single one of his breaths. He adjusts his head on my lap so he's more comfortable, then he looks up at me, his lips curving higher, shifting the tiny strands of hair along his jaw. I run the back of my finger across them, feeling the heat of his cheek against my skin. He bites down on his bottom lip and my hand moves, as if on its own, until I'm millimeters away from his mouth and when his eyes drift shut and he inhales deeply, I blink and come back to reality—a reality I wish didn't exist.

"Go back to my hair," he whispers, his eyes still closed.

I do what he asks, feeling his neck muscles relax against my leg as soon as my fingers weave through his hair.

"So good," he murmurs. "I could fall asleep like this."

I let myself smile because I know he can't see it. "You can't use sleep as an excuse to avoid my question."

His body shakes with his silent chuckle. Then he licks his lips and I curse myself for pulling my hand away instead of touching them like I really wanted to do. As if reluctant, he slowly opens his eyes—eyes that instantly meet mine. They stay on me as he sits up and leans his back against the wall. "Try it," he says.

Something's happening to my heart… like the butterflies in my stomach. Constant, hectic movements that have me struggling for breath. "Try what?"

He pats his lap; that same perfect innocent smile taking over his handsome face.

I lie on my back, hesitating a second, before settling my head on his lap. He removes my hair from its knot and places the band on my stomach. His fingers are rough, just like I remember, but they're warm and gentle. He runs the tips of his fingers from my eyebrows and up to my hairline and when they comb through my hair for the first time, my eyes drift shut, but not before I see his smile form into a frown. I don't open my eyes because I don't want to see his face anymore. I don't want to see the sadness. I want to go back to a few minutes ago when his smile released my butterflies.

I focus on his touch, the sounds of our breaths, the feeling of weightlessness. Then he places one hand on my stomach, the other continuing with my hair. "I'm not really much for talking," he says, and for a moment I'm confused, then I remember what I'd said earlier. I'd already given up on his response, like so many of the unanswered questions I'd asked before. "Unless it's with you for some reason."

Finally, I open my eyes and look up at him. He's smiling again, his fingers now working a rhythm.

"Sometimes I feel like it's just easier to keep my mouth shut. Saves a lot of arguments."

"Like talking about my mom?" I ask, only half joking.

He arches his eyebrows. "Exactly like your mom." Now his hand on my stomach is moving, matching the strokes in my hair. "I guess it's kind of something I got from my dad," he says with a shrug. "And I think that you can tell more from people's actions than their words."

"Like what?"

His gaze shifts, so does his smile. He stares off at nothing in front of him. Both of his hands have stopped, but they're still touching me. "Like when you're at college and you ask the girl you love—the sole reason you're there—if she's happy you followed her path rather than take your own… and when she looks at you, there's a second's pause, a moment's hesitation, right before she says '*yes.*' That split second of silence gave me the truth, right before she spoke the lie."

"Hey Dylan," I whisper, and he drops his gaze, his eyes immediately finding mine. "Do me a favor? Don't talk to me about Heidi anymore."

He doesn't say anything, just continues to stare at me, his eyes roaming my face, my eyes, my lips, and back again. "Hey Riley."

"Yes?"

"Do you want me to kiss you right now?"

A second's pause.

A moment's hesitation.

"No."

Dylan

SHE LIED.

She wanted me to kiss her.

I wanted so badly to kiss her.

I didn't.

Instead, I gave her time.

Time + perspective can change people.

Hopefully.

JAKE ANSWERS AFTER several rings, just long enough for me to start losing my mind. As much as I'm not much for talking, I need to talk to someone. And I *need* to talk about Riley.

"What's up?" he asks, barely louder than the voices in the background.

"You busy? I can call back."

"Nah. You're good. The girls are here for book club so they're drunk and loud and stupid."

"Shut your whore mouth, Jacob!" Lucy shouts in the background.

I laugh. I can't help it. Honestly, after seeing Jake last week, I'd started missing everyone.

"Calm your clit, Luce," Cam tells her.

"The guys are there, too?"

"Yep."

I try to imagine them all there, all together, having fun and talking shit. "Have you told them I'm back?"

"Nope."

"Who is it?" Mikayla shouts.

"Just a guy from the team," Jake says.

I smile to myself, grateful I have someone I can trust in Jake. "Wait. Isn't it Wednesday? Don't they have book club on Tuesdays?"

"Oh man. You don't even want to know..."

"What guy from the team?" Micky asks, and I can picture the scowl on her face.

"No one, babe," he tells her.

"Talk about your stupid book, drink your wine, and let's go!" Logan shouts.

"Fuck you, Logan!" I think I miss Lucy the most.

"Why is everyone there for—"

"So they decided to change from Tuesdays to Wednesdays after last week," Jake cuts in. "Apparently new books come out on Tuesdays and Lucy reads faster than the others. She was done, and Kayla and Amanda weren't and according to Kayla, Lucy spoiled the story for them. This is all hearsay. All I know is I came home from practice and Amanda was on top of Lucy. Hair was being pulled, wine was being spilled, something about some Mason Kade dude and it was fucking hectic, man. I tried to break it up and it'd work for a second and then they'd be at it again so I had to call the guys over to help and shit got real because Logan got mad that Amanda was into some other Logan guy from the book and Cam was trying to get him to calm down. Then Logan and Cam got into a fight about letting their girls swoon over fictional boyfriends and—" He breaks off laughing, his accent thicker than normal when he adds, "It was just fucking crazy, mate, and Kayla was just standing at the side, drunk off her tits, laughing at them and shouting your name over and over and—"

"What!" Mikayla screeches.

Jake pauses a beat. "What?" he asks, and I can hear the fear in his voice.

"You said I was shouting *your* name. As in *Dylan*. I was shouting Dylan's name. Are you talking to Dylan? Is Dylan back?"

He curses under his breath. Static fills the phone and then silence… just for a moment before I hear Amanda's voice. "Dylan?"

I squeeze my eyes shut, preparing for the inevitable. "Yes?"

"How's Afghanistan?"

"I don't know, Amanda. I'm not there."

"So… where are you?"

I smile, and give her a truth I'd been waiting to *feel*. "I'm home."

Fourteen
Dylan

I DIDN'T GET to talk to Jake about Riley last night. After I told them I was back I spent a good couple hours talking with each of them, one after the other. We made plans for them to come over on Sunday. Normally, it'd probably annoy me, but it didn't.

I was on a high—a Riley-induced high.

Speaking of Riley—she hasn't stopped watching me since I stepped foot in her house. It's different from the other times I've caught her looking at me. Most of the time they're quick glances when she doesn't think I'm watching—which is dumb, because I'm always watching. Now, it's different, like she's trying to figure something out. Or like the times I'd unknowingly done something wrong and Heidi would look at me waiting for me to admit to something I hadn't known I'd done.

Riley takes a sip of her wine, her eyes on mine, completely unthreatened by the fact that I'm staring right at her… watching… trying to figure her out… waiting for her to admit to why she's looking at me the way she is.

Oh, what a tangled, fucked-up web we weave.

I'm giddy.

I don't know *why* I'm giddy.

She brings the bottle to her lips and takes another sip.

I'm going to kiss those lips again.

That's why I'm giddy.

She lowers the bottle, her head tilting and her eyebrow quirked.

"What?" I ask.

"Nothing," she says.

Sure, *nothing*.

"So…" I start, getting up from her bed and sitting down next to her on the floor. I like being close to her, touching her, sniffing her. *Creep.* "I have a thing tomorrow."

She turns to me, a glare in place, and I suppress my chuckle because dammit, she's cute. "A thing?" she asks. Another sip.

I move the hair away from her eyes to behind her ear. I keep my hand there for longer than needed, because like I said, I like touching her. "At the VA hospital. Apparently I'm meeting up with someone who'll be in charge of the physical therapy for my shoulder so I guess her and I will be spending a lot of time—"

"Her?" she interrupts, her glare more glary.

Win.

"I was hoping you'd come with. Make it more bearable?"

She opens her mouth, then shuts it, then opens it again—not to speak—but to take another sip.

"It's cool if you don't want to," I tell her, feeling my heart sink to my stomach. "I just thought… I mean, it would've been good to have a friend there, but like I said, it's cool." I start to get up but she presses down on my knee to stop me.

"I can't," she murmurs, her gaze lowered.

I shrug and physically remove her hand from my leg. I stand up and walk to her nightstand where I pick up my phone, keys and wallet. I don't want to risk staying, because staying means talking, and I'm sure whatever we'll end up saying will be something we'll regret.

I need time. Time + *perspective.*

"You're leaving?" she asks, sitting up on her knees, her eyes wide as she places the bottle on the floor next to her.

"Yeah. I think so. I have—"

"You're mad?" she interrupts.

I drop my shoulders and face her fully. "I'm not mad, Riley. But there's a big difference between *can't* and *won't.* It's not like you have plans," I say. "You *can* go, Riley. You just don't *want* to." I make it halfway to her door before I feel her hand on mine and when I spin to face her—there are tears in the eyes the color of sadness.

I drop my gaze, my hands on my hips. "I'm sorry," I tell her. "I'll see you tomorrow, okay?"

"Dylan…" She says my name like some sort of plea. "It's not that I don't *want* to. I do. I really *can't.* I haven't left the house in over a year," she admits. "I'm terrified of what's out there."

I try to breathe through the ache in my chest caused by the fear in her voice. "Why?"

"Just don't leave yet, okay?"

I DON'T LEAVE. I can't.

And I don't bring it up again because I don't want to see that same look in her eyes—the one telling me that whatever she fears is bigger than she lets on, bigger than this room we call our solitude, bigger than *us*.

She goes back to drinking in silence and writing in her notebook.

I go back to watching her.

She doesn't look at me the way she did when I walked in.

I think about the horizon, the *calm*—and I wonder when it is we'll be able to find it. And if we can ever find it together.

The alarm on her phone sounds, warning us that her mom will be home soon and I'll need to go. She reaches for it and taps the screen a few times, silencing it, then she looks at me.

I look at her.

After a while, she gets up and sits on the bed next to me. "I really do wish I could go with you," she says quietly.

"It's okay. You have your reasons."

After a sigh, she says, "Can your dad go with you? Or Eric?"

I turn to her. "It wouldn't be the same as having *you* there."

"I feel horrible." She exaggerates a pout.

"I'm sorry. I didn't say it to make you feel bad."

"I know. I just wish I could give back what you've given me."

"What do you mean?"

"I know what it's like to do things alone. Until you came along, I was drowning in it and now…"

"Now?"

She dips her head.

I throw my arm around her shoulders and bring her into me. "I appreciate it, Riley, but I'll be okay. Promise."

"Will you come by after? Tell me how it went?"

"If you want me to."

"I do," she whispers, then looks up at me, a sad smile on her beautiful face. She leans up and kisses my cheek, her lips lingering longer than necessary. When she moves back, she doesn't move far. So when I turn to face her, she's only an inch away. I bite down on my lip, my gaze moving from her eyes to her wet, parted, perfect fucking mouth. Then I reach up, my hand cupping her face… *please, please let me kiss you.* Slowly—giving her enough time to push me away—I lean down…

"Shit!" She pushes me away.

"Seriously?"

She's on her feet now, whispering loudly, "My mom's home!"

"So what?"

She's pulling on my good arm to get me to stand. "You have to leave." She looks around frantically, then points to her window. "Out there!"

I dig my heels into the carpet. "Riley, I'm twenty-three, I'm not jumping out of a fucking window."

"Please, Dylan."

I cross my arms. "No."

The panic in her eyes escalates when we hear the front door open. "Dylan, *please,*" she cries.

I roll my eyes and start for her window. I lift the damn thing, then climb through it, wondering how it's possible for a twenty-year-old to be constantly drunk but not allowed boys in her room.

She follows after me, sticking her head out when I land on my feet and start to walk away. "Dylan!" she whispers.

I stop and turn to her. "What?"

"Good luck tomorrow. I'll be thinking of you." She rolls her eyes. "I'm *always* thinking of you."

Fifteen
Riley

I THINK I lose my ability to breathe on the third knock. It started the second I stepped foot out of my house and got worse with every step. I have no idea how I manage to keep it together long enough for someone to actually open the door, but as soon as it does, I instantly regret every single step that got me here. She's stunning—blond hair, big brown eyes and legs for days. She's wearing a blue flannel shirt—exactly like the ones Dylan wears—and not much else. If you take away the instant jealousy, I'm pretty sure I have no justified reason to hate her as much as I hate her at the moment. Then she smiles, and I hate her even more. But then she says, "Are you here for Dylan?" and when I nod, her smile gets wider. "I'm a friend of his brother's. We're just having breakfast," she says, opening the door wider. Her smile begins to fade the longer I stand there, completely unsure of what to do next. I want to see him, but I want more to run back to my house, close the doors, drink the wine I hadn't touched since last night and remember all the reasons I'd told him I *couldn't* even though, clearly, I can. I just really, *really* didn't *want* to.

"Are you coming in?" she asks.

I nod again, though my reluctance is clear. "Maybe I should—"

"He'll be happy to see you, Riley," she says, and my breath catches.

She opens the door wider and it's enough for me to take a step forward, literally and metaphorically.

I MUMBLE AN apology for interrupting when I enter the kitchen—feeling the heat of three pairs of eyes on me. I look at everyone in the room, saving Dylan's for last. His dad and his brother are almost identical in their features, minus a beard. Their eyes are brown, though. Dylan's are blue. I'd remember the shade of blue even if I wasn't looking at them right now.

"What are you doing here?" he asks, coming to stand.

I use my skirt to wipe the sweat off my palms. God, I wish I were drunk. Or at least buzzed. It would make this so much easier. But I made my choice, and for the first time since I can remember, I chose someone other than myself. "Your appointment—it's this morning, right?"

He nods. "I thought you said you couldn't—"

My shrug cuts him off.

"Why don't you join us?" his dad says, finally breaking our stare.

"Do you want me to?" I ask, my eyes back on Dylan.

There is no second's pause.

No moment's hesitation.

Just his all-consuming smile. "We have bacon."

Dylan

IT DOESN'T TAKE long for us to finish our meals and drive to the VA hospital. She didn't speak much at the table. In fact, she didn't speak at all. Neither did I. Same goes for the car ride here.

I watched her though. I watched her eyes, clearer than I'd ever seen them, shifting constantly from one spot to another while her hands rested on her lap, her thumbs circling each other. I watched the rise and fall of her chest caused by her uneven breaths… and I watched *her*. Just *her*. And I tried to reason with myself as to why it made me so damn happy that she showed up at my door.

I guess, if you take away my pride, I really just wanted her. How ever she'd have me.

Now, we're sitting in the waiting room at the hospital, her hands still on her lap and mine on top of my knees, stopping them from bouncing. Somewhere, there's a clock ticking, soft footsteps as they move from one area to another, and gentle voices filtering from down the hall where the examination rooms are.

The guy sitting across us clears his throat and I look up at him. He's looking at Riley. Maybe this should piss me off—but the fact he's missing an arm kind of deflates my annoyance. His gaze moves from her to me and he nods once as if we share some kind of unspoken bond.

We don't.

I feel like an imposter.

He's missing an arm. The older guy on my right has scars covering half his face and then there's me. I'm young, I'm fit—and give it a couple months—I'll be back to a hundred percent. I glance at Riley, searching for her reaction. Her gaze is lowered, focused on her moving thumbs. I nudge her with my elbow. "You okay?"

Before she has a chance to respond, the same doctor from my first visit calls my name. I stand up, taking Riley with me. She keeps her hand in mine, her grip tight as we walk down the narrow hallway toward his examination room. We walk in silence, the same silence that seems to have surrounded me all day. Silent on the outside, roaring thoughts on the inside.

A woman stands when we enter the room. She's in her mid-forties, dressed in standard hospital gear. She introduces herself as Tracey, my physical therapist, all while clutching a folder to her chest with *LCpl. Banks, D.* printed on the front. I sit on the bed while Riley takes a seat against the wall next to the door. Her knees are bouncing now, just like mine wanted to out in the waiting room. She looks out of place and I'm sure she feels it.

"Who do we have here?" Tracey asks, motioning to Riley.

"This is my friend Riley," I tell her.

"And you're comfortable with her sitting in the room?"

Riley's eyes meet mine from across the room and she smiles. And that slight smile gives me the encouragement I need to speak the truth—the truth only she can get out of me. "She's the only one I'm comfortable with."

Riley's body relaxes with her exhale and I know I've said the right thing because her knees are no longer bouncing, her gaze is no longer wandering. And me? I realize now why I was happy to see her this morning—because there was a reason I asked her to come with me today. I wanted her here. No. I *needed* her here.

She just doesn't know how much.

"How's the wound healing?"

"Good," I say, but I'm still watching Riley.

"Still bleeding?"

"No, Ma'am."

"That's good, Lance Corporal."

I tear my gaze away from Riley and focus on Tracey. "Dylan's fine, Ma'am."

She nods once. "Okay, Dylan. You ready for me to take a look at it?"

It takes longer than it should for me to shrug out of my shirt and as soon as it's off, both Tracey and Dr. Garvis block my view of Riley to inspect my shoulder.

He checks the entry wound first and then the exit. "It's healing well," Dr. Garvis says while Tracey takes notes in her now open folder. I wonder what it says about me. How much detail goes into medical records of wounded Marines? Does it state how it happened? Not the technical aspects of what bullet or gun caused it but *how*. When. Where. Who.

They speak for a few minutes, their words a jumbled mess of medical terms and timelines. Dr. Garvis moves back to his seat behind his desk, his fingers typing away when I hear the gasp come from Riley. My eyes snap to hers—wide and glazed with tears.

It dawns on me that it's the first time she's ever seen it. Sure, she knows it exists, she's seen it bandaged up, but she's never seen *it*. She raises her hand and covers her mouth and when she sees I've noticed her reaction, she looks away.

Tracey must see it, too, because she stands in front of me, blocking Riley's view. "Still okay, Dylan?"

I nod and look over her shoulder at Riley, who's now looking everywhere but at me. "Riley," I call out.

"Yeah?"

I motion for her to sit on the bed with me and without hesitation; she picks up her bag and sits next to me, her hand immediately on my leg.

Tracey smiles. "I've gone over your file," she says, "and I've come up with a rehabilitation plan for the injury. We weren't sure if you needed more time for it to heal or if your current exercises are helping—"

"He does these spinny things," Riley interrupts.

Tracey quirks an eyebrow at her, her amusement evident. "*Spinny* things?"

"Yeah." Riley holds her free hand to her chest, then rotates her shoulder like she must've seen me doing a few times. "Spinny things."

Tracey smiles.

So do I.

"And these ones," Riley continues, releasing my hand. She has both hands on her chest now, her elbows moving back and forth and I wonder if I've looked as ridiculous as she does at this very moment.

Tracey laughs. "Well, it's good to know you've been doing them," she murmurs, scribbling more notes in the folder.

I cover Riley's hand with mine when she places it back on my leg. Then I nudge her with my elbow. "You been watching me?" I joke.

She shrugs.

"So keep doing those," Tracey says, looking up from her notes. "Give it about a week or so and you can start adding weights. You can start with—" She breaks off when Riley moves quickly to pull out a notebook from her bag. She flips open the cover and sets the tip of the pen on a blank page, her eyes on Tracey. Then she nods.

Tracey looks at me.

I shrug.

Dr. Garvis joins us.

"Go on," Riley says. She looks down at her book, just long enough for her to write: *Dylan's rehab* on the top of the page, and then refocuses on Tracey.

"Riley?" I ask, my gaze moving from Tracey to her. "What are you doing?"

"Taking notes," she answers.

She's already written *Tracey* and *Dr. Garvis* in the time it's taken me to ask a simple question.

The rest of us stay quiet, our eyes on her. "What?" she asks, looking between us.

"Nothing." I shake my head, smiling to myself.

"I'll be giving Dylan a copy of the rehab plan and all the exercises so you don't have—"

Riley waves her hand dismissively. "But that's for him. These are for me."

Dr. Garvis asks, "For you?"

Riley shrugs. "So I can make sure he does it and kick his ass if he doesn't."

"Some friend you have here, Dylan," Tracey says.

"Yeah." I can't stop smiling. "She's just lucky she's beautiful."

WE SPEND A good half hour in the room while Tracey and I discuss my new rehab plan and Riley frantically takes notes. Ten pages of them, last I counted. She asks a lot of questions, too. Questions I would've never thought to ask. Tracey and Dr. Garvis answer every one as best they can and at the end of it all, Doc says, "If everything goes well, we'll have you back to your unit in four to six months."

Four to six months, I think. Riley though—she says it out loud. And having her voice it makes it more real. So does her writing it down, apparently.

THE RIDE BACK home is exactly the same as it was there. Silent.

She sits with her back to the door, her legs crossed beneath her, writing in a notebook—a different one to the one she had at the hospital—and whatever she's writing has her mind so consumed she doesn't even realize that I've pulled into my garage and parked.

"So..." I say, killing the engine.

She looks up and around her and for a moment she's confused. Then she must realize where we are and what we're doing and the reality of the day finally hits her. "Four to six months," she mumbles.

"Four to six months," I repeat.

Blindly, she shoves the notebook in her bag and looks around again. "This your garage?"

"Yep."

She opens the door and steps out. I follow behind her, meeting her at the workbench where my engine parts sit. "What's this?"

"Just an engine I'm working on."

"You think it'll be done in four to six months?" she asks.

"If I want it to be," I tell her. My response has more than one meaning, but she doesn't need to know that. "I've pulled it apart and rebuilt it so many times I can do it with my eyes closed."

"So why not just leave it?"

I shrug. "I don't know. I guess maybe I'm not ready to move on." Another double meaning.

She picks up the toothbrush I use to clean the smaller parts and lifts it between us. "What's this for?"

I grab a random part off the bench and hand it to her. "Scrub it clean."

It wasn't an order, but she does it anyway, and I watch and wait to see if this is it. If this is her way of avoiding the situation and everything we've done to get us to this point. She says, "So you just clean them and..."

I tune her out, my mind too busy screaming all the questions she's avoiding. "Why did you come today?"

Her hands freeze mid movement, just for a moment, before she starts again. "Because you asked me to."

I cover her hands. "Riley," I deadpan. I want her to pay attention. I've moved on from wanting the empty silence of her room and the comfort that comes with it.

She swallows loudly and drops the brush and the part on the bench. Then she faces me. "You had sex with me."

"I'm blindingly aware of that, Riley."

"And you want to have more sex with me."

"Again, I'm positive that's *obvious.*"

Her gaze drops. "But it's not just about sex anymore is it?"

"It's never been *just about sex.*"

"I mean... we feel things..."

I nod. "I feel a lot of things for you. So? What does that mean?"

Rubbing her temple, she sighs loudly. "It means you were wrong, Dylan, about there being a big difference between can't and won't. Sometimes, it's not that easy, especially when it comes to feelings. I wanted you, but I shouldn't have let it happen."

"That makes no sense, Riley. You either wanted to or you didn't."

"I did want you."

"So what's the problem?"

"The guilt! Okay!" she shouts. Then takes a calming breath. "The guilt is the problem." And now she's crying. "I can't let it happen again—the sex *or* the feelings—because the guilt is stronger than the want and it would be okay, you know? For you to be in my room and for us to kiss and touch each other the way we did, but the second you're gone, I'm surrounded by guilt because Jeremy—"

"Is dead," I cut in, and the second the words leave my mouth I hate myself.

She starts to leave, but I grasp her arm. "I'm sorry, Riley. That was wrong and completely out of line."

Her eyes drift shut, her intake of breath long and loud and when she releases it, she opens her eyes—her clear gray eyes. "I need to show you something," she says, shrugging out of my hold and walking out of the garage. I follow behind her, because I can't not. And I know whatever she's about to show me, whatever she's about to say, it's going to change everything. *Everything.*

Sixteen
Riley

There's no emotion greater than fear.

No ache greater than grief.

No sound greater than silence.

Dylan's eyes lift from the notes in his hands and the hundreds on the floor—all the notes I've written to a boy I love. A boy he so simply worded as "dead" and if it were that easy—for me to say he's dead and to move on—then I wouldn't be holding on to him, to the memories of him. Because he's still here, in my mind and in my heart—he's still alive, and the guilt I feel now, which is greater than the guilt I felt after Dylan's kiss is proof of that. Because now, I'm sharing more than just the guilt of our actions. I'm sharing our memories, our lives, our pasts, and our *love*. Not with the boy I loved, but with a man who's making me question that love.

"Do you get it now?" I ask, my voice strained from the sob forcing its way out of me.

"How long have you..." He doesn't finish his sentence. He doesn't need to.

"You know, it's strange... that you can see someone every day for over two years of your life... look into their eyes, touch them, feel their hair between your fingers, see them smile, hear them laugh—and then it gets taken away from you and *nothing*." I wipe my cheeks, my tears flowing unrestrained. "You close your eyes and you try to picture them and you can't. You can't see any of it. You can't hear their voice, hear their laughter, hear them say your name a thousand different ways."

"Riley," he says, his voice hoarse from his own fear—his fear of me and my form of crazy.

"So I write him these letters," I tell him. "I try to remember him, every moment of our lives and I write them down so I don't forget them, because I don't want to forget *him.* I don't want his life and our love to become a generic quote. To one day mean nothing." I take a breath and make sure he's looking at me when I add, "Because he meant *everything* to me, Dylan."

I start to pick up the letters, placing them carefully back in their jars, trying to do everything I can to avoid reading them. Because it's already bad enough that I've bled my heart to Dylan, I don't need the reminder of the guilt to add to the pain.

He drops to his knees in front of me and picks up the notes, opening each one and reading them before handing them to me. He doesn't speak when he does it. He just takes his time, being as careful as I am when he unfolds and refolds them. And when we're done, he leans back against the bed, his eyes on the ceiling and my broken heart weighing heavily in his hands. He stays that way for minutes, hours, who knows? Then he drops his gaze, looking at me silently crying in front of him.

"What happened to him?" he asks, and I shake my head. It's one memory I don't want to remember.

"Will you tell me about him?"

I release a sob. "What?"

He pushes off the bed and moves closer to me, his legs crossed as his hands reach for mine. "Not the memories you have of him or the things you did or the color of his eyes. Tell me about him, the boy who loved you."

I look over at the full bottle of wine on my nightstand.

"No," he says, his finger on my chin, making me face him again. "Let *me* be your alcohol. Let *me* dull your pain."

I cry into my hands, free and uncontrolled and louder than I ever let myself cry.

"Come here," he pulls me with him until he's lying on his back, my head on his chest as he strokes my hair. He holds me to him while I cry. Not from grief. Not from anger. Not from missing someone so badly I don't know how to get through the next hour, let alone the next day, but I cry because it's all too much. Too real. Too raw. And for the first time ever, I allow myself to cry for *me.*

For *my* loss.

"Start from the beginning," Dylan says. "Tell me how you met. How he asked you out. Where he took you on the first date. Your first kiss. Tell me how he made you *feel.* Tell me how he loved you."

I sniff back my heartbreak and look up at him. "Why?"

"Because, Riley," he says, kissing the top of my head. "I plan on loving you like he did."

✧ ✧ ✧

It was English class. Sophomore year. We were studying Shakespeare, watching the "modern" version of Romeo and Juliette. You were sitting next to me leaning on the back legs of your chair messing around with your friends. You were the popular Jock. I was the quiet, get-through-the-day girl. You and your friends started talking louder and louder and I lost it. I turned to you all and told you to be quiet so I could focus. You dropped your chair forward, your eyes wide and on me. "Excuse me?" you asked.

"You heard me. Shut up. Some of us are here to actually learn."

Your friends laughed. You didn't. You just kept looking at me. "Riley, right?"

I rolled my eyes.

You leaned forward, your forearm on my desk and your voice low. "You really think some old dude like Shakespeare wrote this shit so hundreds of years later a bunch of punk teenagers can rip it to shreds in order to get some score out of a hundred… so some self-righteous adult who once ripped the same material to shreds can give said teenager a number in comparison to how he feels about Shakespeare's life's work?"

Shaking my head, I glared at you and pushed your arm off my desk. "I don't need to hear your bullshit opinion. I just want you to shut up."

Your friends laughed again.

And again, you didn't.

Instead, you turned around and told them all to be quiet.

You were their leader—an opinionated ass of a leader.

"Let the lady learn," you shouted.

I yelled at you to shut up.

We both got detention.

And when the class was over I stood up and started packing my bag. You stood, too, right by my table, waiting for me to finish. When I was done, you took my hand in yours and placed your lips on the back of it, kissing it once.

I stood still, not knowing what to do... and annoyed that my first kind-of-kiss from a boy was from you. Then you smiled. "Sweet Riley," you announced. "Parting is such sweet sorrow, That I shall say good night till it be morrow... at detention."

We fell in like in an otherwise empty classroom of detention.

We fell in love in the stands at one my swim meets.

We fell in forever at senior prom, while we danced under the twinkling lights with crowns on our heads at the highest point of our short-lived future. "Riley," you whispered, my hands on your chest and your arms around my waist.

I looked up at you.

Then you spoke. "My bounty is as boundless as the sea, My love as deep; the more I give to thee, The more I have, for both are infinite."

✧ ✧ ✧

I SIT UP and look down at Dylan, his eyes sad and unfocused. He hasn't said a word since I started remembering Jeremy. "I don't think I ever felt worthy of him," I say, wiping my tears.

He reaches up and replaces my hand with his, continuing the job of hiding the pain.

"I want to feel worthy of you, Dylan."

"Riley, you are—"

"Not yet," I cut in. "But I *want* to be. And that's something I haven't felt since Jeremy died. I want to stop drinking and I want to stop feeling nothing but despair when I think of him. I want to be stronger than that. I don't want to feel like the horizon."

His head tilts. "The horizon?"

"I feel like I'm the sky and the earth is reality. And the horizon...

it's just the sky and the earth appearing to touch, but they never do. I want to touch reality, Dylan. I want to live in it. I want to feel like I'm here… in this world, and not just floating around it. And if I've learned anything from Jeremy and from you—it's that life's too short, and no matter how much it hurts, it's better than the alternative."

Seventeen
Dylan

SHE TELLS ME not to come over during the next two days because her mom's home and having her mom question why I'm there may just cause her to drink. She wants to do everything she can to avoid it, which makes me proud. I tell her so and she smiles. "Good. I want to give you a reason to be proud." We exchange phone numbers so she can text me in case her feelings ever get too overwhelming and she reaches for the bottle.

"YOU LOOK LIKE ass," Eric says when I step into the living room.

"It's been a long ass day."

He motions to my shoulder. "Everything okay?"

"Yeah, nothing like that. Where's Sydney?"

"Work."

"What does she do?"

"She's a nurse."

"Seriously?" I ask.

Eric laughs. "Don't let her shitty life choices—aka, being with me—fool you. Sydney's a really smart girl and she's funny and compassionate and… yeah…." He clears his throat. "Hey! Have you seen my balls? I swear I lost them around three weeks ago."

"She probably took them to work with her," I say through a chuckle. "Yo, what's with all the computer shit in my room?"

"It's just work stuff."

"You work?" I ask in disbelief.

He laughs. "I also pay half the mortgage if that means anything."

"What the hell do you even do?"

His eyebrows rise. "Ah, baby brother. If I told you, then I'd have to kill you."

"Fuck off." I throw a cushion at his head. Clearly, I've been hanging around Riley too much. "Tell me."

He throws the cushion back. I catch it. "I work for a secret government agency. I try to find online predators, kiddie porn, all that stuff."

"No shit?"

He nods.

I stare at him. "Yeah. You really look like you're doing a good job with that." I point to him sitting in his boxer shorts with a beer in his hand.

"Fuck off, dickhead. I work nights. That's when the assholes come out." He shrugs. "It works out, though. I get to be home all day and Sydney and I both work the same schedule so we can see each other as much as possible."

"You really like her, huh?"

"Yep," he says, now unashamed. "Thinking of asking her to take it to the next step."

"What? Like marriage?" My voice is loud. Too loud.

"No. Not marriage." He's looking at me like I'm stupid. Maybe I am, but what else could the next step be?

"I'm thinking about asking her to date me, you know. Not just fuck me."

I shake my head. "You're fucking gross."

"Okay, guy who's on The Drug."

"I'm not on The Fucking Drug."

He laughs. "I know. Sydney told me about the girl next door. How's she coping anyway?"

"What do you mean *coping*?"

"After the accident. She kind of went a little…" He spins his finger around his ear and whistles.

"Don't talk about her like that."

"Oh," he says, his eyes wide while he nods slowly. "So you're *more* than boning her?"

"I'm not boning her," I snap. And now I'm pissed. Maybe because he's talking shit—or maybe because he seems to know more about her than I do. Sighing, I drop my head forward. "What accident?" I ask.

"She hasn't told you?"

"Obviously not. How the fuck do you play detective online and you can't even work that out?"

He shakes his empty beer and stands up. "Just look up her name online. I'm sure you can find out."

"Can I borrow a computer?"

He shakes his head as he passes me. "Just use your phone." He smacks the back of my head. "How the fuck are we brothers?"

I pull my phone out of my pocket and search for the Internet app. When I finally find it, I don't type her name. I type his: *Jeremy Walters* into the search window, and when the results load, my eyes scan the headlines, my breath leaving me completely.

Freak cliff jumping accident takes life of promising teen.

North Carolina teen dies after taking "The Leap."

I continue to scroll down the page, my heart beating wildly in my chest.

Then I see it—the one headline that causes my heart to stop and my head to spin.

Pre-college rite of passage tradition ends in tragedy for teen couple. One dead, one injured.

She was *there*.

She was there the exact moment the love of her life took his last breath.

I CLICK ON the link and start to read the article, but a message pops up, blocking my view.

Riley: *Exactly how needy would I come across if I told you I was missing you already?*

I release the breath I didn't know I was holding and read the text over and over. I picture her in her room, in the corner with all her cushions… the way her gaze lifts when she watches me in her bed. I picture her smile when I say something stupid, her head as it tilts back with her laughter. And then I picture her eyes, her clear gray eyes full of hope.

Dylan: *Aboutxas needy asxit would sound ig I tolf you that Is deal wit th wra th of your mpther just to saee you.*

Riley: *What?*

Dylan: *Im reakky bas at this.*

Riley: *Um. Maybe go on your computer because I'm not kidding. I'm needy. And I need you to keep me sane right now.*

Dylan: *Ok. Hanfxin.*

Riley: *What? Lol. Wtf are you on?*

I find Eric on his laptop in his room. "Yo. Can I borrow a computer?"

He faces me. "What? You can't google on your phone?"

"No. I'm texting with Riley and I can't type on my phone for shit."

He laughs and gets up from his chair. Then he opens his closet where more than ten laptops are piled up high. He grabs one and turns to me. "You need me to set it up so you can text from here? Or are you on Facebook?"

I shake my head. "Yeah, set up the text thing."

Riley: *Dylan?*

I start to reply with Eric hovering over me. "Jesus Christ," he says, taking the phone from my hand. His fingers fly across the screen and when he's done he hands it back to me and gets to work on the computer I'll be using. I look down at the text he just sent.

Dylan: *Turns out my brother's a Neanderthal… doesn't understand technology and has fat as fuck fingers. Give him five. I'm setting up a comp for him. Hopefully that'll help his cause. The kid can build an engine in his sleep but he can't fucking type to save his life.*

Riley: *lol. K. Thx.*

I show him the message. "What the fuck does this mean?"

"Laugh out loud. Okay. Thanks."

"Why doesn't she just type that?"

He shakes his head with his chuckle. "You're such a fucking noob, D."

"What the hell is a noob?"

He ignores me and says, "All done." He sets the computer on his bed. I sit down on the mattress and place the computer on my lap.

Dylan: *Can you hear me?*

Riley: *See you? Yes. OMG. Lol.*

Dylan: *okay. What is OMG?*

Riley: *Oh my god. I feel like I'm writing to my grandpa.*

Dylan: *Shut up. Seriously though. What is OMG?*

Riley: *Oh my god.*

Dylan: *Just tell me.*

Riley: *O = Oh. M = my. G = God.*

Dylan: *Oh.*

Riley: *Yeah...*

Dylan: *So...*

Riley: *So...*

Dylan: *What are you wearing?*

Riley: *rly? Lmfao.*

I stay in Eric's room while he works and I type (slower than Riley's grandpa, apparently). I don't know how long we stay in there, occasionally laughing at and with her, while Eric eyes me every so often, but I don't care. I could talk to her all night like this. And I do. Even during Friday night dinner with Dad and E. I have to revert back to my phone when I'm at the table, which makes for more typos than the history of typewriters has ever seen (so Riley says). But now I know what lol, lmfao, omg, k, brb, btw and w00t mean. Though I'm still a little confused on the last one.

I skip the "Friday night insert random sport here" and opt instead to lock myself in my room with the computer Eric has generously let me keep.

Dylan: *Hey. Can you send pictures through this?*

Riley: *Yep.*

Dylan: *Send me a picture of yourself.*

Riley: *A random picture or you want me to take one?*

Dylan: *Take one of you right now. I want to see you.*

Riley: *You send me one first.*

Dylan: *You seriously think I would even know how to do that?*

Riley: *lol. True. It's a little weird, no?*

Dylan: *No, it's not. Unless you're naked or something. Then send me 80 pictures. Please and thank you!*

Riley: *You're such a goof. Okay. Hold on.*

She sends me a picture of her in her room. She's sitting in bed, her back against the headboard just like I'm sitting. It's dark, but I can make out her eyes, still clear, still perfect. Her nose is scrunched a little and her lips… God, her lips. They're wet, a little pouty and fuck she's beautiful.

Riley: *You there?*

Dylan: *Yeah.*

Riley: *What are you doing?*

Dylan: *Taking off my pants. That picture does something to me.*

Riley: *Wow, you're brave when you're talking through texts.*

Dylan: *Yeah, well you can't throw anything at me from all the way over there.*

I wasn't kidding. That picture really did do something—to my cock. Now hard in my pants.

Riley: *God, I wish you were here.*

Dylan: *Me too.*

Riley: *What do you think we'd be doing if you were here?*

I think a moment before responding, trying to ignore the sensation building below.

Dylan: *What I think we'd be doing and what I'd want to be doing are two different things, Riley.*

For a while, she doesn't respond. Maybe I've pushed the wrong buttons. I seem to be good at that.

Dylan: *Sorry?*

Riley: *For what?*

Dylan: *I don't know. Did I say something wrong?*

Another long wait.

Riley: *No.*
Riley: *Are you in bed?*

Dylan: *Yeah.*

Riley: *What are you doing?*

Dylan: *Thinking about you. You?*

Riley: *Same.*

Dylan: *What exactly are you thinking about?*

Riley: *You don't want to know, Dylan.*

Dylan: *I think I do.*

Riley: *Maybe we should stop.*

Dylan: *Stop what?*

Riley: *I'm going to try to sleep.*

Dylan: *Okay.*

Riley: *Good night.*

Dylan: *Good night, Riley.*

I don't go to sleep. Instead, I let my mind continue the conversation. One hand slipping beneath my boxers, the other on my phone, I look at the picture she sent through—my eyes focused on her lips—lips I've tasted. Devoured, almost. They drift shut when my hand circles my cock. I picture her in her bed, her sheets around her waist, one hand on her breast, the other down her panties… *fuck*.

I start to stroke myself, remembering the sounds she makes when she comes, wishing I was there to hear it—or better—be the reason she's moaning, her lips pressed against her pillows and her hand working her to climax.

It doesn't take long for me to blow, and when the buzz fades I heave out a breath and look at her picture again.

With my mouth dry and breaths heavy, I reach for a dirty sock and clean myself up, then smile when my phone sounds with a text.

Riley: *Are you still awake?*

Dylan: *Yes.*

Riley: *What have you been doing?*

Dylan: *Lying in bed.*

Riley: *Me too.*

Dylan: *So.*

Riley: *So…*

Dylan: *What are you wearing?*

Riley: *Nothing anymore.*

Eighteen
Dylan

I SPEND THE next morning in my room talking to her through a computer screen. We don't talk about what happened last night and how close things got to becoming appropriately inappropriate. In the afternoon, Dad and I go out and look for shells for the engine again. We decide on a white '97 Honda Civic and make plans for it to be towed to our house. We also go to the store and get food and drinks for the gang's visit tomorrow. Riley doesn't text as much when I'm out because she says it takes longer for her to try to decipher the messages I type on my phone than it would to actually wait until her mom goes back to work and she can see me again.

AS SOON AS we're home, I go straight back to my room and get on the computer.

Dylan: *Home.*

Riley: *Yay.*

Dylan: *What are you doing?*

Riley: *I just finished reading one of those books you got me.*

Dylan: *Oh yeah? I didn't know you started.*

Riley: *I started when you left earlier today.*

Dylan: *Those are full-size books. Are you a speed-reader or something?*

Riley: *I am, actually. I used to love reading but I hadn't had enough focus (sobriety) since you know...*

Dylan: *That's cool. You and my friend Lucy would get along well.*

Riley: *Lucy?*

Dylan: *My buddy Cameron's wife.*

Riley: *Wife?*

Dylan: *Yeah. They got married last November.*

Riley: *Your friends from school? Aren't they seniors in college?*

Dylan: *Yeah.*

Riley: *A little young, no?*

Dylan: *Love is love, Riley Hudson.*

Riley: *That's true.*
Riley: *I'm actually pretty mad at you.*

Dylan: *Uh oh.*

Riley: *Yep.*

Dylan: *Should I ask why?*

Riley: *That book you got me ends on a cliffhanger, and now I don't know if the couple will ever get back together. Do you know how frustrating that is? When's the next one out?*

Dylan: *No clue. I just picked random ones from the romance section.*

Riley: *And why romance?*

Dylan: *I don't know. Cam's always talking about Lucy reading romance books. Gets her turned on or something. Was hoping for the same effect with you…*

Riley: *You're such a guy. Lol.*

Dylan: *I'm sorry about the cliffhanger.*

Riley: *It's okay. It was more of a pause than a cliffhanger.*

Dylan: *A pause?*

Riley: *Yeah. A pause. Like, sometimes in life you just need a pause before you start to play again.*
Riley: *Like us.*

Dylan: *Us?*

Riley: *Exactly like us. You deployed and I… de—something'd. And now we're playing again.*

Dylan: *Playing?*

Riley: *And you're my favorite toy, Banks.*

Dylan: *I am?*

Riley: *You and the vibrator under my bed.*

Dylan: *?*

Dylan: *!!*
Dylan: *??*
Dylan: *????!!!!!!?????!!!!!*
Dylan: *aehfaincgfiqehrusdlkfjlsdhflkjasdhflkasjhdf*
Dylan: *I mean, what?*

Riley: *LOL. Such a guy. I gtg eat dinner with the mumster. I'll message you later.*

Dylan: *You're mean.*

Riley: *Says the guy who walked out of his house shrugging on a shirt. Nice abs, by the way.*

Dylan: *Stalk much?*

Riley: *Not the first time, Banks. You've always been the boy next door. ;)*

She has me looking at the clock. All day. All night. Even when I try to sleep I wake up every fifteen minutes, checking my phone, hoping for a message. How the hell did I live without this kind of technology for so long? Now it's four in the morning and I can't get back to sleep, my mind running wild with thoughts of her.

Dylan: *Are you awake?*

Riley: *Now I am.*

Dylan: *I wake you?*

Riley: *It's fine. You okay? Did you have a bad dream?*

It dawns on me that I haven't had a nightmare in the past week. Not since I'd been seeing her more and more. Since I spoke to her about it, I guess. Maybe all those years of silence were a waste. Maybe I should've spoken up more.

I switch from my phone to my laptop and sit up in the bed.

Dylan: *No bad dream. Just thinking about you.*

Riley: *Funny. I was dreaming about you when you messaged me.*

Dylan: *oh yeah? What kind of dream? Need me to leave you to play with your other favorite toy?*

Riley: *Lol. No. Not that kind of dream.*

Dylan: *So?*

Riley: *I dreamt we were in your truck. You were driving. I was in the* *middle of the front seat. The sun was out and the warmth of it tickled my skin. You were driving and your hand was on my leg and you were talking to me about the engine in your garage.*

Dylan: *Doesn't sound that exciting.*

Riley: *It was. And you were. You were happy telling me about it.*

Dylan: *And you were bored, right?*

Riley: *No. Why would I be bored?*

Dylan: *Because it's an engine, Riley.*

Riley: *It's also your passion, Dylan. If it excites you, it excites me.*

I think about Heidi and all the times I'd tried to talk to her about cars. She'd shut me down every time. Sometimes it wasn't even verbally, she'd just tune out, grab her phone and ignore me.

Riley: *You okay?*

Dylan: *Yeah. Just thinking.*

Riley: *About?*

Dylan: *Nothing.*

Riley: *Because you're not allowed to talk about her to me?*

Dylan: *lol.*

Riley: *You lol'd.*

Dylan: *I did.*

Riley: *You can talk about her. I was just kidding.*

Dylan: *It's weird.*

Riley: *Says the guy who wanted to hear all about my ex-boyfriend? Not weird at all.*

Dylan: *Valid.*

Riley: *So?*

Dylan: *I was just thinking… She never really cared much about what I was into, you know? Not just cars, but even little things like basketball. Did Jeremy go to your swim meets?*

Riley: *Every single one.*

Dylan: *See?*

Riley: *I'm sorry.*

Dylan: *It's okay. I guess when you say things like that… like you being excited about the things I'm excited about, I kind of just wonder, you* *know? Like, why were we even together for so long?*

Riley: *Can I be completely honest with you?*

Dylan: *Always. I don't ever want anything else from you.*

Riley: *I feel like it's kind of a blessing, you know? That you guys broke up.*

Dylan: *Well yeah, because then I probably would've never met you.*

Riley: *You're sweet, but no. That's not what I meant.*

Dylan: *Then what?*

I can see the little dots on the screen moving. It feels like forever before her message finally comes through.

Riley: *You know those couples in high school who seem so perfect on the outside, but are unhappy on the inside? They spend their teenage years together, go off to college and keep the pretense of perfection going because by then it's all they know. I'm not saying you didn't love each other. You probably did. In fact, I'm sure YOU definitely did, because I can tell when YOU care for someone, you care for them deeply. I just think that maybe time changed you both. At some point you grew apart and you didn't realize it was happening until there was nothing left. And you're probably bitter and angry because you might feel like you don't exactly know how it happened. It's been what? Over two years since you've been together and she's still on your mind.*

I read her text over and over, me and Heidi's history running through my mind like a slideshow of irrelevant events.

Dylan: *Last November.*

Riley: *What?*

Dylan: *I was with her at Cam and Lucy's wedding three months ago.*

Riley: *Oh.*

Dylan: *Sorry.*

Riley: *You don't owe me an apology, Dylan.*

Dylan: *Still.*

Riley: *So you were together when you were deployed?*

Dylan: *Not really.*

Riley: *I'm confused.*

Dylan: *She Dear John'd me when I first deployed and said she wanted* *to see other people. I'm not really sure what she did after that. I don't want to know. But then I saw her at the wedding and we... you know...*

Riley: *What's Dear John mean?*

Dylan: *It's just a term for when your girl breaks up with you in a letter while you're deployed.*

Riley: *I'm sorry.*

Dylan: *Yeah...*

Riley: *But you were together again after the wedding?*

Dylan: *We all went to Vegas for Cam and Lucy's honeymoon.*

Riley: *Hello, Captain Avoidance.*

Dylan: *I broke up with her for good there. She went home. I went back to Afghanistan.*

Riley: *I assumed something happened while you were in Vegas?*

Dylan: *Just don't keep secrets from me, Riley. That's all I ask.*

The little dots on the screen move again.
It feels like forever. Again.
Finally:

Riley: *Good night, Dylan.*

Dylan: *Wait. What did I say? Or do?*

Riley: *It's just a little rich for you to be asking me not to keep secrets when you obviously want to hold on to your own.*

Dylan: *I looked up Jeremy. I know what happened. I know you were there when he died.*

Riley: *I guess some secrets are easier to find than others. Maybe there's a reason we want to keep them a secret instead of pushing the wrong buttons with each other and ending up in a place neither of us want?*

Dylan: *I wish I was in my truck, you next to me, my hand on your leg, sun shining while I tell you about the dumb engine in my garage.*

Riley: *It's not a dumb engine. And I wish I was there, too. Maybe if we close our eyes and go to sleep and wish on it enough it will happen in our dreams?*

Dylan: *I'll make it happen, Riley. Just not in our dreams. In reality. We'll drive toward the calm of the horizon until you feel like you're touching the earth. And we can stay there. I'll show you our reality. Just you and me. And it'll be perfect. You'll see.*

After a long pause, she replies:

Riley: *You made me cry.*

Dylan: *I'm sorry.*

Riley: *I'm falling so hard for you, Dylan Banks.*

Dylan: *I'm already there, Riley Hudson.*

She doesn't respond after that and I don't mind that she doesn't because it gives me the opportunity to work on something I was supposed to do yesterday. I grab what I need and sit in the corner of my room, imagining exactly what she described in her dream. And I let that feeling guide me through my task until I fall back asleep, her dream now becoming mine.

Nineteen
Dylan

I WAKE UP to the sound of my phone ringing. For a second, I get excited, thinking it's Riley. It's not. It's Jake.

"What's up?" I check the time. 9:47. They're not meant to be here until 11.

"Yo. My fucking truck died on the way to your house. Cam and Logan are with me. The girls are coming later. Can you come get us?"

"Yeah, man." I sit up and rub my eyes. "Where are you?"

"Close. We're just at the exit off the highway."

I hang up and shrug on some clothes, still half asleep as I walk through the hallway, past the kitchen, and toward the back door leading to the yard.

As soon as I open the door water splashes my face and my chest. Followed quickly by something brown and soft. And now I'm awake.

Awake and *angry*.

I look down at myself before looking at them. I'm soaking wet, covered in feathers.

Jake and Logan are standing a few feet in front of me—both holding buckets. Jakes drops his. "Oh, fuck," he whispers, eyes wide.

Then Logan breaks out in laughter.

"You know I carry, right?" I threaten, only half-joking. The second I take a step, something wet hits my head. It's white. *Milk*. I start to look up, just in time to see eggs falling from the sky. The first one hits my shoulder, then the rest is a blur. After closing my eyes, I ball my fists at my sides, trying to keep my anger in check. Jake and Logan are cackling like idiots, and now another guffaw from above. I wipe my eyes so I can see Cameron's stupid face hanging over the roof edge, one arm out holding a paper bag. I don't need to see it to know what's inside, I taught these assholes everything they know. He gives me a face splitting grin before flooding me with the entire bag of flour. "Mayhem, motherfucker!"

I SHOWER AND change quickly, leaving them outside to clean up their mess, which they do without protest. "You fucking jerks!" I call out, stepping out from the back door.

Cam stifles his laugh. "It was funny, asshole. Come on. If it were one of us you'd claim that Op. Mayhem genius."

"Dude," Logan whispers, his smile so wide and so smug it takes everything in me not to punch him. "Who's that smoking hot chick I saw leave your house this morning?"

"Who? Sydney? That's my brother's girl." I smirk. "And I'll be sure to tell Amanda you said that."

Instantly, his smile drops. "Don't you dare."

"She'd put your balls in a vice," Jake says.

"Or worse," Cameron chimes in. "She won't touch them ever again."

"Jesus Christ," Logan mumbles, rubbing his face. "Don't talk shit like that. You'll jinx me." He looks at me with fear clear in his eyes. "Seriously, D. Don't fucking tell her I said anything."

Cam chuckles while he taps away at his phone.

"It'll cost you," I tell Logan.

"Name the price."

"Give me time."

"Fine!"

Jake shakes his head. "It blows my fucking mind we're all friends."

"No shit," I murmur.

Logan's phone sounds. "This better not be her," he says, his eyes fixed on Cameron whose phone's still in his hand, smiling like the Cheshire cat. Logan taps his screen a few times, his brow bunching more with each passing second. Then his gaze snaps to Cam again. "Did you get a strap-on sent to my house?"

Cam shrugs and shouts loud enough to be heard over Jake's and my laughter. "You know… just in case you ever feel like being a man again."

✧ ✧ ✧

WE HEAD OUT, in my truck, over to the batting cages while we wait for the girls to arrive. But not before I leave something for Riley at her doorstep.

I don't know why we chose to go to the cages considering I can't even bat. Or pitch. Not that any of us would since we're with Jake. We end up sitting at a table talking shit and watching people strike out.

Cameron drops enough food to feed a small village on the table and sits down opposite me. "You know we're grilling at my house, right?" I tell him.

He nods and shoves half a hot dog in his mouth. Then he tries to speak, but with a mouthful of food it's kind of impossible to understand him. He finishes chewing and makes his attempt to swallow look like the hardest thing in the world. When he's done, he wipes his mouth on his forearm and says, "Lucy's gone all wifey and has been *attempting* to cook every night. And every night it tastes like balls. Side note: I fucking hate Pinterest."

"Me too. Her and Amanda share some fucking board and the other night we had a single piece of ravioli—"

"Raviolo," Cam interrupts.

"What?" Logan snaps.

"Ravioli is plural. Raviolo is singular. One giant piece of pasta: Ravio*lo*."

We stare at him, unblinking.

He throws the hotdog wrapper on the table. "Fuck you, Pinterest!"

Jake laughs. "So what you're saying is that her cooking is bad?"

"I'm not talking *bad-but-still-edible*," Cam responds. "I'm talking, *I-want-to-puke-as-soon-as-it-hits-my-tongue* type bad. Let's just say I've mastered the art of optical illusions—food editing. I'm fucking hungry, man. Like, *all the time*."

Logan goes to pick at the fries on the table but Cam shoos his hand away, then spreads his arms around the food and brings them all closer to him. "I've had Amanda's cooking," he tells Logan. "You can afford to starve. I can't."

Jake chimes in. "Neither of you cook your own meals?"

Cam answers first. "I try to. Hell, I try to do anything as long as it doesn't mean eating ball-sweat-flavored raviolo but she's on these hormone meds to regulate her period or something and she's crazy. As in, *more* crazy than normal."

"You married her," I joke.

"And I wouldn't take it back, D," he says, throwing a handful of fries in his mouth. "Not for a fucking second."

"I cook!" Logan announces, sticking his chest out. "I'm beast-mode with the ramen noodles."

"Beast mode?" I ask.

Jake ignores me. "Kayla cooks for me. She has this weekly plan or something. Certain days she makes me carb-load for training and shit. It's fucking annoying."

"You love it, Jakey. Don't deny it," Cam says.

I laugh and look over at Jake. His cheeks are redder than they were a minute ago, and his gaze is lowered at the phone in his hand. He's most likely messaging his girl about how much he loves and appreciates her. Seeing it makes me grab my phone from my pocket and text Riley.

Dylan: *Hello. Do you cook?*

Riley: *Hello back. Where are you?*

Dylan: *Battingxcages witg thenboys.*

Riley: *And you're texting me? Surely that's breaking bro-code…*

Dylan: *Fuxk bro-code. I miss yiu.*

Riley: *:D :D :D*

Dylan: *wtf is that?*

Riley: *You said wtf! My boy is growing up so fast.*

I laugh to myself.

Dylan: *Chexk yourxdoorstep. I ledt you somwthinf.*

Riley: *And you were doing so well! Go be with your friends! I'll be here when you get done! :D :D :D*

Dylan: *:d?*

Riley: *GO!*

Dylan: *Wait. Still no drink?*

Riley: *Not a drop!*

I put the phone away and look back up to see three sets of eyes watching me. "What?"

Logan sighs and bats his eyelashes, then sits his chin on the back of his hand. With a high-pitched voice, he croons. "Soooo… who are you textiiiiing?"

Cam laughs. Jake doesn't. He just continues to watch me with a slight smile.

"Riley."

Logan asks, his voice back to normal, "Who's Riley?"

I keep my eyes on Jake, sending a silent message. "Just a friend."

JAKE GETS A call from Micky telling him they're close to my house so we wait for Cameron to finish all the food and head back. Amanda's car's parked on the street when we pull up and her, Lucy, and Micky are standing around it, holding up signs that say *Welcome Home* and *We Missed You* and *Team Silence.*

"What the hell is Team Silence?" I ask Jake as I park in the garage and get out.

He doesn't get a chance to respond before the cheering starts and the girls charge me all at once.

"Whoa!" Jake stands in front of me, his hands up. "His shoulder! Jeez, I told you guys about this."

"Sorry." Micky laughs, slowing down just in time. "We got a little excited."

Jake steps to the side allowing each of the girls in for a hug and a few words.

"The gang's all together again," Lucy squeals, her arms around her husband. We all ignore the fact that, technically, she's wrong, because for as far back as I could remember the gang always included Heidi. Considering how we left things—at a hotel room in Vegas with me telling her to get the fuck out and that I never wanted to see her again—it would be insane of her to even attempt it.

"I hope you're ready to eat," I tell them, leading them through the garage into the back yard.

The second I turn my back; I hear her voice. "Sorry," Riley says, and I spin on my heels and face her.

She's weaving her way through my friends, who part like the Red Sea to make room for her. Her eyes lock on mine and there's something about the way she's looking at me that keeps the breath in my lungs and my hands at my sides. Her eyes are filled with tears, but her smile—her smile tells me the opposite. God, I love it when she smiles. She doesn't speak. Not a word. She simply walks toward me as everything but my heart seems to slow and by the time she reaches me, the only sound I can hear is the the blood pulsing in my eardrums. She places her hands on my chest and rises to her toes. Then she kisses me. Right on my mouth. And now her arms are around my neck and her lips are parting and when her tongue brushes along mine, I pull her into me with my arms around her waist and I kiss her back—our tongues, our lips, our bodies uniting as one and I don't know how long we stand there, her body bent back from the force of my kiss because time doesn't exist when it comes to Riley. Neither does the outside world, apparently. After a while, but not long enough, she pulls away, her lips red and raw from my attack. She smiles again, the tips of her fingers going to her lips. "Hi," she whispers.

"Hi."

She grins wider and releases me completely. "Bye."

I hold her tighter. "Stay."

She removes my arms from around her waist. "Can't."

I grab her hand. "Please?"

She pulls out of my hold. "Sorry."

And just like that, she walks away. But she's not gone. I can still feel her with me. Every single fiber of my being feels her with me.

I watch her leave. We all do.

"Who was that?" Logan asks when she's no longer in view.

"That was Riley."

"Holy shit," he says, "I thought Riley was a dude."

"Also," Amanda joins in. "That was the weirdest verbal exchange I've ever witnessed."

Twenty
Riley

I WAS TWELVE when my mom made me go with her to welcome the new neighbors. He and his dad were shooting baskets in their driveway when we showed up.

He stood next to his Dad with a basketball under his arm wearing sweatpants and a Tar Heels basketball jersey. He was wearing a cap, too, one he took off as soon as he saw my mom and I coming toward them. My mother introduced us both and our parents shook hands. Then his dad said, "This is my boy, Dylan."

Dylan.

Dylan.

Dylan.

His name ran on repeat in my head.

Then he nodded at me and shook my mom's hand. "Pleased to meet you, Ma'am," he said to her and the first set of butterflies I'd ever felt swarmed in my stomach. I remember his voice being deep, especially for a fifteen-year-old. He was tall and he had muscles—muscles that shouldn't belong to a boy his age. His dark hair fell across his brow, and he palmed it away from his deep blue eyes. I think I was drawn to his eyes first. Then he looked at me. Right at me. And he smiled. And for the first time in my life I wondered what it would be like to kiss a boy—that particular boy—and that particular mouth.

When I got home, I went straight to my room and threw myself on the bed, my hands on my lips. Then I *imagined* what it would be like to kiss him.

Kissing Dylan Banks, the boy next door, was nothing at all like I imagined.

It was so, *so* much more.

I PRACTICALLY RUN to my house and straight to my room, where I close the door and throw myself on the bed like I did when I was twelve. Then I place my hand on my lips and close my eyes, reliving the kiss over and over again. It was different kissing him this time. My mind was clear, and so was my heart—clear and open and ready for him.

My phone vibrates on my nightstand and I quickly reach for it, as well as the glass jar he'd left at my door. I read his text first.

Dylan: *You stole my kiss!*

Riley: *Because I'm worthy of it.*

I set the phone down and pull out the two notes he'd left in a jar. I unfold the one he had written the number "1" on and take a breath, knowing what his words will do to me. It'll be the third time I read it, and even though I know I'm going to experience the same things I do whenever Dylan had been involved—Butterflies, emptiness, guilt—there's one more emotion I can now add to it. *Love.*

I'd come home for the weekend during my sophomore year of college. When I spoke to my dad earlier that day, he mentioned he was going away so I knew I would have the house to myself, which was something I'd been craving since I moved away. I liked being alone, liked the quiet I knew the house would provide. He was standing outside at the end of our joining fence pacing the sidewalk when I pulled into my driveway. I recognized him from high school but I couldn't for the life of me remember his name. So it was kind of odd that when I got out of my truck, he looked over at me and stopped in his tracks. I wasn't sure what he was doing so I walked over and asked him. He didn't respond to my question. Instead, he said, "Banks, man. How's UNC?"

I must've given him a look that terrified him a little because he laughed nervously and said, "I'm Jeremy. You went to my high school. I played on Varsity with you a few times."

"Sorry," I told him, and lied. "I didn't recognize you."

"All good," he said, but he still seemed nervous. And distracted. He kept looking over at your house.

"Is there something I can help you with?" I asked him.

His entire body stilled and he slowly looked from your

house to me. "Maybe."

"Maybe?"

"I have this problem," he told me.

"What kind of problem?"

I remember looking at him, and then at your house, and then at mine, because I just wanted to get inside and away from the world and all the stupid talking and even stupider questions.

"Riley, my girlfriend..." He pointed to your house. "She broke up with me. Again."

"Again?"

He laughed. "She's always breaking up with me."

"Maybe she doesn't actually like you, dude," I told him.

He raised his chin. "Oh, she does. She loves me. She has no choice but to love me."

I laughed with him, which now kind of makes sense. At the time, I was pretty sure Heidi and I were done, though we never vocalized it. It was a just a feeling—the kind you get in your gut, you know? And I remember being jealous of him—that he was so confident in your relationship and in himself that he could say that. "So what's the problem then?"

"I'm pretty sure she thinks I'm going to leave her when we go off to college or some shit. So she's trying to get a head start. Which is stupid—I'd never leave her. And I sure as hell won't let her leave me."

"Has she said anything to you?" I found myself asking.

He shrugged. "She says she doesn't feel worthy of me. I don't know." His gaze dropped. "I feel like it's my fault. Maybe I haven't shown her how much I love her or how much she means to me and how sometimes I walk with her hand in mine and I get that sense of pride, you know? Not because I want to show her off or whatever, or the fact that I think it's amazing that she doesn't mind being seen in public with a kid like me but because she's fucking smart, man. And she's beautiful, and funny and passionate and opinionated and a complete pain in the ass but, fuck, I love her. I love all those things about her and it hurts she can't see that. That she can't love herself the way I do. I don't know. Is it my fault?" he asked, his eyes back on mine, pleading with me to give him something.

I didn't have anything to say. It'd been a long time since I felt what he was feeling. That kind of pain at the thought of losing someone he loved with everything he had. And it wasn't a show, Riley. It was just me and him—two guys talking out on the street—him pouring his heart out, and me, not able to give him whatever it was he was looking for. "College is a long time away, bro."

He just shrugged. "Time means nothing when forever's in play."

Then he looked over at your house again and I could see the desperation in his eyes. "Maybe don't show her." I told him.

His gaze trailed back to mine. "What?"

"Don't show her. Tell her. Everything you just told me, say it to her."

He squared his shoulders and took a long, deep breath. "You think it's enough?"

"It has to be, right?"

He nodded and sniffed once and for the first time since I'd been speaking to him, I saw the fear in his eyes. He was so afraid of losing you, Riley.

Then he smiled and shook his head. "Under love's heavy burden do I sink," he mumbled. And then he was gone. He marched right up to your house and pounded on the door. I turned around and went into the house, not wanting to witness your moment of love and (hopefully) clarity.

I sat in my room in the silence of my thoughts, having no fucking idea what I was doing with my life. But that kid on the street—he knew. He wanted you to be his life. His love.

And at least you get to have that, Riley. At least you get to walk away knowing his heart belonged to you and that he was so afraid of losing you, so desperate to show you your worth, that he bled his heart out to a stranger. He loved you, Ry. He loved you so damn much. And I was so jealous of him, not because he had you at the time, but because he was so passionate about you and love and life and the future you'd share, and I didn't have any of that.

What I had wasn't enough.

I wanted more than enough.

I enlisted the next day.

And I found something I was proud of, like he was proud of you.

Jeremy Walters—he changed both our lives.

I cover my mouth with my hand to stop the sobs from escaping. Each read seems to hurt more, but not the kind of hurt that has me reaching for the bottle. It's the kind that lets me know I'm breathing and that I'm alive, and that eventually, it'll be okay. I fold the note and place it on the bed next to me, then I reach into the jar and pick up the second letter, already smiling as I unfold it.

Riley,

I'm sorry for making you cry with the last letter. I hate seeing you cry. I hate even more knowing I caused it. But, I thought you should know about that night because I know for sure it's not something you can write to him about. I wonder if he'll be pissed that I told you about it. Looks like I'm breaking bro-codes all over the place when it comes to you.

Anyway, there's something I've been meaning to tell you. I haven't really had the chance to say it in person, so I thought I'd write it to you. And with any luck, take away some of that hurt I just caused (I'm sorry—again).

Okay.

Here goes.

I find it completely appalling that you seem to love bacon. It's weird. You're weird, Riley. I mean, out of all the food in all the world, you ask for bacon? It just doesn't make sense. But, because I'm trying to get in your pants, here are some random facts about bacon:

1. International bacon day is September 3rd. I mean… what the hell? There's an actual day to celebrate bacon!

2. Bacon cures hangovers. Okay… so maybe that explains why you love it so much.

3. There's bacon-scented cologne. Jesus Christ, what has the world come to?

4. There's a bust of Kevin Bacon… made of bacon. Is now an appropriate time to use WTF?

5. And last, but not least. You, Riley Hudson, are bacon me crazy.

✧ ✧ ✧

Riley: *You're such a goof, Lance Corporal Banks.*

Dylan: *Jesus. You just mafe me hard…er. The thinga I'd like toxbe doing to you wgen you call me that in person…*

Riley: *omg…*

Dylan: *Also, if youcever kiss me like thaf in front ofxall my friends again…*

Riley: *…*

Dylan: *I won't let youxleave so easily. I can't fuxking focus on anythinf else now.*

Riley: *Because I'm bacon you crazy?*

Dylan: *:D :D :D !*

"Riley!" Mom shouts. I quickly put the letters back in the jar and move just in time to hide it under my bed before she opens my bedroom door. "There's someone at the door for you."

I race past her, cutting her off, my heart already soaring at the thought of seeing Dylan.

Only it's not Dylan.

It's his friend Jake.

My footsteps slow, my mind does the opposite. "Hey Riley," he says, eyeing Dylan's house quickly before returning to me.

My heart races as I step outside, closing the door behind me. "Hi," I whisper.

I know why he's here.

I *hate* that he's here.

He clears his throat and shoves his hands in his pockets, looking down his nose at me. "Are you going to tell him or should I?"

Dylan

APPARENTLY THE WHOLE bucket and feathers mayhem wasn't enough. While I was at the cages with the guys, the girls were here—in my house, and with the help of Eric and Dad, they managed to turn my bedroom into a My Little Pony shrine. I'm not just talking about a few figures in there. No. That would've been too easy. I'm talking at least a hundred of them. And glitter. Every-fucking-where. And pink and purple streamers stapled to my goddamn ceiling. It was the first thing I noticed when I walked in. Followed closely by the full-length wall decal. A silver, glittery unicorn. And if that wasn't bad enough… the unicorn had Logan's face, while Jake and Cameron rode it. I would've beaten their asses had I seen the room while they were all still here, but I didn't come in here until now… an hour after they'd left.

"I think it suits you," Dad says from behind me.

Eric laughs, his head popping up over Dad's shoulder. "So worth it just for the look on your face."

I slump down on the mattress and rub the back of neck, ideas of retaliation already coming to mind. "I'm going to fucking kill 'em."

Dad joins in on Eric's laughter. "Those boys ain't right," he says shaking his head. "Sleep well, Princess." He closes the door after him and I let out a frustrated groan when I see the giant *High School Musical* poster taped to the back of the door. And more glitter.

I reach for my laptop and open it. Then pull all those fuckers' names into a group message.

Dylan: *You know the rules of mayhem, right?*

Logan: *Retaliation. Fight or die, brother.*

Lucy: *Every little girl wishes for a pony. You got eleventy-three of them. What's the big deal?*

Cam: *LOL.*

Jake: *Just so we're clear, I knew nothing about this.*

Amanda: *LIES!*

Mikayla: *LIES!*

Logan: *Jake supplied us with the glitter and High School Musical poster. He won't say how he got it, though.*

Jake: *Shut up.*

Mikayla: *Jake stopped liking Zac Efron after 17 Again.*

Jake: *Wow, babe. There's a bus. Just throw me under it.*

Lucy: *Lol. It's okay, Jake. Amanda told me she thinks about him when Logan's on the bottom.*

Logan: *WTF!*

Amanda: *LIES!*

Dylan: *Yo, Luce.*

Lucy: *Yeah?*

Dylan: *I got Riley this book. She said it ends in a cliffhanger and wants to know when the next one's out.*

Lucy: *You got a girl a book? Mother fucking swoon.*

Cam: *I'm right here.*

Dylan: *So it's a romance book, I guess.*

Lucy: *OMG. She reads romance? Wtf! Totes my new bff. Does she have a fave bbf?*

Dylan: *I don't know what any of that means.*

Lucy: *Title? Author?*

Dylan: *No idea.*

Lucy: *?*

Dylan: *The cover's blue.*

Lucy: *Seriously?*

Dylan: *Yeah. Like a light blue.*

Lucy: *You're a shit kid, Banks.*

Amanda: *He seems happy, Heidi. I'd leave it alone.*
Amanda: *Crap.*
Amanda: *Wrong chat.*
Amanda: *Ignore that.*

Logan: *I shouldn't let her out of the house.*

Dylan: *I'll see you guys soon.*

I close out of the screen, ignoring Amanda's comment. It's irrelevant. And if Heidi wants to know how I am, she knows where I fucking live.

Dylan: *Message me as soon as your mom leaves tomorrow. I'll be waiting. I can't wait to see you.*

Riley: *K.*

Dylan: *You good?*

Riley: *:(*

Dylan: *?*

Riley: *Hang on. I know you hate seeing those dots so I'm just warning* *you that the next one will be a long message.*

Dylan: *K.*

Riley: *I wanted to wait until I told you in person, but I don't think I can. I know it's been less than a month since we've really known each other, but what's time, right? Because in that short time you've become the most important person in my life, Dylan. You're the reason I actually get out of bed in the morning, the reason I haven't had anything to drink all weekend—no matter how badly I wanted to. You're the reason I want to face reality head on and not just float through it. There are going to be things that happen, things we'll probably share that'll change the way we think or feel about each other, or at least the way you feel about me... but I just wanted you to know that you matter. You matter so much to me. And regardless of how things will end up between us, that's never going to change. You'll always be the boy who changed my course in life. The one who changed ME. The one who gave me a reason to look for something more than just the "enough" I was struggling to get through. I'm grateful you showed up on my doorstep that day—pissed off and angry at the world. Because if you hadn't... I wouldn't be here. And I don't just mean here, writing to you. I mean here, in this world.*

Twenty-One

Riley

I SPEND THE entire night wide-awake, tossing and turning, and then tossing and turning some more. Before I know it, the birds are chirping, the clock is ticking, the sun is rising, and my heart… it's sinking.

Dylan stands on the other side of my door, looking the same as he always does. Sweats, white grease stained tank under a flannel shirt—sleeves rolled up. But his eyes, his smile, they're different. They're settled. Like our conversation last night and the two days apart has given him the same sense of calm it gave me… until Jake stood exactly where Dylan is right now.

"Hi," he says, and I release a breath, stand on my toes, and throw my arms around his neck. I squeeze tight, because I don't know if it'll be the last time.

Guilt. Guilt is such a fucked-up emotion, because it's not one I should be feeling when his arms wrap around my waist, pressing my body flush against his. "I've missed you, Riley."

"Me too," I whisper, pulling away.

He grasps my top and brings me into him, like I'd done with him so many times before. "Come back," he says, his smile getting wider. "You give such good hugs."

We repeat the process, holding each other a little longer until his low, sweet chuckle reverberates in my ears and he releases me.

His smile falls when he looks at my face, the bags under my eyes, the redness from the thousand tears I've shed. "Has Jake spoken to you?" I ask.

With his eyes on mine, he slowly shakes his head. "What's going on, Riley?"

"We should talk."

His face falls. "I figured as much."

I take his hand and lead him to my room, but there's resistance. When I turn to him, he's looking at my bedroom door. His throat bobs with his swallow. "Can we maybe go somewhere else? I just… I don't think I want whatever is going to happen next to take away from the memories I have of us in your room."

Nodding, I slip on my shoes and walk past him and outside. I don't deflect from his prediction. I don't tell him that it's okay—that it's not what this is about. I don't say anything, because I don't want my next words to be a lie. I want to give him the raw—and until today—unspoken truth.

He closes the door after him and takes my hand, then leads me to his garage. The same garage I once declared my clear and unquestionable need for him.

I stay silent as he opens the passenger door of his truck and I get inside, waiting—my heart slowly breaking—for him to join me.

He drives.

I don't know how long he drives for but it's not like it is in my dream because the idea of teasing myself with that moment, that wish, doesn't just break my heart. It completely disintegrates it.

So I sit with my side against the door, as far away from him as possible.

We don't say a word.

Not out loud.

But in my head, I shift through the jumbled mess—a dictionary of apologies and explanations—and I fight the tears, the sob brewing in my chest because the memories hurt, and I don't have anything to dull the ache besides the man sitting next to me. And right now, he's not enough.

Out of all the places he could possibly take me to, he takes me to a cemetery. Not the one I'm familiar with. It's smaller, older and a little less well kept. He stays quiet as he gets out of the car and makes his way to my side where he opens the door for me and takes my hand to help me down.

I'm in a daze, too caught up in my own thoughts that I don't even realize he's walking ahead of me and I'm following cluelessly behind until he stops at a plot and starts picking at the weeds surrounding the headstone. Faded and damaged, the words on marble are hard to make out, but I read them.

Every single one.

Ruby Banks

My wife, my friend, the mother dear

In dreamless sleep repossess here

May those whose love to her was given

All meet and live with her in heaven

I try to cover my gasp, my tears falling with my blink as I look up at him. "Dylan," I whisper, my breath as shaky as my hands.

"I wanted her to meet you," he says, taking a seat on the dirt in front of the marker, "In case I don't get this chance again."

I sit down next to him and take his hand.

"It's been so long since I've been here," he tells me, shifting our positions so his arm's around me and his other hand is on my leg. "My dad and Eric and I used to come here a bit when I was younger. I always felt out of place, you know? Because they knew her and could talk to her the way they would if she were alive. They could picture her, see her reactions to their words and I—I couldn't do any of that. I couldn't describe her to you, what she looked like when she smiled or the sound of her voice or the way she smelled."

"I'm sorry."

He shrugs. "My dad—he used to say, *'It's better to have loved and lost, than never to have loved at all.'* I guess you just reminded me of it when I saw your face earlier. I kind of knew, you know?" He finally faces me, his eyes as sad as my heart. "Is this it, Riley? Am I losing you?"

I sigh. "Losing me would mean that you had me to begin with."

His lip curves on one side. "I had you, Riley. Even if it was for a second, I still had you."

I look away, because the hope in his eyes is too detrimental to my soul. "I messed up, Dylan."

"How bad?"

"*I don't even know where to start* type bad."

He blows out a breath so heavy I can feel his entire body shift beside me. "You've been keeping it a secret from me?"

"Yes."

"So why is it so important you tell me? Because Jake knows about it?"

"No… because you deserve to know."

"And what if I told you that I don't want to know? That I hold a secret I don't want to tell anyone. Especially you. And what if I told you that we could both keep them for eternity and it wouldn't change a thing?"

I don't hesitate. "I'd still tell you."

"Why?"

I turn to him. "Because you were the one who asked me to."

He doesn't respond, just looks right at me. After a while, he looks away. "Heidi had an abortion while I was in basic training. It was my child. She didn't tell me about it. She didn't even tell me she was pregnant. Not until Vegas a few months ago. That's why I left her for good."

All air leaves my lungs. "Jesus. I'm sorry, Dylan."

"We spoke to each other while I was in basic at Camp Lejeune and even when I deployed. She wrote me letters even after she broke up with me. She should've said something. And when she did, she tried to put it on me like it was my fault because I enlisted and left her. I didn't leave *her*. I just enlisted. There wasn't an either/or decision. We could've still made it work. The worst part is that she knew she was pregnant when I left. She didn't even tell me then. She just let me go. She should've said something, you know? I should've had a say at least."

I take a calming breath—one that gets caught by the lump in my throat. "That's not your shame to carry, Dylan. It's hers."

"I think deep down I know that. But it doesn't stop it from hurting. And it's not even about her. She stopped being the reason I hurt the night I found out. I think it's more about my decision to leave." He faces me again. "You think it was selfish? For me to go?"

"For you to search out something more for yourself? Not at all."

"But I didn't tell her I enlisted until it was too late."

"And you think it would've changed anything? You think that by you not going you would've been happy together, with or without a baby?"

He shrugs. "No. I wouldn't have been happy. Not together anyway."

"So now? When you look back on it all… what do you think?"

"It's irrelevant."

"Of course what you think is relevant."

"No, Riley." He shakes his head. "I mean, when I look back on it… none of it matters anymore. I thought it did. Then I met you. And now it's irrelevant." He pulls me closer to him. "And you—your secret. Is it relevant?"

I think about his question for a long time and I come up with nothing. A yes or no answer would be too simple. So instead, I give the complicated. "After Jeremy died, I lost it. Like, mentally lost it."

"You were grieving."

I shake my head. "No. It wasn't just grief. It was *everything*."

"Like what?" I look down on his hand on my leg and I get lost in the warmth of his touch and his voice when he says, "It'll only change us if you let it."

I heave in a breath and let it out in a *whoosh*, along with everything I've wanted to say but never had anyone to say it to. "He was so scared up on that cliff, Dylan. He was scared and I laughed at him. He told me he loved me. I never said it back. They were the last words he ever said to me and I never—" I break off on a sob.

"Riley…"

I sniff through the pain and find the courage to continue. "I still remember the moment it happened. The rocks when they landed on my shoulders and the impact of the water when we hit the lake. I remember the exact moment I knew something was wrong." The pain is already unbearable, but I push through it. I have to. For both Dylan and Jeremy. "His grip on my hand tightened… he was supposed to jump. He didn't jump. He fell. He fell all the way to the bottom and he didn't come up. The medical reports say he hit his head on the edge of the cliff and was already unconscious when he hit the water." I wipe my eyes across my forearm. "It only took a day for the rumors to start and another day for them to get back to me. Kids in our class were saying that it wasn't an accident. That I *pushed* him. That I *drowned* him. I would never hurt him, Dylan. *Never*."

"Fuck them, Riley."

"Mom kept telling me that they were just bored and needed something else to focus on to take away from the pain of losing someone. And I just kept thinking, *what about me?* What about *my* pain? Then it escalated to the point where people began questioning why I didn't call for help right away…."

Dylan's eyes are wet when he rubs them across my bare shoulder. He sniffs once. Twice. His hands going behind my knees and lifting me onto him so he can hold me tighter. Closer.

"And I tried to talk to my mom about it. When the nightmares became too much, I tried to talk to her. I tried to talk to anyone who would listen but no one would. No one cared. And then the generic *I'm sorrys* mixed with accusations started coming through and I lost it. I was so mad, so angry, so lost. People stopped talking to me. Friends I thought would be there stopped being my friend because they were never really mine, they were his. His parents stopped talking to me. And the girls—they were the worst. The messages I'd get pushed me over the edge."

"What messages?" he asks, a single finger wiping my tears away.

"The truth. That I was never worthy of him to begin with. That it was my fault his life was taken too soon. That he was such a promising kid and I ruined it all. I took it all away from him."

"That's not true, Riley."

"And after a while, everything stopped. The messages, the fake sympathy, all of it just stopped. And when I couldn't find it in myself to go off to college and start a new life that was supposed to be ours, my mom stopped caring too. She just got mad and impatient and she didn't understand that I wasn't ready. That I was still grieving. I could see it in the way she looked at me… she didn't understand why I was still stuck there—in my hell—when the world was moving around me. I started to lock myself in my room. I didn't eat. Didn't shower. Didn't talk to anyone. And then one night she came into my room and said, '*It's time to move on,*' like it was that fucking easy. And I lost it, Dylan." I break off on another sob. "It's not like I planned on any of it. I hadn't even started drinking then. I stole her car in the middle of the night. I just wanted to hurt her like her words had hurt me. And when her salon came into view, I stepped on the pedal and I drove up the curb and over the sidewalk and right through the front window. Just to fuck her, you know?"

"Riley..."

"But I didn't stop, I couldn't. I just kept driving, hitting wall after wall until there was nowhere else left to go and the car wouldn't move and I just sat there with smoke around me and my mind gone and my heart dead in the bottom of the lake."

Dylan clears his throat. "And then what happened?"

"Cops came. Fire trucks. Ambulances. Apparently I'd gone through five different businesses in my fit of rage. Jake's dad's law practice was one of them. That's how he knows about it. I got arrested and charged with so many felonies, I can't even name them. Mom hired a lawyer to try to get me out of it using temporary insanity as a defense, but it's a small town. I ruined people's businesses, their incomes, their livelihoods. It didn't matter that I was still hurting. I caused more suffering than Jeremy's death had caused me. It was like a witch-hunt, pitchforks and everything. They probably would've burned me at the stakes if they could. But not Jake's dad. For some reason he felt for me and he helped my mom get rid of her hired lawyer and he offered her a deal. Pay off what the insurance doesn't cover for the damage caused and six months of home-arrest. Ankle bracelet and everything. My mom took it. I was too fucked up to care. Mom lost all her clients. Then she had to sell the salon to pay everyone and I started to drink. After a while, I couldn't stop drinking. And Mom didn't stop supplying it. It was easier for her to deal with me in a sedated state of constant semi drunk than deal with watching my emotional pain."

Dylan takes a huge breath, his chest heaving and pushing against my side. "Riley. What happened to you, the way people treated you... that's their shame to carry. Not yours," he says, repeating my words.

I face him, watching him blink back his own tears. "It took me a long time to work that out. A really long time. And when I did, I just got more pissed because they weren't fucking there, Dylan. No one was. They weren't there when I was sinking, drowning, trying to search for Jeremy. They weren't there when I finally found his body, eyes open, laying cold and still under the water. They weren't the ones who tasted the blood in their mouths... or woke up for weeks after... dreaming of that same blood-stained water drowning them and killing them. They didn't feel the burn in their lungs when they screamed for help, their mouths and lungs filling and dying for air. I swam to the shore and screamed and screamed and nobody came. Nobody heard me. Nobody saved him. *I* was the one who dived back in, who kicked and kicked and used every single bit of strength I had to get him out. His eyes were still open, Dylan. His beautiful lifeless eyes were still there, but they were dead. And so was he. His head was on my lap, his blood on my hands, and I knew he was dead. I just cried and held him. I didn't know what else to do. People came, people shouted, people cried. And the next thing I knew, I was being pulled away from him—the boy I love. They were taking him away from me. And the first thing they did was close his eyes." I choke hard on the sob and finally release it, my breaths as weak as the rest of my body. "Those eyes were *mine*. They belong to me and they took them away from me."

He kisses away my tears, his body warm against mine.

We breathe through the pain, apart but together, and we hold each other. We hold on to the only thing that makes sense in an otherwise messed-up world and we allow ourselves to hurt and to grieve and to love and to forgive. We watch the sun move across the sky, feel the wind envelop us. And we keep close the chaos we created and the truth that releases it.

We bleed our hearts, bare our souls, and in the end, we hold on to a once untouchable reality.

He pulls away, his hands cupping my face and his eyes searching mine. Then he smiles—a childish innocent smile his mother gets to witness. And somehow, some way, he finds a way to release my hurt. "That's it? That's all of it?" he asks.

"That's it," I tell him.

He kisses my lips. Just once. "You're just a little broken, Riley Hudson. That's all. Now you just have to let me be the glue that keeps you together."

Twenty-Two
Riley

WE DRIVE HOME in the complete opposite setting to the drive there. I sit in the middle of the seat, his hand on my leg, the afternoon sun beating down on us while he tells me about the engine that's been sitting in his garage since he was sixteen. Occasionally, he'll ask if I'm sure I want to hear about it. I tell him he's stupid and to keep going. Of course I want to hear about it. I write down what type it is so I can google it later and prove it to him. Then I tell him about seeing him the first time when I was twelve and he was in his driveway and how I went home and thought about kissing him. He eyes me sideways, a clear smirk on his lips, then he calls me a juvenile horn-bag and pushes me away. A second later, though, he pulls me back and apologizes. Then he adds that had he known I felt that way, he probably would have walked around shirtless a lot more. I remind him I was twelve. He reminds me of his bacon joke and uses it to prove that in his mind, he's *still* twelve.

It's perfect—better than any dream I've ever had.

He talks about his friends and what they got up to yesterday, his generally good mood switching for a moment when he tells me about what they did to his room.

I laugh. I can't stop laughing. "I have to see it," I tell him.

So when we pull into his garage, he opens my door, helps me to step out and holds my hand as he leads me through his house. The one and only time I'd been inside, I only really saw the hallway and the kitchen. He shows me through the rest of the house, which is basically just the living room. It's nice. Neat. But definitely *very* male. The one thing that stands out are the pictures framed and hanging on the walls. So many pictures of Dylan, of his brother, of his mom and dad, and then of the three Banks Military Men. From babies, to kids, to teens to adults. There's even a glass case in the living room with all the boy's trophies and participation ribbons. Basketball for Dylan. Academics for Eric. I point to one of him standing next to his truck, Jake next to him, with the bed loaded. "What's that?"

"That would be the day I left for UNC."

"I bet your dad was proud."

He smiles. "Honestly, I could've flunked out of high school and pressed metal over at the factory like he does and he'd still be proud." He places his hands on my waist and kisses my shoulder. "Okay. My room. Promise not to laugh?"

"I can't promise that. *At all.*"

He rolls his eyes but guides me, his hands staying where they are, through the living room, past the hallway, and to his closed door. "Ready?"

"I don't think I'll ever be ready," I joke.

He reaches across and turns the handle, then stops. "I just want to make it clear that this isn't some kind of personal joke or anything. Never, and I mean *ever* have I mentioned anything about ponies or glitter or—"

"Just open the door," I say through a laugh.

I try. Truly, I try not to laugh, but how can I not? It's ridiculous. He gently pushes me inside, while I continue to cackle with laughter, my hands out, moving the streamers out of the way. He stands in front of me shaking his head. "It gets worse," he tells me, grasping my shoulders and spinning me around to face his now closed door. "*High School Musical*?" I almost shout, turning to him. But before I can laugh, before I can breathe, his mouth is on mine, his hands gripping my waist, pushing me slowly until my back's against the door. His tongue parts my lips and I welcome it. I welcome him and his entire body as he pushes up and into me, his leg between mine, his hands gripping my wrists and moving them above my head. He doesn't stop kissing me, not for a second. When he needs air, he moves from my lips down to my neck and I gasp for breath, but he doesn't give me long before his mouth covers mine again and I get lost. Completely lost. In this moment and in his kiss and in our mixed moans. He steps back, just enough to shift so his hips are between my legs and I can feel his excitement pressed against my stomach. He takes his hand off my wrists and uses the other to keep both my hands pinned against the door, trapped with his force. His free hand glides down my side, past the swell of my breast and my waist, ending on my bare thigh. He lifts my leg, forcing them both off the ground, using his body to pin me in place before his mouth is on my jaw, my neck, my collarbone, his tongue sliding across my skin.

Using his body, he shifts me higher until his hardness is exactly where I want it.

"Dylan…"

He responds by moaning into my skin, his hand pressing harder on my wrists.

I try to break from his hold. I want to touch him. I want to feel every single inch of his body but he's too strong. Too overcome by lust.

His hips start thrusting, slow, smooth movements and I'm wet. So damn wet.

"Dylan…"

He covers my mouth again, his tongue soft and warm and relentless. He keeps thrusting, keeps pushing me closer and closer to—

"Dylan!" For a second I'm confused because I didn't speak his name and it's not my voice. "Dylan!" *Bang bang bang.* I get pushed forward by the force of the door opening.

Dylan curses and drops me to the floor while his hand slams against the door. "What, Eric?!"

I wipe my lips with the back of my hand, my eyes wide in panic.

On the other side of the door, Eric shouts, "I left some shit I need for work in there."

Clearly reluctant, Dylan plants his hands on my waist, guiding me in front of him with his hard-on pressed against my back. He opens the door for his brother, whose eyes widen when he sees us.

"Oh," his brother says. Then he smirks. "Riley, right?"

I nod.

Dylan's grip on my waist tightens.

His brother asks me, "You still got that mole on the inside of your left thigh?"

"What?" I pant.

"He's fucking around," Dylan says from behind me. "Get your shit and leave, E."

Eric steps forward, his strides short and slow, his eyes staying on us. Dylan moves us as one, turning slightly to follow him across the room.

"I can't for the life of me remember where I put it," Eric says, index finger tapping his chin as he slows his steps even more. "Maybe it's under your bed…" He stops moving.

So do we.

"No." Finger on chin again. "We cleared that out for your she-male porn."

"Get the fuck out," Dylan snaps.

I giggle. Then trap my lips between my teeth when Dylan grunts. He adds, "I didn't see your car out front. I didn't know anyone was home."

Eric smiles, his eyebrow quirked. "Baby brother, you been sneakin' girls into your room when no one's home?"

Dylan scoffs. "No. And *girl*. Singular. And still no."

"Swear, it's the first time I've been here," I stammer.

Eric laughs, his head tilting back with the force of it. "Riley, Dylan's a grown man. He's allowed to bring girls home."

Dylan sighs. "Seriously. What do you want?"

Eric's grin widens. "Your truck."

"What?"

"You want alone time with your girl? I want your truck. You've never let me drive it. Dad even hid the fucking keys while you were gone."

"Fine," Dylan huffs, throwing him the keys.

His brother's face shifts from humor to shock when he looks down at the keys he just caught. "Seriously?"

"Just go!"

Eric shrugs as he pockets the keys. "I might just stay."

Dylan grunts again.

Apparently Eric finds this funny.

Me? I'm just confused.

Eric says, "Retaliation is a bitch, Dylan. Have I taught you nothing?"

"I might go home," I tell them.

"No," they both say at the same time.

Eric's tone turns serious. "I'm leaving." He taps Dylan's shoulder as he passes. "It's good to see you happy, man."

I unknowingly hold my breath as I watch him leave, only releasing it when I hear the front door close.

"You're so cute," Dylan says through a chuckle.

I face him. "What?"

"You were so scared, like we were busted or something." He raises the pitch of his voice when he mocks, "Swear it's the first time I've been here." After I smack his chest, he tries to pretend to be hurt, but he's too busy laughing. "You do realize we're adults, Riley? I've been allowed to have girls in my room since I was sixteen."

I stick my tongue out in disgust. "I guess that's why you were so confident in your attack of me just now."

He releases a chuckle from deep in his throat, his eyes on the ceiling as he starts to pull down the streamers. "Sorry about that. It's your fault, though. You shouldn't look so hot sitting in my truck." He drops the streamers on the floor—the floor covered in glitter. "You're lucky Eric walked in when he did. I probably would've fucked you against the door."

"Dylan!"

He laughs again, louder and unrestrained as his gaze moves to mine. Then he steps forward, his hands cupping my face. "You're blushing."

"You're purposely embarrassing me," I admit.

"So you didn't like it?"

"I didn't *not* like it."

He nods. "You want to stop?"

I shrug. "Maybe just slow down?"

He bites down on his lip, then exhales loudly. "We better do something else then because you, in my room, looking as pretty as you look right now…" He leans down, his mouth finding mine again. But it's different than earlier, it's slower and sweeter. When he pulls away, he curses under his breath and releases his hold on my face. "Yeah. We should *really* do something else. Or get out of here."

"Eric has your truck."

"Right." He nods. "Want to help me clean this crap up?"

We spend the next half hour pulling down streamers and vacuuming glitter as much as we can. There's not a lot in his room. Just a mattress in the corner—not even a bed—a desk and chest of drawers.

We bag the trash and change his sheets (flannel, just like his shirts) and when we're done, he opens a drawer and tells me to pick something to change into so I don't have to go home covered in glitter. Then he lies on his bed, his left hand behind his head, his right on in his stomach, and his eyes on me.

I run my finger through his clothes, T-shirts with the USMC logo and even his combat uniform. I choose a flannel shirt, blue and white, like the one he wore the second day he showed up at my door. When I turn away from him, I shrug out of my top, leaving me in nothing but my bra and denim shorts. I button it up quickly and remove my shorts, not bothering to replace them. The shirt's so big it ends just above my knees. I push away the memories of wearing Jeremy's shirts for the past year and a half and turn to him, my gaze lowered and my thumb between my teeth.

"Riley," he murmurs, and when I lift my eyes, I see his gaze moving down my body. "Come here." He pats the mattress on the spot next to him.

I chew my lip as I take the slow steps toward him, trying to hide my hesitation. I sit where he indicated, one leg beneath me on the mattress, the other stretched out on the floor in front of me. He places his hand on my knee, then begins to slowly stroke up and down my leg. He smiles, his eyes on mine. "You look scared."

I let out a nervous laugh. "A little."

His brows knit. "Why?"

I shrug. "I don't know. The day was just overwhelming, I guess. And now I'm here and I feel like an old weight's been lifted and a new one's in its place."

He sits up slightly, leaning on his left elbow. "What do you mean?"

"I just mean the physical stuff."

He arches his eyebrows in question.

"You're just a lot more experienced than I am, I guess, and that's terrifying."

"I've only been with two people my entire life," he tells me. "You included."

"Yeah, but you've probably slept with that other person over a hundred times and I'm… *almost a virgin.*"

"Almost?" he asks, his amusement evident.

"Well, once with Jeremy and once with you."

"Shit," he says in a clipped tone. "I'm sorry. I didn't know…"

"It's okay. I didn't stop you, remember?"

After a moment, he lies back down and says, "I'm not going to promise I'll keep my hands off you because you're beautiful, Riley. And I like you. I like being close to you and touching you and reminding myself that you're mine. So if I get inappropriately handsy just tell me to fuck off or throw something at me. But I probably still won't stop, especially now, because seeing you in my shirt like this, it does something to me."

"Something?" I whisper.

He takes my hand and places it on his stomach, then slowly guides it lower and lower, until I'm grasping him, my fingers instinctively wrapping around his hardness. I inhale a huge breath and hold it for as long as my lungs can handle, then I release it with the strength of my unspoken twentieth wish.

Dylan.

I wished for Dylan.

I lean down slowly, watching his eyes drift shut right before mine do. And like he'd done to me, I kiss him, soft and slow. He removes his hand covering mine and places it behind my neck, holding me to him while his mouth parts, his tongue meeting mine. After a while, his free hand finds my bare thigh, moving higher and higher until he's cupping my panty-covered ass. He shifts my entire body until I'm lying on top of him. With each of my legs on either side of him and his cock pressed against my center, he thrusts up, pushing into me. We moan into each other's mouths until we find a slow, perfect, rhythm. Then his hand on my butt moves, higher this time, onto my bare back where his fingers find the back of my bra.

I lift my head and look down at him, eyebrows quirked in question.

He grins, chuckling at the same time. "You know why I chose basketball when all my friends played baseball, Riley?"

"What?" I pant, confusion clear on my face.

"Because I sucked at baseball. I could only ever get to first base."

My head drops with my laughter. "Are you telling me you want me to let you get to second base because you sucked at baseball?"

He kisses my neck, moving slowly to my shoulder. "Actually, I'm *begging* you to let me get to second base."

"That's such a pathetic attempt to woo a girl," I tell him, tilting my head to the side to give him better access.

His lips shift against my skin. "I'm pretty sure the handbook states the wooing begins after third base."

"Oh, you're not getting to third base today."

He drops his head back on the pillow. "Well, no shit. Not if you don't let me get to second. That's just cheating, Riley. Do you want me to be a cheater?"

God, he's funny. And so fucking hot. I sit up completely, pressing down on him.

His hands find my waist, underneath the shirt, and his eyes are lowered, focused on our joined parts.

"My eyes are up here, Rookie."

He smiles a lazy smile and lifts his gaze to mine.

"You first," I tell him.

"Me?"

"Shirt off, stud."

Smirking, he sits up and I help him remove first his shirt, and then his tank. I eye his chest, the dips of his abs—the skin covered in a golden glow. Then I eye the wound, now completely healed on the outside. "Does it hurt if I touch it?" I ask.

He runs his thumb across my lips. "Fuck, your pout is sexy."

"Seriously," I whine. "Does it?"

He shakes his head, his hands moving higher and taking the fabric of the shirt with it. "It's scar tissue. I can barely feel it." He licks his lips, his eyes right on mine and his breaths shaky.

"What if I kiss it?" I whisper.

His gaze drops, but he doesn't respond. I reach out with my finger first and run it over the hard lump of skin, feeling his exhale fall on my neck. Then I lean down, and press my lips to it, fighting back tears that came out of nowhere. I kiss it again, and again, while his grip on my sides tightens, his thumb brushing the bottom of my breasts. I keep my lips on him, skimming from his shoulder and up his neck, kissing and licking, and sucking slightly. He groans, a sound filled with need and want and overwhelming lust.

I know because I feel it too.

Slowly, I reach up, undoing the buttons of my shirt until it splits open in the middle. Then I pull back and grasp each side of the shirt revealing myself to him—my bra and panties the only thing covering me.

"You're so fucking beautiful, Riley."

Beneath me, his cock stirs.

As does the vibrating phone in his pocket.

He grunts in frustration and I shift to the side, allowing him access to it. Before he can read it, I take it from him, annoyed that someone had the audacity to ruin our perfect lust-filled moment. Dylan doesn't fight it, so I read the text out loud.

Dave: *I hope you're getting money and fucking bitches. Hugs and Kisses - Your gimp.*

I look over at Dylan, who's sitting up and shaking his head. "It's not what it looks like."

"Who's Dave?"

"My buddy in Afghanistan."

"Uh-huh." I type out a quick message while Dylan watches.

Dylan: *He's trying, you cock-blocking gimp.*

Dylan says, "You make it impossible not to like you as much as I do. You know that, right?"

Dave: *Pic or I call bullshit.*

Dylan laughs. "Just ignore him, babe."

"Or we could have fun with him," I respond, pulling him by the back of his neck until his face is buried between my breasts. I snap the pic and send it, all while Dylan watches me, his eyes wide in shock.

Dave: *Carry on, my man. Carry the fuck on.*
Dave: *Also, I wish you were more technically minded. I could use you right now.*

Dylan's face turns serious when he reads the text. He takes the phone from me and I witness first hand his snail-speed typing.

Dylan: *You good?*

Dave: *Yeah, man. We're on base at the moment so if you can tear yourself away from your girl for a minute, set up Skype and we can organize a time to call.*

Dylan looks up at me. "What's Skype?"

"It's like a video chat thing. I have it on my phone." I get off him and grab my phone from the pocket of my shorts sitting on the floor. "Tell him to add me."

He looks at me confused.

I take the phone from him.

Dylan: *Hey. It's Riley. The girl in the pic. You can add me on Skype. I have it on my phone. xoxR1L3YHxox*

Dave: *Oh. Seriously, it's cool. You guys do your thing. I didn't mean to interrupt.*

Dylan: *We can continue any time. I don't mind.*

Dave: *Thx so much. Honestly. I kind of just want to see his ugly face, you know?*

Dylan: *lol. I'd miss him too.*

"What are you writing?" Dylan asks.

"Nothing."

Dave: *Okay. Added you.*

Dylan: *I'll get him to call now.*

I open the app and accept the add request, then hand the phone to Dylan. "Just press the green video camera icon to call him. I'm going to raid your fridge. You want anything?"

Shaking his head, he says, "Thanks, babe." Then kisses me quickly, but I can already tell his mind is elsewhere. I button up my shirt as I exit his room, leaving him to talk to his buddy.

THERE ISN'T MUCH in his fridge. Milk, butter, bologna, and a block of cheese. Shutting the fridge, I look around the kitchen. It's as bare as the fridge is. The table in the middle isn't even a real table; it's one of those foldout poker ones. I open the cabinets, searching for the glasses and when I find one, I turn on the tap and fill it with water. I take it with me to the garage and sit it on the workbench where the engine he's told me all about sits in pieces. Grabbing a smaller piece, I ignore the shaking of my hands, matching the shakiness of my breath. And for the countless time since we got back in his truck, I try to ignore the day's overwhelming emotions.

Surely, it can't be that easy to go from one extreme to another. To wake up knowing that the secrets of your past could be the undoing of your future to this—being insanely attached and falling in love with a boy I barely know—a boy who's declared time and time again that he feels the same way. He's shown me his heart; I've shown him mine. And the best, or maybe the worst part is that I haven't felt an ounce of guilt.

Grief, yes.

Longing, definitely.

But *guilt*? No.

I don't know how to explain it—what it's like to be in unfamiliar arms, kiss in an unfamiliar way, laugh with an unfamiliar sound… but I haven't felt this connected since the moments before I climbed that cliff. And I don't mean connected to someone, but connected to the world.

I wipe the tears, the emotions flooding me as the excitement builds. The thrill of waking up every morning with more to look forward to than the next sip of alcohol. I want to drive in his truck, I want to see the world again, and I want him next to me, keeping me safe and sane and knowing that when things get too hard, too rough, and the guilt becomes too much to bare—not just the guilt of my feelings for him but the guilt of my past and the pain I'd caused others, he'll do exactly what he said he'd do: he'll be the glue that holds me together.

He calls my name from somewhere in the house, and I tell him where I am. He shows up a moment later, his eyes going from me to the engine. "What are you doing, babe?" he asks.

I love that he calls me babe. "Just tinkering with your engine, Lance Corporal Banks."

"Oh my God," he murmurs, his grin wider than I've ever seen. He steps forward, looking in my eyes, and then he runs the back of his finger across my cheek. "You got grease on your face, Riley. So fucking hot."

I roll my eyes and keep him at a distance. "How's everything with your buddy?"

Shrugging, he releases a long drawn out sigh. "He's in a war. It's as bad as you'd imagine it would be."

"I don't imagine it as anything. You don't really talk much about it."

He takes the part from my hand and holds it in his, palm up as he looks down on it. "You know when you're having a nightmare and you know it's just a dream so you try to wake up but your body fights it, so it keeps going and going until something finally happens which forces you up, and you wake up in a pool of sweat but your mind is still there, stuck in the nightmare?"

"I know it well," I whisper.

"War is like that, Riley. Only the things that wake you up are the cause of the nightmares."

"So why do it?" I ask.

"Because sometimes you need to have nightmares to appreciate the dreams."

I don't know how to respond, so I don't. I just stare at him, watching his features soften as he stares back, his smile growing with each passing second. Then he bends down, plants a chaste kiss on my cheek and places my phone in my hand. "Your mom's going to be home soon. I should get you back."

"Already?" I complain, checking the time.

"Time flies when you're having fun."

Twenty-Three
Dylan

Riley: *You know what I miss?*

Dylan: *Me?*

Riley: *Please. I only saw you an hour ago.*

Dylan: *I still choose the answer to be ME.*

Riley: *I miss playing basketball.*

Dylan: *You play?*

Riley: *I dabble.*

Dylan: *Dribble?*

Riley: *Dabble. It's a figure of speech, Dylan.*

Dylan: *I know. It was a joke.*

Riley: *Your typing's gotten better. And faster.*

Dylan: *I'm on the computer.*

Riley: *I figured.*

Dylan: *But swimming was your thing, right? You don't miss swimming?*

Riley: *I haven't been in the water since... you know.*

Dylan: *Oh.*

Riley: *Besides the bath, I mean.*

Dylan: *You kill me with your visuals, Hudson.*

Riley: *Unintentional.*

Dylan: *Sure.*

Riley: *I do miss you though.*

Dylan: *Needy much?*

Riley: *lol. Shut up.*

Dylan: *I miss you too. My room smells like you now.*
Dylan: *I could come over. We can drive to the elementary school and shoot hoops.*

Riley: *I wish.*

Dylan: *You're twenty, Riley. Surely your mom can't tell you what to do.*

Riley: *It's not that she tells me what to do. I don't know. Guilt + respect, I guess.*

Dylan: *I call bullshit. I say it's fear.*

Riley: *It's not.*

Dylan: *It makes no sense.*

Riley: *Doesn't have to make sense to you.*
Riley: *Besides, it'll be dark soon. We can do it tomorrow when she's at work.*

Dylan: *Put your sneakers on. I'll be over in five.*

Riley: *Don't you dare!*

I don't bother replying. Instead, I go over to her house. I knock on her door and fake a smile when her mother answers. "Good evening, Ms. Hudson. I'd like to see Riley. Actually, I'd like to take Riley out of the house. Not just now, but a lot of times in the future so you should probably get used to me knocking on your door and requesting her presence to join me. And I'm sorry if this will cause problems for you, but—"

"What are you doing, Dylan?" Riley says.

I look past her mother to see her standing just outside her door. Then I ignore her question and speak to the woman in front of me. "But I like your daughter. A lot. And if I don't get to see her now, then I don't know what I'll do. Honestly, I'll probably revert to being a teenager and toilet papering your house." I shrug. "Sorry."

"Dylan!" Riley snaps.

Her mom doesn't speak, so I keep going. "I guess I'm not really here to ask for permission. I'm just here to pick up your daughter." I glance up at Riley. "Let's go."

Her gaze moves from me to her mom. "I can't," she says.

"Just go," her mom says. "We'll discuss it when you get home."

I thought Riley would smile, but she doesn't. She looks hesitant, but more than that, she looks pissed. *At me.* "I don't have to go," she tells her mom, like she's a grounded teenager.

Her mom looks me over from head to toe. "You're a marine, right?"

I square my shoulders. "Yes, Ma'am."

"And you're home for what? R&R?"

"No, Ma'am. Medical."

She nods. "Afghanistan?"

I lift my chin. She's trying to be intimidating. It's not going to work. Not on me. And not when it comes to Riley. "Yes, Ma'am."

"So medical leave… that means you're going back, right?"

"Yes, Ma'am."

"So what is it exactly you're doing with my daughter, Mr. Banks? Are you just looking for a good time with her before you redeploy? And then what? You leave her behind as just another notch on your belt?"

Now I'm pissed. "That's not at all—"

"You can show up at my door and act as tough as you want," she cuts in. "But regardless of what she's told you, I love my daughter and I do what's best for her. And what's best for her is definitely *not* you. Because you're not staying, you're going back. Back to a warzone where it's your job to put your life on the line every single second you're there. She's already lost someone she loved. Someone we *all* loved. And look at her. This is how she dealt with it… how she's *still* dealing with it. If you really like her like you say you do, you'll leave her alone. So she doesn't have to go through life worrying how she's going to handle the next death that comes her way."

I don't know how long I stand there, my hands in my pockets looking at the woman who I thought I hated, wondering exactly when it was in her speech that my hate turned to admiration, but it's a long ass time.

And time + perspective can change people.

Instantly.

Because she's right.

Through the chaos Riley and I created within the four walls of her bedroom, and the overwhelming feelings I let overshadow our reality… I never thought about it like that.

Not once.

But then I look over at Riley, her eyes right on mine, full of hope and promise and a complete contrast to how she was a month ago, and I take a breath. And then another. And I wonder what events in all our lives, her mother included, were The Turning Points? The points where we all determined that the fear of our pasts and the uncertainty of our futures were greater than our need for happiness.

Here.

Now.

While time and everything around us stood unmoving… who's to say we couldn't have it all?

I look at her mother again, right into her eyes, clear and gray just like Riley's. "I'll come back tomorrow. And the day after that. And the day after that. I'll keep coming back until you allow me to see her. I won't be sneaking around behind your back. I won't be calling or texting her without your approval. She matters a lot to me. More than a lot. So I'm here. Now. And I don't plan on that changing until you both realize that Riley's happiness is just as important as everyone else's."

I turn and walk away, leaving them standing there. I don't hear the door close. Not until I'm on the sidewalk and half way home. Once I'm back in my room, I get a message on my phone.

Riley: *Why the hell would you do that?*

Dylan: *Retaliation. Fight or die, Hudson.*

Then I grab a notebook, a pen and another empty jar.

Twenty-Four
Dylan

I WAKE UP early the next morning prepared for battle. I shower, dress, and make my way out to Riley's house, where I lean on her mom's car, jar in hand, and I wait. I'm only there a few minutes before she appears from the door, stopping in her tracks when she sees me. "Mr. Banks," she says in greeting.

"Ma'am."

I push off the car and stand tall, waiting for her to get to me. When she does, I offer her the jar. "For you," I tell her.

She eyes it curiously for a moment. "What's this?" she asks.

"A gift."

"Like Riley's jars?"

"Yes, Ma'am."

Her eyebrows narrow in confusion. "I'm late for work," she mumbles, using the keyless entry to unlock her car.

I open the door for her and wait until she's seated before saying, "Have a phenomenal day, Ma'am."

I give her an over exaggerated grin, along with a pathetic wave as she reverses out of the driveway. Then I turn to her front door—where I know Riley will be standing, watching with the same narrowed eyes, same look of confusion.

And as hard as it is, I keep my promise to her mother: I walk away.

TWENTY MINUTES LATER, Riley calls. Not texts, but actually calls.

"Mom just called me," she says.

I hold the phone tighter against my ear, my anticipation building. "And?"

"She asked if you wanted to come over for dinner tonight? What the hell, Dylan?"

RILEY ANSWERS THE door with the same look of confusion that I left her with. But it doesn't last long before she smiles—this all-consuming, heart-stealing smile that has me doing the same. She throws her arms around my neck, forcing me to bend down and she squeezes tight, so tight it begins to hurt. But she doesn't need to know that. "Sorry," she whispers, releasing me. She points at the flowers in my hand. "For me?" she asks.

I cringe slightly. Crap. *I should've gotten two.* "For your mom, actually."

She shrugs. "It's cool. You already got me flowers on my birthday."

"I picked you dead flowers," I remind her.

"But it's the thought that counts." She pulls me by my shirt and practically drags me down the hall and into the kitchen where her mom's busy on the stove. Whatever she's cooking smells amazing, better than the frozen dinners we have at home. I tell her that, and when she hears me, she spins around with a smile that's almost identical to Riley's. She wipes her hands on a cloth and makes her way to us.

She hugs like Riley too. "Good evening, Mr. Banks."

"Dylan's fine, Ma'am."

Riley says, "Is someone going to tell me what happened?"

"I'm getting to know your boyfriend," her mom says, releasing me.

WE SIT DOWN for a meal at an actual dining table, with an actual freshly cooked meal, and salad, and iced tea. My enjoyment is obvious by the constant moans of pleasure. Something they seem to think is hilarious. I don't even realize until I've polished off my plate that they haven't even touched theirs. I lean back in my chair, my hands on my lap and look down at them, trying to suppress my laughter. "Sorry. I'm a growing boy."

Ms. Hudson, who has told me to call her Holly, says, "I hate to break it to you but there's no possible way you're growing anymore. How tall are you now, Dylan?"

"6'3", Ma'am."

"Hmm. That's not much taller than you were when we first met you, is it?"

I shrug. "I don't know. Ask Riley. She seems to remember that moment quite well."

Riley's jaw drops.

I squeeze her leg under the table.

Her mom laughs. "So that's why you spent the next few weeks glued to the living room window."

"Lies!" Riley squeals. Then her eyes narrow at me. "I was going to give you my food but after that…" Slowly, she puts her entire hand in her plate, using it to scoop up the lasagna and shoves it in her mouth, smearing bits of it around her lips.

I choke on my guffaw, pick up my napkin and start to clean her face.

"You're a mess, Ry," her mom tells her.

"And so cute," I add.

She waits until I'm done cleaning her before leaning forward and kissing me quickly. Then she places her plate in front of me. I welcome the food and look across the table at Holly. She's watching Riley with a frown on her face. Then she blinks and as if coming to, she notices me watching her. Riley's hand's on mine now, still on her leg under the table.

Holly clears her throat. "So do you guys have plans for tomorrow?" she asks.

Riley's eyes widen slightly when her gaze shifts between us. "Nothing solid," she says hesitantly.

Holly nods.

I chime in. "I was actually thinking of going into town. I need to get some supplies. But I need to be home in the morning," I tell them. "I'm expecting a delivery."

"Oh yeah?" Riley asks. "Of what?"

"Car shell."

"For the engine?" She smiles. "You're ready to move on?"

"Yep. Moving on. With you, Riley Hudson."

✧ ✧ ✧

Riley: *You in your garage?*

Dylan: *Youxstalking again, Hudson?*

Riley: *Open the door.*

I open the garage door just high enough for her to duck underneath and then close it again. She's wearing my shirt from yesterday and I'm pretty sure not much else. "What's up?" I ask as she walks past me and toward the workbench. She uses the stepladder set up in front of it to climb onto the bench and sits down to face me. "Nothing. Just wanted to see you."

"Yeah?" I walk over and clean my hands on an old rag, throwing it over my shoulder before standing in front of her and rubbing my hands on her bare legs. "I just left you an hour ago. Already missing me, huh?"

She places her forearms on my shoulders and spreads her legs, bringing me closer to her. "My mom came and spoke to me after you left."

I kiss her quickly. "How did that go?"

"It was… *freeing*, I guess."

"Freeing how?"

"She told me you wrote her a letter."

I nod.

"She didn't tell me what was in it though. She just said it helped open her eyes to what was happening with me. And the fact that she had no real clue what was going on was a huge wake up call for her." She lowers her arms and places her palms flat on my chest, her eyes focused on the touch. "She admitted some stuff that kind of had me realizing that I'd been pushing her away since the night I lost it. I think we were both drowning in so much guilt—guilt I didn't know she was carrying—that we lost focus on ourselves and each other and even though we lived together, we couldn't be further apart."

My eyes narrow in confusion. "She carries guilt?"

"Apparently," she says, her gaze and her hands dropping. "She said she felt responsible for the accident. Not with Jeremy, but with me. She thinks she should've noticed my self-destruction as it was happening instead of when it was too late. She knows I tried to talk to her… It was hard for her to hear what I'd gone through that day at the lake so instead of listening she chose to ignore me. It was easier for her that way, but it's something she regrets. I feel horrible, Dylan."

"Why?"

"Because I should've seen it. I shouldn't have walked around pretending to be blind to it all. She could've let me go to court, had them deal with me… she sold her salon that she worked her entire life to create, sold her pride to the town, lost clients. Now she rents a chair from a chain salon and makes half the money she used to and she did that because she cared about me and she loved me. At the time, I thought she did it to hide her shame." I let her speak, because it's important she talks about it, maybe remove some of the weight that's constantly pushing her down. She adds, "I chose to become a recluse after the mandatory house arrest because I didn't want people looking at me and judging her. I don't even know how the drinking started. She hates that she let it go on for so long, encouraged it even. I guess she was trying to help dull the pain, you know?"

I hold her closer, her chest pressed against mine.

She cries more than a year's worth of tears, releases more than a year's worth of pain, and when she pulls away, her eyes red and unfocused, she says, "Jeremy—he was such a good kid." And I can see the smile breaking through caused by the memory of happiness only they could share. "He was always happy. Always smiling. He'd talk to anyone and everyone that approached him and he'd stick up for the shy quiet kids. I wondered if it was because of me that he did that, so I asked him once and he just shrugged and said 'if all the quiet ones have as much to say as you do, then the world needs to hear it.' He was always thinking about other people, but beneath that—there was something deep brewing, like he wanted to change the world somehow. He wanted to leave a legacy when he died, you know?"

More tears.

Bigger smiles.

"He had this one postcard in his locker he got from Myrtle Beach and it said '*facta non verba.*'"

"Actions speak louder than words?"

She nods. "I shouldn't have let the words of others control my actions. If he was around to see how badly I let it ruin me, he would've been so mad. Not so much at them, but at me. And I'm just pissed off because it's not what he would've wanted, you know? I should've done better. For him. I should've done more. Like, what's his legacy now?"

I keep my eyes on hers, watching the sadness and desperation consume her. "So *you* be his legacy."

Her eyes snap to mine, her breath completely leaving her. "But… I thought I belong to you now?"

"It doesn't have to be either/or, Riley. It never has to be. You can have us both. You can have it all."

Twenty-Five
Riley

FOR THE NEXT week, we spend every spare second together and when we're not together, we text—something he's gotten a lot better at. We leave the confines of my room and spend most of the days in his garage working on putting the engine in the shell that had been delivered. He's been over twice since. Once with his dad and brother.

I still don't know what he wrote to my mom. I stopped "nagging" as he puts it, after a couple days.

We keep up with his shoulder rehab. I force him to. I keep all records in the notebook from his last visit and make sure I have everything I need for when we go back next week. Maybe it's dumb to assume it's important, but it is to me. Besides, I love watching him do it. The best part is when he takes his shirt off and does one-handed push-ups—using his left arm, obviously.

There's definitely a difference between a boy's body and a man's. Or maybe it's just Dylan. Yeah. I'm going to say it's just Dylan.

His buddy in Afghanistan has called twice using my Skype. I leave the room when they talk. It just seems too private and, to be honest, I'm not sure I'm ready to hear what he has to go back to when he finally does go back.

We don't talk about it—what will happen with us when he leaves. Because like he said, he's here. Now. And that's more than enough.

"You're turning into a grease monkey," he says, eyeing me from under the hood of the Honda.

I look down at my clothes and the grease stains smeared on my white shirt. "I am!"

"It's hot, Ry." He stands to his full height, stalking toward me with a wrench in his hand. He has that look in eyes. You know, *that* look.

The one that tells me he's pretty much done with the car for the day and the rest will be spent with me in his arms while he makes me laugh. I love that time of day. Almost as much as I love him.

He pulls his phone out of his pocket and takes a picture. (Side note: it took me fifteen minutes to show him how to use it.) Then he drops his wrench on the bench next to where I'm sitting and settles his hands on my legs. "Feel like helping out?"

"Not right now. I just like watching you."

"Quit treating me like a piece of meat, Hudson. Jeez. I have feelings you know."

Giggling, I lift his tank up and peek at his abs.

He slaps my hand away. "My eyes are up here," he jokes, then pulls the collar of my shirt down and peers down. "Is there some sort of Dylan-gets-to-be-in-my-pants schedule you're working with that I should know about?" He nuzzles his face into my neck, kissing it gently. "Throw a kid a bone here."

My fingers part through his hair—hair that's gotten longer since he came home. "You have to earn your bases, Rookie."

He mocks an exaggerated sob.

I roll my eyes. "There's no crying in baseball!"

"That reminds me," he says, reaching behind me. He drops a book on my lap. "I got you this."

I smile. "Part two of the pause?"

"Yep. Luce called this morning and said it came out today so I went to the store and got it. Now you can see how it ends."

"You're the bestest boyfriend ever," I announce.

He laughs at that, just as his phone sounds with a text.

I reach for it before he can get to it and when I read the text, I wish I hadn't.

> ***Heidi:*** *Hey… So, I'm in town for the weekend. I heard you were back. I'm free now. Just seeing if you wanted to catch up. For old time's sake.*

"For old time's sake? What does that even mean?" I ask.

He moves away from my neck, his eyes already narrowed. Then he takes the phone from my hand and reads the text. He looks up.

"Have you been talking to her?" I ask.

"No. This is the first time she's contacted me." He's still holding the phone. He wants to reply.

"I'm not going to stop you from talking to her. Or seeing her. Or doing whatever it is..." my voice drops to a whisper. "...for old time's sake."

He shakes his head. "It's not like that, Riley."

"But you *want* to see her."

He shrugs, his response giving me nothing. "If it's going to cause issues then I'll just tell her no."

"It's fine," I say, my tone clipped.

"Obviously *not.*"

"I just don't get why you'd want to see her. Do you miss her?"

"No!" His head drops forward. "Jesus, Riley. You're making this impossible. I could've lied. I could've ignored her message now and then seen her behind your back but I don't want to keep anything from you."

"Well, you are!"

"What?!"

"You *are* keeping something from me!"

"What the hell are you talking about?"

"*Why* do you want to see her?"

"Closure," he yells. Then softer, "I just want closure. We left things at such a shitty point and after you and I talked about it, our relationship made more sense to me than it did when I was actually part of it. So I just... I don't know *why.*"

I push aside my petty jealousy, just for a moment, and I think about him—how broken he was because of her—and I see things from his perspective. I jump off the bench and wrap my arms around his waist. "I'm being selfish."

"Honestly? A little."

I pull back and pout at him.

He smiles, running his grease stained thumb across my lips.

"Just don't like... sleep with her. Or touch her. Or try not to even look at her."

"You're not being fair, Riley."

"Yeah, but I'm also not blind and regardless of how badly I wish, I don't have amnesia. I remember what she looks like, Dylan. And you're a guy."

He shakes his head with his intake of breath. Then he looks down at me. "I'm also a guy who's madly in love with you, Riley."

"What?" I whisper, my breath leaving me.

"You need me to repeat it?"

"No." I try to suppress my smile. I can't. "Maybe?"

He doesn't skip a beat. "I'm madly in love with you, Riley."

"Again?"

He laughs. "You want me to write it down?"

I can't stop smiling. "Yes."

With a chuckle, he releases me and gets a marker from one of the drawers on the bench, then grabs my arm. I watch his face as the pen presses down on my skin, marking me, making me his.

I love you, Riley Hudson.

Then underneath;

Semper Fidelis.

"Isn't that the Marine Corps motto?"

He nods. "Know what it means?"

"No."

"*Always faithful.*"

Dylan

THERE WAS ALWAYS a level of fear when it came to Heidi. From the first time she talked to me sophomore year and even after we'd started dating. It's completely fair to say she was the hottest girl in school, at least on my radar. When I finally took enough of her hints and worked up the courage to ask her out—I was still surprised she said yes. It was no secret she dated before me. Guys who were older, even Logan (if you can call what they did dating).

I guess what I'm trying to say is that I always found myself kind of in awe of her beauty and presence. Being with her was intimidating, to say the least. Maybe that's why I kept my mouth shut around her—in fear that I'd say something dumb or try to joke around and she wouldn't find it funny like Riley does.

But as I hear her car door close a good half hour after Riley left, followed by the clicking of her heels against the concrete of my driveway, I don't feel intimidated. I don't feel afraid. In fact, I don't feel much of anything at all.

I wipe my hands on the rag and pop my head out from under the hood of the Honda, faking a smile as she walks toward me, her familiar hips swaying from side to side. She hadn't changed much in the few months since I'd seen her. Not that I expected her to. I guess what's changed is my perspective. Not just *of* her, but of *us*.

"Hey," she says, her perfectly applied red lipstick curving with her smile. Her bright blue eyes take me in as she flicks her hair over her shoulder—hair that seems to glow gold from the orange of the sunset.

I stand next to the car, my hands in my pockets and I nod once. "Hey."

"You still messing around with the cars, I see."

Maybe I should be annoyed at her choice of words, but I'm not. That's just Heidi. "You home to visit your parents?" I ask.

She nods and looks around the garage. "I don't think I've ever really been in here."

"You haven't," I say curtly. It comes out harsher than intended but I don't back down.

Her smile falls, just for a moment, before returning. "How's your dad?"

"He's good."

"Eric's home now, right? How is he?"

"Also good." I lean back against the car and cross my arms. "And you?"

She inhales a breath through her nose, her hands by her sides. Her jeans hug her waist and continue that way all the way down to her ankles. "I'm okay. You know, senior year. Getting by. You miss college?" she asks, a slight laugh bubbling out of her. Probably because she already knows my answer.

"Not a single fucking minute of it."

Her smile drops, her hands now clasped together in front of her. "I'm sorry, Dylan. I didn't think it would be this awkward."

I shake my head. "It's not."

"I just wanted to see you, I guess. Make sure you were okay. I heard you got—"

"You heard?" I cut in.

She shrugs. "I asked. I knew the guys were coming to see you so…"

"So you could've contacted me yourself."

"I wanted to, Dylan," she says, her tone pleading. "I didn't think you'd want anything to do with me after the way we left things."

"I was angry back then."

"And you had every right to be," she rushes out. "I betrayed you in the worst possible way, not just by what I did but by not telling you about it to begin with. I was scared—"

"I don't really care," I interrupt.

"Dylan."

"No." I exhale loudly, trying to keep my emotions in check. "I don't mean I don't care about your apology or whatever this is. I'm just saying that I don't care about it; what happened in the past. I'm not mad. Not anymore."

"You're not?" she asks, clearly surprised.

"I've moved on from it, Heidi. I had to."

She blows out a shaky breath, her hands at her sides again. "We never really talked about it, you know… what happened to *us*?"

I shrug. "We grew apart."

"That's it?"

I nod.

"Before or after you broke up with me?"

I shake my head, slightly annoyed. "I didn't break up with you, Heidi. I enlisted."

"You asked if I wanted to stay with you even though your future was uncertain!"

"Exactly!" I take a calming breath. "Heidi, I *asked* you. I did it for *you*. I didn't say I wanted to break up. You read into that what you wanted. And you can't deny that even after that there was a part of you still holding onto us like I was because you broke up with me in a damn letter while I was deployed!"

Her mouth opens. Her eyes widen. It seems like words are caught in her throat and for a few seconds, she stays that way. Then, slowly, her features soften, as if she's remembering the conversation for exactly what it was. "When did we grow apart?" she asks.

"I can't answer that, Heidi."

She frowns, her gaze dropping. "Did I do something, Dylan? Was there a certain incident that made you wake up one day and realize I wasn't enough for you?" When she looks back up, her eyes are clouded with tears.

For a second, I almost go to her. *Almost.* "No, Heidi. It wasn't anything you did. But it wasn't anything I did either. It was just us. We weren't working. You knew I didn't want to go to college but I went for you, and that life—" I take a breath. "That life is perfect for you. It wasn't for me. And that's how we would've spent the rest of our lives had I not made the choice to leave. We would've both been unhappy."

"I didn't ask you to follow me there," she says.

"I'm not saying you did."

"Then why do it?"

"Because I loved you, Heids."

She wipes her tears. "You did?"

"Of course, I did. I don't regret being with you all those years."

"Do you regret how it ended?" she asks.

I shrug. "I really only regret not telling you sooner."

"Telling me what?"

"That I thought we'd fallen out of love."

"I still loved you," she says quickly.

I shrug again. "Yeah, but it was a different kind of love. It was familiar and—"

"Safe," she cuts in. "You always made me feel safe, Dylan."

I find myself smiling, though I don't really know why. "Why'd you really want to see me, Heidi?"

Now it's her turn to shrug. "Closure, I guess. Why'd you *let* me see you?"

"Same reason."

"So you don't hate me?"

I shake my head.

Then she says, "You look good, Dylan."

And I look away.

She sighs. "Your dad helping you with the car? That was something you did together, right?"

"Yeah, it *was.*" I smile again. "Riley's helping me with the rebuild."

"Riley's… a guy from your unit?"

I chuckle. "No. Riley's my girlfriend."

Her eyes widen. "Your *girlfriend*?"

"Uh huh."

"Sorry." She laughs. "I thought Riley was a guy."

"Common mistake."

"So…" Her shoulders relax. "How'd you meet?"

I jerk my head toward Riley's house. "She's the girl next door."

"How cliché."

"Says The Prom Queen."

She laughs louder and pats her hair. "I still wear my crown when I want to relive my greatest moments."

Shaking my head, I tell her, "That doesn't surprise me at all."

"You're such a jerk," she jokes. Then adds, "So can I meet her?"

I pull my phone out of my pocket and shoot Riley a text.

Dylan: *Come over.*

"Whoa, you learned how to text?" Heidi asks.

"Yeah. Riley's a texter. Besides, it's about time, right?"

"You must really like her."

"You have no idea, Heids."

RILEY SHOWS UP a minute later, stopping at the end of my driveway when she sees Heidi in the garage. She's dressed exactly as she was when she left: a plain white shirt underneath one of mine. I make her wear them when we're working on the car so it doesn't ruin her clothes.

Slowly, she walks up the driveway, her gaze everywhere but on us.

"Hey babe," I say in greeting.

She glances at Heidi quickly before looking back at me. "Hey. I'm sorry. I thought you meant to come over *now*. I didn't know you still had company."

"I asked him if I could meet you," Heidi cuts in, raising her hand in a wave. "I'm Heidi."

"I know," Riley rushes out, then recovers, "I mean, I know you—recognize you—from high school, I mean." She presses one foot on top of the other—a sign I've learned means she's trying not to run.

"We were in the same class?" Heidi tilts her head as she looks Riley up and down.

"No. You were older," Riley answers. *She's so nervous.*

I speak up. "Riley was a sophomore when I was a senior." I say *I* instead of *we*, because I want Riley to know that when it comes to Heidi and I, there is no *we*.

"Oh cool," Heidi responds, smiling at the both of us. I don't know if it's fake. I don't care if it is.

"I was just telling Heidi how you were helping me with the re-build," I tell Riley.

She nods. "Just the things his injury prevents him from doing. He's got the rest under control."

"So you're into cars?" Heidi asks her.

"Not before Dylan," Riley says, her voice louder and more confi-dent. "But it's his thing and it makes him happy so of course I want to be part of it." It's for sure a dig at Heidi, though Heidi wouldn't have a clue.

Heidi looks between us, before pointing to Riley's arm. "What's that?" she asks.

Riley lifts her arm, my messy hand written declaration of my love prominent for all to see.

Seconds of silence pass while I look between the two girls. Heidi—with her so-called perfect hair and perfect make-up and perfect clothes, and then I look over at Riley, whose hair is a messy knot on top of her head, make-up free, wearing my shirt and a pair of old workout shorts, standing barefoot in my garage. They couldn't be more opposite if they tried and if you asked me a thousand times over to choose between them, my answer *is* and *always will be* Riley. Because while Heidi might seem perfect, she's not perfect for me. Riley on the other hand… well, she's *my* Riley.

And I'm madly in love with her.

Obviously.

Twenty-Six
Dylan

WITH MY EYES closed, I blindly reach for the phone on my nightstand. I'd gotten used to Riley's messages in the middle of the night so it didn't surprise me at all when her name popped up. What did surprise me was the message.

Riley: *Are you up? I'm outside. Let me in.*

Dylan: *kjd*

Riley: *It's cold, Dylan.*

I kick the covers off and stumble down the hall and toward the door. "I need you," she says as soon as I open it. She presses her freezing cold hands against my bare stomach and I squeal—like a girl—and swat her hands away. She laughs and grabs my hand, then drags me through the house and into my room. Keep in mind, I'm still half asleep, so I don't really realize that I'm back in my room and she's thrown me on the mattress and started removing her top until she says, "I *need* you, Dylan." And then everything becomes clear, even in the semi-dark of my room. I sit up, my heart racing and my dick already at half-mast when her bare breasts come into view.

I smack my cheek, forcing myself to wake up because I don't want to miss this. Not a single second.

Now she's standing in front of me, wearing nothing but bright white panties and *holy fucking shit.*

I smack my cheek again just in case this is a dream.

"What are you doing?" she asks, wrapping her fingers around my wrist to stop me from doing it again.

Now her bare legs are between mine and I don't think I'm breathing. *At all.* I run my thumb at the sweet spot between her legs, feeling the heat emit against my skin. She moans softly, her forearms on my shoulders and her head tilted back, her eyes closed and her tits on full display. I reach up with my free hand and cover one, then dip my head and replace my other thumb with my mouth, tasting her over the fabric of her panties. They're silk—soft and wet against my lips.

"Wait," she whispers. She must be fucking crazy. There's no way I'm waiting. Instead, I run my hands down the arch of her back, to her ass, beneath her panties and I squeeze hard, bringing her mound closer to my open mouth. She's gripping my hair now, squeezing her legs together and trying to push away.

Yeah, she's fucking insane if she thinks it'll stop me.

I lower my hands, past her ass and to her thighs, pushing her panties down. I bite my lip when they drop to the floor, giving me a perfect view of her pussy only inches away from me.

"Dylan, I've never—" She breaks off on a moan when I kiss her there, tasting her for the first time. I grab her leg and place her foot on the mattress beside me, opening her up… just for me. Then, like a man possessed, I dive in. She pulls on my hair, but she's not pushing me away this time, she's holding me to her… *as if there'd be anywhere else I'd rather be.*

I run a single finger between her folds, touching our combined wetness. Then I put it inside her, feeling her contract around me. She's so tight. So fucking wet. So perfect. "Jesus Christ," I groan between licks. I take my finger out, replacing it with two, while my mouth moves up and covers her clit.

She moans again, her hips rocking back and forth, matching my fingers as they move in and out. It doesn't take long for her release and the second she's done she drops her leg back to the floor, and then drops to her knees, her hands already on the band of my boxers. I lift slightly; just enough for her to pull them down and free my cock. Her eyes widen slightly and inside I'm fucking beaming with pride. Outside, I'm forcing myself to breathe. I lean back on my arms; grateful she makes me do those fucking shoulder exercises so I can actually hold my weight. Then she looks up—her eyes hazy, filled with lust—the tip of my cock an inch from her mouth.

I lick my lips and drop my gaze to her now warm hand curled around my dick and I swear if this is a dream I'm going to cry. Legit, *cry.*

It's not a dream, though. Because my dreams of this moment don't come close to the feeling of her warm mouth around me, her lips spread thin. Not gonna lie, I've thought about this moment a lot. A little too much. Every single time she pouted, my mind pictured those lips exactly where they are. And now it's happening. And I'm close. Closer than I wanted to be.

She's hesitant, it seems, which just makes my cock throb in her mouth because her inexperience mixed with innocence makes her even hotter. She pulls back, takes a breath and then resumes her position, her eyes focused on her task. I place my hand in her hair and slowly guide her, not to be forceful, but to be.... helpful. Yeah. *Helpful.*

I lean back on my outstretched arm, the other hand still in her hair and I wonder how the fuck it is I got so lucky. Then she looks up again, her eyebrows raised as if asking if I'm enjoying what she's doing. That one look—that single second—is my undoing. I push her away and reach for a discarded shirt. "Like this?" she asks, making a fist around my dick and pumping to the same pace as her mouth only seconds earlier.

"You're fucking incredible, Riley." And then I blow. I come harder than I have since the first time I was inside her, my breath catches in my chest as she keeps her strokes going and "*Holy shit!*"

She laughs as I throw the shirt across the room and wipe my brow on my forearm. Then she climbs onto the mattress, her legs on either side of mine, straddling my waist.

"Hi," she says.

"Hi," I say back, feeling the wetness of both our parts as they touch, my still hard cock between her folds. She kisses my neck, making her way up to my jaw, before finding my lips. Her hips circle, grinding herself into me. It's too much. Too fucking much. Because I'm already close to coming again and I need her to get off again. At least twice.

I am a gentleman, after all.

So, I flip her onto her back, her hair splaying across my pillow. I kiss and suck and lick my way down from her neck, stopping at each of her breasts, paying them equal attention before I move to her stomach, my tongue dipping into her belly button. She writhes beneath me, her hands fisted in the sheets as I move lower again, her moans of pleasure filling my ears and making me harder. I taste her again, because I didn't get enough the first time. Her back arches off the bed, her legs squeezing the sides of my face as I bite down on her clit. I place my arm across her stomach, keeping her in place so I can get my finger inside her again.

She's close. I can tell because her breathing's stopped, her stomach muscles have tensed and her thighs are pressed hard against my ears. She's trying to lift off the mattress, trying to get more of me.

I give her more.

Fuck, I give her *everything.*

"Oh shit oh shit oh shit." She says this over and over while my fingers work faster and faster until they're completely soaked with her juices and so is my mouth. She drops back on the bed, her hands releasing the sheets, her entire body covered in sweat and nothing—not a goddamn thing has ever, EVER, turned me on as much as watching and feeling her hand around my cock, guiding me to her entrance while her eyes lock with mine. I reach across her and open the drawer of my nightstand to pull out a condom and, with one of her hands still around my cock; she uses the other to take the packet from me. She bites down on the corner, tearing it open and then, as if she wasn't sexy enough, she rolls it on for me. Then she places one hand behind her head, the other covering her breast as she bites her lip and nods once. I push up on my left arm, my right hand gripping her leg and wrapping it around my waist so she's wide open for me. I wasn't kidding when I said she was tight—because she wasn't kidding when she said she was "almost" a virgin. On the first thrust, I'm inside her and on the second, she leans up, her hands on my shoulders and her mouth by my ear when she moans, "Fuck me, Lance Corporal Banks."

WE LAY TOGETHER, her head on my chest and my arm around her, completely naked and covered in sweat. Our bodies stick to the sheets but we're both too exhausted to do anything about it. "What the hell got into you, Hudson?" I joke.

She laughs and presses her face into the crook of my neck. "I read that book you got me."

"Yeah?"

"It was a little more... *erotic* than the first one."

I chuckle, making her half sit up and look down on me.

"What?" she asks.

"Nothing." I reach for my phone and send Cam a text.

Dylan: *FUCK YEAH BOOKS!*

Twenty-Seven
Riley

THE NEXT COUPLE months go by in a blur. Mom jokes that Dylan may as well move in with the amount of time he's over. We spend every night together, either at his house or mine. Sometimes I wonder if it's his way of keeping an eye on me—making sure I don't drink. But then I realize that it doesn't matter. Either way, I'm grateful for him. Each day we spend together, we learn and we laugh and we love more than the last.

I push him to maintain his rehab. He pushes my buttons. Same old. But he also helps me to push my boundaries. He encouraged me to go into town, which I did, with him holding my hand, our chins raised and ready for whatever would come my way.

Nothing came.

It seems that to a degree, Mom was right. People just needed something to talk about. Apparently, the current "talk" is some priest having an affair with a housewife. Whatever. *People are stupid.*

That night, I wrote letters to everyone I affected with my actions, put them in a jar, and walked into the stores or offices and handed them to the owners, Jake's dad included.

Mr. Andrews was happy to see Dylan, and happy to see that I was happy. We also went to see Dr. Matthews, his friend's dad, and got me on birth control.

We go to Dylan's check ups together (I'm on my third notebook) and his doctors are happy with his progress. And even though we know the clock is ticking on our current time together… we don't talk about it.

We don't look at the clock.

We're having too much fun.

My mom brings it up sometimes, but never to the point where she's the one pushing the wrong buttons.

A few nights ago we drove down to UNC for "Operation Mayhem: Retaliation Edition." I didn't really know what this meant, but it involved me dressing in black, fishing wire, a fishing rod, sixteen cans of cat food, a crowbar, the *High School Musical* soundtrack, a shit ton of eggs, a blow up doll, and five huge black dildos. That's just what was in the front seat. I don't even want to list what was in the bed of his truck. Nor do I want to think about the dent this made on his credit card.

"Mo money, mo problems," he said when I casually mentioned it, which made absolutely no sense but he'd been talking to Dave a lot more lately so I guess that might have something to do with it.

I beg him to leave Lucy alone since her and I had started texting a bit, mainly about books. Oh. I forgot to mention, the morning after I showed up at his house in the middle of the night, Dylan went out and got me a Kindle and had Lucy load it up with "her" types of books. He just kept saying, "Read, Riley. Read as much as you want, whenever you want." So I did. And now Lucy and I read books together—something she loves because we're both quick readers. Anyway, his response to my request to leave Lucy alone was quite disturbing. "But then what would I do with three of the dildos and the five feet of chains?" So… I left that alone.

I also left him to do most of the mayhem himself considering I already had a record for disorderly conduct. We left UNC as the sun was rising and headed back home. I asked why he didn't stay to at least watch one of the reactions. He said it wasn't the point. The point is to plant, not to witness. That's rule number four.

Did I mention that I think I'm in love with him? Because I think am. Soul-crushing, heart-stealing, life-changing, guilt-free L.O.V.E in *love* with him.

"ALL RIGHT, BABE," he says, sticking his head out from under the hood of the Honda. "Turn her over."

I put my Kindle on the seat next to me and reach for the keys in the ignition. Then I crank it. It starts first go, causing a giant grin to form across Dylan's face. I start to celebrate but he presses a finger on his lips to silence me, then he closes his eyes and listens to the quiet roar of the engine for a minute. I guess hoping it doesn't die.

I'd learned from our chats that he's a 1342 Small Craft Mechanic. I'm sure I got my wording wrong but it basically means that that's what he chose his job to be when he enlisted and while he was deployed. Besides, you know, saving the world and all that.

So I guess it's safe to say that he'd be pretty disappointed in himself had he not connected the engine to the shell properly. But going off of the widening of his grin, he's done all right.

He rubs his hands together as he makes his way to the passenger seat, carefully placing my Kindle in the glove box. Swear, he thinks that Kindle is made of unicorn leather or something. He handles it with more care than he handles me… but then again… the books I've read have taught me that not all lovemaking should be sensual. Sometimes, you just want a good, hard, rough spanking. True story.

"Let's take her for a spin," he tells me.

"You want me to drive?"

He looks at me like I'm stupid. "Of course you're driving. It's your car."

"What?!" I shout.

"Why the hell do you think I've been working on it?"

"You can't give me a car! Did Afghanistan give you brain damage?"

He rolls his eyes. "I have a car! What the hell am I going to do with this one?"

"You can't buy me a car, Dylan!"

He scoffs. "Technically, I didn't *buy* you a car. I *made* you one." His smile widens as he pretends to write in the air. "Dear Jeremy," he says, his voice high pitched. "Dylan made me a car and I love him so much."

I laugh. I can't help it. Because I know he's not mocking me. He's just being Dylan.

"Seriously," he adds. "What am I going to do with this?"

"You didn't buy it with the intention of giving it to me, though."

"I beg to differ."

"You got it a few weeks after you got home. We'd barely started dating."

"Yeah, and I wanted to get in your pants back then. This was my go-to if all my other plans failed me."

"What? Give me a car in the hopes I'd put out?"

"Yep."

We argue about this for another five minutes before he finally gets sick of my nagging and tells me to shut up and be grateful. So… I shut up and be grateful.

WE'RE GONE A couple of hours before we get back to our neighborhood, but he tells me to turn onto a street two before ours. He doesn't tell me why. Just says it'll be worth it. Then he tells me to stop in front of nowhere familiar and gets out of the car. I stay. Just in case this is one of his crazy Operation Mayhems and I need to bail quickly. He walks to my side of the car, opens my door, undoes my belt, and holds my hand, helping me to get out. "What's going on?" I ask, looking around me.

He's pulling one of his shitty pranks. I can feel it. My heart can feel it. It's already hammering in my chest. I suspect his crazy friends will retaliate his retaliation and throw shit at me. Probably under his advisement. I do tend to throw shit at him often.

He must sense my concern because he chuckles. "Don't worry, Riley. Nothing bad is going to happen." He walks up a path leading to a single story house, similar to ours, but a little bit bigger.

"Are we visiting with someone?" I look down at my clothes—my standard grease stained shirt underneath one of his and my torn denim shorts and I grasp his hand tighter and dig my heels into the ground. "I'm not dressed for this."

He laughs again. "There's no one here."

"Oh my God, you're going to kill me in this abandoned house."

He shrugs. "Maybe," he says, pulling a set of keys out of his pocket and stopping at the front door. Then he proceeds to open it. "But that would be a really bad way to start out in our new home. Not to mention the resale value."

I stop in my tracks, my breath leaving me and running far away to the land of sense, abandoning me in the land of—"What's going on?" I ask.

This makes him laugh harder. "I spoke to your mom about it," he tells me. "She was hesitant at first, but after an hour or so of me convincing her that it was a good idea for you to get out of the house, get on your feet, and maybe even get a job… if you don't plan on going back to college, that is..."

My eyes roam the space of the empty living room, but they're not looking at the house. They're still looking for my breath. And the sense. Because right now, neither exist.

"So?"

I look over at him, standing a few feet in front of me with his hands in his pockets and his eyes on mine. "Huh?"

He shrugs, his voice lowering, and I can see the insecurity masked behind the cockiness. "I bought us a house, Riley. I want us to move out and move on. I want us to do it together."

"But the car..." I whisper stupidly.

"The car goes with the house, and both come with me. If you want them."

"I want them," I squeak, feeling it impossible to breathe through the lump in my throat, the overwhelming emotions and the love I have for the man in front of me. "But what happens... I mean, when you leave?"

"That's why I got one close to your mom, so you can visit and if things ever get too hard, you can always go home... to *her* home." He takes a step forward, licking his lips as he does. Then he takes my hand and dips his head so we're eye to eye. "But I'm hoping we can make this *our* home, and while I'm gone, you'll continue to keep it that way. So that when I'm done, I can come home, Riley. To you. You're my home now."

WE MAKE LOVE on the hardwood floors of our new living room, our sounds of pleasure echoing off the walls and into my heart. I cry. I've never cried when we've made love before—but then again, he's never made me feel like this. There was always a question between now and the day he redeployed... what would happen to us? And he cleared up that question with an act that defies logic—an act that denied permission. He didn't ask if I wanted these things. He didn't *need* to.

He knew I wanted it.

Wanted him.

And for the first time since he knocked on my door—angry and pissed off at the world—we found what we were looking for. And it sure as hell wasn't in the bottom of a bottle.

It was in each other.
We found the horizon.
He found his calm.
And I found my reality.

WE DRIVE. HIS hand on my leg. The sun beaming down on us. While we talk about *my* new car and *our* new house.

Dreams—they do come true.

Twenty-Eight
Riley

DYLAN ROLLS UP the sleeves of his shirt, his eyes on mine and his lips pressed tight.

I take another look around the empty kitchen. "Well," I ask him. "Where should we start?"

He smirks. "Probably where it all began. On the kitchen counter. Then the bedroom floor. Oh, and the shower. I've always wanted to fuck you in the shower. The possibilities are endless, Hudson."

He jumps back, avoiding my smack on his stomach. Then he laughs. "I don't know, babe. It's your house."

"Our house," I tell him.

Shrugging, he says, "Yeah, but I don't care what it looks like. Anything will be better than how I've been living."

I rub my hands together. "My Little Pony it is!"

He shrugs again.

"You seriously don't care, do you?"

"Nope." He steps toward me, his arms going around my waist. "Just as long as you're happy."

"I feel horrible," I admit. "We're spending all your money."

He shoves me away jokingly. "Yeah, go get a job, gold digger."

An excited burst of laughter bubbles out of me. "I can't wait to move in and make this our home."

"So let's do it then. What do we need? Bed? We can bring one of ours. Fridge? I have a spare in the garage."

"Mom said she'd give us her kitchen table and any linen we needed."

Dylan smiles. "Then that's all we need. We can get everything else as we go."

I cover my lips with my hand, hiding my smile as I look around the empty house again. "I can't believe you bought us a house."

He places his hand on my back as I walk from room to room. "I can't believe I'm lucky enough to have you all to myself."

I turn to him, my hands on his chest. "Shut up. I'm the lucky one, Dylan."

He takes my wrists, and kisses the palm of each hand. "We're both lucky."

"I'll get a job to help pay for things."

"It's not necessary, but I do think it'll be good for you."

I nod.

"So are we moving in today or what?" he asks.

"We're here. Now. Why not?"

ERIC AND HIS dad help us move my bed and his fridge using Dylan's truck. Mom raids the house for whatever she can give us. I can tell she's sad to see me go and I'm sure she was more than hesitant when Dylan brought up the idea, but she's doing exactly what she's always done. She's doing what's best for me. I'm sure the fact that I'm only a ten-minute walk away helps. Dylan makes plans with Logan and Amanda to come over the next day so Amanda can give us ideas on how to decorate since she's apparently into that stuff. I don't tell him that the idea of getting to know his friends on more than a "*Hey, I knew you in high school*" level absolutely terrifies me. It's not so much that they're intimidating, because I don't think they are. I think it's more my worry about being compared to Heidi. I don't know. I just hope they like me. And accept me. Because I don't plan on going anywhere.

We make love on the kitchen counter. And in the shower. And finally in our bed. And we make plans. Stupid plans. Things like turning the guestroom into storage for random clown and moth paintings.

I hate moths.

He hates clowns.

We spend the night laughing, not bothering to stifle them in case we wake anyone, and when exhaustion finally takes over, we fall asleep the way we do every night—with his arms around me, and my arms around him—keeping each other safe.

✧ ✧ ✧

I HIDE OUT in the bathroom when Dylan tells me Logan and Amanda are close. I don't know what else to do with nerves so high and my hands so shaky.

Dylan knocks on the door. "Babe, Amanda's here."

"I'll be out in a minute."

I check my make-up free face in the mirror—once pale, now a little tanner since I've started leaving the house. I check my eyes, gray and full of hope, and I look down at my dress, hoping it's enough. I curse myself for not being more like my mother—a woman who enjoys the wonders of hair and make-up. A woman like *Heidi*.

When I finally gain the courage, I head out of our room. They're all standing in the kitchen while Dylan tells them the details of the house. The age, the build, and a bunch of other stuff I tune out when Amanda turns around. She's in denim shorts, a tank, and flannel shirt, sleeves rolled up like she's ready to work. She's dressed exactly like I do. Her hair's in a knot on top of her head and when she smiles at me, her eyes smile too. She places a giant folder on the kitchen table as she makes her way over to me, arms outstretched when she says, "Hi Riley!"

She pulls me into a hug, not too over-affectionate, but not underwhelming either. "It's good to see Dylan let you out of his grasp long enough to finally meet you."

Logan's next to her now, his arms out just like hers were. "'Sup, Riley?" he asks, pulling me in for a hug.

Dylan breaks us apart while Logan and Amanda laugh. "That's enough of that," Dylan says, not a hint of humor in his voice.

Just so I'm clear, Jealous Dylan = Hot Dylan.

"Did you want to show me around the place first and then we can go through some ideas?" Amanda asks, stepping up next to me. She waves off the boys as she picks up the folder and the next thing I know we're talking Scandinavian versus Modern Eclectic and picking out paint samples at the hardware store.

At some point while we're there, Logan gets a call from Cameron and by the time we get home, all of Dylan's friends are waiting out front. Apparently they'd all come home for the weekend because they wanted to help us get settled in, and they wanted to see Dylan.

"I brought the food," Mikayla (Jake's girlfriend) says, lifting boxes of pizza in her hands.

"I brought the booze," Lucy adds.

And now we're having a paint party.

"Do you mind?" Dylan says when he finds me in the bedroom. "It's just that we don't get to see each other often and—"

"I don't mind at all!" I replace my dress with what I normally wear, smiling as I see him watching me from the corner of my eye. I'll never get sick of his reaction to my body. *Never.*

We eat first, then end the night painting and dancing and singing to the *High School Musical* soundtrack. I get to know his friends; they get to know me.

The only rule Mom had when Dylan spoke to her about me moving in was that no alcohol was to be kept in the house. It was a no-brainer for Dylan, and even for me. He once asked if I thought I should go to AA for my drinking problem. He even offered to go the meetings with me, but I didn't think I needed it. Truth is—Dylan had become what he once offered. He became my alcohol. Only he didn't just dull my pain—he *cured* it.

I guess the rule was just Mom's way of making sure I don't fall off the edge, and regardless of how I may have acted months ago, I truly appreciate her thinking of it.

I don't have an issue with other people drinking. I don't even mind watching other people drink. Especially Dylan. Because Buzzed Dylan = Handsy Dylan = Hot Dylan.

LUCY GETS DRUNK and curses like a sailor, which everyone finds hilarious. Me, especially.

She then goes on to tell Dylan the details of *Operation Mayhem: Roxy-Is-A-Slut-Of-A-Fucking-Whore Edition (aka Ho-peration Whore-hem),* and even though I'm sure the fumes from the paint contribute to our mood, I'm having a good time. A *really* good time.

Because Lucy and I had been chatting about books, I kind of felt like I knew her already. And because Amanda and I had spent the day together, we had bonded. So I find it a little odd when Mikayla stands next to me, paintbrush in her hand and a Tar Heels cap pulled low on her brow and says, "I remember my first night meeting these guys. Swear, I thought they were all crazy, but crazy *good*, you know?"

I nod. "You didn't go to our high school, did you?"

"Nope. I met them all the night of senior prom. We had it on the same night. It's long story. I'm sure Dylan can tell you about it." She drops her gaze, just for a second before looking back up at me. "I don't know," she mumbles. "I kind of felt compelled to reach out to you and let you know that they're all good people. They're accepting of anyone, no questions asked. They're the type of friends who become family, Riley." She looks over at Dylan quickly. "And if you ever need anything, you can always call us. Especially when…"

"Yeah," I finish for her. *When he deploys*, she wanted to say.

She smiles again. "I just didn't want you to think that because you're only dating Dylan, it doesn't make you part of our family. Because you are now." She laughs. "Whether you like it or not."

Behind us, Lucy squeals, pulling our attention away from each other.

"You're just causing more work for me, Luce," Cam huffs. "You got streaks everywhere. Go sit in the corner like a good little girl."

"Oh, *Dylan*!" She snaps, puffing out her chest. "Don't tell me what to do!"

"What?" Dylan asks, turning to her from his spot on top of the ladder. "Did you say my name?"

Lucy yells. "You can *Dylan* too, Dylan!"

"She's so wasted," Mikayla says through a giggle.

"Why are you saying my name?" Dylan asks again, his brow bunched in confusion.

Confused Dylan = Hot Dylan.

"We've been through this," Jake tells him.

"I forget," Dylan mumbles.

Amanda chimes in. "Like that time Lucy forgot that we don't all read like her and spoiled an entire book."

"You can *Dylan*, too, AmanDuh!" Lucy shouts.

Now everyone's laughing. Me included. "Why is my boyfriend's name a verb?" I ask.

Mikayla speaks first. "It means to shut up or stop, I guess. Or, like, don't talk about it."

"Really?" Dylan asks. "Funny. When Riley says it, it means '*Don't*

Stop. Please. More. Keep going. Yeah. Just like that!"

"Dylan, Dylan!" I yell, throwing my brush at his head.

Funny Dylan = Hot Dylan.

And Hot Dylan = *Mine.*

Twenty-Nine
Dylan

WE SPEND THE next month getting settled into the house. I see Riley a lot less since she got a job. I told her she didn't have to, that I had enough income plus Mom's life insurance leftover from the deposit on the house that she could wait, at least until I was gone. It was selfish, I know, but I just wanted her for myself.

She works at an animal shelter—which is perfect for her because she really doesn't like people. This way, animals don't judge her. She spends eight hours a day cleaning dog shit and mopping up piss and feeding them and giving them meds and she couldn't be happier.

And I'm happy she's happy.

NOW, IT'S SUMMER and Jake and Mikayla, and Cameron and Lucy have graduated. Logan and Amanda still have another year because of the year they both missed—Amanda at the start and Logan when he took the year off with Doctors Without Borders. Jake is… well, Jake is taking his year off now. Everyone questioned why the hell he would possibly take a year off between college and all the possibilities the MLB are offering him and his answer is simple: Baseball's been his and Kayla's and his family's life since he moved back to the states. Now it was his chance to give them the attention they'd been giving him. Everyone thought he was crazy. Everyone but me. I understood completely. The income they have from renting out the house by UNC is enough for them to live off for the next year before things get hectic again with him, so he's taking the time. If the decision bites him in the ass, then so be it. Baseball is a career. It's not his life anymore. He and Kayla have plans to travel and see the world, and me? Well, I'm just taking every horizon I can get.

"WATCHA GOT, OLD man?" Riley says, her arms spread out as she watches me dribble in front of her.

From the stands, Logan shouts, "Yeah, Grandpa Banks. Whatcha got?"

We decided to put the house stuff on hold for the day and spend it with our friends at the sports park. We normally hit up the batting cages, but today we gave it a break and played basketball instead. Well, Riley and the guys and I played. The other girls sat in the stands arguing about some book something. Unless the book gets me laid, I don't really pay much attention.

Now it's just me and Riley, one on one, and she's in short shorts, a sports bra and lose tank that barely covers said bra. She's sweating though. Not because it's hot, but because she's down 12-2. She doesn't like losing. It helps I'm almost a foot taller than her and my arm's almost at a hundred percent again.

"Who you calling old?" I ask, dribbling around her for another lay up.

She narrows her eyes at me, just for a moment before she pouts.

"Don't think you can distract me with your hotness. That shit won't fly on the court."

The pout turns to a smirk as she makes her way over to me, taking the ball from my hands. She drops it to the ground, then stands on it, using my neck for leverage. "Next score wins?" she asks.

I roll my eyes.

Lucy shouts, "Use the girl card!"

"What girl card?" I ask.

She smirks. "No sex for a month."

"Pshh. You can't live without sex for a month."

She quirks an eyebrow. "Want to test me?"

I remove her arms from around my neck. "Nope."

Her head throws back with her laugh. "I didn't think so."

She scores.

She wins.

I get guaranteed sex for the next month.

I win.

I'd call that a win-win.

I SIT BACK down with the rest of the guys while Riley gets us drinks. "You let her walk all over you," Cameron says.

Lucy glares at him.

He apologizes.

"Where does she hide that whip she's constantly beating you with?" I ask him.

"In her magical pussy," he says, earning him a slap on the back of the head from Lucy.

We all laugh as Riley returns with drinks. She hands the waters out to all of us and takes her seat on my lap. Then she places her bottle on my shoulder. "How is it?"

"Fine," I tell her, kissing her neck. "I'll rest it when we get home."

She smiles. She loves it when I say *home*.

"So, do you know what the deal is, Dylan?" Amanda asks, her hand shielding the sun as she looks up at us. "Like, any idea when you go back?"

"Not sure." I shrug. "I have a check up next week and we'll go from there."

Riley adds, "They're really happy with his progress, though, so that's a good sign."

"And what? You go back to your unit?" Logan says.

"Yep. If everything goes to plan."

"I can't believe we're all home for the summer," Micky chimes in.

"It'll be good," Jake says. "We haven't all been together like this in forever."

"Minus Heidi," Lucy says.

There's no awkwardness at her statement. Not anymore. Riley and Heidi seem to have formed a weird only-a-girl-would-understand mutual respect for each other. We've even hung out as a group. They don't say a lot to each other, but they don't claw each other's eyes out either. Granted, if it ever got to that, I'd put my money on Riley. Every single time.

I tune them out as the girls go back to talking books, the guys go back to talking about Cameron's inability to score a free throw and I go back to looking at the girl I love, watching her smile and join in on both conversations.

She faces me, her smile still in place. "You okay?"

I nod.

Then, for some random reason, I shout, "Yahoo!" Weird, I know. But Dad used to say it and… dammit, I guess I am Grandpa Banks.

"What the hell was that?" Riley says through a fit of laughter.

"Did you just *Yahoo*?" Jake asks.

Next to me, Cameron's holding a hand to his chest like I just scared the shit out of him.

I laugh with them. Then loudly exclaim, "It's a beautiful day, boys!"

Now they're all looking at me like I'm crazy. I am. Riley—she bakes me crazy. Okay. That didn't have the same effect as bacon but whatever.

Down on the court, I see two teenage boys eying me like my friends are. "What?" I yell. "It is a beautiful day! The sun's out… everyone's on break. I got a beautiful girl in my arms."

"Well," one of the kids says. "You do have a beautiful girl."

"Watch your fucking mouth," I shout, getting up to go to him.

Riley grabs onto my neck with one hand, the other covering my mouth. "He's sorry," she tells them, before looking back at me, a laugh bubbling out of her. "What's gotten into you?"

"I'm happy," I tell her.

"You're crazy," she retorts.

"You bake me crazy." *Nope.* Still not the same effect. Maybe this is why I kept silent for so long.

WE LEAVE THE guys at the park and I drive Riley to work. She's on the afternoon shift for now, but she'll be taking over the nine to five next week. Most days, I drive her there and pick her up because even though she has her own car, she prefers I drive. Reminds her of how dreams can become a reality. I don't mind. But I do get lonely. Some days I just go over to Dad's house and mess around with Eric. Other days I work on our house. It's old, but the bones are good, and with enough work we can get it to where we want. That's what I'm doing—replacing the air-conditioning unit—when I get an unexpected phone call.

Dr. Garvis is on the other end, his tone a mixture of hopefulness and something else I can't quite decipher. He tells me he'd like to fast forward my appointment to tomorrow and that something has changed with his scheduling. I agree, even though I know Riley can't get the day off and she likes to go with me to all my check ups. He ends the conversation by saying, "Hopefully your shoulder's still where it was and I can sign off on the paperwork sooner rather than later."

I SPEND THE next couple hours writing a list of all the work the house needs and head over to Dad's. I tell him and Eric about the phone call, ignoring their identical solemn looks, and get Eric to make copies of the list on his printer. I ask them for help to get the work done in case I can't get to it all before I leave, and then I give them spare keys—to the house and the cars. I give them the information to my bank accounts to forward on to Riley because if it happens sooner than I want, I don't want to waste our time together going over these petty details while she whines about not needing it until I tell her to shut up. Then I visit Holly next door. I sit with her and have a quiet meal and I tell her what I know. I ask that she not tell Riley yet, that I want to be the one to do it, and then I tell her that my dad and Eric have spare keys in case she, too, ever needs anything. I don't know why I tell her that. I don't really know why I do any of it. Then I go back home and get started on the list. I finish the air conditioner, fix the jammed garage door and clear out the gutters. And then I shower, grab my keys, and put on a mask so I'm ready to face Riley with the plans of keeping the appointment to myself. She doesn't need to know yet. She'll just worry—and the fact that she won't be there will make it worse. I'll tell her when I know for sure what the plan is. If there even is a plan.

"SHE'S OUT BACK," Edna, the shelter receptionist, tells me.

I go behind the desk, like I'd done many times before, and make my way through the aisles of cages and crying animals until I see Riley squatting in front of a cage, patting a tiny dog so ugly I swear I would've mistaken it for a giant rat.

"Ry," I call out, walking toward her. "What's going on? I've been waiting in the car for fifteen minutes."

She looks up, her eyes glassy. "He always cries when I leave. I hate it," she mumbles, looking back at the dog.

"They're sad animals," I remind her. "They cry."

"Not like this one," she says. "He's all scared and alone and he has no-one." She motions for me to squat down next to her. "Look at him, Dylan."

I roll my eyes and sigh at the same time. Then I look at the dog. He looks like every other homeless dog. Nothing but skin and bones and spots of fur. His head rests on his front legs, the fur around his eyes wet from all the crying he's done. "He's… cute," I lie. "I'm sure someone will come in and take him. Let's go. I've got stuff to do at the house."

"Okay," she says, reluctantly getting up. The dog whimpers as soon as her hand leaves him. "See, baby?"

"Riley."

"Bye, puppy," she says, followed by a pout.

She grabs her stuff and starts to leave, looking back at the dog every time it lets out a whimper.

I grasp her shoulders. "Come on, we have to go."

SHE'S SILENT ON the way home.

She's still silent when we have my second meal for the night.

She stays silent as we get into bed, her beautiful pout still in place.

"What's wrong?" I ask, even though I know the answer.

"I can't stop thinking about him."

"What's his name? I'll kick his ass."

She fakes a laugh and settles her head on my chest. "It's sad, that's all. I know he's not going to get picked up and they'll have to put him down. I just hate that for him—like the world's already given up on him, you know?"

"So what do you want to do about it?"

She looks up quickly, then drops her gaze. "There's nothing we can do." She pauses a beat. "Is there?"

"Riley, we can't have a dog. Not now. I'm going soon—or whenever…" I recover quickly. "And we'd need to train him. We don't have time for that right now. I'm trying to get the house dealt with and you're still redecorating or whatever and you won't be home so I'll have to deal with him—"

"They said I could bring him to work," she cuts in.

I sigh. "You've spoken to them about it?"

"I was just thinking out loud." She kisses my chest. "But you're right. It's too much right now. I'm sorry I brought it up."

Half an hour later, we're still awake, still in the same positions. "Riley?"

"Hm?"

"You still thinking about him?"

She leans up on her elbow. "I know it sounds stupid, but I just feel connected to him somehow," she rushes out. "I feel like at some point, we were at the same place in our lives… like he's lost and sad and he has no one. He has no family, no friends, everyone's left him and he just exists. He'd probably rather die—"

"Ry…"

She lies back down, her head on my chest again. "I know. I was just thinking… time's ticking, you know? And who knows where you'll be in a month? Who am I going to have to keep me company when I'm missing you and unable to contact you?" She shakes her head. "It's stupid."

I stroke her hair, letting her words sink in. "And they said you could take him to work with you?"

Her body stills, but she doesn't look up. "Yes…"

"And you promise to take care of him? As in, I don't have to do anything?"

She covers her mouth, still not looking at me. "Yes…"

"And you're going to train him and keep his claws clipped because these hardwood floors are original and—"

"Yes!" she shouts, jumping up, her eyes filled with tears and her smile bright. "Are you saying…"

"I'm not saying anything. I'm just asking questions…"

"Dylan!" she laughs out, slapping my chest. "Be serious." She takes off her top.

My laugh matches hers. "What the hell are you doing?"

"Preparing my payment," she tells me, her hands already on the band of my drawers.

"Man, you should've stuck to reading. It would've been a lot cheaper."

She removes her hands, her body bouncing with excitement. "I don't know what you're saying! What are you saying?!"

I reach up and cup her face, my smile fading with each second I touch her.

Fuck, I love her. I'm going to miss these moments. I'm going to miss her.

I grasp the back of her neck and bring her lips to mine. "Get the dog," I whisper. "On one condition."

"Anything," she says, her smile wide as she starts to remove her panties.

I stop her. "Riley."

"What?"

Then I release my last secret, my last justified fear. "Semper Fidelis."

She tilts her head, her smile waning. "Always faithful?"

I nod. "Promise me."

"Always, Dylan," she whispers. Her mouth covering mine as she lies on top of me. Then she pulls back, holding my face in her hands. "Always."

Thirty
Riley

"LET'S GO MEET your daddy," I whisper in our puppy's ear, walking out of work and toward Dylan's truck.

Dylan smiles as we both get inside. "Have you named him?" he asks.

"Bacon."

He chuckles. "You named the dog Bacon?"

"Yep." I lean up and give him a kiss. "I just brought him so he could meet his daddy. He has to stay in here for a few days for medical checks before we can bring him home." I hand him Bacon.

"Did you just call me his daddy?" he asks, awkwardly holding Bacon in his arms.

I laugh. "What would you rather?"

Dylan shrugs. "Master."

I take Bacon from him and hold his face next to mine. "You can't be Master. He's our baby."

With an eye roll, Dylan says, "Let's go."

"Daddy's gwumpy, baby," I whisper in Bacon's ear. "He be better when you come home. Pwomise." I look up at Dylan, waiting for his amused response. There's nothing there. "Everything okay?"

"We need to talk, Riley."

I WOKE UP this morning with a clear head, a clear plan for the day. We'd wake up, have breakfast, and then I'd spend the day with my new puppy. I'd come home, Dylan and I would have dinner, and we'd make love like we do most nights before falling asleep.

I didn't expect to be sitting opposite him at the kitchen table while he told me that he went to see Dr. Garvis. I didn't expect him to say that he was given the all clear. And I *definitely* didn't expect him to tell me that he was going to go back *tomorrow*. Had I known that, I probably wouldn't have woken up at all.

"So that's it?" I ask him, his hands covering mine between us. I'm trying not to cry. I don't want to. Crying shows weakness. Weakness gives him something to worry about. I don't want him to worry.

He swallows loudly, his eyes fixed on mine. "That's it."

"And you can't, like, delay it or anything?"

He shakes his head.

I inhale deeply and look away. I look at the kitchen cabinets with three different color samples painted on one of the doors. I look at the floor, the black-and-white checkered floors we once deemed ugly but are now kind of attached to. I look at the kitchen sink, a single bead of water hanging on to the tap for dear life. I look everywhere but at Dylan.

"Ry?"

"We knew, right?"

"What?"

I tear my gaze away from the tap and look back at him. "We knew it was going to happen…"

"We just didn't prepare for it," he finishes for me.

"So what do we do?"

"I have to pack."

"Right now?"

He nods. "I leave first thing."

STANDING BETWEEN HIS legs, I place a towel around his neck to catch the hairs as I take the clippers from him, my fingers shaking from my overwhelming emotions.

His hands find my legs, bare underneath one of his flannel shirts. He rests his head against my stomach. "I didn't think…" he murmurs, his words dying in the air.

"You didn't think what, baby?" I run my hands through the back of his hair; hair so much longer and thicker than it was five months ago.

"It didn't hurt like this the first time I left."

I smile through the force of the tears begging to be released. "It'll be okay. I'll be here when you get back."

He wraps his arms around my waist squeezing tight and I take the opportunity to breathe through the pain and wipe the tears from my cheeks—tears I've held on to since he told me he was leaving. That this was it. This was the last night in our new home until… we don't even know when.

I sniff back another sob and fake a strength we both know doesn't exist. "You ready, Lance Corporal?"

He pulls away, lifting his glassy eyes to mine. His smile matches mine, and he nods once.

We're both lying to each other, *for* each other. Because in this moment it's impossible to feel anything other than heartache and despair.

My hands shake from the force of my contained sobs when I pull his head forward, placing the clippers on the back of his neck and slowly guiding it up his head. I pray the sound of it will drown out my quiet cries. My tears fall, blurring my vision, but he just holds me tighter, his shaky breaths warm on my stomach. I shave his head, row by row, the ache in my chest all-consuming. His shoulders shake, his own cries muffled by his shirt that I'm wearing and when I'm done, we need a moment to recover. Still hiding our emotions, still faking our strength. I wipe my eyes on my shoulder. He wipes his on my stomach. We take another moment. And then many more. Until all the moments of silence consume us and we're crying, openly, but unwilling to witness it. I grasp his head, keeping him to me. He grasps my legs, holding me to him. "I don't want to leave you, Riley."

And just like that, I find the strength I'd been searching for.

Because he said "*I don't want to leave you.*"

He didn't say "*I don't want to be apart.*"

He didn't say "*I don't want to go.*"

He doesn't want to leave *me.*

I take his face in my hands and tilt his head back, containing my sob when I see his eyes filled with tears, his face red from holding back his emotions. I run my hands through his clipped hair, just like it was when I met him.

"We should have talked about it," he says. "I should've thought about *you.*"

> ***I fell in like in my kitchen, surrounded by twenty wishes.***
>
> ***I fell in love in his garage, once when I kissed him, and then again when he wrote love on my arm.***
>
> ***I fell in forever right now, when a man I love put my happiness first and made me finally believe that I Am Worthy.***

Through tears, through heartache, and through love, I find courage in my self-worth. "I'll be okay," I tell him honestly. "And there never has to be an either/or with us, Dylan. You can live your purpose. And I'll create my legacy. We can still have each other. We can have it all."

Thirty-One
Dylan

WE PACK AND go to bed soon after.

We don't sleep, though. I think it'd be impossible to find the calm needed to actually do that. We hold each other close and we talk. A lot. About everything.

We talk about our past, about how we met, and about our future. Because if we didn't make plans for our future, it would feel like a goodbye.

And neither of us want or are ready for that.

We declare our love for each other, over and over, and show each other that love, over and over, beneath the flannel sheets of the same bed I once lay in, watching her cry and promising myself that I didn't want to know what caused those tears.

It was a lie.

Even back then, I wanted her.

But I didn't just want her. I wanted to give her a reason to stop crying.

And as I lay here now watching her sit up on her elbow, her gaze focused on the finger she's using to trace the outline of a scar—a scar created from a bullet that brought me to her, I finally release the heartache that's consumed me since I told her I had to leave. And when she looks up, her gaze locked on mine, and she whispers another I love you, I wonder to myself… what was The Turning Point? From me standing in my garage and writing love on her arm to this…

Who would've thought that finding my calm and creating my happiness would hurt so much?

✧ ✧ ✧

EVERYONE'S ALREADY AT the bus station when we show up. Dad, Eric, Holly and all my friends. We walk up to them, our hands joined. She releases me so I can say my goodbyes, first to the girls, then to the guys, then to Holly, and finally to Dad and Eric.

The words we speak are generic.

The feelings are not.

She waits at the end of the line, her head lowered and her hands clasped together.

I square my shoulders. "Hudson."

She looks up, tears already forming in her eyes.

"I'm going to miss you the most," I tell her.

She smiles and pushes on my shoulder. "You better," she says quietly. "And you better stay safe, Lance Corporal." Her voice wavers, betraying her light-hearted words.

"I will, baby." I wrap my arms around her waist and bring her into me. "I have something valuable waiting for me."

She sniffs back her tears and raises her chin. "I'm not going to cry over you, Banks."

I chuckle. "I don't expect you to."

We fake it, because there's only so many times we can say goodbye without actually saying the words.

She leans up, pressing her lips to mine. Softly at first, then both our emotions take over, our holds get tighter, our kiss gets deeper, and our love grows stronger.

We release each other only when the last-call announcement for my bus sounds over the speakers. "I'm not going to cry," she repeats, more to herself than to me.

"Don't cry," I tell her honestly. "I couldn't leave you if you did."

She raises her chin and sucks in a breath, showing me the strength I know she carries. "I'll be home before you know it, Ry." Again, the words are generic. The feelings are far from it.

Her features soften, her act put aside. "I love you so much, Dylan."

"Wait for me, okay?" I whisper, my weakness shown in words only she can hear.

"Dylan…"

"Promise me"

"Semper Fidelis. Always."

Another announcement.

Another non-goodbye.

I pick up my bag. "I have to go."

She nods as Jake stands beside her, throwing an arm over her shoulders.

I give everyone a casual salute before looking back at Riley. Then I cup her face, my thumb skimming across her lips when I force her to look at me. "I never told you."

"Told me what?"

"That I'm glad you're *here*, Riley. Not just *here* with me, but *here* in this world." Then I nod once at Jake—an unspoken understanding, before turning quickly and walking away.

It's not until I'm on the bus and the engine's started and the brakes are off that I finally look back at them: At Dad and Eric standing side by side, at my friends in a line, all holding hands. At Holly, standing to the side of Riley. And Riley—crying in Jake's arms, her head on his chest and his hand rubbing her back, letting her know what I always knew—that he'll take care of her.

They all will.

If I wasn't sure of it, there's no way I'd be leaving her.

Riley

IT'S THE FIRST time in a really long time that I've thought about drinking, but there's a big difference between thinking about it and wanting to. I don't want to. I won't. Because Dylan was right. Whatever I'm looking for, I'm not going to find in the bottom of a bottle. I'm going to find it in him.

"I'm sorry, sweetheart," Mom tells me, hugging me tight. "I have a client waiting for me. Will you be okay?"

"We'll take care of her, Ms. Hudson." Jake answers for me.

I look up at him, a little confused.

She's holding out a glass jar, a single folded up piece of paper inside it. "Dylan wanted me to give you this."

I release another round of tears as I take it from her, feeling the eyes and presence of everyone around me.

"What is it?" I ask.

She smiles, warm and comforting. "It's his heart, baby."

THE JAR SITS on my lap as I drive carefully, my anxiety building with each passing second. I pull into the garage next to his truck, now covered to keep it safe from dust. He said I could drive it, but the thought of being in it without him didn't sit right with me. I get out of my car and go straight to his workbench—the second thing we brought over from his dad's house along with all his tools. With the jar gripped tightly in one hand, I run the other over his tools, smelling the grease that comes to mind whenever I think about him. I wait for my heart to settle—a million thoughts racing through my head. When I feel like I can actually read his words without my heart shattering to pieces, I place the jar gently on the bench and stare at it. And that's all I do. Minutes pass. I don't move. I barely breathe. It's his voice in my mind "*Come on, Hudson!*" that gives me the courage.

I unscrew the lid and as carefully as possible, I take out the letter.

Dear Ms. Hudson,

I'm sure you already know who I am. Or, at least, you think you do. Maybe in some aspects, you're right. I am the boy next door. I am a Marine.

And I am hopelessly in love with your daughter.

You don't know that last part yet.

Neither does she.

I'm hoping one day she'll give me a chance to show her.

And I'm hoping even more that I can do that with your blessing.

So, I thought I'd write you this letter, introduce myself properly so you can get to know me—Dylan Banks—not the boy next door. Not the Marine. But the boy who loves your daughter.

I never knew my mom. She died during childbirth. Sucks, I know, but I'm not telling you that to gain your sympathy. I'm telling you because my dad raised both me and my brother on his own… he was both parents for us… and he did a damn fine job of it.

He taught us to be honorable men, to love and respect everyone equally, and he showed us, more than taught us, to

love fiercely. My dad, though quiet, has always had a voice when it came to putting us first.

He left the military as soon as my mother passed and became the strength we all needed to move on from her death. Then took a job at a factory pressing metal so that he could support and raise us the best way possible.

I'm getting off track.

I guess what I'm trying to say is that my dad loves us something fierce and he's always done what's best for us. Which, I know now, is something you'd understand.

See, for the past few weeks, I've woken up every day and Riley's been the first thing on my mind. She's the last thing I think about when I go to sleep, and she's pretty much all I think about while I'm awake.

Swear, Ms. Hudson, I'm not a creep. I just really like her.

She's smart and witty and funny and a complete pain in the ass—which, I guess, just adds to her charm. And she's pretty. Real pretty. And she's so strong. The fact that she hasn't had anything to drink the past few days (not sure if you knew that or not) just shows how strong she is. I'm sure you know all those things about her, though you may not have witnessed it since the accident, I just thought I'd remind you.

Riley told me about her dad (jerk, right?) and it kind of made me angry—that there was some guy out there who'd had a hand in creating such a perfect girl and he didn't even know her. I felt bad for him—that he was missing out on all things Riley. Then I thought about Riley and how she missed out on having a father in her life. But then I realized, she didn't miss out.

She had you.

To be completely honest, Ms. Hudson—and please don't take offense to what I say next—I didn't like you. Not at all. I didn't understand why a mother would let her daughter drink her days away and do nothing to stop it. It wasn't until you practically kicked my ass and called me out while I stood on your doorstep desperate to see Riley that it finally registered—you're just like my dad: You do what's best for your kids, and you love them something fierce.

So I guess what I'm trying to say is that no, Riley isn't now, nor will she ever be… how did you phrase it? "Another notch on my belt."

Riley gives me a reason to wake up in the mornings.

She gives me hope.

She gives me answers.

She gives me the calm I can't seem to find anywhere else, not even in my own head.

Yes, I will be going back to Afghanistan to serve my country.

Yes, I will be leaving her at some point.

Yes, I will miss her when I do.

But here's the thing you may have misjudged about me: The reason for me joining the Marines wasn't for the money or because it was some sort of family legacy. The reason I didn't think twice about my answer when you asked if I'd be redeploying is simple:

One day I'd like to get married and have children. Lots of them. (Children, not marriages.) I'd like for my wife and my children to not be afraid to leave their homes or turn on the news at night after dinner and see warzone after warzone and wonder when it is that it'll all end. I want to wake up in the mornings, our minds clear of hate and racism and injustice and terrorism. I want to kiss my wife, play with my kids, and know that I did everything I could so that we can be together without fear of what will happen when we turn ours backs.

Sure, I wanted all those things pre-Riley, but it wasn't until I met her that all my reasons—my purpose—had a face.

I'm not saying that I'll be the one to marry Riley one day (I could be so lucky). I'm just saying that the person Riley is—past, present and future—is the kind of person I'm fighting for. The reason I chose a career that puts my life on the line every day to serve my country.

I just want more, Ms. Hudson.

I want more for your family, and I want more for mine.

Don't you?

Yours sincerely,
Lance Corporal Dylan Banks.

Thirty-Two
Riley

THERE ARE CERTAIN things a person does that you don't actually realize are things until you start missing them. For example: Reach over you to silence your alarm every morning, and then become your personal snooze button. Or switch on the coffee pot while you're in the shower so it's ready by the time you got out. Or remember all the occurrences from the night before so you can find where the hell you misplaced your keys. These are all things Dylan did. All things I'd learned in the first half hour of the next day. All things I'd taken for granted now that he was gone.

I even walked to his truck, too preoccupied on my phone, and stood by the passenger door for him to drive me to work. I stood there for a good minute before realizing he wasn't behind me. I hadn't even closed the back door.

THE DAYS ARE okay.

The nights are hard.

We'd spent every night for the past five months together so it was difficult getting used to being alone. His friends, or *ours*, I should say—they message me often to check in on me and make sure that I'm doing fine but my work schedule doesn't give us a lot of time to catch up. Besides, it's only been three days. *Three days.* I finally get what Dylan meant when he said the time is identical for everyone, but at the same time it's not. Because my version of three days feels like an eternity.

Eric: *You bringing home The Bacon tonight?*

Riley: *Um. What?*

Eric: *Your dog…*

Riley: *Oh! Yes, he's coming home with me.*

Eric: *Can we visit? Dad and Sydney are here. We'd love to meet him. It's cool if you're busy though. Or just want him to get settled. We understand.*

Riley: *No! Come by! I'd love some company!*

Eric: *Okay. Should we bring frozen dinners or…*

Riley: *Lol! Um…*

Eric: *Jokes. Pizza or Chinese?*

Riley: *Chinese, please.*

Eric: *Same order?*

Riley: *Yes, please.*

Eric: *Have you heard from him?*

Riley: *No. :(*

Eric: *We'll be over at 6:30.*

Riley: *See you then!*

I GET THROUGH the rest of the work day, excited to bring home Bacon and hang out with Dylan's family. I'm only home ten minutes when they knock on my door.

We sit at the table and talk about anything Non-Dylan-Deployment related while Bacon charms the pants off everyone. "We should get a dog," Mal says.

"We had a dog once, didn't we?" Eric responds.

Mal shakes his head, his eyes narrowed at his son. "We've never had a dog."

"I'm sure we did. When I was younger. It used to cry and piss and shit everywhere. Oh wait. That was Dylan."

I choke on a laugh just as there's another knock on the door. I get up to answer it, but Eric stops me. "I don't know that I like you on your own answering doors late at night."

I look at the time. It's only seven. I tell him that, but he just shakes his head and motions for me to sit. Then he gets up and answers the door for me, speaking over his shoulder when he says, "I'm going to set up a security system in here. Cameras and everything on the outside. Just in case."

"You're being a little dramatic, no?" I ask, but he's already out of the kitchen.

"It's not a bad idea," Mal chimes in.

"Besides," Sydney says, shrugging, "Once Eric has an idea in his head, you can't change it. Just give him that peace of mind."

"I don't know that I can afford that," I tell them.

"Don't you worry, Riley," Mal says. "Dylan would've wanted it."

I look down at my plate, knowing full well they're right.

"We didn't know you had company," a deep, familiar, accented voice sounds from the kitchen door. Jake stands in front of the rest of the gang, pizza boxes in hand.

My smile is instant. So is the swelling of my heart, because even though it can get lonely, I know I'll never be alone.

✧ ✧ ✧

WEEKS PASS AND I try not to think about it too much. Bacon helps. The dog. Not the food.

Dylan had warned me the night before he left that communication would be limited. Especially if he's remote, and he won't really know what he'll be doing at any given time. He told me he'd most likely get to the base, be given orders, and be shipped out as soon as possible. His unit was a man down, which is why he was rushed off. It's also why I worry so much. I asked a lot of questions that night and he did the best to answer them. Then he came up with the best response possible: "It's the life of a military wife, Ry." It's not to say that I hadn't thought about a future with him, but the word "wife" had never been spoken before. And that single word set off the butterflies.

BACON CRIES AT night so he sleeps in bed with me, which I know is something Dylan may not be happy about when he gets home, especially the first few days, or weeks in our case, but I can't help it. I hate hearing those cries. Besides, it's nice to have someone in bed with me. It helps take away from the heartache of his absence.

Dylan

"I THOUGHT YOU'D be too busy with your girl," Dave says, leading me toward the USO office. Apparently he'd been R&R for a couple weeks while I was home and never bothered to tell me.

Now we're united again at a base a few miles north of Ghazni. I'd left the night I got to Camp Lejeune and was temporarily set up with another unit until mine found their way back here.

"I would've come to Pittsburgh to see you."

"And do what?" he asked.

"I don't know. Meet your mom. Your brothers."

"And Riley. She would've come, too?"

I shrug, opening the door of the tent and stepping inside. "Probably."

"Yeah," he says, following behind me as I sit down at one of the free computers. "I don't think I could've handled you all loved up and settled when I had to come back to this shithole."

I face him quickly. "She would've fucking loved you."

"Oh yeah?" He licks his finger, then rubs his nipple over his combat uniform. "I would have made her *love* me."

"You're fucking delusional." I point to the laptop. "What do I do?"

Shaking his head, he leans over me and opens a program on the screen, then begins to type faster than I thought humanly possible. A second later, a picture of Riley pops up on the screen.

"Why the fuck do you have a picture of my girl?"

He laughs loudly, his head throwing back with the force of it. "It's her profile picture, dumbass."

I wait for his laughter to die down before asking, "Now what?"

"Now press the video camera icon."

"And that's it?"

"That's it."

I wait for him to leave and when I can tell he has absolutely no plans to, I hover over the damn icon, trying to hide my excitement, because fuck I'm excited. I haven't spoken to her since I left and dammit I miss her. I miss everything about her. I miss the way she smells. The way she moans when her alarm goes off. The way she falls back asleep right away while I watch her, occasionally attempting to wake her so she's not late for work. I miss the way she looks when I tell her she has to get up, and I miss her cursing at me when I forcefully pull her out of bed. I miss the way she'd smile when she got out of the shower, all fresh and clean and perfect when she'd lean up on her toes to kiss me good morning. I miss the way she'd always choose to sit in the middle of the seat and place my hand on her leg, half distracted by her phone when I'd drive her to work. I miss touching her. I miss kissing her. I miss—

"Are you actually going to call her or what?" Dave says, pulling me from my thoughts.

"I don't know," I mumble, my excitement turning to worry.

"Why not?"

"I feel like this will do more bad than good. Like having a little piece of her is worse than not having her, period."

"Have you spoken to her at all?"

"Nope."

"How long have you been back?"

"Three weeks and two days," I tell him.

"She'd be wonderin', man. I'd want to hear from you. Even when you were home I was thinking about you. And she may not love you as much as I do—"

"Shut up." I chuckle.

"Just call her, dude."

Inhaling deeply, I square my shoulders, preparing myself. Then I click the icon.

It rings once.

Twice.

And by the third time I've almost given up.

Then it connects and all I can see is black. But her voice... I can hear her voice. "Hello?" she croaks. "Dylan?"

There's a dog barking in the background and I can make out shapes but nothing else. "Babe? Can you see me?"

"Oh my God," she whispers. "Hi baby."

The dog's barks turn to whimpers. "Can you see me?"

"Yes."

I lean closer, trying to make out her features. "I can't see anything, baby. It's dark."

"You're cutting out. Hang on, I'm going to turn the light on."

Dave taps my shoulder. "It's 3 a.m. there."

A moment later, the screen lights up and all I can see is the flannel of our bed sheets. Then it moves to a dog, and then finally, familiar bare legs I've dreamed about more times than not since I got here.

"Nice legs," Dave says.

"You can fuck off now," I retort.

I can see the side of her face, her hand as it wipes her eyes, either from sleep or from tears. Then she lifts her phone in front of her and I release a shaky breath. She's staring at the screen, her lips parted—curved slightly—her beautiful gray eyes wide and her hair a complete mess. My heart, my world, my breath—all of it stops.

"Hi baby," she whispers again, and I drop my gaze, just for a moment so I can gather my thoughts. I struggle to swallow and wipe my eyes on my collar.

Dave settles his hand on my shoulder and squeezes once. "Everyone's cleared out," he tells me. "I'll be out front and try to give you some privacy."

I nod, thankful for his actions and wait until I hear the door close before finally looking up at the flickering image of the girl I love, the girl I've missed more than words could ever convey.

"Dylan?" she asks, her once wide and hopeful eyes now narrowed in confusion.

"God, Riley. You are a sight for sore eyes."

She laughs through her tears. "I've missed you so much."

"Me too, baby."

"I love you so much."

I smile. "Me too, baby."

"What are you—I mean, are you allowed to say where you are?"

I shake my head.

"But you're safe?"

"I'm safe."

The dog barks again. "Is that Bacon?"

She nods. "He's biting my feet."

"I don't think I've ever been jealous of a dog before."

She smiles, her eyes clear again. "You want to see him?"

"Yeah."

She moves off screen for a moment, then returns with the puppy in her arms, his face next to hers. "There's Daddy, Bacon. Say hi." She grabs his paw and makes him wave.

"You better be taking care of Mamma," I say.

He jumps out of her hold and she frowns. "I think he needs to go on a potty break."

"You need to take him out?"

"No. Cameron installed a doggy door and he's trained to go out on his own."

My smile widens. "Cameron's been around?"

"They all have. And your dad and Eric, too. Eric set up a security system—"

"He did? Why didn't I think of that?"

She nods. "He didn't like me answering the door when I was home alone."

"He's a good man," I tell her. "What else has been going on?"

She shrugs. "Not much. Just missing you."

"But they're all taking care of you?"

"Yes, baby."

"And you—you're okay?"

She nods.

"And the drinking?"

"No. I'm not drinking."

"No urge?"

A second's pause. A moment's hesitation. "No."

"Riley. Don't lie to me."

She inhales deeply and lets it out in a *whoosh*. "I've thought about it. But I wouldn't do it, Dylan. Not after everything we've been through."

"Good."

"Don't worry about me, babe. Not with everything else you have going on. I'm okay. I promise."

"Okay."

"Hey, is there somewhere I can send you stuff? Do you guys need anything?"

"Probably. Dave will know—" and right on cue, I hear him say, "We gotta go. Meeting."

"Fuck," I spit.

"Already?" Riley whines. "That was so fast."

"I know, Ry, but I have to. I think we're still here tomorrow so I'll try to call again."

Dave walks over and bends so his face appears on camera. "Hey Boo," he says.

Riley laughs and waves at the screen. "Hi Dave."

I cover Dave's eyes. "Ry, flash me your tits real quick."

"Dylan!"

Dave tries to pry my fingers off his face. I don't budge. "Come on!" I plead. "I'm a desperate, deployed man and I'm missing my girl."

She bites down on her lip, her gaze lowered.

Dave's trying to shrug out of my hold now. I keep him in place. "Quick, baby," I say through a chuckle. "If you love me you would."

"You just love my boobs," she retorts. "Bye boys!"

"Did I miss it?" Dave yells, his view still covered by my hands.

Riley adds, "You're lucky I love you so much." Then she reaches up, quickly unbuttons my shirt she's wearing, grips the sides and spreads her arms wide, smirking as she does.

Swear, I'm the luckiest asshole in the world.

Thirty-Three

Riley

I PACE THE kitchen, checking the time for the millionth time. It's 6:00 a.m. On the dot. I haven't slept. He said he'd call. Last night he called at 3. He should've called already. I check my phone again. 100% charge. Full volume on the ringer. I open the Skype app to quadruple check there are no missed calls. There aren't.

Panic sets in.

Tears fill my eyes.

He wouldn't have said he'd call if he couldn't.

Something's wrong. I can feel it.

I look at Bacon, fast asleep on his bed. I check the time again. 6:01.

I pace faster, my hands balling and straightening at my sides.

They'd tell me, right? If something were wrong, they'd call? No. They just show up at the door. I've seen it in movies. Read it in books. They don't call.

Did he even change the address on his forms? Or whatever the fuck they have to do to let whoever the fuck know to go to wherever the fuck so they can notify if something happened.

"Oh my God," I whisper. He probably didn't change the address.

Without a second thought, I grab my keys, not bothering to dress and jump in my car.

I pull up to Dylan's dad's house and check the time on the dash. 6:02.

If it's physically possible to have your heart beat and die at the same time, that's what mine's doing. I step out of the car and march to the front door, my adrenaline and fear overshadowing any sense in the situation. I knock, hard and loud, and when a few seconds pass and no one answers I start to yell and pound my fist.

Eric answers wearing nothing but his boxers, his eyes half asleep at first but when he sees me and my obvious state, he seems to wake up. "What's wrong?" he rushes out, pulling me inside.

"He didn't call!"

"What?"

"He said he'd call and he didn't call. Have you heard anything?"

"Riley!" He grasps my elbows. "Slow down." Then over his shoulder, he shouts. "Dad! Riley's here." He bends down and looks in my eyes—my tear-filled, panicked eyes. "Take a breath, try to calm down. And start again. Please."

Mal appears down the hall, tying his robe. "Sweetheart, what's wrong?"

I try to take Eric's advice.

Breathe. *Calm*. Speak. "Dylan called last night." I shake my head quickly. "Not last night, but the night before. And he said he'd call again and he hasn't. Something happened to him. Did you get a call or—"

"Riley," Eric cuts me off, grasping my elbows tighter. "Did Dylan say he would definitely call? Or did he say he'd try? Because we can't make those kinds of promises."

"I—" I try to think of Dylan's exact words but nothing comes to mind.

Sydney's up now, her look of worry matching everyone else's.

"Sweetheart," Mal says, coming to me and placing his hand on my shoulder. "I'm sure he would've called if he could. There are just so many uncertainties over there, it's impossible…"

Eric releases his hold on me and leans against the wall, his chest rising and falling as he runs his hand through his hair. "So you haven't heard anything? *Official*, I mean."

"No but—"

His dad and he share a look—one of relief.

Sydney asks, "Do you want me to get your mom, Riley?"

I nod, tears releasing with my sob.

"Come on," Mal says, his hand still on my shoulder as he leads me to the kitchen. He sits me down on a chair and switches on the coffee pot. Then leans against the counter, Eric beside him. They're looking at me with pity in their eyes and I know what they're thinking, because I think it too. I've just never voiced it. Not until now. "I don't think I'm cut out for this."

"For what?" Eric asks.

"For this. This military life."

Silence fills the air as I look down at the table, my tears flowing fast and free. Then, unable to keep it in anymore, I release a truth that even I didn't want to believe. "I thought I could handle it but I can't. I wanted to believe so badly that I was strong enough for this but I'm not. I can't deal with another death and I feel like that's what I'm waiting for. For someone to knock on my door and tell me that another person I love is dead and I can't. I just can't." I wipe my tears, my words strained as I look up at them. "I love him. I do. You know I do, but—"

The back door opens and my mom appears. She's in her pajamas, her eyes glassy as she looks over at me, Sydney behind her. "Oh, honey," she coos. Then she smiles. "You've had a bad night, huh?"

I nod, releasing yet another sob.

She lifts the packet of bacon in her hands. "Will this help?"

I nod again, and even though I feel like a child—a sad, heartbroken child—having them here, having them understand—it helps.

In hushed tones, Eric, Sydney and my mom make breakfast while I focus on the table, waiting for my heart to settle.

"Riley?" Mal says, standing on the other side of the table. His voice is low, barely a whisper. "I'd like to show you something, if you don't mind."

HE LEADS ME down the hallway to his bedroom. I'd never been inside before but I just assumed it would be like Dylan's—sparse and covered in flannel. So you can imagine my surprise when he opens the door to a beautiful dark timber setting and white cotton sheets with a knitted throw at the end. He must see the shock on my face because he chuckles, low and gruff, just like Dylan. "It helps remind me of Ruby; Dylan's mother. It's the only space in the house that has any form of feminine touch." He sighs. "Twenty-three years she's been gone and I still can't find it in myself to change the washing detergent she used. Smells like her, you know?"

It's the most he's spoken about her and I wonder why. *Out loud.* Then kick myself for doing so.

He doesn't seem to mind though. He just points to a beautiful armchair in the corner of the room and indicates for me to sit while he goes to his closet. "I made the decision early not to talk about her too much around Dylan. I didn't want him feeling left out if Eric and I speak about our memories of her since he never knew her."

"I've met her," I tell him, my hands gliding across the fabric of the seat.

From inside his closet, he asks, "Oh, yeah?"

"Dylan took me to meet her right when we started dating."

"He did, huh?" he responds, walking out with a shoebox. Then he stops in his tracks. "Has he mentioned anything… about us not talking about her too much? Would he like us to?"

I shrug. "To be honest, I think it's something he thinks about but doesn't really talk about…"

He nods and continues his path toward me. Then, carefully, he places the shoebox on my lap. "Take a look," he says, sitting on the edge of the bed a couple feet away from me.

I lift the lid. *Letters.* So many letters addressed to *My love, Malvin*, but no addresses. I look up at him.

"She wrote me all these letters while I was deployed in Panama. I never knew about them until she passed and I was clearing out the closet to move here."

I take a calming breath, wondering why he's telling me all this. Not just telling me, but showing me. "So you'd never read them before then?"

He shakes his head. "She didn't write them for *me*, Riley. She wrote them for herself. I guess it helped keep me close and make the distance easier to deal with."

"And why… I mean, why are you showing me?"

He smiles. "I think there's a lot you can learn from these letters. If not learn, then at least understand. No one is *cut out* for this life but we make it work. Because that's exactly what life is, sweetheart. Work. And in the end, it pays off. I know—I have two amazing boys as proof."

I SPEND THE rest of the day in Dylan's bed, surrounded by tissues and letters filled with immeasurable heartache and longing and fear, but also joy and love and excitement and questions of the future. And plans—

there were so many plans Ruby Banks made with a man oceans away, doing exactly what Dylan is—helping to provide a life better than the one we know.

Every letter starts the same. She loves him. She misses him.

Some are sad, some are funny, but most of them just spoke about him. About her memories of him which she missed dearly. Memories that reminded me so much of Dylan that I spent most of the time with my hand to my mouth to stop from crying out loud.

There were also a few pictures in the box. Mainly of her taken over the years, even one of her pregnant with Eric going by the date stamp.

But there was one letter that hit me right in the feels. One that changed my outlook on everything. She told him about all the unsent, unread letters and she promised he'd never see them. At least not while he was deployed. She wanted him to focus on absolutely nothing but getting home to her. Safe. So they can continue making the memories she holds so close.

And when she ended the letter with "Fuck the oceans," I lie down on the bed, her letter against my chest, listening to the silence that surrounds me and release the fear of grief.

I connect to a woman whose words give me a sense of calm, of hope and of understanding—long after her last breath.

Ruby Banks—she was something else.

She was brave, she was funny, and she put love first.

She was an exceptional woman.

And she was everything I hope to be.

Thirty-Four
Dylan

"YOU THINK THIS is enough?" Dave mumbles, sitting against a wall of what I'm sure was once someone's home… now ours for the night.

I pocket the picture of Riley I'd been staring at and face him. "What's enough?"

"What we're doing? You think we're saving the world?"

I shrug. "You think that's our purpose?" I ask him, my weapon to my chest, finger off the trigger. We hadn't heard anything since the sun set. Our duties are done for the day—at least me and Dave's—and I plan on spending the next couple hours trying to get some sleep.

Apparently Dave has other plans. He likes to save these philosophical conversations for the times when we're alone. He ignores my question and asks, "You ever regret it?"

"Regret what?" I shuffle further down the wall until I'm lying on my back looking up at him.

He shakes his head. "Nothin'." After a pause, he smiles. "I miss my fuckin' mom, man. And my brothers." He reaches into his pocket and pulls out some photographs. "Ricky had a birthday party. They sent me photos."

"Ricky's the youngest, right?" I take the pictures from him.

"Yep," he says, his pride evident. "Just turned seven." He points to the picture. "They all dressed up as Minions."

I study the photograph: Three boys standing next to each other in bright yellow shirts underneath blue denim overalls. They have the same red hair and freckles as Davey. Same identical smiles. "They look happy," I tell him, moving to the next picture of Ricky blowing out the candles on his cake and I find myself smiling. "Maybe being here is different for everyone, Dave. Maybe we're not here to save the world, or maybe we are. But in the end, you saved them—your mom and your brothers. You think they'd be smiling like that if your old man were still home beating the shit out of you and your mom? They're your *purpose* and you're their *reason*."

He's quiet as he takes the pictures from me, a solid frown on his lips. "Yeah… you're right. I guess sometimes I forget that."

"It's real easy to forget when you're here. I'm sure they don't forget what you're doing for them, though."

He nods slowly, carefully placing the pictures back in his pocket. Then he smiles when he looks back at me. "Yo. What do you think our girl's doin' right now?"

"A: She's *my* girl. Not *ours*. And B:…" I close my eyes and settle my head on my rucksack, trying to picture her smile, hear her laugh, but the only thing I can see are eyes the color of sadness. I release a breath, my heart aching for her. "I just hope she's finding the strength she needs to get through the day."

Riley

TWO YEARS.

That's how long it's been since I'd driven up this road. Since I've seen the clear blue of the lake. Since I've sat on these rocky embankments watching the sun filter through the water.

Two long years.

And I don't know how I feel.

I glance down at Bacon sitting on my lap. "Well… I'm here. That's something, right?"

He pops his head up, just for a second, before settling back down on my arm.

I take a breath, ignoring the thundering of my heart as I slowly tear my gaze away from him and up to the edge of the cliff, a thousand questions running through my mind. I wonder if it knows the heartbreak it caused—the life it took that created an onset of events that brought me here. "Time to make Daddy proud," I tell Bacon, setting him on the ground beside me. I stand and turn my back on the cliff and the lake and focus on him. "I bet you're sick of me talking about him, huh?" I clip the leash on his collar. Squatting down so we're eye to eye, I say, "You'll love him, Bacon. And he'll love you. And when he comes home, we'll be a happy family and I'll be free of all this. That's why I'm here… for closure. You understand, right?"

He spins in a circle, tangling the leash around his legs. I lead him toward a tree and tie the leash around it. "I'll be back." Then I point at him. "Sit," I order. He sits. He's a champ of a dog, well-behaved and completed puppy training first in his class. I told Dylan all this in one of the letters I'd never send him.

I face the cliff again, my heart now beating out of my chest. I shrug out of my shirt and shorts and stand in my one-piece swimsuit, preparing myself for the battle ahead of me. For a second I think about Dylan, think about what he's doing right now and if he ever feels what I'm feeling. When he's face to face with danger, weapon drawn… does he ever feel ready?

Probably not.

But he does it anyway.

Because he's tough and he's brave and he's everything he encourages me to be.

With tears welling in my eyes, I take the first step.

Toward the cliff.

Toward my past.

Toward my pain.

My fists ball at my sides, my footsteps heavy as I make my way up the path I'd tried so hard to forget.

I try to ignore the voices in my head. Not mine. Not even Dylan's. But Jeremy's.

"*I think I'm afraid of heights.*"

"*This is bad. This is really fucking bad.*"

I wipe the tears released with my sob and put one foot in front of the other, my mind screaming to turn around—my heart doing the opposite—until the tears are endless and the sobs are loud and I'm standing at the top of the cliff, the otherwise perfect sky clouded with memories of Jeremy.

"*I love you.*" I hear it over and over—the last words he ever spoke—words I laughed at and never repeated.

Not to him.

I stand in the middle of the clearing, my eyes drifting shut and my fingers digging into my palms. I feel the heat of the sun warm my skin, feel the wind whirling around me, hear the ebb and flow of the water beneath me. I inhale deeply, hoping it'll help to calm my nerves and the immense emotions hitting me, drowning me, slowly killing me.

I cover my mouth, muffling my cry and turn swiftly.

Away from the edge.

Away from my past.

Away from my pain.

"I was wondering if you'd ever come up," a deep male voice says from behind me.

I know the voice.

I've heard it so many times since Dylan left.

I close my eyes before slowly turning to him. Behind my lids, the tears are begging, fighting to be released. He adds, "I've been waiting for you."

My eyes snap open to see Jake standing in front of me wearing nothing but board shorts and a sad smile. "What are you doing here?" I squeak.

He shrugs, his hands at his sides.

"But how did you know—"

"Dylan."

I bow my head, not for a moment of silence, but for a moment of clarity. My knees go weak and I collapse to the dirt, my hands over my eyes as I release every single emotion possible.

Sadness.

Longing.

Heartbreak.

Fear.

Grief.

Then I look up when I hear Jake's footsteps moving toward me. He sits beside me, his head lowered and his arms resting on his raised knees. His gaze is distant when he says, "Sometimes I have these moments where I look at myself and my life and I realize how good I have it. I've never had to experience the kind of loss you have. I've never had my heart truly broken, never had my life ripped out of my hands, never had to deal with devastating news that would ultimately change the course of my future. And sometimes I think I don't belong. Like I'm an imposter in an unforgivable world and I keep waiting for something bad to happen to me directly and nothing does." He pauses a beat. "Not that I'm not grateful for that," he adds quickly. "I'm just saying I wish I had something better to say, or a piece of advice that would somehow help you in this situation. But I don't. The only thing I can say is that while it's hard to watch the people you love suffer… loving them during those times is easy." He turns to me. "So that's why I'm here, Riley. Because you're one of us. And we love you."

Another sob.

Another round of tears.

He throws his arm around my shoulders, bringing me to him as he continues to speak. I try to listen; try to pay attention, even though my cries make it almost impossible. "You know the phrase *actions speak louder than words*?"

I wipe my cheeks. "I know it well," I tell him. *Facta Non Verba.*

"That was my motto when it came to Dylan."

"Because he was so silent?"

Jake nods. "He never voiced it, but I could tell something was up the few weeks leading up to him enlisting. It was hard to get him to speak when we were with the others and college didn't give us much free time to catch up on our own. So one day I loosened a spark plug on my truck and called him to have a look at it. I could tell he knew what I'd done as soon as he popped the hood, but he didn't mention it. He just kept fiddling with the engine because he knew I wanted to talk and I knew he'd let me. I knew if I asked if he were okay he'd nod and move on so I chose my words carefully. I asked him if he was happy."

I face him. "What did he say?"

He turns to me. "He said he was happy *enough*, but I could tell he wanted more because he stopped his task and just stared at nothing for a long time. Then I finally asked him if *happy enough* was good enough. He shook his head and without another word, he replaced my spark plug and dropped the hood. The next time I saw him was the day before he left for basic. The others don't know this but he showed up at my house the next morning and asked that I ride with him back home to his dad's house. He spoke more to me on that two-hour drive than all the years I'd known him. He admitted to hating college, he admitted to falling out of love with Heidi and he admitted that for the first time in a long time, he was actually looking forward to something."

I sniff once. "So you're telling me this to remind me that he's not here for a good reason?"

"No." Jake smiles—the same sad smile he greeted me with. "I'm telling you this because I was there. I was there when he said goodbye to his friends. I was there when he told his dad he was leaving. I was there when he got on the bus for the first time, waving goodbye to us and to his old life. And I can tell you, for certain, that his actions were louder than his words the day he said goodbye to you. He didn't find his *more than enough* by enlisting and deploying, Riley. He found it in *you*."

WE STAND AT the edge of the cliff, hand in hand, staring at the calm of the horizon. "You ready?" Jake asks.

"I'm ready."

"You sure?"

I face him, nod, and through the giant lump in my throat, I ask, "You think Dylan would be proud of me?"

Jake smiles. "Riley, Dylan would be proud of you regardless."

I inhale deeply. Then, "One. Two. Three."

We jump.

We fall.

There's no resistance. Just air surrounding me until I'm submerged, the warmth of the water filling my mouth and my ears. I open my eyes, squinting, searching for him. His hand takes mine, his smile wide beneath the blue of the lake as streams of sunlight create a show of lights. His hand stays with mine as we swim up, gasping for air as soon as we're clear.

Then the water in my ears is replaced with shouts and cheers and my name being called from the embankment. Our friends stand at the edge, their fists raised in triumph. "Yeah, Riley!" Lucy shouts, her hands cupped around her mouth.

I look over at Jake, but he just smiles. "We're all here for you, Riley."

"Are you going again?" Logan shouts as we swim to shore. He's already shrugging out of his clothes. They all are, though Kayla struggles with Bacon in her arms.

I nod. My smile matching Jake's from just a minute ago. "I think I am."

WE TAKE THE Leap a few more times, each time getting easier. And we spend the afternoon talking, laughing and swimming in the lake with Bacon.

They've even brought a portable grill so I think they plan on staying for a while.

When the sun's at its highest, more people show up at the lake. People I recognize. People from my class. One of Jeremy's friends—Lucas—approaches, walking right up to Lucy. "What are you doing here?" he asks her.

She stands up from her sun bathing position and hugs him quickly. Cam shakes his hand. They all look over at me. Lucas's smile falters momentarily, before shoving his hands in his pockets, his gaze lowered as he makes his way over.

I square my shoulders, not knowing what to expect.

"Hey, Riley." He stops a few feet in front of me, his eyes meeting mine. "It's been a long time…"

I nod, wiping my sweaty palms on my wet legs. "You know Lucy?"

He laughs once. Not from humor, but probably from the same nerves I'm feeling. "Yeah, she's my sister."

"Really? I didn't know…"

"Yeah. She's not big on claiming me." He pauses a beat. "So you and Banks?" He smiles up at me, hoping for a reaction, one I don't have. When enough time passes and he must realize that, he rubs the back of his head and adds, "I'm a sucky friend."

My eyes narrow in confusion. "What?"

"I should've reached out to you after everything happened. Especially with the crap people were spreading about you. I knew it was bullshit and I should've done something to stop it, but I don't know…" He shrugs. "By the time I got the balls to do it, you'd already left."

"Left?"

"Yeah. That's the rumor. That your mom shipped you off somewhere to serve your house arrest…"

I shake my head in disbelief.

"Really?" he asks.

"I've been home all this time."

"But I came by once—"

"You did?"

"—and nobody answered," he finishes.

"Oh." I don't bother telling him that I was probably too drunk to hear it.

"I'm sorry, Riley. You would've hurt the most of all of us and we just..."

I shrug and look away. "It's fine."

"It's not fine. We were all hoping we'd see you here last year but understood why you weren't."

My eyes shift back to him, my head tilted. "Last year?"

"We came here last year to pay our respects. And we've made a pact to come here every year until we're old and gray," he says through a chuckle. Then he points to the rest of Jeremy's friends standing twenty yards away. They're all watching us. "They're probably too afraid to come and talk to you."

"Why?"

"Because they all feel the same as I do. They feel guilty that we weren't there for you like we should've been... like Jeremy would've wanted us to be."

I feel the tears prick my eyes, the impact from his words, and the acceptance of forgiveness hit me all at once. "We were all grieving," I tell him.

"I suppose. Coming here, remembering him, it helps."

I don't know what to say, so I smile.

Jake's beside me now—my substitute protector should I need one.

Lucas adds, "So listen. We all chipped in and got a plaque made up. We got permission to put it up on the cliff. It's a piece of Jeremy for eternity and it'd be an honor if you were the one to put him to rest."

In loving memory of Jeremy Walters

Your life is your legacy.

We will never forget.

Thirty-Five

Riley

AMANDA SCRUNCHES HER nose in disgust as she looks at Mikayla first, then Lucy, then at me. We have Kindles in our hands. They have wine. I have soda. It's the first time I've hosted a book club at my house, which, by the way, is only a book club for the first half hour.

Amanda sighs, throwing her Kindle on the carpet in front of her. "You know… I don't mind anal play in books, if that's what you're into, have at it! But like, fucking wash the thing before you put it in your mouth. The fucking germs." She sticks out her tongue, gagging at the thought.

"That's what you got from the entire book?" Lucy asks through a laugh.

"I couldn't finish it after that. I just kept running to the bathroom to use mouthwash."

Mikayla laughs, stopping momentarily to look down at her ringing phone. Her smile fades. "It's Heidi," she announces. She takes a breath and holds it, eyeing us all as the phone continues to ring.

"Are you going to answer?" Lucy asks.

"I don't know. I hate lying to her about where we are."

"Why would you lie?" I ask.

Her eyes widen. "I didn't mean to offend, Riley. I'm sorry. It's just… it's…"

"Awkward," Lucy chimes in. "It's nothing against you. I think we make it more awkward than it is."

"Wait." I rear back in surprise. "You guys don't feel like you have to choose or keep secrets because of us, do you? I mean, if it came down to it, she was your friend first. I'm not going to get in the way of that. Besides, we've been in the same room together before—"

"Yeah, but Dylan has always been there so…" Amanda's words die in the air.

"This isn't middle school. We're adults," I tell them. The phone stops ringing, and then starts again a second later. I pick it up and hand it to Micky. "Tell her to come over."

"What?!"

"Yeah. I can be nice."

"It's not you we're worried about," Amanda says.

"You don't think I could take Heidi?" I roll my eyes. "Please."

"Who would win in a fight?" Lucy asks, lost in thought.

"Amanda," Micky answers.

"She's not fighting," I tell her. "Tell her to come over and that I want to fight her. I'll set up a ring in the back yard. We can settle this right now."

"Really?" Lucy says, her eyes wide as she sits up higher. "Fuck yes!" She's excited. Way too excited.

Amanda laughs.

"I was kidding, Luce. Calm down," I tell her.

"You really want me to tell her to come over?" Micky asks, her thumb hovering over her phone.

"Yes."

"Okay. It's your funeral." She answers the call and brings the phone to her ear. "Hey." Pause. "Yeah, we're at Riley and Dylan's." A longer pause. "Book club. But Riley said you're welcome to come over." An even longer pause. Micky's eyes shift to me. "She wants to fight you."

My jaw drops.

Micky laughs. "I'm kidding. We're just sitting around now. Amanda killed the book for everyone." The longest pause in the history of the world. "Sure. I'll text you the address." She hangs up and drops the phone to her lap. "She'll be here in fifteen. She's bringing gloves."

"Gloves?" I ask.

"Boxing gloves."

"Fuck yes!" Lucy shouts, now on her knees, her arms raised in victory.

Micky laughs. "I'm kidding, Luce."

"Stop messing with my emotions!" Lucy yells.

FIFTEEN MINUTES LATER, Heidi shows up, causing the most awkward half hug in the history of half hugs. She's carrying a huge duffle bag and holding a plate of brownies. "What's in the bag?" I ask her, hoping to God she didn't plan on staying the night. "Just cosmetic stuff." She shrugs. "I know this is your night—the whole book club thing… it's just that I don't really read so…"

I return her shrug. "Cool."

She nods. "Cool."

"Hey," Lucy whispers, her eyes already half hooded from the booze. "Are you guys going to fight? Because I need to make room on my phone to record it. And if you do could you do it in your underwear? Cameron and I would really appreciate it."

TEN MINUTES LATER and a now empty plate of brownies, we're all lying on the floor. I'm light headed, and the room is spinning, and Lucy is loud. So damn loud.

"I could eat an entire truck of faces," she says.

"Me too," Amanda says.

Micky adds, "Did you guys watch that thing on the thing about the lady who eats her hair?"

"But did she die?" Heidi asks.

Lucy says, "My hair smells like the morning dew on a holy sunset and praying elephants."

I sit up quickly, gasping, and looking at Heidi. "Where did you get those brownies?" I ask.

She sits up too, a lot slower than I did. "They were in my fridge. They weren't that good. My mom sucks at baking."

"Heidi." I shuffle on my knees until I'm in front of her. Reaching out, I shake her shoulders, hating that her hair stays as perfect as her face while I do it. "Is there weed in those brownies?"

She slaps my hand away, scowling at me. "Why the hell would there be weed? It's just my parents at home. Why would they have weed brownies? Why is it called weed? And what is *brown*?"

Amanda chuckles. "Heidi's parents are stoners."

"Shut up," Heidi retorts, her face paling as realization sets in.

Mikayla gasps. "We're stoners!"

Heidi clicks her tongue. "You're all full of shit," she says, swaying on her feet when she stands up. She walks over to her gigantic bag. "Let me do your face now."

"With your vagina?" Lucy asks.

"Luce!" Heidi squeals.

Lucy sighs. "I have such strange lesbian tendencies. I apologize."

WE ALL GIGGLE like schoolgirls, watching Heidi attempt to apply make up on Mikayla's face.

"You look like a clown!" Amanda shouts. She's louder than Lucy.

"A sexy clown," I add, seeing Micky's frown.

"You look like a fucking whore!" Lucy yells.

Micky gasps. "Fuck off. I'd rather be a lesbian with Roxy than with you!"

Lucy's gasp matches Micky's. "That was a low blow."

Micky's gaze drops, her frown back in place. "It was. I'm sorry."

"Who's Roxy?" I ask, fisting a bunch of compacts in Heidi's bag. I pull them out and drop them on my lap. Then I open one—blue eye shadow. I smear it across my lips and find a brush to apply what I think is blush across my entire face. Because my mind tells me to. And the brush feels so damn good against my skin.

Lucy says, "Roxy is a fucking cunt of a whore and we shall never speak her name again."

"Yeah, Riley," Amanda spits. "Her name is Dylan."

"I thought her name was Roxy," I mumble using a tube of mascara to paint my nails.

Heidi turns to me. "What are you doing?"

"What are *you* doing?"

Amanda giggles.

Out of nowhere, Lucy says, "Hey. Is Dylan a moaner?"

I throw a brush at her face. "What?"

"A moaner," she says, ignoring the brush. "In bed, I mean. Like… does he moan?"

"I bet he's just silent," Kayla says.

"He's not a moaner," I snap.

And they all shut their mouths and looks down at their hands.

I add, "He's more of a grunter."

Lucy tries to stifle her laugh.

"And a talker."

"Dylan talks?" Amanda shouts.

"Yeah, he says dirty, filthy shit in my ear right before I come."

"So hot," Lucy mumbles.

"Dylan talks?" Amanda shouts again.

Micky laughs.

"He never did that with me," Heidi murmurs.

Lucy scoffs. "As if you'd be into that anyway."

Heidi shrugs. "True."

I nudge Heidi's elbow. "You missed out, Heids."

"I bet you're missing the D," Micky says.

"I miss him a lot," I admit.

Lucy laughs. "Not D, as in Dylan. She means The D. As in The Dick."

My eyes widen. "Oh." Then I shrug. "Not as much as I miss him."

"It must be hard," Lucy says, a seriousness taking over. "Cam and I spent a few weeks apart and it was hell."

"I had a year away from Logan," Amanda chimes in.

"A few days, max, for me and Jake," Kayla says.

Heidi asks, "What do you miss the most?"

For a moment, I wonder why she's asking… if it's because she's trying to compare us to see who missed him more. She must realize what I'm thinking because she adds, "I just thought you might like to talk about him. Lucy's right. It must be so hard." She smiles, warm and gentle. And I know right away there isn't a single ounce of malice in her words.

She's trying to cross a bridge, and I choose to meet her in the middle.

I suck in a breath and let it out in a *whoosh* as I lie back down. The others follow.

"I miss everything about him. I miss the way he touches me, the way he smells, the sound of his voice—"

"Dylan talks?!" Amanda yells again, and I laugh.

"He talks a lot," I tell her. "And he's funny. So funny."

"Dylan's funny?!" she shouts.

We laugh as one, mine ending sooner than the others. I'd done everything I could to ignore how much I've been missing him lately but the days are just as hard as the nights now and I've tried not to think about what he's doing and where he is and if he's safe. I try not to get angry when I think about how hard it is for him to call, just once, just so I can hear his voice and tell him I love him. I tell the girls all this without realizing it, but they never interrupt, never ask questions.

I wipe my eyes, the pain of longing unbearable. I release another round of tears. Another sob. I'm not the only one crying now, but we do it quietly. Together but apart. "I'm so grateful that he gave me you guys, too, because I don't know that I'd be able to get through all this without you and the boys and I appreciate you all so much and I'm sorry if I've never told you that."

Next to me, Kayla lifts her head. She smiles but she doesn't speak.

I add, "I think, what I miss most, is the way he makes me feel. I don't think he even realizes how important he is in my life. He was my strength when I had none and sometimes I find myself getting lost and I have to dig deep to find my way back. The only way I can do that is because he's shown me that I can. He has this way of making me smile, making me happy. He makes me laugh when I feel like I can't. But the best part is that when I believed it to be impossible, he made me love again."

Kayla takes my hand, holding it between us as we lay on our backs, looking up at the ceiling. "He'll come back to you, Riley. He loves you so much."

"He *made* you a car," Lucy says.

"And gave you his home," Amanda chimes in.

On the other side of me Heidi sighs. "But Riley knows. Right, Riley?"

"Knows what?" I ask, rolling my head to face her.

"That it's not about him giving you a car or a house. Those are just material things—things Dylan doesn't care about. That was just his way of showing it."

"Showing what?" I whisper.

Her eyes lock on mine. "That he loves you and that he's creating a future with you, Riley. One that he plans on lasting forever."

Thirty-Six
Riley

I WAKE TO Sydney in my bed. She wasn't there last night.

She's smiling, *creepily*. Real creepily.

Honestly, it wasn't really a surprise to find her here. Eric had a key to the house and she did tell me she had plans for a belated birthday celebration.

She takes me clothes shopping, which is odd because it's rare you'd find me outside of work in anything other than Dylan's shirts.

It's lunchtime by the time we get back. I park in the garage like I do every other time, but when I open the door to the yard and the shout of "Surprise!" fills my ears, I kind of just stand there, shocked. Everyone's here; Mom, Mal, Eric, a few people from work and the rest of the gang.

"What—why?"

"Dylan," Mal states.

And they all lower their heads for a moment of silence. Until Lucy laughs. "I couldn't hold it in," she says. Then claps at everyone's skilled synchronization.

Sydney smacks my ass. "Go get changed into your new clothes," she orders, and suddenly it all makes sense.

"HAVE YOU HEARD from him?" Sydney asks, patting her stomach.

I lean back in my chair, my belly full from all the food Mal prepared on the grill. "I'm sure he would've contacted me if it were possible."

She grins. "Oh, I'm sure. He'd hate to be missing out on your twenty-first birthday."

"And our one-year anniversary," I tell her, my smile wider than hers.

"Oh yeah?"

"I mean, technically, probably not. But it was the beginning of it all."

Lucy approaches, phone to her ear. She hangs up when she gets to me. "That was Cameron. He wanted to apologize. He got held up at work but he's on his way."

THERE'S THAT AWKWARD moment at every party when everyone circles the cake while they sing Happy Birthday, all eyes on you, and you kind of just sit there waiting for the song to be over and the focus to switch to anything else so you're no longer embarrassed.

The first song seems to go on forever.

Then mom states that she hadn't recorded it properly and we need to do it again. So everyone laughs and they repeat the song, a little less enthused than the first time. When it's over we all look at mom, making sure she's not so Dylan with technology and when she gives a thumbs up and says, "Make your wish, Riley," I lower my gaze and take a calming breath.

I wonder for a second if I should blow out the candles individually. Would twenty-one wishes for Dylan have the same effect as one big one?

I lean down, feeling the warmth of the candles against my cheek. Then I close my eyes, suck in a breath, and I think about the boy I love. The boy I miss more than anything. My lips part—his name on repeat in my head. Then I make my wish, and I blow.

"Happy Birthday, baby."

My eyes snap open. There's a figure to my right—one I swore wasn't there a minute ago but I'm too afraid to look because as much as I believe in wishes, they don't happen this fast.

I struggle to swallow as I look up at everyone watching me, their eyes on mine, their smiles in place.

Nothing has changed.

It's in my head. It's gotta be.

I close my eyes again, letting the disappointment set in.

"What did you wish for, babe?" Same voice. Only louder.

I open my eyes and look for Jake. "Jake," I whisper, my body shaking. I'm too afraid to turn to the imaginary sound. To the imaginary

Dylan. Tears fight their way out of me. As do the butterflies. "Jake," I say again. "I can hear him."

Next to him, Mikayla's crying. Jake doesn't seem to hear me though. Or at least he pretends like he doesn't because he won't respond. I stand quickly and march over to him, still refusing to let my hopes control my senses. I stand in front of Jake, my eyes locked on his. "Jake. Is he real?"

Jake nods. "Yes, Riley. He's real."

I push on his chest because I'm angry he's saying such a thing, even in my dreams. Because I'm sure that's what this is. A dream. A big, fat, stupid, heartbreaking dream. "Don't lie to me, Jake. Is. He. Real?"

I don't know why people are laughing when I'm crying and it's *my* damn dream.

Jake grasps my shoulders and bends so we're eye to eye. "Riley," he says, his voice calm and soothing. "Dylan's home." Then he spins me around until I'm face to face with a boy I've missed more than words could describe. He's standing in front of me; head to toe in camo and he's so much more than I remember him to be. So much. He takes a step forward, his hand already raised, his deep blue eyes locked on mine. Then he smiles. And everyone and everything else disappears and it's just me and him and the power of wishes. "Hi," he says, and I jump forward, my arms and legs around him. I kiss him. Every single inch of his beautiful face. His lips—lips I'd missed so much and the second he comes to, his arms go around me, holding me to him, returning every one of my kisses with his own. I pull back, just long enough to ask, "What are you doing here?" But he doesn't get a chance to respond before my mouth covers his and I can hear people laughing, hear Eric call out for us to get a room but I don't care because he's *home*. Dylan's home. Why is he home?

I release him quickly, my feet finding the ground. "Why are you home? Are you hurt? What happened?" I check his body for any sign of injury, running my hands over his shoulders and stomach and God, I missed him.

"I'm on R&R," he tells me. "And I came home for you."

"For me?"

He shakes his head, his teeth clamping down on his bottom lip as he eyes me up and down. "God, baby. I didn't realize how much I missed you until now."

I throw my arms around his waist and squeeze and squeeze until all air's left both our lungs. Everyone's still laughing and I still don't care. "I'm never letting you go again," I tell him.

He chuckles. I missed his chuckle the most. "You're going to have to in twelve days."

My eyes widen as I look back up at him. "Twelve days?"

A frown pulls on his lips. "Yeah. I couldn't get any more—" My grin must cut him off. "You're not disappointed?"

"Dylan! I have you for twelve whole days!"

Eric chimes in. "Can I say hello to my baby bro now?"

I let Dylan say hello to everyone and I introduce him to my friends from work he doesn't know. The entire time I hold onto his arm, afraid he'll fly away if I let him go.

HE LOOKS AT me mid-conversation with our friends before bending down to my ear and whispering, "I'm going to take a shower. Bedroom. Five minutes."

I watch him walk through the back door, nudging Eric as he does. Whatever Dylan must say to him has him looking over at me and nodding. I pull my phone out from my bra and check the time. And I continue to do so—watching the minutes tick away.

IT'S NOT UNTIL my hand's covering the handle of the bedroom door that the nerves kick in. Along with the same butterflies from earlier. I take a breath. Or ten. And check the time again.

Six minutes.

With all the courage I can possible muster, I press down on the handle and peek inside.

He's just gotten out of the shower, his shoulders still wet as he goes through his drawers, his back turned. He's wearing a towel around his waist and nothing else. Then he does the worst (or best) thing he can possibly do. He drops the towel, giving me a perfect view of his beautifully toned ass.

I moan.

I don't mean to, but holy shit I've missed him.

Every square inch of him.

His shoulders tense when he hears the sound that can only be described as pure lust. Slowly, he turns to me, not bothering to cover himself. Then he smirks. "You're late."

"I'm sorry." I can't stop looking at his—

He clears his throat.

I lift my gaze, pausing for a moment at the perfect V just below his perfect abs and perfect chest and FYI, Naked Dylan = Hot As Fuck Dylan.

He stalks toward me, his body on show, and when he's close enough he reaches for my hand and pulls me into the room, shutting the door behind me.

"Hi," he says, pushing me gently until my back is pressed to the door.

The nerves and the butterflies return and I drop my gaze, too afraid to look at him.

He moves forward again, his warm body pressed against mine as he dips his head, his mouth to my ear. "What's wrong?" he asks.

I inhale deeply, feeling his chest press harder into mine. "I'm nervous," I admit.

His lips curve against my neck as he kisses me softly. "Why?"

"I don't know." My body melts into his when his hands find my waist, his thumb stroking my bare stomach between my shorts and my shirt.

Then, slowly, one of his hands move from my waist and up my sides until he's cupping my face. His mouth moves from my neck, up my jaw, and across my cheek, his kisses relentless. Then he pulls away, just enough to run his tongue along my lips, begging for entrance.

If it wasn't for him pressing me against the door, I'd be on the floor in a puddle of my own need and desire.

Literally.

He kisses me. Softly at first, then all at once we lose control. Of the need. Of the lust. Of the longing. Of ourselves.

One of his hands is in my hair, pulling gently, making my head tilt back to make my mouth more accessible to him. The other's on my shorts, making fast work of the button and the zipper. And me? I have no idea what to do with my hands so I grasp his hardness, upright between us, and I stroke gently, smiling against his lips when he curses into my mouth. Now my shorts are on the floor, his fingers inside me and his mouth around my nipple. I don't even remember him pulling up my shirt. "Riley," he murmurs, moving up from my breast and to my mouth again. "Promise. Tonight I'll worship your body. But right now, I need inside you. I need to fuck you, Riley."

He removes his fingers from inside me and uses both hands to cup my ass as I kick off my shorts and without effort, he lifts me, pinning my body against the door with him between my legs while I guide him to where I need him the most.

My cry of pleasure is stifled by his shoulder when he fills me—my eyes rolling to the back of my head—my head that just hit the door behind me. He pauses inside—letting our bodies get used to the sensation—our foreheads touching as his eyes search mine. "You're so beautiful," he says.

And then he moves. Pulling out slowly just to thrust into me again. And again. And again. With so much force the door bangs against the frame. Over and over. And over again.

My fingers curl, gripping his shoulders as immeasurable pleasure washes through me. He pulls back from the kiss, replacing his tongue with his thumb and I suck on it, making it wet, knowing that he's about to do something he's done so many times before. Leaning back, my body still pinned to the door, he uses his thumb to circle my clit, all while he pumps into me, his other arm around my back to keep me in place.

My breaths are heavy, my body on fire from the onslaught of pleasure he's creating.

My fingers dig deeper.

"So fucking wet," he murmurs. "So fucking beautiful."

Bodies covered in sweat, we move as one until I come, a loud moan escaping before I can stop it. A second later, he follows, his muscles tensing beneath my touch. I collapse into his arms while he lowers me gently back to earth—to reality. A reality so perfect I don't want to be anywhere else. Then he laughs, hugging me in his arms. "You were so fucking loud, Riley. Neighbors three streets down would've heard you."

I look up at him, shock clear on my face. "Shut up."

He smirks, his eyebrow quirked. Then he smacks my bare ass. "I don't know how you're going to face everyone now."

"But… it wasn't just me," I whine.

He laughs again. "Riley, I'm a guy. That makes me a fucking boss. You on the other hand…"

I kiss him quickly. "I'm a girl who's missed her man. Besides…" I shrug. "It's my party and I'll fuck if I want to."

Thirty-Seven

Riley

MOST OF THE guests clear out soon after. I'm not sure if it's because Dylan's here or because... well... let's put it this way: Mom refused to make eye contact and Mal blushed fifty shades of red whenever I was near him.

THE ONLY ONES who hang around are our friends. We have a few quiet drinks (sans me) around the fire pit while the afternoon sun begins to dip. They talk a lot, mainly about Jake and Kayla's travels around the states and their overseas ones coming up. I sit with Dylan, his hand on my leg as we listen to them speak, neither of us really talking. Then when Jake chuckles and points to Dylan, I realize why.

Next to me—my boyfriend's sound asleep—his mouth parted and his chest rising and falling peacefully.

"He must be so tired." Lucy pouts.

I look from Dylan to her. "Did y'all know he was coming?"

Jake answers, "Yep. Cam picked him up from the airport."

My gaze moves to Cameron. "So you weren't held up at work?"

He shakes his head.

Logan says, "That's why your mom got us to sing Happy Birthday twice. They didn't show up the first time."

I smile, remembering my initial embarrassment. "I can't believe you guys kept it a secret for so long."

"He really wanted to surprise you, Ry. It was important to him," Jake tells me.

Dylan's hand on my leg shifts as he lets out a single snore.

Amanda says, "Let's clean up so Riley can get Grandpa Banks to bed."

We all stifle our laughs, hoping not to wake him, and we continue to do so while we clean up. With all of us working on it, it doesn't take long. I say goodbye at the front door, telling them that we'll be in touch when Dylan's up to it and then I go back out to the yard, my smile growing with each step closer to him. "Come on, Grandpa Banks," I whisper, squeezing his hand.

Slowly, his eyes open, his attention on me before looking around us. "I fell asleep?"

I nod with my smile.

"Where is everyone?"

"They left."

"I'm sorry, baby. I ruined your party," he says, his disappointment evident.

"Shut up." I pull on his hand until he's on his feet. "Let's go to bed."

He looks at his watch. "It's only five."

I lead him toward the house. "I said *bed*, Dylan. Not sleep."

We don't even make it to the bedroom before Bacon's running circles around Dylan's leg trying to get his attention. "It's like he can sense another man's about to take his place in the bed," I tell him.

"He sleeps in our bed?" Dylan asks, bending down to pick him up.

"I got lonely," I tell him.

"So where the hell is he going to sleep now?" He lifts him higher until their noses almost touch. To Bacon, he says, "So you're the man who's been keeping my girl warm at night? I have some choice words for you." Bacon licks Dylan's cheek. He scrunches his nose and places the dog back on the floor before looking at me. "Seriously, though. Where is he going to sleep?"

"Watch," I tell him, and then point to Bacon's bed in the kitchen. "Bed," I order. Bacon moves to the bed. "Sit." Bacon sits. "Stay." Bacon stays.

"Holy shit," Dylan mumbles, grabbing my hand and dragging me to the bedroom. He slams the door shut behind us. "Order me around like that."

I laugh and point to the bed. "Bed!" He moves to the bed, containing his smile. "Strip!" He removes his shirt. I quirk an eyebrow. "All of it." He drops his shorts and boxers in one move. "Sit!" He sits. "Stay." He laughs, loud and free.

I watch his eyes widen and his beautiful smile spread when I drop to my knees between his legs, preparing to show him just how much I missed him.

WE LAY NAKED, on our sides, our bodies clean and fresh from the shower and finally satisfied. He runs a finger down the middle of my forehead, between my eyebrows and past my nose. I kiss it when it passes my lips. He laughs quietly and runs the back of his fingers across my cheek. "I didn't plan on coming home and doing… you know… what we just did… five times…" He presses his lips to mine and pulls away slowly. "I really missed you, Riley. Not just the physical side, but you. I missed this, lying with you and just looking at you and talking to you and everything about you."

"Me too," I whisper, moving closer until my forehead's on his chest. "I still can't believe you're here."

He starts to stroke my hair, resting his chin on top of my head. "Riley?"

I look up at him. "Yeah?"

"My dad told me about what happened the day after I called you and he said—"

"It's nothing, Dylan. I'm sorry. I didn't know he was going to tell you about it." I sit up quickly, covering my breasts with the blanket as the panic sets in. "It was just a moment of weakness. That's all."

He leans up on his elbow and rests his head on his hand. "How many moments of weaknesses did you have?"

"What?" I ask, tears pricking in the back of my eyes. I can already hear the disappointment in his voice. "If you want to ask something just come out and ask, Dylan."

"Did you drink while I was gone?"

"No."

"Not even—"

"Nothing, Dylan. Not a drop. And to be honest I'm a little pissed—"

"I'm sorry," he cuts in, sitting all the way up and bringing me to him. "I'm sorry," he repeats. "I just worry. It has to be hard for you and

I just don't want anything to set you back, that's all."

"I'm fine," I tell him, my shoulders tense. "You have enough to worry about over there, you don't need to worry about me."

"I'm always going to worry about you, Ry."

"What if I said that I had been drinking, or that I couldn't handle it? What would it change?"

"I'd leave."

"Leave what? Afghanistan? You don't have a choice!"

"The military."

"Don't be dumb."

"Wow, Ry."

"You can't leave the military, Dylan. It means too much to you. And I wouldn't let you."

"You won't *let* me?" he asks incredulously. "I hate to break it to you, babe, but if I had to make the choice between you and the Marines, I'd choose you. Every time."

"That's not what I want, though!" I shake my head, my gaze lowered when he finally releases me. "Dylan, that's not what I want this relationship to be—you always watching out for me, worrying about me, giving up your life for me. I'm so much stronger than I was when you met me. And you helped me become that. I don't want to go through the rest of my life knowing you're watching my every move and me walking on eggshells always afraid I'm going to disappoint you."

"That's not what I meant," he mumbles, his finger on my chin forcing me to look at him. Then he smiles. "The rest of your life?"

"Huh?"

"You said the rest of your life. So you plan on being with me forever."

I roll my eyes. "I thought that was obvious, Dylan, and that's not the point. The point is—"

"The point is you love me and I love you and we really suck at talking."

I laugh. I can't help it. "We really do."

He grasps my shoulders, bringing us both back to our lying positions. "Dad told me he showed you some letters—the ones my mom wrote him while he was deployed but never sent?"

I nod against his chest.

"I never got any letters from you."

I sit up slightly. "Were you expecting them?" I ask, my heart dropping.

He smiles, moving the hair away from my eyes. "I *was*. But now I know why and I get it."

"You do?"

He nods, pulling me back down to him. "Did you write to me?"

"Maybe."

A smile pulls on his lips. "Are you going to show me?"

"One day. Maybe."

"That's good enough," he says, then changes the subject. "So what's the plan for tomorrow?"

"I have work—"

"No you don't."

"What?"

"I didn't tell you?"

I roll my eyes again. "Tell me what?"

"Eric organized for you to have the time off while I was back. They were all in on it, too."

I sit up quickly, pick up my pillow and throw it at him. "Shut up!"

He groans, his eyes shut tight. "Quit throwing shit at me."

"Are you serious?"

"Yes," he says through a chuckle. "But I don't know anymore. Maybe you should go to work." He puts the pillow back in place. "I think my life's safer in Afghanistan."

"Dylan," I deadpan. "Seriously? I don't have to work?"

"No. For the third time. I wanted you all to myself."

I pick up the pillow again because, obviously, I do stupid shit when I'm excited.

Before I have a chance to throw it, he takes it from me, throws it across the room and grasps both my hands, flipping me onto my back at the same time. His entire body covers me, his hands holding mine above my head. "I told you to quit throwing shit, Riley."

I giggle and try to squirm out of his hold, knowing full well it's useless. He's too strong, too demanding.

"Quit fighting it," he says, using his knees to spread my legs apart. He settles between them, his hard-on rocking against my center.

I lean up and kiss him quickly. "What's my punishment, Lance Corporal?"

He groans from deep in his throat, dipping his head. "Aren't you sore?"

"A little," I admit.

"Need me to kiss it better?"

I nod.

He smirks.

Then his phone goes off.

Dave: *What are you doing, handsome?*

Dylan: *Gettingxmoney and ducking bitches.*

He throws his phone across the room.

Then he kisses me better.

So much better.

Thirty-Eight
Dylan

I CAN'T TELL you how many times I tried to remember her exactly the way she is; sleeping peacefully on her stomach, her hair a mess, her mouth parted, her breaths even.

So many nights I'd try to picture it.

And my memories didn't do her justice.

THE SECOND I saw her yesterday sitting on a chair, the flames of twenty-one candles lighting her beautiful face, eyes closed and her entire body tense with the strength of her wish, something in me switched. I'm not exactly sure what it was or how to describe it, but somehow, saving the world didn't seem as important as saving her.

I LEAN DOWN and press my lips to her temple. "I'm going to take Bacon for a walk," I whisper.

She mumbles something incoherent. Then a second later, she sits up, fully alert. "I thought you were a dream," she says through a smile.

"No dream, baby."

She stands quickly and moves to the bathroom. "Twelve days and counting. Give me five. I'm not missing out on a second with you."

We take Bacon for a walk to Dad's house. We have breakfast with Eric and Dad and catch up on everything that's been going on since I've been gone. Not a lot has happened, apart from Eric taking over my old room again and Sydney moving in. I guess that last one's kind of a big deal. Apparently Sydney had been living with her ex (awkward), which was something Eric wasn't too happy with. They argued for a long time about it. In fact, it was the only thing they argued about. Eric wasn't willing to leave Dad so he asked her to move in. Eric says she's been slowly making the house a little homey. You know, besides the two recliners and frozen dinners. Her and Dad get a long well. They always have. And I'm glad Eric thought to stay with him because honestly, Riley wasn't the only reason I chose to stay so close to home. I'd hate to think what his life would become if we were both far away.

Bacon sits at the table. Literally *at* the table. He'd come with Riley to visit often and now they have a baby's high chair all set up for him. His favorite food? Bacon.

"Doesn't that make him a cannibal?" I ask.

Eric laughs. "It's not like he's a pig eating pig, D."

"Oh yeah."

RILEY SMILES UP at me on the walk back home. "Have I mentioned that I'm happy you're home?"

"A few times."

She squeezes my hand tighter. "It doesn't seem like enough."

"It is, babe. I'm just glad you're not shacked up with some other guy."

"Shut up," she says, her head throwing back with her laugh.

"Seriously, Ry. Were you tempted?"

"Not for a second."

"Anyone try?"

Her face falls, her nose scrunched a little.

I stop walking and turn to her, eyes narrowed. "Who?"

"Dylan, it's so not important."

I know it's not, but watching her squirm and seeing the blush form on her cheeks is fun. Regardless of how I felt when I left her, the time away had given me perspective. I trust her with our love. I trust her with my life. It won't stop me from acting like a dick just for shits and giggles though. I dip my head, looking into her eyes. "Riley. Name and address?"

She looks away, her cheeks getting redder. Fuck, she's cute. "He's just that student vet who volunteers at the shelter. You met him yesterday. Bryce…"

I keep a straight face, feigning an anger that doesn't exist. "He asked you out?"

She nods.

"And what did you say?"

"I said I was yours, Dylan."

I suppress my smile at her words. "And he left it alone?"

She nods again, her throat bobbing with her swallow. She's so nervous. So cute. "Swear he never brought it up again."

"And you still see him?"

"He's a volunteer, D."

"Right."

She grabs her phone from the pocket of her sweatshirt and starts typing away.

"What are you doing?"

"I'm sending him a text to warn him."

"About what?"

"I don't know. That he's probably going to wake up one day with a dildo glued to his ear."

I can't help but laugh. She puts the phone away and a second later, my phone chimes with a text from her—his name and address.

"He asked Heidi out at my party."

"He did?"

I nod. "And I like Heidi and I like him, so just don't do anything permanent, okay?" She leans up and kisses me once, and when her feet find the ground I just stare at her. At her perfect smile, her perfect messy hair, her perfect eyes, her perfect everything.

"You're being very understanding," I tell her. "And very forgiving of my future actions."

She shrugs. "It's because I know you, flaws and all, and I'm madly in love with you anyway."

WE SPEND THE rest of the day at home while I take in everything new about the place since I'd left. She'd chosen a color for the kitchen cabinets and had unscrewed, unhinged, cleaned, sanded and painted them all on her own thanks to something called Pinterest. I'd heard Cam talk about it in the past so I asked her what it was.

Guys.

This is really important.

If you ever read this... Never, under any circumstance, and I mean ever, ask your girl to show you her Pinterest. Ever.

SIX HOURS LATER, my eyes are bleeding. Not literally. But come on. There are only so many different techniques a throw can be thrown on a bed before it just looks like a fucking piece of fabric thrown on a shitty fucking bed.

I wonder if she ever thought that about cars.

"So you're into all this stuff now?" I ask, shutting the laptop screen to aide my bleeding eyes.

We turn to each other from our seats at the kitchen table. She shrugs. "Not really. I just do it when I'm bored. I thought *you* were into it!"

"What?"

"Yeah. You were asking all these questions and telling me to google stuff," she says.

"I was just trying to sound interested, Ry. Like you did with my car stuff."

"What?" she says.

"Huh?"

"Did we just waste…" she looks at the clock on the wall. "… six hours!"

I laugh. "I was trying to be nice!"

She stands quickly and stomps her foot. "You know what we could've been doing in those six hours?"

I get up, grab our mugs off the table and put them in the new dishwasher. "What would you rather be doing?" I ask, leaning back on the counter and facing her.

"Anything."

"Anything?"

"D. Seriously. I've puked stuff better than some of the prints on those boards. I'd rather wallpaper the house with Bacon. The dog *and* the food."

I laugh, my hands finding her waist before pulling her between my legs. "You know what I love most about you, Riley?"

She smiles "What?"

"Everything. You're so damn perfect."

Sighing, she says, "I'm far from perfect, Dylan."

"You're perfect for me."

"Then that's all that matters."

Riley

I'D LOVE TO say that we made the most of the two weeks he was back. We spent most of the time at home, in the bedroom or garage, keeping to ourselves. We did make an effort to see our friends and family, but mostly, we just wanted to be together. Alone. We drove, a lot, and we talked. He told me about what he'd done, leaving out details I'm sure would be too much for me to handle. And he told me about Dave—about the shenanigans they'd get up to. He did mention that Dave had changed a little while he'd been gone on medical leave. Most likely because he wasn't as close to any of the other guys as he had been with him. It makes sense, I told him. It would be lonely out there and without the presence of your best friend, it would be hard. I knew that first hand.

I told him about the brownie incident with the girls and how Heidi and I had gotten closer that night. He gave me a weird look that had me asking what he was thinking. "You guys didn't like… compare notes or anything?" I gagged a little, and then smacked his gut. He laughed. "I was just making sure," he told me. He may have found it funny. I didn't. In fact, I was pretty upset over it. I think maybe because the thought of him being with someone else, as long as and as often (puke) as him and Heidi… I can't even finish that thought. He knew how unsettled it made me feel—which, honestly wasn't hard to work out considering I didn't bother hiding it. He held me in his arms, and told me he loved me, and only me, and that I was being dumb. I waited until he was in the shower on his own and threw a bucket of cold water at him, followed by glitter. Because glitter solves everything. It sure as hell solved my bad mood.

He paid me back though, of course. Because the first rule of Mayhem is retaliation. He asked me to go out and get him something from the hardware store to fix our jammed windows. Want to know what it's like to walk into a hardware store and ask for a tube of Slip Airy Deep Sock-It? Trust me, you don't. I repeated it for the fifth time, my eyes moving to the note in my hand and back up at the three guys with confused faces staring back at me. Then it clicked for the youngest one. He repeated it over and over again. He even announced through the store speakers, "Rodney, please come to the front desk. We have a Slip Airy Deep Sock-It enquiry." They all seemed to be in on some kind of private joke as they typed on their computers, repeating the word over and over again, smirking and chuckling to themselves. It wasn't until the hundredth or so repeat of the product's name that it finally dawned on me.

Yeah.

I'm slow.

Slip Airy Deep Sock-It = Slippery Deep Socket = Wet vagina.

I kicked his ass when I got home.

He didn't stop laughing.

Not until he had my pre-flailing arms held behind my back, my chest sticking out in front of me. "We even now?" he asked, smiling down at me.

I called a truce. I had to.

Hey, don't judge. You've never been captured in the arms of Dylan Banks while his perfectly blue eyes looked down at you like he was ready to devour you. And devour me, he did.

✧ ✧ ✧

TIME IS AN asshole, I've decided.

The ticking and the consistency of it.

Because as much as I wanted it to slow down, it doesn't. In fact, the harder I wished, the faster it went. Until we're back here, standing hand in hand saying goodbye to each other. Only now we're at the airport. "I'm going to miss you, Banks."

"I'll miss you more, Hudson," he says, stepping forward and wrapping his arms around my waist. He lifts me off the ground, kissing me as he does. When he places me back on earth, he pulls away. "I'll be back before you know it, Ry."

"Promise?"

He nods.

I nod.

He kisses me once more.

And then he's gone.

Thirty-Nine
Dylan

THE TIME AWAY from Riley isn't as bad as it was the first time because a lot of it's on base, which means I have more contact with her. Still not as much as I'd want, which is every second of every day, but hey… it could be worse.

FOR SOME REASON, I'm not really sure why, but I'd become the target of all the guys' pranks. It started off as them streaking behind me on one of my many Skype calls to Riley, and then it kind of just escalated. I guess I'm a good target because I'd get unjustifiably pissed off after each one. I'm not used to being the target. I'm used to aiming the grenade, so to speak.

They could happen any time, anywhere. Some were stupid. Some were smart. Some were on the fly and some were planned. They included, but were not limited to: honking the tank horn while I was working under it, equaling a gash on my head. They put shaving cream over my clothes and then set it on fire—while I was sleeping. This one wouldn't have been so bad had they chosen anywhere else besides my dick because what's the first thing you do when you realize you're on fire? Try to put it out with your hand, that's what. This subsequently led to my new nickname: *Flaming Battered Cock.* They also poured hot sauce in my mouth while I was sleeping—the consequences of that are self-explanatory. They wrapped my bed in Saran wrap—while I was in it. They did a lot of things while I was sleeping, hence why I don't sleep much any more. There were a lot of water ones. You know… open doors… bucket of water. Open tank doors… bucket of water. Eat… bucket of water. Sleep… bucket of water. Breathe… bucket of fucking water. The worst one, though, just happened recently. There I was, sitting on the toilet, minding my business, pants down to my ankles, picture of Riley in one hand… you can imagine what was in the other when FLASH BANG.

A flash bang is exactly what it sounds like. It's a device that goes off with a flash and a bang… it's meant to be used to stun and disorientate the enemy. But when you're in fuck-knows-where, Afghanistan, in the middle of a warzone, a flash bang could easily be mistaken for many other things.

So, while my eyes tried to refocus and my ears rang, I did what anyone in my situation would do, I ran out—pants still around my ankles wondering what the fuck was going on. It's not until I heard the laughter of eleven men when realization set in.

So for three months I've been constantly looking over my shoulder. Well, more than I normally would.

Also, that last prank is on YouTube now. I've watched it. Conway was the mastermind; Leroy was the leader. One guess who was holding the camera. Yep. Dave.

Swear, there's no shame greater than running out of restroom, tripping over your pants and falling on your face while trying to hide your still semi-erect cock.

"It's not funny, Ry!"

Through the screen, she covers her mouth attempting to stifle her laugh.

"Ry!"

Now she's on her back, her hands on her stomach. Her laptop shifts, making the camera tilt so I'm looking at the ceiling, her laughter filling my ears.

"Ry!" I shout.

Slowly, she sits up, wiping her eyes as she does. "I need the link, babe."

"Not a chance."

She grabs her phone from the nightstand and crosses her legs beneath her. "I'll just get it from Dave," she says through a smile.

I shake my head, succumbing to the inevitable.

"Do me a favor, okay? Watch it when you're alone. I have enough shame to deal with."

"Promise," she says, her grin getting wider when her phone sounds. She reads the text quickly and looks back up at me. "So any more I should know about?"

"None that I haven't told you. Hey, you better not be relaying this back to the guys."

Her mouth clamps shut.

"Riley!"

"I'm sorry! It's too funny not to share."

I shake my head. "Babe! I need to talk to you. It's serious."

Her face falls. Then her eyes narrow. "What's her name and number? I'll fly over there and kick her ass!" she jokes.

I don't. "We got our orders."

She clears her throat, all humor gone. Then she picks up her laptop and brings it closer to her face. "What does that mean?"

"It means I'm coming home."

For a moment, I think the computer's frozen. It hasn't. But she has. Then, slowly, she lifts her hand to her mouth. "Home?"

I nod, a slight smile breaking through. "I'm coming home, baby."

"When?"

"I'll be home in a month. But I'll be on base, babe. Until my contract's up in a few months."

"What does that mean?"

"It means I can come home on weekends. I was thinking we could alternate. I'll come up one weekend, and you can come up the next? We can stay at a hotel close by."

Her smile is slow, like she's still trying to comprehend exactly what she's feeling. "That sounds amazing. Did you just find out?"

"No. I waited to tell you so time wouldn't go by so slowly."

"And when your contract's up? What happens then?"

I sigh. "I was hoping we could talk about it in person? Discuss our future then."

Her smile widens. "*Our* future."

✧ ✧ ✧

I DON'T SLEEP. I *can't.* I'm way too fucking excited. I told Riley we were leaving in a week. Well, two weeks of debriefing on base and then I'd come home to her. I lied. We leave tomorrow.

I wanted to surprise her.

She fucking hates surprises.

Apparently the other boys aren't as excited as I am because they're well and truly passed out for the night. Everyone but Dave who told me he was taking a piss over—I look at my watch—over an hour ago.

Sometimes, especially at night, "taking a piss" means "jerking off" so there's a little leeway in how much time should pass before worry should set in. An hour, though? That's way too fucking long. Even for Dave and *The Desperate Housewives.*

I get out of bed and slip on my shoes, before grabbing the 9mm and stepping out of the tent. I look around, trying to listen to the faint voices yards away, but I don't recognize any of them. Then I head to the toilet blocks, my eyes on my surroundings. It doesn't take long to find him sitting in a chair by himself. He's got his gun in one hand, piece of paper in the other. Slowly, I walk toward him, hoping not to spook him. "That's a long ass piss," I murmur, sitting on a chair opposite him.

He looks up, his eyes a complete contrast to mine. "Sorry, Lover. Didn't know you'd be waiting up for me," he says, using his weapon to scratch the back of his head.

I get more comfortable, ready to spend the night talking with him. Maybe it seems stupid considering everything I have waiting for me at home, but I'll definitely miss Dave. Actually, he's the only fucking thing I'll miss about being here. "I couldn't sleep," I tell him.

He gives me a half-hearted smile. "Yeah man, I bet you're excited to get home to your girl."

"Yep," I admit, unashamed. "She's going to lose her mind when she sees me. More than the last time."

"You didn't tell her you were coming?"

"I said I'd be home a week later than planned."

"She hates surprises. You know that?"

"*I* know that. How the fuck do *you* know that?"

He shrugs. "We talk."

"You talk?"

"A little."

"About?"

He chuckles, his eyes focused on the ground. "Girl stuff, Banks. Mainly what it's like to be bottom."

Shaking my head, I tell him, "I was thinking after things get settled for us back home, we'd love to visit you. Meet your mom and your brothers."

He looks up and for the first time, I don't see Dave the barely-man forced to be here. I don't see a scrawny, cocky Irish kid whose words are laced with constant jokes. I don't really know who I see. "You okay?"

"Mike sent me an email." He lifts the piece of paper in his hand, his gaze returning to his shoes.

"Yeah. He's second oldest, right?"

Nodding and kicking at the dirt, he says, "My old man got out of jail early. Came right to the house. Beat the shit outta Mom. Lucky school was on otherwise my brothers…"

"Jesus Christ, Dave." I lean forward and swallow the lump in my throat. "I'm fucking sorry, man."

He's silent for so long I think he's fallen asleep. Then he inhales deeply, his eyes moving to mine. "I don't fucking know…"

"Know what?"

"Anything," he says, dropping his head again. "I don't fucking know anything, Banks. I thought I did, but I don't. I thought I was doing the right thing—enlisting, deploying, taking care of my family, at least financially, and I thought it'd be enough but it's fucking not. I'm fucking here. They're there. I couldn't stop it from happening and there's this ache…" he says, a sob forcing its way out of him. His head bobs as he sniffs back his tears, tears twenty-one fucking years in the making. He holds his gun, barrel pointed to his heart. "…right in here. This pain I can't fucking take anymore. It's like fear and anger and fucking hurt and guilt. The fucking guilt is the worst!"

"Dave, man, you can't have known—"

"I should've been there!"

"But you were here," I remind him.

He ignores me. "And now I have to somehow go home and face them. Face my brothers and my beaten mom and know that they fucking hate me because I'm here, fighting someone else's war when there's already one in my own fucking home."

I watch him stand and begin to pace, every single justified emotion coursing through him.

Fear.

Anger.

Hurt.

Guilt.

"I fucking failed, Dylan!" he shouts, spit flying from his mouth.

"Shut up. You did—"

"I can't fucking go home, man. I can't face them."

I stand up, panic clear in my words. "You can stay—"

"I can't!" He looks up at me, his tear soaked cheeks reflecting the moon… his childish innocence portrayed in his loud cries. "I don't know…" he says again.

I take a breath, and then another, my entire body shaking. "Know what?" I whisper.

His shoulders square, his lips pressed tight, he looks right in my eyes.

Then he lifts his gun.

My stomach drops.

My hands reach out.

And I don't know what's louder—my shout of his name or the gun going off—but I'll never, ever, forget the sound that follows.

Silence.

Part II
The Breaking

Forty
Riley

"I FEEL LIKE my face is on fire!" I yell.

Heidi laughs, continuing to apply whatever the hell concoction she just made up. A face peel, apparently. Which, by the way, just seems like the dumbest name for a beauty product in the history of the world.

"It stops burning after a few seconds," Mikayla says.

I open my eyes to try to look at her, only to be told to keep them shut by Heidi. "You're twenty-one, Ry. Surely this isn't the first time you've had one. Didn't your mom own a salon that did all this stuff?" She hasn't stopped laughing since I laid down on the floor in front of her surrounded by pizza boxes, wine, and enough fruity smelling products to give me an asthma attack. I don't even have asthma.

"My mom and I are of a different breed. Obviously."

Lucy adds, "My mom was a real homey type mom. You know, the one who had everything organized, drove all of us to our activities, never forgot an important date. The house was always clean and dinner was on the table at the same time every night. I think that's why I try to cook and stuff—because I want to be like her. I don't know how she did it—raised seven kids plus Dad. I can't even take care of Cameron."

Mikayla laughs. "Cam's the equivalent of ten children sometimes."

"I just want to make you pretty for when Dylan comes home next week," Heidi says.

"Are you excited?" Amanda asks.

"Excited and nervous and I don't know."

"Nervous?" Amanda says.

I smile. "When he came home for R&R, I had all these butterflies and I was so nervous. Dylan's so..."

"Intimidating?" Lucy asks.

I nod.

"So fucking hot," she responds.

We all laugh, then stop when we hear the key turn in the front door.

"We're all going to die," Amanda whispers, grabbing the item closest to her—a cushion.

"This is how all scary movies start," Mikayla says, eyes wide.

"And hot as fuck pornos," Lucy retorts.

I'd laugh, but I'm too busy wondering what the hell Amanda plans on doing with the cushion. Smother an intruder to death?

It's not until I hear Lucy gasp, her eyes on the entryway that I finally follow her gaze. With my face still burning, my eyes widen when I see Dylan standing in the doorway—his lips pressed tight, his shoulders rigid, and his eyes on all of us. He looks down.

"Hi," I whisper, a smile forming, cracking the peel on my face. "I thought..." I use Heidi's shoulders to help me stand. "I thought you weren't coming home for a week."

I pick at my shirt, wondering a: what he's doing here and b: how much of an ass I look like.

He doesn't respond though, he just walks further into the house, down the hallway and toward our bedroom.

"We should go," Heidi says, and I nod, too confused to give any other reaction.

I don't wait for them to leave before going to the bedroom and knocking. I don't know why I knock but I have this feeling in my gut that something's off. *Really* off.

There's no response so I quietly open the door and peek inside. He's sitting on the edge of the bed, his gaze distant. It's so different to the last time I did this. There's no happiness to see me, no lust filled eyes welcoming me. There's *nothing*. Not a single emotion on his face that lets me know he can even see me. "You came early," I say, moving inside just a step and leaning against the wall. My body's telling me to run to him, to kiss him, to hug him, to show him how much I've missed him. But my mind? My mind is telling me to stay put. And I have no idea why.

He bends down and slowly unlaces his boots.

I swallow nervously. "Did something happen or..."

He licks his lips as he looks up. Not at me, but through me. He still doesn't speak.

I try to fake a smile, and when I do, I'm reminded of the gunk on my face. "I'm going to shower," I tell him. "Then maybe I can heat up some food?"

He drops his gaze again and continues with his task of removing his shoes.

I take a breath. A loud one. One that has his eyes snapping to mine. And even though I know he can see me, he still doesn't speak. His eyes follow me as I move across the room and to the bathroom. I leave the door open as I switch on the shower and undress, letting him know he's welcome to join me. It's not until I'm in the shower, my face clear of the peel that I finally see him move. He kicks off his shoes, then removes his pants, and finally his shirts. It's all slow movements, like he's in no rush to join me. Then he just sits there, his head lowered again. When he must hear the shower switch off, he gazes up at me. With my naked body on full display, I step out from the fog of the shower. He stands, his footsteps slow as he approaches. Then he leans against the counter, watching me dry myself. He waits until the towel is wrapped around me before taking my hand. My eyes drift shut at the contact. I've missed him. But the man in front of me is not the man I've been looking forward to seeing. His eyes—so blue—once full of hope and humor… they've changed. In the few weeks since I'd spoken to him—*he's* changed.

Gently, he pulls me to him until my chest is flush against his, his breath warm on my forehead but his hand cold on my cheek as he tilts my head up, forcing me to look into his empty eyes. "Hey baby," he finally says, his voice weak.

With a shaky exhale, I lean up and kiss him. Slow and gentle, just like his touch. "I've missed you," I tell him.

He looks away. "Me too."

He holds me to him, his arms around my waist and his chin resting on my head.

"Why are you home early?" I manage to ask.

He doesn't respond, just holds me tighter.

"Are you hungry?"

"I'm tired, Ry," he says, releasing me. "I'm so fucking tired."

I take his hand and lead him to bed, my mind racing with so many thoughts I can't focus on one. He climbs on the bed and gets under the covers, his hands behind his head as he looks up at the ceiling. I remove the towel and stand still, just for a moment, trying to gauge his response. Again, there is none. His eyes, his body, his everything remain still. I walk over to the bedroom door, switch on the hallway light, and turn off the bedroom one, before making my way back to the bed, wondering the entire time what the right thing to do is. It's obvious his mind is elsewhere. It's also obvious he's not interested in me. I lie next to him, my arm around his waist and my leg over his while I rest my head on his chest. I wait for his hands to move, to touch me, even if it's not for sex but we've always, always fallen asleep in each other's arms but tonight… nothing.

He doesn't move.

Doesn't bring me closer.

Doesn't react to my naked body wrapped around his.

Almost four months he's been gone and nothing.

The childish, immature side of me wonders momentarily if there's someone else. But I know Dylan. He wouldn't. He *couldn't.*

Tears fall from my eyes before I can stop them because I don't know what the hell has happened to him and worse, I don't know how to fix it.

Three weeks.

It's only been three weeks since I last spoke to him. Since we made plans. Since we told each other we loved one another and that we missed each other and now this. What is *this*?

I wipe my eyes, hoping he doesn't realize, but the shaking of my shoulders gives me away. He sighs. Loudly. As if he's annoyed that I'm lying here, naked, in the arms of my boyfriend and I'm lost. I'm so damn lost.

"I'm just tired, Riley," he mumbles.

"That's all?" I ask.

He sighs again. Then he does something which causes my next flood of tears. He moves my arm and lifts his knees, pushing me off him before turning his back to me. "That's all," he mumbles. "Now leave it alone, okay?"

I don't know how long I lie in restless silence, eyes closed, fighting silent sobs, releasing silent tears, wondering how I went from laughing with the girls to trying to predict his next move, next words.

After a while, his phone rings. Silently, he reaches over me to get it from my nightstand. He doesn't even look at me when he answers, "Yeah?"

A slight pause. The male on the other end speaks, but his voice is low, muffled by Dylan's face. Another, "Yeah," from Dylan. Followed by an, "Okay."

He hangs up, throws the phone on the bed, then slowly gets up and moves toward the closet.

I sit up, holding the blanket to my naked chest. "What are you doing?"

"Going out."

I shift and start to get up too. "Who was it? Was it Dave? I want to meet him. I can be ready in five."

"No."

"No to what?" I ask, sitting on the edge of the bed now.

"No to all of it, Ry."

Ignoring the shattering of my heart, I whisper, "I thought you said you were tired."

He finishes shrugging on his jeans before looking at me, his jaw tense. "And I thought I said to leave it alone."

"Dylan…"

He puts on a shirt and then a hoodie. Then he sits on the edge of the bed and slips on his shoes. Sighing, he rubs his eyes with one hand, the other reaching for his phone. "Don't wait up, okay?"

"Is there someone else?" I blurt out. Because nothing makes sense. *Nothing.*

His shoulders tense, so does his entire body. "Jesus fucking Christ, Riley. This is the last goddamn thing I need. Especially from you. They're guys from my unit—"

"You just left your unit, Dylan," I interrupt. "I haven't seen you in months." I wish I was stronger. I wish my words came out stronger, too. But they don't. They're weak and pathetic and needy, which is exactly how I feel.

He inhales deeply, as if doing so will give him the calm he needs when he actually looks at me. But it doesn't do either of those things, because all I can see is anger. He shakes his head, his angry eyes on mine. But he doesn't speak. *Why the fuck won't he talk to me?*

Suddenly, he marches to the open bedroom door and slams it shut behind him. I cringe, listening to the rattle of the windows from the force of his actions.

Then another door slams—the front door. Followed by a screeching of tires out on the street. And then…

Silence.

I reach for my phone, my first impulse is to call Eric and ask him if he knows anything. If he has any advice that may help in the situation. But I don't. Instead, I start to type out a message.

Riley: *Dylan's Home*

I stare at the flashing cursor at the end of the words that once meant so much to me… now making absolutely no sense. This doesn't feel like *home.*

With tears blurring my vision, I delete the text and write another.

Riley: *Dylan's back.*

It still feels wrong. Because the man who just stormed out of the house isn't Dylan. I don't know who he is.

Riley: *He's back.*

Eric: *?*

Riley: *Dylan.*

Eric: *He is?*

Riley: *I think something's wrong, E. I don't know. Something's happened.*

Eric: *What do you mean? Is he hurt?*

Riley: *Not that I know of.*

Eric: *Ask him.*

Riley: *He's gone.*

Eric: *Gone where?*

Riley: *Out with some guys from his unit, I guess.*

Eric: *When did he get home?*

Riley: *A couple hours ago.*

Eric: *And he left you?*

Riley: *Yes.*

Eric: *Hold on.*

Dylan: *Really, Riley? You telling E about ourxbusiness? How close did you guys get while I was fuxking gone? Don't accuse me of shit when you'fe talking to my brother behind mycback.*

Riley: *I'm worried.*

After fifteen minutes of no response, I get out of bed, throw on some clothes and clean the living room, the kitchen, the bathrooms, the toilets, the garage, the everything. Because I'm lost.

So lost.

And scared.

I'm so damn scared.

IT'S AFTER THREE in the morning when I hear the front door open. I know because I'm sitting in bed, Kindle in my hand pretending to read like I've been doing for the past four hours. His footsteps are heavy as he trudges down the hallway, his body crashing into the walls. Muffled grunts belonging to two voices I don't recognize get louder as they approach the bedroom.

Dylan stops in the doorway held up by two other guys.

He's drunk.

Beyond drunk.

He doesn't even see me watching him, his head lowered as he takes the few steps to get to the bed, falling chest first into it.

"Hey Riley," one of the guys says. He's built like Dylan with dark skin and even darker eyes. He doesn't step foot in the room, just holds on to the doorframe. "Banks said we could crash in your guestroom."

The leaner guy standing next to him laughs.

"What did you do to him?" I ask, shifting my gaze from Dylan's passed out frame to them.

The darker guy struggles to stand upright, his hand going to his forehead in an attempted salute. "We didn't do anything, Ma'am Sir Ma'am," he almost shouts.

Frustrated, I kick off the sheets, ignoring Dylan's moan as I stand up.

"Nice legs," one of them says. I look up to see the leaner guy watching me, his eyes focused on my bare legs. "His pictures of you didn't do justice, Ma'am."

"Watch your fucking mouth, Leroy," Dylan mumbles, his words muffled by the bed. He still hasn't gotten up. His torso's on the bed, his knees are on the floor.

I grab spare blankets out of the linen closet and open the door to the guestroom. They thank me, politely, before moving to opposite sides of the bed. Leroy murmurs something about how good it'll be to sleep in an actual bed. I step into the room, closing the door behind me as they start to strip out of their clothes. "Did something happen over there?"

Leroy looks at me like I'm stupid. "Everything happens over there, Ma'am."

"Quit calling me Ma'am. I'm younger than you are."

He chuckles. "Sorry."

"Where's Dave?"

Leroy smirks. "What? We not good enough, Riley?"

"No." I shake my head. "I just assumed that he'd be… where is he?"

Conway answers. "Dave's… unavailable."

"What happened in the past few weeks—"

Leroy sighs, cutting me off. "Good night, Ma'am."

Forty-One
Dylan

"THANKS FOR LETTING us crash here for the weekend, Riley," Conway says as Riley places the plate full of bacon, eggs and toast on the table in front of me. Even though I refuse to look at her, I know she's watching me. I can *feel* it. She's probably wondering when it was exactly that she agreed to having two strange men stay in our house.

If I could find it in myself to look at her, to actually speak to her, I'd tell her the answer was never. She never agreed to it, but I had no choice. Besides, I wanted them here. Because they're the only ones who understood.

They called last night and asked if I wanted to escape. They didn't ask if I wanted to hang out, go drinking or go somewhere and fucking talk. They said *escape*.

So we did. We escaped to a bar full of military veterans who didn't fucking judge us. We drank and we drank and we drank some more, until the numb caused by the alcohol overpowered the fucking pain living and breathing in each of us.

But I felt it the most, and they knew that. I could tell by the way they looked at me, by the way they bought drink after drink after goddamn drink until I felt nothing.

And I wanted to feel nothing—especially after they kept patting me on the back, toasting to Dave and to me—his *best friend*. Every time they mentioned it I drank some more, praying that they were fucking wrong. Because I wasn't his best friend. I wasn't worthy of it.

If I was, I should've been able to stop him. But more than that, I should've been able to see it coming way before he bled his heart out to me.

All those times he wanted to talk. All those missed calls and messages I never fucking returned... He even sat and listened to me talk about Riley while he was fucking dying on the inside and he never said a word.

He shouldn't have had to.

I should've known.

"I have to get to work," Riley says, bringing me back to reality. "I'll be home just after five but I can come by on my break if you guys need anything."

"It's the weekend," I mutter and almost look up at her. *Almost.*

But what would I say?

How would she look at me?

"I've been working an extra day so I could get Fridays off for the next couple months... I wanted to drive down to see you earlier."

My guilt and my fear outweigh everything else. I keep my eyes lowered but wide fucking open. Because if I close them, there's darkness. And with darkness comes the need for light. And the only light I see is the one caused by his gun... right before he blew his fucking brains out.

One week.

He just needed to make it one fucking week and we could've survived the hell he thought would've been waiting for him at home. We could've done it together. Every single step.

Just one fucking week.

Why couldn't he fucking handle it?

I stand quickly and march to the bedroom, slamming the door shut behind me. I need space. I need time. I need fucking sleep.

"I'd just leave him, Riley," Conway says from the other side of the door.

"But if he's—"

Leroy cuts her off. "Just trust us, okay? We know what we're doing."

I'm glad they fucking think so, because I know nothing.

Not a goddamn thing.

✧ ✧ ✧

GRIEF IS LIKE a constant daze of a million fucking emotions and I don't want to feel a single one. But it's there. All of them. Eating away at my insides until all I want to do is fucking punch something. Maybe it's a bad idea to have my brothers here—in my personal space—because they just seem to make it worse. Seeing them, knowing what we've been through, knowing what we're one day going back to… I can't fucking handle it.

We sit in the living room, watching mind-numbing TV because we can't think of anything else to do that'll take our minds off the pain.

The news has stopped reporting the events that go on over there. Apparently it's not as important as some psycho chick in Texas claiming to have been impregnated by a fucking pig. Or a new flavor at Starbucks. Or Kanye. Who the fuck is Kanye? Whoever he is—he needs to get the hell off my television.

Conway and Leroy look up at me when the back door opens, their eyes as tired as mine. Then they shift to the empty packets of food and cans of soda splayed out all over the place. We probably should've cleaned up before Riley got home—but I can't find it in myself to care.

Riley seems to though. I can tell by the shock mixed with disappointment on her face as soon as she's in my vision. It only lasts a second before she smiles. I look away and focus on the TV again. Now some woman with a huge ass is standing next to that Kanye dick. *Great.* I almost yell, "*My fucking friend committed suicide serving this fucking country and this is the shit you come up with.*" I don't, of course, because that would make me insane.

Maybe that's what grief does.

Makes you insane.

And that doesn't even include the voices or the images plaguing my damn mind.

FROM THE CORNER of my eye I see Riley squat down, placing Bacon on the floor. He runs straight to me and parks himself on my lap. I don't know why he comes to me. I've barely spent time with the damn dog.

"Hey guys," Riley says quietly.

They both wave—adding a smile faker than hers. "'Sup, Ry?" Conway replies.

"I take it you guys have eaten?" she asks.

We nod simultaneously, then go back to watching TV. "*Kentucky Man Tries to Dig Up Dad So He Can 'Go to Heaven,'*" the reporter reads.

"What the fuck?" Conway mumbles.

Exactly, Conway. What the fucking fuck?

In the kitchen, I hear Riley opening and closing the fridge, and then doing the same with the cabinets. I'm pretty sure they ate everything in the house. Probably the only reason they stopped eating. She returns a moment later with her phone, keys and wallet in hand and another fake smile. "I'm going to the store to grab something for dinner. You guys want or need anything?"

Leroy says, reaching into his pocket, "A case of beer would go down well."

Riley freezes.

I sigh. "We don't keep alcohol in the house."

"Why?"

I stop stroking Bacon and point to Riley. "Recovering alcoholic."

Her gaze drops, her shoulders tense.

"Oh, shit," Conway chimes in. "Sorry."

"It's fine," Riley says. But there's a scowl on her face directed right at me.

I don't see what the big deal is. It's not like it's a fucking secret. Besides, I could use a drink.

"Is it all right to leave Bacon here?" she says.

"Bacon?" Leroy asks.

"Our dog," Riley replies.

"You named your dog Bacon?" he quips.

I sit up slightly. "*Her* dog. Not mine. And she fucking named him."

"I'll be back," Riley says.

Leroy waits until we hear the front door close and Riley's car start in the garage before turning to me. "Riley's a nice girl, Banks."

"I know that," I say quickly.

"Do you? Because you're kind of being an ass."

My eyes snap to his and whatever he sees has his hands going up in surrender. "Sorry, man. Not my place."

"I fucking hate Kanye," Conway says, changing the subject.

They go back to watching the television, and I go back to drowning in a million different emotions. But there's one that never seems to fade, always forefront, always leading the charge.

Guilt.

Riley

EVEN THOUGH IT wasn't a lie—that I am a recovering alcoholic—Dylan's never used that term before. Not to me, and hopefully not to anyone else. It hurt. It hurt so damn much that now I'm sitting in my car—a car he *made* me—crying my eyes out in the almost empty parking lot at the store.

I can't be angry, I try to convince myself, because he's not being himself.

"It isn't you," I whisper, wiping the tears off my cheek. I flip the visor and check my face in the mirror. "It isn't you," I repeat, looking at the sad, broken eyes staring back at me.

If I say it enough, I might finally believe it.

I take my time in the store, not in any rush to go back to what awaits at the house. I push the cart aisle by aisle without really seeing anything through the tears clouding my vision. I grab enough food and snacks to feed an army—or three Marines—and make my way to the register. Still slow. Still avoiding.

"How you going, Riley?" Sally, the elderly clerk, asks.

I fake another smile. Maybe if I smile enough, I might finally believe I have a reason to do it.

She turns to me, clueless of my heartbreak. "How's that boyfriend of yours doing?"

"Good," I lie.

"You tell him we appreciate his service."

"Yes, Ma'am." I smile and nod.

She continues to make small talk as she checks out all the items. *Her brother's cousin's son's girlfriend's sister's boyfriend is a marine. Does my boyfriend know him? Am I having a party? What's with all the food? Did I see the game over the weekend? Am I still swimming? There's a sale on canned green beans if I wanted to stock up.*

I want to roll my eyes.

I want even more to tell her to shut the hell up.

I do neither.

I stand.

I nod.

I smile.

I wait.

Which is exactly the same thing I do around Dylan. Because anything else would mean I'm letting the pain win.

I keep it together, just long enough to get out of the store and push my cart to my car. And then I let it out. Again and again. Over and over. Sob after sob. Tear after endless tear.

Then a message comes through on my phone.

Dylan: *You been gome forever.*

Riley: *Leaving the store now, babe. I'll be home soon.*

Dylan: *K. You get beers?*

I inhale deeply, waiting for the calm to set in. It doesn't.

Riley: *Yes.*

Then I go back into the store, buy a case of beer which is forbidden in *our* home, and listen to Sally tell me about her cat's urinary tract infection.

I cry the entire drive home—only stopping when I pull into the garage. And then I repeat the same process I had when I got to the store. I wipe my tears, tell myself that it isn't me. That it can't be.

I CARRY THE case of beer, struggling to unlock the back door, and walk into the living room. Nothing's changed. "Here," I say, opening the box and handing them one each.

"You're the best, Riley. Honestly," Conway says, reaching into his pocket. He pulls out his wallet but before he can do anything, Dylan interrupts.

"We got it." He looks up at me, his right hand stroking Bacon. "Can you put the rest in the fridge?"

I'm getting really sick of fake smiling. "Sure."

Once all the beers are put away, Conway walks into the kitchen, trashing his empty bottle. I reach into the fridge and grab another one for him but he declines. "I was just seeing if you needed help bringing any bags in."

"Please."

It takes both of us two trips to bring in all the groceries. He helps put them away before turning to me. "I take it this food's for us?" he asks.

I nod.

"We really don't want to inconvenience you in any way," he says.

"It's no problem. Make yourself at home."

"We're assholes. We ate all your food and didn't even think about you. I really am sorry." I can tell by the plea in his eyes that he means it. "It's been a while since we've had access to that much food, you know? Occasionally we'll get packages but they don't last long between twelve men so…"

I shrug. "It's honestly fine."

He nods, his hands going in his pockets. But he doesn't leave. He just stands there, as if waiting for me to say something more. I don't. Finally, he breaks. "My parents moved up north when I left for basic. My girlfriend broke up with me while I was deployed. We shared a house. Now she's living with her new boyfriend and I kind of got nowhere to go so Dylan's really helping me out here…"

I turn around and run the water into a pot so I can start on my dinner. "I'm glad," I tell him over my shoulder. "Not about the girlfriend thing. I'm sorry about that. I meant that Dylan's able to help you out. He's a good man."

And right on cue, Dylan walks into the kitchen holding Bacon under his arm like a football. He doesn't speak, just opens the fridge, grabs another beer, and walks back out.

I switch my gaze back to Conway.

He shrugs. "You need help with dinner?"

"It's fine. I was just going to make pasta real quick."

He grins from ear to ear and rolls up his sleeves. I don't think it's me he's smiling about. I think it's the prospect of more food. "Put me to work, boss," he says.

I tilt my head, eyeing him curiously. If something as simple as food can make him happy, then why doesn't it do the same for Dylan?

Why can't I make him happy?

WE EAT THE pasta at the kitchen table after Conway clears it of all the other trash it was covered in. Leroy and Conway talk about the news they'd just seen. Dylan stares at his untouched plate. I stare at him. Then suddenly, he stands. "I'm going to bed," he announces to no one in particular. He grabs another beer before he leaves, leaving me sitting with two people I know nothing about. I quickly finish my meal, tell them to leave everything and that I'll take care of it in the morning.

DYLAN'S ALREADY IN bed, facing the wall when I enter the bedroom.

I go straight to the bathroom and turn on the shower. I spend as long in there as I did in the store and ignore the fact that he is now sitting on the edge of the bed watching me. And I avoid the thoughts running through my head—the million questions I'm too afraid to ask.

I step out when the water turns cold, reaching for the towel before I'm even fully out. I dry myself, my back turned to him. Watching him watch me would be too much, too intimate, and intimacy is the last—or maybe the *only* thing I want.

I can't decide.

"Riley," he says, his voice deep and demanding. I can feel him behind me, feel his heavy breaths on my neck.

Slowly, I turn to him, grasping my towel tighter.

I look into his eyes, look for a sign of what he's feeling, what he's wanting.

He gives nothing.

I move around him and stand in front of the mirror, forcing the tears away. "It's good to see you're getting on well with Bacon," I murmur. "He really missed you while you were gone."

"What the fuck is that supposed to mean?" he barks.

I shut my eyes, searching for strength. Searching for calm.

"What do you want from me, Riley?" His voice is loud. So loud it echoes off the walls. He grasps my shoulders, my eyes snapping open at his harsh touch. He spins me around, forcing me to face him. He stares down at me and slowly, the scowl fades and his grip loosens along with his shoulders.

He licks his lips, his eyes on mine. I watch the rise and fall of his chest as his head dips, his nose brushing against mine and I release a sob I'd been holding since I walked into the room. "Is this what you want?" he whispers, his hands moving from my shoulders, down my side and to my waist. His touch is soft, giving me the calm I'd been dying for. He presses his lips, soft and wet against mine, catching my bottom lip between his. I melt into him, into his touch, into his arms, into the single moment of affection I'd been searching for. His lips part, his tongue sliding across mine as he pushes into me. His hands are on my neck now, holding me to him as he strokes my jaw with his thumb. "Is it?" he asks.

I tilt my head up, my mouth desperate for the kiss. "I want you," I tell him, my palms flat on his bare chest, moving lower and lower. I finger the band of his boxers, his mouth hungry against mine. Then I reach beneath the fabric like I'd done so many times before. Only this time, it's different.

He's not turned on. Not even the slightest.

His muscles tense, his hands on my neck releasing me quickly.

My eyes snap open and land on his. Eyes locked—his with anger, mine with fear.

It is me.

"Fucking shit!" he yells.

"It's not a big deal." I try to calm him down. "It's—I'm—you probably have a lot on your mind, baby." I grasp his face, watching the anger ignite… from his eyes to the rest of his body.

"Fuck!" he shouts, raising his fist.

I cower, my eyes squeezing shut, right before a gust of air hits the side of my face and the sound of shattering glass fills my ears.

I gasp for breath, my tears instant.

Bacon barks.

The bedroom door opens, slamming against the wall behind it.

Dylan pushes my hands away just as Conway and Leroy appear in the bathroom doorway.

I grip my towel tight, my eyes wide and on the floor. My heart, my poor, erratically beating heart…

I cover my mouth, muffling my cry.

"Are you okay, Riley?" Conway says.

I look up at him… my entire body shaking with fear. "I'm fine," I manage to get out. "It was just an accident."

He nods before looking at Dylan. "Dude. Maybe—" He doesn't get a chance to finish before Dylan storms out, roughly pushing him out of the way. He puts on pants and shoes and nothing else and a second later, a door slams shut and his truck roars to life. His tires screech, and what follows is a sound I've come to fear.

Silence.

All but for our heavy breaths, mixed in the tiny room.

"He's been through a lot," Leroy tries to reason.

"I just need to be alone."

Conway pushes Leroy out of the room and away from me. "We'll be out here if you need anything."

AFTER DRESSING QUICKLY, I find tape in one of the kitchen drawers and use it to keep the broken pieces of the mirror in place. Then I clean up the mess on the bathroom counter and floor. When I get back out, Leroy and Conway are tidying the living room of the mess they'd made earlier. I find myself cleaning up after them. The living room, the kitchen, the guest bathroom, and the fridge because apparently cleaning is my replacement for drinking.

"My mom cleans when she's upset," Conway says, leaning on the counter next to the sink as I wash the dishes.

"I'm not upset," I tell him.

"Leroy and I were talkin'. We thought maybe we could take Dylan to a hotel or something, just for the night—"

"What?" I ask, my fear turning to confusion. "Why would you do that?"

"Just to give you space, Riley. For him to find—"

"But this is his home," I whimper, patting my chest with my wet hand. "*I'm* his home."

Conway doesn't seem to believe me.

And neither do I.

He pats my shoulders as he walks past. "Good night, Riley. Thank you for everything."

I wait until he's gone before opening the fridge and grabbing a beer.

Just one, I tell myself.

I need it to dull the ache.

DYLAN RETURNS A few hours later, his entire frame freezing when he sees me sitting in the middle of the bed staring at the unopened bottle of beer.

I couldn't do it—not after everything we'd been through to get me here.

I can feel him approach, but I don't take my eyes off my temptation. He leans over the bed, grabs the beer and takes it away. "I went for a drive," he says, walking out of the bedroom. I hear the fridge door open and close and his footsteps returning. He sits on the bed, right in front of me, legs crossed just like mine, but I'm too afraid to look at him. "It wasn't the same without you, Ry." He takes one of my hands in his, the other going to my chin, forcing me to face him. The anger in his eyes is no longer there. Now replaced with sympathy and regret. I wish I could believe him. "I missed you riding in my truck, sitting in the middle of the seat like you always do." The corners of his mouth lift as he wipes my tears, adding, "I had nowhere to put my hand."

I ignore how his touch makes me feel, how his words seem to remove the effects of his actions. "Dylan, you can't just do what you did, then come back and act like it never happened," I say, the shakiness of my voice defying the strength I needed to fake.

He just stares at me, all emotion wiped from his features.

"Babe," I beg. "You have to give me something here. I don't know what happened." I reach out to cup his face, but before I can even touch him, he pulls back.

For a split second, the fury flames in his eyes again but it disappears as soon as he must see the hurt in mine. He studies me, for seconds that feel like minutes, he just looks at me. "I'd never hurt you, Riley," he says, his voice barely a whisper. He releases a single tear, letting it fall, bringing my defenses with it. "You know that, right?"

"I know, baby." I spring forward, my arms going around his neck, his going to my waist.

We hold each other tight, finally succumbing to the exhaustion of our emotions.

And I fall asleep in the safest, most dangerous way possible; in the arms of a boy I love, a boy I no longer know.

Forty-Two
Riley

I WAKE UP to the sounds of Dylan moving around the room, his footsteps heavy. The bed dips, causing me to open my eyes. He's sitting on the edge of the bed, fully dressed, slipping on his shoes.

"You're leaving?" I ask, checking the time on my phone. It's barely seven in the morning. We'd only been asleep for a few hours.

After sighing loudly, he says. "Since you found it so necessary to tell Eric I was back, they want to see me." He glances at me quickly. "You coming?"

It's hard not to feel the sharpness of every word spat, each one used to create a wound in my already shattered heart. My voice timid, I answer, "Do you want me to?"

He shakes his head and looks up at the ceiling. "It'd be pretty pathetic if I showed up without you, right?"

I quickly get ready and fake another smile as he tells the guys we'll be back and to make themselves at home—as if they weren't already doing that. I take Bacon with us, because I don't trust him with them, and we get in his truck and drive, me sitting in the middle—both his hands on the steering wheel. I'm glad he chose not to walk, because I don't think I could handle all that silence.

He turns to me as he puts the truck in park. I can tell he wants to say something and I'm almost positive of what it is. *Keep faking it, Riley.* So I do. I grasp his hand as he opens the front door to the house and smile beside him like the perfect girlfriend I'm supposed to be, but inside… I'm slowly dying, and right now, all I can think about is running back to my room—not *ours*, but *mine*—and letting my emotions get lost in an entire bottle of wine. Or four. Because I miss everything we created in the four walls of that room when the darkness of my grief overshadowed everything else. Until he showed up.

IT DOESN'T TAKE long for everyone to fall into a natural routine after the initial greetings. We sit at the kitchen table—Bacon in his high chair—and we eat. Eric, Mal and Sydney talk. We listen. Occasionally they'll ask something of us. We reply as best we can. Dylan takes my hand resting on the table and holds it in his.

Keep faking it, Riley.

"What happened to your hand?" Sydney asks, pointing to Dylan's hand. I hadn't even noticed the cuts and bruises until she mentioned it.

Next to me, Dylan tenses. I cover his hand with mine, hiding the evidence, but it's too late.

"Did you get into a fight?" Eric asks him.

"No," Dylan snaps.

Sydney stands up and gently moves my hand, inspecting the cuts. I let her. Because the alternative would've caused more problems. Or so I thought.

"Is that glass?" she says, but it's not a question.

"Dylan?" Mal asks.

He pulls his hand away and hides it under the table. "It's fine."

"No it's not, D. If it's glass you need to get it taken out. Let me look at it." Sydney's waving her hand in front of him. "I've got a first aid kit. I can do it here."

And Dylan loses it. Really, truly, loses it. "I said it's fine, Sydney! Leave it the fuck alone!"

"Don't fucking talk to her like that. She's just trying to help you," Eric yells. He's on his feet now, walking around the table to Dylan. I look down at my plate, my heart hammering in my ears because I know what's going to happen next. I can feel it.

"Fuck this," Dylan spits, standing so quickly his chair tips and falls to the floor. "I don't fucking need this shit! I knew I shouldn't have come here!"

"What the fuck is your problem, man?"

I cringe at the loudness of both their voices.

"Fuck you, Eric!" Dylan roars.

And I don't see what happens next. I don't want to. I shut my eyes and keep them that way. Even when I hear the scuffle go on next to me.

Even when I feel a body press to my side. Even when Mal and Sydney's screams become louder than the pulse pounding in my ears.

"Enough!" Mal shouts so loud my ears ring.

I finally open my eyes and lift my gaze. Eric's on the floor, leaning against the kitchen cabinets while Sydney attends to his bloody nose and cut lip. Dylan's arms are being held back my Mal, his chest rising and falling, his eyes burning with the same anger that created the cuts on his knuckles.

Dylan shrugs out of his dad's hold, his eyes still on Eric. "Let's go, Riley," he says, grabbing his keys from the table.

I look back down at my plate and stay silent. I do nothing. I feel nothing.

His voice is further away when he repeats his words, even angrier than he was.

I cringe, but I don't move.

"Fuck this. You can fucking walk home!" He slams the front door and a second later, I hear his truck rev, tires screech, and then he's gone.

Slowly, I stand up and pick up Bacon from his seat, feeling the intensity of three sets of eyes on me.

Eric gets up, going after me as I start to leave the room. "Riley," he says, his hand on my arm freezing me to my spot.

With a gentle touch I crave from his brother, he turns me to him. His head moves from side to side, his eyes scanning me from head to toe. "Riley, if Dylan is hurting you… I mean, physically…" He doesn't finish his sentence. He can't. The thought itself is incomprehensible.

I shake my head quickly, hoping it's enough to convince him that Dylan's not. And then I drop my gaze, because I don't want him to see the fear in my eyes—the one that says that even though he's not… *yet*… it doesn't mean that I'm not terrified he will.

"Sweetheart," Mal says, "you're always welcome to come here."

Sydney adds, "You can always call me, or *us*, any of us. Anytime. No matter what."

I bite my lip to stop the sob from escaping, but I can't do the same with my tears. I force myself to look up at them. I want nothing more than to hug them, to kiss them, and to tell them how grateful I am that they've accepted me into their family. That they loved me like Dylan did… but I don't. Because doing so would mean that I'm admitting it's over. And it can't be over.

He's only been back for two days.

Two stupid days.

Keep faking it, Riley.

"Thank you for breakfast. I'll see you soon."

DYLAN'S SITTING ON the couch in the living room with his buddies when I get back home. I don't speak to any of them. I simply go to my room, shower and get to work early.

The work day goes by quickly, unfortunately, while I dodge the million text messages from Sydney asking if I'm okay. If I want to hang out after work. If I want to see a movie. If I want to have a good old fashioned slumber party. I don't want any of those things. What I want is my fucking boyfriend back.

I want it so badly that I do something I've never done before. Something so extreme and stupid. I go to the store, pick out a cupcake and a single candle. I light it in the car with Bacon on my lap. And just like I did the last two times I'd done this—I wish for Dylan.

My Dylan.

I DON'T GET my wish because the house is exactly the way it was the day before. It's a fucking mess. Only now the place smells like beer—maybe because of all the empty bottles around the room—some on the floor, spilled over and soaking into our brand new carpets. They're all facing the TV playing a car racing game on a PlayStation. A PlayStation we didn't have yesterday.

I greet them quickly and keep Bacon in my arms as I make my way into the kitchen. I make dinner for myself, happy they at least left me something, and eat alone in the bedroom, wishing for a moment that I'd taken up any one of Sydney's offers. When I'm done, I go back out to the kitchen, ordering Bacon to sit and stay in his bed so I can start to clean the mess they'd created. I clear every surface I can see throughout the house, swiftly moving around their lazing bodies in the living room and trashing what I can. Three trash bags later, I roll up my sleeves and start on the dishes. I've started doing it by hand for some reason—maybe because I find it therapeutic. That's when Dylan decides to walk in, leaning against the counter next to me, his arms crossed.

I don't speak.

Speaking seems to make it worse.

"I tried to use my bank card today. It got declined."

My shoulders tense. Not because I'd done anything wrong, but because of his accusatory tone. I don't look at him. Just continue with the dishes. "I transfer your wage into the mortgage to offset the interest."

"So you don't have to pay your share, you mean?"

I push down the lump formed in my throat. "No, Dylan. I still pay the same amount. Half, sometimes more."

"Whatever," he mumbles, pushing off the counter.

I drop the plate in my hand and finally face him, trying to keep my emotions in check. "I thought I was doing the right thing," I tell him. "We can still access the money in our mortgage. I just thought it would be good to—"

"*My* mortgage, Riley. It's *my* house."

My jaw drops, just slightly, my eyes instantly filling with tears.

"Fuck, baby," he murmurs, pulling me into him. "I didn't mean that. I'm sorry."

He's angry one minute. Sorry the next.

Regretful one minute. Frustrated the next.

He's a million different emotions wrapped in irritability.

"Did you hear me?" he asks quietly, holding me tighter. "Did you?" he asks again, a little louder, a little firmer.

I glance at the fridge longing for the alcohol stocked inside.

"Ry," he says, trying to get my attention. "We're going to take off. Head back to base."

I switch my focus to him. "Now?"

He kisses the top of my head. "We've been waiting for you to get home so I could say goodbye."

I try to contain my tears. Try to stay strong. For the same reason I kept all those letters to myself. For *him*. "Okay."

Forty-Three
Dylan

THERE WAS A ceremony the moment we landed—one I hadn't invited Riley to. I'd only be able to see her for a few hours before having to leave her again and a few hours wouldn't have been enough. I don't regret the decision.

The next day the debriefings started. Meetings and classes focused on making sure you handle your PTSD, make you aware that you're on home soil and not to fucking kill anyone, and specifically, don't fucking kill yourself.

My unit had a private class that basically went: What happened to Dave O'Brien was unfortunate, don't let it happen to you.

It wasn't until when Leroy, Conway and I were sitting around talking shit that things became clearer. At least for me.

"I'm not saying this to be an asshole, so don't take it the wrong way, but obviously Irish was fighting demons. Ones we had no fucking clue about. All I'm saying is that it made sense he did it there, you know? The day before we were supposed to leave. If he'd done it at home, the military may not have covered his funeral costs and his family may not have been eligible for the death gratuity payment. Not for suicide. There'd be a shit ton more red tape and they'd probably have to fucking fight for it. Besides, this way, he gets to go home a hero," Leroy said.

I requested leave the next day. I wanted it in time for the funeral but they couldn't make it work. Now, two and a half weeks later, I finally get to see him.

✧ ✧ ✧

I'D BEEN TO a military cemetery before. Once. With my dad. I was seven. I had no idea what it meant or what I was doing there. At that age, there were only two things on my mind. Why did Dad make me dress like him and why was every plot exactly the same?

Now, I'm older, a little wiser, but the relevance of those thoughts are still the same.

I follow the guard's instructions until I find the fresh dirt sitting six feet above Davey's dead body. My steps are slow as I approach, glass jar in my hand containing words I hope hurt him as much as he hurt me. After placing it in front of the white cross, I sit with him, in silence, because really? What else is there left to say?

✧ ✧ ✧

DAVE RARELY SPOKE about his home life on a personal level. He talked about his brothers, the kind of kids they were and what they were into, and he spoke a lot about his mom. But never his actual home or the area he grew up in.

I don't think anyone ever wants to admit they're ashamed of their upbringing, so they kind of just choose to ignore the facts instead.

I did it a lot with Heidi and it sucked. Not because I was ashamed of my dad or brother or the way he raised us but given the way Heidi lived in comparison, I was definitely on the low end of the economic scale. I guess when you're fifteen, you look at the world differently. She had a nice white mansion with both caring parents who'd spend money on her in a drop of a hat. I'm sure, if asked, my dad would've too, but we were raised to believe that material things weren't important and what we looked like on the outside didn't determine who we were on the inside. I'm not saying that Heidi's like that, I'm just saying that the younger version of me was afraid I wouldn't be enough for her, and that maybe the older version of me continued to believe that.

Maybe that's where we went wrong.

THE HOUSES THAT line the roads leading to Dave's become smaller and more congested, from single story homes to apartments to larger complexes created for public housing.

I drive around the block a few times, confused by the numbers until I finally find his complex. I park the rental on the side of the road and make sure I've locked the car. There are way too many buildings, too many numbers, and I find myself standing in the middle with absolutely no direction.

"Need help?" a female voice sounds from behind me.

I turn swiftly, trying to hide my reaction to the girl standing in front of me. She can't be more than fifteen, wearing a crop top, no bra, cigarette in her mouth and the kind of devilish grin I'd seen from the classy females in the veteran's bar.

I tell her the house number I'm looking for. She points to a building behind me. "Third floor," she says with a thick Pittsburgh accent.

After thanking her politely, I make my way to the O'Brien's door, remove my hat, and I knock.

My heart drops the minute Dave's mom answers. The cuts and bruises that cover her face are faded, but they're still there. And even if I hadn't seen pictures of her from Dave, there's no mistaking who she is. Same red hair. Same freckles. Same damn smile. "Dylan Banks?" she asks, her hand going to her mouth.

"Yes, Ma'am."

"He told me if anything would happen, you'd be the first to check in on me," she cries, opening the door wider for me.

I don't step in. Not yet. Instead, I find myself reaching out to her, my arms going around her thin, frail body and I hug her. I continue to hug her as her cries get louder and my heart becomes weaker. After a while, she pulls back, grasping my arms as she looks up at me. "You were his best friend, Dylan." She cups my face with both hands. "How are you handling it?"

I stare, unblinking, wondering how it is a woman who's just lost her pride and her eldest son in the worst possible way can possibly be thinking of anyone or anything but the hurt and the pain, because that's *all* I've felt.

THE BOYS ARE at school, which is good because it gives us time to sit and talk.

They hadn't always lived like this, she tells me. They had to move somewhere they could afford once Dave's dad went to jail. Dave gave the majority of his income to his mother while he was serving and never once asked for anything in return. It wasn't much, but she made it work. With three boys in school, it was hard to keep up with all the bills. A single bedroom public housing home was all they could afford. The boys share the room. She sleeps on a mattress in the hallway, and Dave took the couch whenever he was home.

It's strange, the way she spoke about it. There was pride in her voice, in her demeanor—the way her shoulders sat straight and her chin lifted as she told me about things I would consider hardships—only she didn't consider them that. She considered them battles, ones that she came out of alive and fighting, waiting for the next hurdle to cross.

She's an amazing woman, strong and defiant and not once did she use the term "suicide" or the fact that Dave took a bullet to his own fucking head. The closest she came to it was "*he lost his battle*" and maybe that's what it was. Maybe that's how she chooses to honor him.

He lost the damn battle.

Now I just need to stop reliving the sight and sound of it and maybe I can overcome it too. Because as we sit on the well-used couch of the tiny living room, pictures of Dave staring back at me, all I can see is the fear in his eyes, his finger as it pulls the trigger, and then the blood as it erupts from the side of his fucking head.

✧ ✧ ✧

I ONCE TOLD Riley that war was like being unable to wake up from a nightmare. Your body fights it, so does your mind, until something happens that forces you to wake up.

War is what you wake up to.

And it's also the cause of the nightmares.

And so it goes.

On and on.

And on.

An endless cycle of nightmares.

I don't sleep.

Because just like the times when I first came home, the nightmares are real and they're raw and they cause me to plead with my body to keep my eyes open because a single moment of darkness creates the hell in my mind.

✧ ✧ ✧

Dave,
I think I hate you.

Do you even know what you did?

You left your mom and your brothers behind.

You left me behind.

And I hate you because you haven't really left me. It's like everything I do now, I think about you and how you would react to it. What would you say to me?

I know you hate me.

I can tell from all the guilt I carry.

Not from the guilt of not knowing you were suffering, because I've come to terms with the fact that you were just really fucking good at faking it. I don't know why you faked it. You should've known I'd be there. Sometimes I think there were signs, you know? And in my mind I go through all the conversations we'd had and all the things we'd done and I come up blank.

It's the guilt from the way I treat Riley.

Because I see you.

I hear you.

You make me hurt her.

You and your inability to leave me the fuck alone.

Yeah.

I don't think.

I'm positive.

I fucking hate you.

Forty-Four
Riley

I ASKED HIM on the Monday if I should book the hotel for the following weekend or if he had one in mind. He told me he'd get back to me with the details. Four days later he finally replied with an address. I reminded him that I'd taken Fridays off for a while so I'll be at the hotel as soon I could check in. I told him that I missed him. And that I loved him. Because I felt it important for him to know… just in case he'd forgotten.

NOW, IT'S CLOSE to midnight on the Friday and I'm sitting alone in the hotel room he told me to go to. He should've finished at the car pool on base at five, according to his dad, and would have been able to leave soon after. The base is a twenty-minute drive away. At the most.

I look down at my feet kicking back and forth on the edge of the bed, my hands clasped on my lap and my heart in my stomach. I listen to the sounds of my quiet cries echo off the walls of the tiny room and I go through the hundred questions rattling in my head. The same ones which have been there every minute, every hour, slowly stealing every ounce of sense and strength he'd once given me.

Riley: *I love you. I miss you. I'm here. I hope you're okay, baby.*

I spend the next morning doing exactly the same thing I did the night before. Sitting on the bed, missing the boy I love. Multiple voices from outside my room have my ears perking and my mind racing. My phone beeps with a text and I rush toward it, my hands shaking as I read it.

Dylan: *Room?*

Riley: *208.*

I open the door and pop my head out, moving side to side. The voices get louder. And then I see him walking toward me, his hand around the straps of an overnight bag with Leroy and Conway behind him. I step out completely, leaning against the door to keep it open. I swear, for a second, I see him smile. But then he murmurs a "hey" as he walks past me and into the room and I know I imagine it. I had to have.

Conway and Leroy nod, say my name in greeting, and continue their walk down the hallway. I take a breath, my gaze on my feet and I try to prepare myself for the unknown. As slow as possible, I step back in the room and close the door behind me. Dylan's in bed, his back turned. "Hi," I say, my lips trembling.

He rolls onto his back, his eyes on the ceiling.

I stand on the other side of the bed, one foot on top of the other, forcing myself to stay, and not run away like I really want to. Four and half hours and I can be home. *Home.* I don't even know what home is anymore. I thought it was him. I thought I was his. But now…

"Ry," he says, his voice low. He places his hand out toward me as he closes his eyes. "Thank you."

I stand. Still. Not knowing what to do.

"Please, Ry," he begs, his hand raised and his sad, tired eyes on mine. "I'm so tired," he mumbles. "Just let me hold you."

I take his hand, my knees on the bed as he sits up, his arms going around my waist. He kisses my neck. "I missed you, baby," and just like that—those simple words—my defenses drop, my fear fades, and I give myself over to him.

Because I love him.

And I miss him.

Even when he's right in front of me.

FOR HOURS I lay with him while he sleeps peacefully next to me, until someone bangs on the door, and he sits up quickly, reaching first to his ankle then to the nightstand.

"Banks!" *Bang bang bang.*

Dylan sucks in a breath, his feet thumping on the floor as he sits on the edge of the bed. His hands go to his head, pressing tight against his ears. With my heart racing, I come up behind him and place my hand gently on his shoulders. He flinches, moving away from me.

"Banks!" *Bang bang bang.*

"Fuck off!" Dylan yells.

"Ten minutes. Let's go," Conway shouts on the other side of the door.

Dylan stands quickly, moving to the bathroom. Over his shoulder, he says, "Get ready."

"Okay." I shuffle out of bed and follow him to the bathroom where he's splashing water on his face. I stand next to him, reaching for my hair brush. When he's done, he wipes his face on a towel, then just stands in front of the mirror, his hand gripping the sink, his head dipped, causing the muscles in his shoulder to flex against his shirt.

"Sorry," he says, his gaze shifting to me. His body seems to relax as he turns slightly, his hand going to the small of my back. "Thanks for lying with me just now."

I smile. I can't help it. "It's okay."

After taking my hair out from its knot, I start to brush it. Through the mirror, I see him smile. *Real.* For the first time in so long.

He moves behind me, his hands going to my waist as his lips press against my neck. "You smell so good," he says.

"Your friends said we had ten minutes."

He groans, his forehead on my shoulder and he wraps his arms around me.

"What's in ten minutes, babe?"

Sighing, he releases me and moves back to the room to slip on his shoes. "We're meeting the guys in the unit."

"Oh yeah?" I ask, tying my hair back up and applying some lip gloss.

"Yep. We're all saying goodbye to Dave."

I step out of the bathroom and go through my bag for something to change into. "Is he going home? His contract's not up yet, is it?"

For a while, he doesn't speak. When I look over at him, he's looking right at me, as if he'd been waiting for me to make eye contact.

"Dylan?"

"Ry. Davey killed himself."

I freeze mid-movement, my breath caught in my chest.

Dylan grabs his phone and wallet from the nightstand, kissing my forehead as he walks past. "I'll meet you by the pool."

He exits the room, leaving me standing there, my feet glued to the floor and my heart right next to it.

My vision clears—not of sight—but of mind. And everything makes sense. *Everything*.

How did I not see it?

Me? Of all people.

How could I not see grief standing right in front of me?

The anger and the hurt and the continuous emotional back and forth.

I've experienced it all… the constant spiral of heartbreak and despair and guilt and bargaining and hurt—the fucking hurt that leads you to the unexplainable. The never-ending thoughts tormenting your mind, bringing you to your knees and kicking you while you're down.

I should've known.

✧ ✧ ✧

I SIT ON Dylan's lap as he sits with the guys from his unit and a couple of their girls drinking beers around the hotel pool. They tell stories about Dave, relive memories he'd created and celebrate the life of the fallen.

The others talk.

Dylan doesn't.

He simply sips on his beer, his jaw tense as he listens to their stories. His knee begins to bounce, his breaths becoming harsher with each minute that passes.

Then he taps my leg, hinting for me to move. And even though I can already feel the anger emitting from him, feel the rage from his shaking body beneath me, I get up quickly and stand by his chair. "This is fucking bullshit," he mumbles, throwing his beer behind him and walking away.

"What was that?" Leroy asks.

Dylan's fists ball at his sides, the anger raging in his eyes again. I count the number of empty bottles by his chair. He's only had three. "You heard me, Leroy. Don't fucking talk about him like you knew him. You didn't fucking know him." He eyes everyone before adding, "None of you did. You didn't give him the time of day when he was breathing, don't act like you give a shit now when he's dead."

"Banks, he was in our unit! We spent every fucking day with the kid," Leroy says, his eyes narrowed in disgust. "You think we'd all fucking be here if we didn't give a shit?!"

Two steps.

That's all it takes for Dylan to get to Leroy, fisting his collar and pushing him up against the chain-link fence behind him. "How old was he?" Dylan snaps, his forehead pressed against Leroy's.

Leroy grabs Dylan's wrists, trying to push him away. Dylan doesn't budge. "What?"

"How fucking old was he? What were his brothers' names?" Dylan yells, spit flying from his mouth. "Answer me!"

"Fuck you!" Leroy shouts.

The other guys are on their feet now. But it's like they're waiting for a reason to break it up, as if what's happening isn't reason enough. My heart's pounding in my ears now, tears streaking down my cheek caused by fear. Sob after sob, after fucking sob escaping me. No one sees me. No one hears me.

"Dylan!" I shout, moving toward them.

"You didn't fucking know him!" Dylan yells.

Leroy's eyes narrow more, his anger matching Dylan's as he tries again, in vain, to get out of Dylan's grasp. "And you're such a fucking hero, Banks, you couldn't—"

I've never heard what a punch to someone's jaw sounds like. I never want to again. But I do. Again and again, all while the guys shout, trying to get between them. I scream. Conway yells. We all try to calm him down but the rage inside Dylan is too strong, too loud. He doesn't hear. Or maybe he chooses not to.

I step forward, holding my breath to stop the cries. My vision blurred, I grab his arm right before he goes for the fourth punch. His strength is unmatched when he pushes me back, his palm finding my chest as his eyes stay on Leroy. "Fuck off!" he shouts, and I stumble on my feet, my hands in front of me, reaching for something. *Anything.* Conway shouts my name. Dylan turns, his mouth open, his eyes on mine. Right before I fall.

My back hits the water, my lungs instantly filling with it. So do my ears. My nose.

I shut my eyes and close my mouth, then I hold my breath, listening to the water whirl around me. It feels like an eternity before my feet find the tiled floor, and for a moment, I want to stay down here. Because being underwater—the source of *my* nightmares—seems safer than being up there… where my reality *is* my nightmare. Then I remember Dylan, I remember his eyes. The rage first, then the shock. I find the courage to push off my feet and I gasp for air the moment I feel it hit my face, my head spinning. I blink back the water as I search for Dylan. He's standing by the edge, his arms held back by three men. "Riley," Conway says, and I tear my gaze away from Dylan to see Conway squatting by the edge of the pool, his hand out for me. I swim toward him, gripping his hand when I reach him. He helps me out of the pool, his hands instantly on me. One on my shoulder, the other on my cheek as he forces me to look at him. "You okay?" he asks, his dark eyes penetrating mine.

I try to calm my breaths, try to soothe the ache in my chest. I glance at Dylan, looking for some form of remorse. There is none. The rage is back. "Get your fucking hands off her!" he yells, trying to get loose.

"Stop!" I shout at him, my hand up between us. "Just stop." I look at Conway. "I'm fine."

Someone hands him a towel; one he wraps around my shoulders. "I'll walk you up to your room." He turns me away from Dylan, from my *love*, my *heart*, from my *hurt*, and with Conway's words meant only for me, he says, "We're going to clear out and give Banks some time to settle down. He's had it rough."

I glance over my shoulder, my body shaking from the cold. Dylan's watching me, his jaw set, his eyes on mine. There's still no remorse. But there's no longer rage. There's *nothing*.

And I don't know what I fear most.

✧ ✧ ✧

I WATCH HIM from the hotel room window, alone, sitting in the same chair we'd been in hours ago. Besides reaching for the numerous beers, he doesn't move. He keeps his head down, his eyes on the pool, taking sip after sip, drowning in heartbreak.

I take a breath, my gaze lowering as I try to think of the right thing to do. Conway said to give him time.

I gave him that.

I gave myself that, too.

And yet here I am, exactly where I'd been since he came home. Time doesn't change anything. But love will. It *has* to.

Without another thought, I slip on my shoes and make my way out to him.

He looks up when he must hear the pool gate open and quickly looks back down. He doesn't make eye contact. I know he won't. Still, I take slow steps toward him, stopping in front of him, giving him the opportunity to acknowledge my existence. After a few seconds of nothing, I take a chance and sit on his lap like I'd been doing before everything went to shit.

The sun went down five hours ago, taking the light and warmth of the day with it. Now it's cold and dark and the atmosphere is miserable. Even more miserable than the events of the day. It's quiet, though, all but for Dylan's heavy breaths.

I loosely wrap my arm around his shoulders and stare straight ahead, not wanting to make eye contact in case it sets him off.

I know that it's wrong to live my life in fear—especially of him—but I also know that it won't be forever. We just need to get through this. We *have* to get through this.

He doesn't touch me.

He doesn't hold me.

But after a while, he finally speaks. "Was it thick?"

I tense in his arms, confused by his words. "Was what thick?"

"His blood. Jeremy's. When you held his head on your lap, was it thick?"

"Dylan…" I finally face him, but he's staring right ahead. Right at nothing.

"Dave's was thick, Riley. And I don't know. I guess I'm just trying to work out exactly what I had on my hands."

My breath catches in my throat as realization sets in.

He continues, "See, his head was on my lap, and it just…" He lets out a breath through his nose, his shoulders dropping, "…it felt thick. So I'm assuming it was just bits of his skull and… what? His brain? I mean… with Jeremy—"

"Stop it," I whisper through clenched teeth. I'd tried so hard to forget and now he's here… making me remember.

He swallows loudly, and leans back further in his chair. "I get it now, Riley. I get what it's like to be you. To have blood on your hands—to have that guilt weighing on you constantly. I should've fucking seen what was going on with him and I didn't. Or maybe I chose to ignore it. Just like you did on that cliff."

"Stop," I cry.

He doesn't stop. "And the worst part is that I keep seeing it. Keep hearing it. I look into the mirror and I see him standing there, his head fucking blown off, begging me to see him. To hear him. To realize how much he was suffering. But it's too late, right? Because he's fucking dead now. What the hell am I supposed to do, Riley? Tell me."

"I don't—"

"You think I should drink? I mean, it helps. It blurs the visions a little so it makes it more dream-like. It tricks your mind into believing that's all it is. A dream. Not a memory. Is that why you did it?"

I open my mouth. Nothing comes out.

Finally, his gaze meets mine. "Or do you think I should write stupid letters even though he's six feet under? You think that'll bring him back to life?"

I don't respond. I can't. Because when your heart's breaking, being ripped out of you by the person who caused it to beat in the first place, there's nothing left. Nothing to say. Nothing to do.

I start to get up but he holds me down. "Or maybe I should go home, get in my truck and drive it right through my dad's house. Maybe your mom's, too. Just because. Maybe that'll help. You think I'll get jail time?"

I wipe my eyes, my sobs uncontrolled. "Why are you being like this?"

"Because I'm hurting, Riley," he mumbles, his gaze shifting, his hold tightening. "And I'm allowed to be angry. I'm allowed to be drunk. I'm allowed to hate the world and everything in it. That's how you dealt with it, right?"

"I never pushed away the people who loved me," I bite out.

He scoffs. "Maybe you should have. Then we wouldn't be here. Now we have to go back to our fucked up lives and pretend like none of this matters. I'm not serving my goddamn purpose any more than you're out there creating a legacy. We're just two fucked up people with blood on our hands, faking our happiness."

Forty-Five

Dylan

GETTING RILEY TO fall in love with me was easy. Getting her to hate me is the hardest fucking thing I've ever done.

As I sat alone, beer in hand, watching the murky blue water of the hotel pool splash against the edges, I made my choice.

Something in me snapped that night and I'd hurt her. Again. Physically, emotionally, all of it. And there was no way I was going to let her allow me to continue to do it. So, I said things I didn't mean. Things I knew would destroy her.

I wanted her to hate me so that it didn't hurt so much when she left.

But she didn't.

She kept her arms wrapped around me the entire night in that hotel room. She kept her smile in place as she said goodbye to the guys she'd met the night before… guys whose opinions of me had no doubt changed and she held my hand as I walked her to her car for the long ass drive back home.

On the outside, her love for me had never wavered, even after what I'd done. Inside though, she was hurting. She *had* to be. I *needed* her to be.

THE WEEK ON base went by slowly. Too fucking slowly. My friends who I'd once taken a fucking bullet for no longer respected me. They left me alone.

Riley didn't. She called often. Messaged even more. She asked if I was coming home or if she should come here. After five on the Friday, I finally called her. She answered the phone like she did every time. Her voice high pitched and happy to hear from me.

I guess it's true what they say; ignorance is bliss.

Why don't you hate me, Riley?

I SHOWED UP five hours later and went straight to bed. No words spoken. No affections shared. Just like I'd planned.

I never looked at her. Never acknowledged her.

Like I said, I wanted her to hate me.

Doesn't mean it didn't hurt like hell.

No worse than after the fourth hour of lying in our bed—the bed I spent days in, watching her, falling in love with her… she has her arms wrapped around me, her breaths warm and even as they hit my bare chest. I reach over and switch on the lamp on the nightstand, my heart breaking as I look at her sleeping peacefully. My fingers twirl in her hair—her messy hair I'd always loved. Her lashes fan across her cheeks, cheeks I've kissed so many times before and for a moment, just one single moment, I second guess myself, wondering if I'm doing the right thing. I run the back of my fingers across her face… so beautiful and so innocent and so damn perfect and I know, deep down, I know she doesn't deserve anything I'm doing to her.

I don't deserve her.

AS GENTLE AS I can, I remove her arms from around me and get out of bed. I look toward the bathroom, to the still-smashed mirror and I feel my heart shatter. Not just for her, but for me too.

It'll hurt.

Her.

Me.

Everyone around us.

I switch off the light, grab my bag and head for the door, taking one more look at the girl I'd planned on spending forever with. The light from the hall filters through the room, landing on her. Slowly, her hand moves, feeling around the bed, her eyes snapping open when she feels the emptiness. The same emptiness I feel inside me.

Then she sits up, her eyes slowly moving to me.

She covers her mouth with the back of her hand, a single sob escaping her. She doesn't speak. She doesn't need to.

But I do. Because it's the last thing I'll ever say to her. She needs to know. I owe her that much. "I'm so sorry, Riley."

I CHECK INTO a hotel nearby because I'm too fucking tired to drive.

The more time that passes, the more I see Dave. Yes, I know he's fucking dead. Doesn't stop him from making an appearance in my life.

Most of the time it's in the mirror. I should be seeing me. I see him. Right now, I don't know what's worse.

Sometimes I hear his voice, the sound of his cry right before he pulled the trigger.

Sometimes—and these are the worst—he just appears out of nowhere. Today he sat in the car next to me. I had an entire conversation with a dead man, out loud. He told me about his brothers, how many birthdays he missed and how much he missed them. I told him he was a fucking pussy. That if he really felt that way he should've thought about how much they'd all miss him. It's not like he'd come home and they'd be able to make up for lost time. He was dead. He was also a fucking asshole.

I blame it on lack of sleep. There's no other explanation for it. Apart from the fact that I might possibly be certifiably insane.

"I THOUGHT YOU liked Riley."

"I love Riley," I tell Dave, or the ghost of him, or my vision of him, or whatever the fuck is happening right now.

"You've got a pretty fucked up way of showing it."

"What the fuck would you know?"

"Man, she would've been better off with me."

I rub my eyes, trying to fight off sleep. "You're fucking delusional, dude."

"Says the guy who sees dead people."

Forty-Six
Riley

I DROP THE pen on the notepad and read my letter to Dylan over and over again. Sighing, I tear out the page and put it in the new jar and set it on the bench.

I run my fingers across his tools, my lips pressed tight to suppress my cries.

I'm sick of crying.

I'm sick of wiping away the tears.

I'm sick of hurting.

I'm sick of not finding a solution to the pain.

I'm sick of all of it.

"Ry?" Jake calls from behind me. His grin widens as he walks up the driveway and I curse myself for leaving the garage door open. "Dylan inside?"

I fake a smile and shrug.

His eyes narrow as his footsteps slow. Then he laughs nervously. "Where is he?"

"I'm not sure," I tell him.

He drops his gaze to the boxes on the floor—the real reason I'm out here. "What's all this?"

I smile, a real one, and for a second I forget about the hell I'm living in. "It's a new work bench… some state of the art thing. I was hoping it would be here before he got home but they were a few days late on the delivery. Not that it matters." I shrug. "He's been home a month."

Jake rears back a little. "I'm confused. Kayla said… wait. So he's been home a month?"

I nod. "On base. But he's—" I can't lie. He's not *home.* "Around."

"Asshole didn't even tell me he was back. Did he just want to spend alone time with you or something?"

I laugh. I can't help it. And then I cry. Something else I have absolutely no control over.

He settles his hands on my shoulders as he dips his head, his eyes right on mine. "Are you okay, Ry?"

"I'm fine," I lie.

"You don't seem fine."

I wipe my eyes and take a breath. And then another. Looking for the strength that's not-so-slowly diminishing. "I'm okay. Really." I point to the boxes by my feet and release another lie. "It's just overwhelming. I'm trying to grasp how I'm going to build all this and remove the other one and I don't know…" I scratch my head and look back up at Jake. "I just want to make him happy. That's all."

He tilts his head, as if searching for my hidden meaning. He won't find it. It's the only piece of truth I've voiced since he's been back. I do want to make him happy. It's all I've ever wanted.

"I can call the guys to come and help if they're around. I know Cam's here. He might be able to get one of Lucy's dad's workers and we can get it done in no time."

"Yeah," I whisper. "That'd be good."

Jake gets on the phone and fifteen minutes later, Cameron shows up with Lucas—Jeremy's friend from high school and Cam's brother-in-law.

"I brought a professional," Cam says, tapping the back of his hand on Lucas's chest as they walk up the driveway.

"That's good," Jake says to me, "I'm good at lifting heavy shit, Cameron's good at designing it, but neither of us are great with tools. That was always—"

"Dylan," I cut in, and Jake and Cam instinctively bow their heads.

"'Sup, Hudson," Lucas says, nodding in greeting.

"So you know what you're doing?" I ask, shuffling on my feet.

He nods again. "Yep. I'm working construction full time for the old man now."

"And me!" Cam says, pointing to himself. "I'm his boss."

"Fuck off."

"You're fired!" Cam booms.

Lucas picks up his tools he'd just set on the floor and spins around.

"Laters!"

"No!" I yell. "I need your help."

He turns around, his smile wide. "I'll do it for you, Hudson. I owe you this much."

I drop my gaze at the memory of Jeremy he instantly invokes in me. Another sob rises from the pit of my stomach, catching in my throat before it leaves me.

"You okay?" he asks.

"Yeah. I'm fine… just…"

"Jeremy?" he asks.

I nod. "Jeremy." I don't know why I'm thinking about Jeremy the way I am. Why I suddenly find myself missing him the way I do.

Jake clears his throat. "So how long do we have until D gets home? You want it to be a surprise, right?"

"He won't be home tonight," I let slip, but don't bother to right my wrong.

"Where is he?" Cameron asks.

I look up, three sets of eyes on me—their expressions matching that of Dylan's family as I stood in their hallway. They look worried. I *am* worried. I don't know what to say, so I give them a half truth. It's better than the constant lies falling from my lips. "I think he just needed to get away for the night."

IT DOESN'T TAKE them long to demolish the old bench and put the new one up, and it's only when I see it in pieces on the back of both Jake and Lucas's truck as they drive away that I realize I've made a mistake. Dylan has a personal attachment to that bench—the years and years he spent working on it and I just took it away. He won't see the good I'd tried to do… he'll only see the bad.

He only ever sees the bad now.

I curse under my breath, already fearing his response. And of all the emotions that could possibly lead me to what I do next, fear is the greatest one.

Dylan

RILEY'S CALLING.

I don't know why she's calling.

I ignore the call only for it to ring again. And again.

Then a text comes through.

Riley: *I've been pulled over. The brake lights were out, I guess, and it's registered under your name. The officer asked you to come and bring some identification.*

I sit on the edge of the hotel bed and check the time. It's nine at night. I don't know if I've slept or if I've just been in a daze but last I knew it was light out. I call her back, but I don't speak.

"Dylan?" she asks, her voice barely a whisper.

I grab the beer sitting on my nightstand and take a few sips. "Where are you?"

She gives me her location and I take another sip. Then I dress, grab my keys and go to her.

She's not hard to find, the flashing lights of the police car give her away. I park behind both cars and get out, pulling out my wallet as I walk toward them. A part of me is angry she's driving without brake lights, not just because it's fucking dangerous, but because I'd specifically asked Dad to take care of that shit because I knew she wouldn't.

She's still sitting behind the driver's seat and when I walk up, the officer turns to me, aiming his flashlight in my eyes. "You're the owner of this vehicle?" he asks. He's my dad's age, same build, no beard.

"Yes, Sir," I tell him, pulling my military ID from my wallet and handing it to him.

He flashes his light on the ID and looks up at me. "Camp Lejeune?" he asks.

I nod. "Yes, Sir."

"Did Ms. Hudson tell you why she was pulled over?"

"Yes, Sir. Brake lights. I'll take care of it first thing."

He steps closer as he hands me back his ID, then freezes in his spot. He shines his light at my face again. "You been drinking, Lance

Corporal?"

I suppress my eye roll. "I was having a beer when I got the call, officer."

"How many beers?"

"Just the one."

"I'm going to trust you," he tells me, his voice stern.

I stay quiet, because everything I want to say would just get us in more trouble. I'm not intoxicated, but I've definitely had more than one beer.

He turns and starts walking back to Riley's window.

I lean against the car, my arms and legs crossed, waiting. I just want to get back to the hotel. Back to solitary. Back to silence.

"Here's your license back, Ms. Hudson. You're going to have to leave the car here and get it towed. It's illegal to drive it the way it is."

Shit. Now I have to sit in the fucking car with her.

"Is that a bottle of liquor on your passenger seat, Miss?" the office asks, and my head whips to the side, my ears perked, waiting for her response.

"Yes, Sir," she says quietly.

I push off the car and stand next to the cop, my forearm resting on the roof. I don't look at her. I can't.

The officer sighs. "Hand it over."

It takes a long time before I see Riley's hand out the window, holding the bottle of Boons Farm wine she used to inhale to survive.

The officer lifts it higher, his flashlight shining on the screw cap. "This seal's broken, Ms. Hudson. You are aware it's an offense to drive with an open container of alcohol in a vehicle, aren't you?"

She sniffs once. "Yes, Sir."

The officer opens her door. "Please step out of the vehicle, Miss."

I keep my gaze lowered, and re-cross my arms, doing everything I can not to look at her. If I see her—see the plea in her eyes—her eyes the color of sadness, I don't know what I'll do. I'd probably cut the bullshit and reach out to her, hold her and tell her that it'll be okay. But it won't last long until I fuck up, until I hurt her, until Dave's in my vision again—pushing me to the brink of insanity.

"Have you consumed any alcohol tonight?" the officer asks her.

She sobs again, the single sound causing the destruction inside me. I finally look at her, her cheeks stained with tears as she stands in front of the police officer, her hands shaking at her sides.

"No, Sir. I mean yes, Sir. Just a sip. In the parking lot at the store where I got it. That's all."

My stomach falls, my breath releasing as my head drops forward, Riley's words completely ruining me.

Her shoulders shake as she covers her eyes, releasing another round of sobs.

The officer says, "I need to do a sobriety test, Ms. Hudson."

"Okay," she says, her face contorting with another cry.

The cop's shoulders drop as he stands in front of the girl I love, his authoritative demeanor waning. "Miss. If you've only had a sip, you'll be okay. You'll get a fine and it will all be over, okay?"

She drops her head in her hands, her shoulder lifting with each sob.

"Riley," I whisper, but she doesn't hear me.

"*Go to her!*" Dave's voice rattles in my head. But I can't. My feet are glued to the ground, my heart with it. Because I destroyed her. *I caused this.*

She looks up, wiping her tears on her arm. She straightens her shoulders as she looks between the cop and I.

"Miss?" the officer says again.

Her words are muffled by her forearm—using it to hide her cries. "That's not why I'm crying."

"Then why?" the officer asks gently.

She stands taller, looking at me for a long time before going back to the cop. "Because I'm a recovering alcoholic, Sir. Fifteen months and I haven't had a drop and tonight, I failed." Every word is forced. Every sob is restrained. Every breath is a struggle. "I failed myself and I failed him." She points to me. "I'm a disappointment, Sir." She cries harder, attempting to hold in her breaths to keep them quiet, but it doesn't work. "I'm a fucking disappointment."

"Riley," I breathe out.

She places her arms in front of her. "You can arrest me," she whimpers. "I don't mind."

The officer looks between us, not knowing what to do. After a while, he sighs, his focus on me. "Take your girl home," he says. "Show her she's loved."

SILENTLY, I LEAD Riley to my truck, opening the passenger door for her. After making sure her car is secure, I get behind the wheel.

She doesn't sit in the middle like she always does, she sits with her side pressed against the door as far away from me as possible.

I start the drive back to our house, my head spinning, my jaw tense.

"*Be nice,*" Dave says and I squeeze my eyes shut, trying to block him out. The last fucking thing I need is his dead voice adding fuel to my guilt.

Riley doesn't stop crying. As hard as she tries to stop, I hear every single one, feel each one like a bullet straight through my heart. "I'm sorry, Dylan," she says.

"*She's fucking sorry, man.*"

I press my thumb to my temple, begging, pleading for the voices to stop.

"Dylan?" she whispers.

"*She needs you, man.*"

"Not now!" I yell, punching the steering wheel.

"I'm sorry," Riley shouts, cowering against the door again.

I face her quickly. "Not you!" And when I focus on the road again, Dave's standing in front of the car, his head blown off, his voice loud in my ears. "*Stop fucking yelling at her!*"

I slam on the brakes to avoid hitting him, my hands gripping the wheel as the tires spin, burning rubber against the concrete. I lose control, just for a moment, the car fishtailing across the narrow road before finally coming to a stop. Smoke surrounds the car, fog rises through the headlights.

I turn to Riley, her eyes wide, her hands gripping the door. She's breathing heavily, just like me.

Fear.

It's all I see.

All I feel.

In her.

In me.

"Fuck!" I hit the steering wheel again. Feeling the rage build. "Get out, Riley!"

"I'm not leaving!"

I reach out and open the door, forcefully pushing her out of the car.

"Get out!"

"I'm sorry, Dylan!" she shouts through her sobs, standing next to the car.

"Go home!"

She shakes her head, her hands in her hair. Then her face turns white. "Dylan!"

Forty-Seven
Dylan

MY BREATHS ARE weak. My body weaker. I try to open my eyes, but I can't. I can hear her voice. She's screaming my name. Over and over. I can feel her with me, but she sounds far away. So far.

My lips part, her name barely a whisper.

She's crying. She screaming and she's crying.

White light flashes behind my eyes. More distant voices. But none louder than Dave's. "*What the hell did you do, man?*" I follow his voice because I have no choice. My breath leaves me. It doesn't return. It's dark. So damn dark.

Forty-Eight
Dylan

THERE'S A BEEPING sound, something pressing down on my fingers, faint voices, and the familiar smell of hospitals. I know where I am before I open my eyes.

I try to remember what happened, about as much as I try to forget.

I remember Riley's face—the white caused by the headlights behind me. Then the sound of crashing metal right before the car spun and spun and spun some more. I tried to control the steering wheel but I couldn't.

"Riley," I breathe out, my eyes snapping open. I search frantically for her, but she isn't here. No one's here. "Riley!" I shout, starting to get up. There's weight on my chest, keeping me down, and pain in my right leg that shoots up to my hip.

Dad steps into the room, his eyes wide when he sees me half out of bed. He starts to speak, but I cut him off. "Where's Riley?"

He places a gentle hand on my chest, keeping me down.

"Where is she!" I demand.

"She's here. She stepped out for a minute, but she's here. She'll be back. She hasn't left your side for two days."

"Two days?" I whisper.

He nods.

I ignore the beeps from the monitor next to me, the sounds fast and frantic. "Is she okay?"

"She's okay. Do you remember anything that happened?"

I shake my head. "Yes. No. Some."

"The other car hit yours on enough of an angle that it barely clipped her. She's got a bruised hip. That's all. A few cuts and bruises from trying to get you out. But she's okay."

I rip the monitor off my fingers and try to get up again.

"Son, please," he begs. "I know it's hard. You need to stay down."

Tears build in my eyes, my heart aching more than the physical pain I'm in. I try to take his advice, try to breathe through the guilt.

Dad inhales a breath, his hands slowly rising when he knows I'm not going anywhere. "I contacted your First Sergeant. They approved your leave until your leg heals. I think it's best you stay close. You have a concussion and a punctured lung. Broken leg—"

"I don't care. I want to see Riley. Where is she?"

"She's just—"

"You're up!" It should be physically and emotionally impossible to feel so much from the sound of one person's voice, but hearing her, seeing her smile as she walks toward me, coffee in her hand… I feel everything. I feel the air fill my lungs, feel the pain leave my body.

"Baby," I whisper, my hand out, reaching for her.

She glances at Dad quickly before looking over at me.

And her touch—her touch doubles everything I felt when I heard her voice, when I saw her face. She reaches up, one hand on mine, the other still holding the coffee when she uses the back of her fingers to glide across my forehead. I gaze into her eyes, looking for the calm. It isn't there. Neither is the smile anymore. "How are you feeling?"

"Sore," I croak, my throat dry.

Both her hands leave me, returning a second later with a cup of water and a straw. She lifts my head gently until my mouth surrounds the straw and I drink slowly, my throat aching when I swallow.

Dad steps back from the bed, taking a seat in the corner of the room.

"You've been out a while," Riley says.

Where did her smile go?

Where is the calm?

My head spins, my breaths ragged as I try to remember.

I don't remember anything. Just the headlights shining on her face and the spinning of the car.

And Dave.

I remember Dave.

Slowly, it all comes back to me. I remember why we were there in the first place.

I *ruined* her.

Destroyed every ounce of strength she had.

I wanted her to hate me.

I wanted her to leave me.

I took away her smile.

I stole the calm in her eyes.

And I replaced them both with *fear*.

I rest my head back on the pillow and look her in the eye. "I'm so sorry, baby."

"It's okay," she whispers, her lips warm and wet as she leans forward, taking my hand and kissing it. "We'll get through it, Dylan. Always."

"I love you."

"*I know.*"

✧ ✧ ✧

A FEW WEEKS ago, if you'd asked me what moment in my life caused me the greatest shame, it would've involved a flash bang, a picture of Riley and Dave behind the camera. Now, it's the presence of my family, Riley plus two cops as they proceed to tell me that my license has been revoked for thirty days—not that it matters with my broken leg. What matters is *why*. I keep my eyes on Riley as they go through the standard process, her eyebrows bunched in confusion. They'd tested my blood alcohol level once I arrived in the ER. I was 0.09. One point above the legal alcohol limit. I lied to the officer that night—the same one standing silently next to his partner who's doing all the talking. He probably feels guilty—that it's his fault it happened. That, maybe, he should've given me the sobriety test instead of letting me walk away. I'll keep his secret—I've ruined enough lives. None more so than the girl standing by my side, her grip on my hand loosening with each word spoken.

Eric shouts, moving closer to the cops. "My brother earned a Purple Heart serving this goddamn country and you're going to …" I tune out the rest when Riley turns to me, the tears in her eyes clouding but not at all hiding her disappointment. I don't look away. I won't. I want her to see me. To know that I'm sorry. That I regret it. That I love her. That I *need* her.

EVERY ONE LEAVES. Everyone but Riley.

She doesn't talk to me. Doesn't look at me. But she stays by my side, my hand in hers.

And in my mind, in my heart, I can feel it. She's slipping away from me.

HOURS PASS. DAD returns.

He won't look at me either.

I sit up when Holly walks in, her smile tight when she sees me. "How you doin' there, Marine?" She smiles sadly as she stands by the bed. "He's okay," Riley answers for me.

Dad gets up from his seat and moves the chair next to Riley's offering it to Holly. She takes it, her eyes on mine and Riley's joined hands.

Then she sighs, scooting her chair closer to the edge of the bed. "Guys." She pauses, her mouth opening and closing a few times. Dropping her head, she heaves in a breath. "I know this is bad timing. But we need to talk. Well, I need to. To both you. And I'm just going to say what I need to say and I'd like for you to only interrupt if anything I say is incorrect and if it is, I apologize. Okay?"

I look at Riley, whose eyes are lowered and I nod, my heart racing, making the beeping of the monitor more frantic.

"Maybe now isn't a good time, Holly," Dad says.

Holly glances up at Dad, and then at the monitor, and then back to me. Riley stays quiet, as if she knows what's about to happen. She squeezes my hand, trying to comfort me. It doesn't work. Her eyes… I need her eyes. She won't look at me.

"I'm sorry, Mal," Holly says, "but I think it has to happen now."

Dad nods.

My heart races faster—so painfully I find it impossible to breathe.

She says, her hand on my arm, "I went by your house to collect some things for Riley because she refuses to leave your side." She swallows loudly, her eyes on mine. So much like Riley's, but not at all the same. "I went to your bathroom and I saw the shattered mirror. It looks like direct contact with something, most likely a fist. I'm going to assume that you caused it, and again, interrupt me if I'm wrong…"

She waits for me to say something.

I don't.

I can't.

"Dylan?" Dad says, and my entire body goes slack. My head falls back on the pillow and I gaze up at the ceiling because there's only so much shame a person can handle before it becomes too much.

I'm filled with it.

Holly says, "I'm going to be honest with you. It scared me, Dylan. It made me afraid to think that my daughter was living in a home with someone who would do that—but not just that—it made me afraid to think that she'd be in that situation and not tell me about it."

"Mom, stop," Riley cries.

Holly doesn't. "I know she loves you. I know we all love you. And I know you saw her suffering from the aftermath of a death and that you were able to help her get through it just by being there, so it worries me that you didn't think it okay to come to us—any of us—if you felt like you were struggling. I'm not afraid to admit that that fear caused me to snoop around your house, Dylan. I saw the bottles of beer in your fridge, which doesn't make sense because you know my daughter and you allowed that in a home you share with her."

Her words crush every ounce of hope I'd wished for. Every ounce of dignity I had left.

"And then I went out to the garage and saw a jar on the floor, like the ones she used when she wrote those letters to Jeremy."

Riley's chair scrapes against the floor as she stands quickly. "No!" I look over at her, her eyes frantic.

Holly continues, "I didn't think anything of it at first, but I'm a mother and I care about her. So I picked it up and I read it. I won't apologize for doing it."

"Mom," Riley cries, her hands covering her face. "Please don't!"

Dad's on the other side of the bed, his hand on my chest to stop me from moving.

I won't move.

I can't.

Holly reaches into her purse, pulling out a folded piece of paper before handing it to me.

My fingers shake as I unfold it, unaware of the devastation it's about to cause.

To me.

To her.

To everyone around us.

To the lives we'd built and the promises we'd created.

Riley's watching me, tears flowing fast and free. She's shaking her head and I don't know why. Not until I read her words—words written from the hate I created.

Dylan.

I love you.

I miss you.

You left me last night. I checked your online bank statement and there was a payment listed for a hotel ten minutes away. I called the hotel. They said it was charged for two nights. It's strange—when you're not with me, I feel the longing swelling in my chest, but when you are with me... I can feel your presence crushing my heart.

I figured you booked a hotel because you hate me and you couldn't stand to be around me.

That, or you're cheating on me.

And right now, I don't know which is worse.

I read the letter over and over, focusing on each and every word until Riley's loud sob pulls my focus away from the letter and up at her. "I didn't mean it," she cries, her hand back on mine. "Please, baby, you have to believe me."

"Dylan," Dad says, and I don't need to see him to feel his disappointment.

"So," Holly says, standing up. She looks between Riley and I. "Is any of it a lie?"

I drop my gaze, folding the letter before placing it under my pillow. "I'm not cheating on her, Holly. I would never do that."

"See?" Riley shouts.

Her mom ignores her. "But you hate her?"

"No." I shake my head, my eyes drifting shut. "I wanted her to hate me."

"Why?"

The force of my tears cause my eyes to open. I don't look at Riley. I look at her. "Because I was hurting your daughter. And I wanted her to leave me."

Holly's brow furrows in concentration, or maybe confusion. "Can you give us a minute, Riley?"

"No!" Riley shouts, her hand holding mine so tight it begins to hurt.

Dad moves around the bed and carefully pries Riley's fingers from my hand. He grasps her shoulders. "Come on, sweetheart," he says, guiding her to the door.

She looks over her shoulder at me. "I didn't mean it, Dylan!"

Holly waits until she's out of the room and the door is closed before looking back at me. I keep my eyes on hers, because I deserve to see the sadness, the anger, the disappointment. After a while, she leans down and presses her lips to my forehead. When she pulls back, she's smiling—a sweet, sad, pathetic smile. "I love you, Dylan. I love you for everything you've done for my daughter. I love that you loved her when she'd given up on love, and I love that you saw her when I was blind. I gave you my blessing and you broke her heart." She takes a breath, her tears matching mine. "You created a fine line between honor and betrayal, Dylan. And you walked with a foot on either side. I'll be taking her home with me. So, I guess, in the end you got what you wanted."

THERE ARE NOW two sounds I'll never forget. The gunshot that took Davey's life, and Riley's screams at her mother, begging her to let her stay, yelling that she was wrong—that she didn't mean what she said in the letter. But the worst… the worst is when she cried, long and loud—*She loves me.* She'll *always* love me.

Forty-Nine
Dylan

DAD GOES BACK to work.

Eric shows up less and less.

They assure me it has nothing to do with the DUI.

I don't believe them.

The guys come by.

So do the girls.

Only Sydney's a regular and that's because she works here.

She zips up the bag that Eric brought when he still gave a shit about me. "You ready to get out of here?"

I've been stuck in the same room for over two weeks. I'm well and truly ready to get out of here. When I tell her that, she spins me in the wheelchair until I'm facing the door. Two bodies dressed in black appear in the doorway, dropping to the floor as soon as I see them. They both look up, and even though they're wearing black beanies pulled low on their brows, their faces covered in war paint, I can still tell it's Logan and Jake.

Logan holds his wrist to his mouth as they slowly army crawl toward me. "All clear for Operation Banks Robbery. Target identified. Do you copy, Juliett Alfa?"

Jake does the same with his wrist as they continue crawling toward me. "Roger that, Lima Mike. Shit!" He looks up at Sydney standing behind me. "Target compromised."

"Goddammit, Juliett! You had one fucking job!" Logan yells.

I shake my head and ignore how ridiculous they are. "What the fuck are you assholes doing?"

They stand quickly, brushing down their clothes. Then in unison, they grin from ear to ear.

"We're busting you out," Jake states.

Logan rolls his eyes. "Obviously."

"I've already been discharged."

The height of Logan's repeated eye roll forces his head to roll back. "Obviously," he says again.

"You know the rules, boys," Sydney says, moving around me. "He stays in the chair until he's off hospital property."

Their cocky smiles drop as they stand straighter, puffing their chests. They salute her, followed by a united, "Sir. Yes, Sir!"

Sydney shakes her head. "Your friends are idiots, Dylan."

Logan waits until she's left the room before offering his fist for a bump that I return. He asks, "How you feeling, bro?"

Jake's behind me now, slowly rolling me forward. I shrug. "Could always be worse, right?"

Logan grabs my bag off the bed and the crutches leaning against the wall. Six more weeks I'll be using them while the cast is on my leg. "You ready?"

I nod.

Logan walks.

Jakes pushes.

I EXPECT THEM to drive me straight home. They don't. Instead, they take me to the garage where my car was towed. "What are we doing here?"

Logan turns to me. "Perspective."

THE PHYSICAL DETAILS of what my truck looks like are irrelevant. But the visions, the memories of what happened that link to the damage—that's why they brought me here.

"Poor Bessie," Jake mumbles, standing beside me, hands in his pockets.

On the other side, Logan speaks up. "You're kind of lucky to be alive."

I look away from the truck, adjusting the crutches beneath my shoulders and face him. "You mean she's lucky I didn't fucking kill her?"

Logan's gaze drops, his foot kicking the dirt we're standing on. For a moment, I think about Afghanistan, about the seconds right before we entered the house of hell. The seed that planted the events that brought me to *her*. "I know it's not the same," Logan says. "But I get where you're coming from. I understand the guilt. Your girl's hurt, you think it's your fault." He removes his beanie, running his hands through his hair before adding, "I've been where you were man, sitting in a hospital room, drowning in guilt, the realization of your lack of self-worth eating away at you until you feel like it's on you to save her from the pain you created."

I listen to his words, each one meaning more than the last.

"So you feel like you need to run away to save her. You block her and everyone out to save them all from the destruction you'll cause." He sniffs once, his eyes lifting and locking with mine. "It doesn't work though, D. I spent a year running away and the guilt is a thousand times worse when you're doing it alone."

"I don't plan on running away," I tell him.

"Maybe not physically, but emotionally."

I stay silent.

Jake says, "Obviously something happened, man. From the time you came back for Riley's birthday to now. And we're not here to get you to bare your soul to us so please don't think that. We're just here to let you know that no matter what it is, we're here." He picks up a few rocks from the ground and starts pitching them at the truck. "I didn't want to wait until it was too late like I did with Logan."

"Shut up," Logan snaps.

"I'm serious."

"There's no way you could've known. I didn't even fucking know," Logan says.

For a few moments, we stand in silence.

"Is it like…" Jake hesitates. "PTS—"

"No," I snap. "Don't fucking say it."

Logan stands in front of me, his hands on his hips. "There's nothing wrong with—"

"Shut up!"

I turn swiftly and hobble back to the car. I don't wait for them to follow me before throwing my crutches in the back seat and getting in. I stare at the clock on the dash, watching the minutes tick by until I can be alone again. So I can drown myself in the guilt and the hate that make it impossibly easy not to see her.

Not to hold her.

Not to tell her that I'm sorry.

So fucking sorry.

But it doesn't matter that I love her and I miss her and I'd do anything if she would just get in my truck that's no longer drivable and sit next to me while we drove to the calm of the horizon.

After a few minutes, they both join me. I don't know what they had to say to each other. I don't care.

"Take me home," I tell them.

"All right, man," Jake says, turning the car over.

It doesn't take long before they start talking again.

"I used to see my dad," Logan says. "My real dad. In my nightmares. He'd come and beat the shit out of me and I'd wake up in a pool of sweat and sometimes piss, and I'm not talking when I was a kid, man, I'm talking two fucking years ago. I had a break down when I was with Doctors Without Borders and a psych diagnosed me with PTSD. I was on meds for a long time. And then I came home and Amanda—"

"So you're saying I go running back to Riley and hope she forgives me?" I ask, my tone flat. It's not like I don't appreciate what he's saying, and there's a part of me that feels like the biggest asshole in the world that I didn't know any of this about him considering he's one of my best friends, but nothing he's saying is relevant. At least not to me.

"That's not what I'm saying."

"So what then?"

"You know after what happened with me before I left, Amanda changed her major."

I lean back in my seat and look over at Jake, sitting silent, driving like a fucking grandma. I wonder if he at least knows where the fuck this conversation's going.

Logan continues, "She changed her major to psychology."

And there it is.

"She's actually pretty good," Jake finally chimes in. "My dad sends some of the kids he works with to her. Not so much for sessions but more as a mentor."

"So?" I ask. "She's going to braid my hair and everything'll be better?"

Logan faces me, a scowl on his face.

I look out the window.

And I stay that way until the car pulls up in front of my house.

They start to get out but I stop them. "I just need some time," I tell them honestly.

And silence.

Fuck, I need the silence.

Fifty
Dylan

MARTIN LUTHER KING once said "In the End, we will remember not the words of our enemies, but the silence of our friends" and as I sit on the couch, the TV on mute, and my mind on Riley, I wonder if it's true.

I wonder if I'll remember about the recent events in my life and be able to recall The Turning Point. I wonder if I'll look back on Dave as an enemy, because right now, that's what he feels like. I wonder if the silence of my friends for the past week was their form of showing me they care.

"I just need some time," was the last thing I told them. And I meant it.

But now I'm here, surrounded by silence so loud it's deafening. And I'd give just about anything to feel something else.

THE FEAR IS still here.

So is the grief.

But the silence I crave is nowhere to be seen.

I DIDN'T THINK coming home would hurt this much. Actually, I didn't think about it at all. Had I done so, I probably would've found somewhere else to stay, just until someone could come in and remove everything so I could sell it and move out. The second I walked in, I was filled with memories of Riley. She'd picked out every single piece of furniture, chosen every paint color, decided on the placement of everything. We even stood in the flooring store for three hours while she debated over the carpet that lay under my feet. I'd give anything to have those three hours back.

I haven't left the house. I haven't needed to. Eric and Dad bring me enough food to feed an army. I barely eat. I can't. I barely sleep. I can't do that either. I definitely can't sleep in our bed. I realized that the moment I stepped in there. It got worse when I walked into the bathroom to see the shattered mirror. It seemed like forever ago since I punched that fucking thing while she stood right in front of me, her eyes wide, her body shaking from fear. It was three weeks post Dave. Two weeks since I'd been back. Two nights since I'd been home.

Time.

Time is fucking stupid.

A knock on the door pulls me from my thoughts.

Dad and Eric have a key and let themselves in.

Sydney always calls before she comes.

The knocking starts again and I sigh. Finally, I get off my ass and limp over to the door.

The second I see her, time stops.

So does my heart.

"Hi," Riley whispers, raising her hand. She's even more beautiful than I let myself remember.

I inhale deeply. Hold it. And wait for the world to start spinning again.

It doesn't.

"Hi," I finally manage to say, my entire body rigid.

Her gaze moves from me to inside the house. "Are you busy?"

I shake my head, my words caught in my throat.

"I just came by to get a few things if that's okay?"

I open the door wider for her, my stomach flipping as she steps inside, her bare arm skimming mine. There's a weight on my chest, about as heavy as the one on my shoulders. My mouth's dry, my mind's spinning. My heart—I don't know… I don't have possession of it. I did. And then she showed up, reached inside, and stole it without me even realizing.

"My mom came by, as you know," she says over her shoulder as she makes her way to the living room. She starts to pick up a few of Bacon's toys. *Bacon.* I haven't even thought about Bacon. She adds, "She got some of my things, but not everything I needed so…" She turns around, her eyes on mine while I just stand there, crutches under my arm, wondering how it is she's functioning the way she is when I feel like death.

What a stupid saying.

No one feels death.

It just happens. One second you're breathing, the next you're not.

Dying, yes. You can feel like you're dying, but the actual death part—no. Or, at least I choose to believe that.

Because I'd hate to think otherwise.

What a morbid fucking thought.

"Anyway, I guess that's why I'm here," she continues. "I'll be quick. Just ignore me."

Right. That should be easy enough.

I sit on the couch and continue to stare up at the ceiling like I was doing before she decided to ruin me.

I ignore her familiar scent as she walks past me. I ignore the sounds of her footsteps as she moves around the house. And I ignore the fact that I can't fucking ignore her at all. Her steps, her sounds, her moves, her very presence is everything. *Everything.*

Something scrapes against the tiles of the kitchen and before I know it, I'm choosing not to ignore her. My steps are rushed, or as rushed as they can be when I'm on crutches. She's dragging a chair across the room. "What are you doing?" I ask, finally finding my voice.

She smiles at me.

She.

Smiles.

At.

Me!

Hate me, Riley. Why don't you hate me?

"I couldn't reach something in the bedroom."

I hobble over to the bedroom, hesitating for a second to prepare my heart for the onslaught my next move will create. I step into the room, stopping just inside and I inhale deeply. It was supposed to be calming. It's not. The room smells like her. Like us. Like us *together*.

I stay still as she walks around me, her side grazing mine when she steps in front of me. She faces the wall opposite the bed and points up. "Dylan?"

I shut my eyes, my stomach dropping, my mind fearing my body's reaction to the way she says my name.

It's not just the memories that cause the fear.

It's the longing.

It's her.

"I just wanted to take these frames with me if you don't want them…"

My eyes snap open, my gaze on her first, before I follow the length of her arm, her finger pointed to two black and white photographs hanging on the wall.

I'd never seen them before. Never even knew they were there.

I reach up, grab the first frame and hand it to her, then I grab the other. I don't give her this one. I can't. Not yet. Instead, I stare at it. And that's all I do.

My emotions keep me anchored to my spot, my heart heavy, my breaths heavier.

I skim my thumb across the glass. Behind it, there's a black and white image of her smiling face, a familiar one I'd only seen through the screen of the computer. There's an inset of me in the corner from when I was deployed, staring back, smiling right along with her.

"I took a screen shot when we spoke once," she says.

I tear my gaze away from the image and look at her. She's looking down at the picture she's holding—identical to mine, only I take up the frame and she's the inset.

She releases a breath as she sits on the edge of the bed, her fingers stroking the glass. "I kind of just wanted to remind myself that even though we were oceans apart, we were still together, you know?" She looks up at me, her eyes no longer clear but glassy, filling with tears.

I sit down next to her, ignoring the voices in my head that tell me not to—that it'll just make it worse, but I'm drained—of will and of sense—and I can't find the strength to stay upright.

"I hung them a few days before you got back. I figured you didn't see them because you never mentioned it."

"I'm sorry," I tell her, my focus back on the frame I'm gripping so tight my knuckles are white.

"It's okay," she says quietly. "You had a lot on your mind."

The room fills with the sounds of our heavy breaths and the silence of our incredible heartbreak.

"Is it true? What you said to my mom in the hospital?"

I inhale deeply, the sound echoing off the walls.

"That you wanted me to hate you?"

I nod once.

"Why?" she whispers. She's fighting to contain her cry but I feel it. I feel every ounce of pain she's trying so hard to hide. "Why not just tell me to leave?"

"Because I'm a fucking coward, Riley." I sit up, my hands stretched behind me as I look up at the ceiling. "I wanted to plant the seed in your head—the seed of loathing. So you were convinced it's something you wanted. Because I know you, Riley. I know if I'd say that you'd come back. You'll beg and you'll plead and I'll give in because I love you. I love you more than anything. And it's not enough. It never will be."

"That's a fucking lie, Dylan."

My eyes snap to her, but she's still looking at the frame. "You know I love you. You know I'd always put you first. *Always*. If you didn't want me anymore, I would've left. If you were suffering and you wanted to do it alone, you could've said that. If you needed time, I would've given it to you. You didn't come to me, Dylan." She stands up and faces me. Then takes the frame from me. "You didn't let me be the glue that held you together, and that's all I wanted to be for you. I'm sorry if that wasn't enough."

I find the strength to reach for her, but she moves away.

"My mom once told me that the hardest part of her day was the few seconds her hand would cover my doorknob and…" She pauses, wiping tears with the back of her hand. "…she was so afraid I wouldn't be able to find the strength to get through the day and I'd do something I couldn't take back."

"Ry, I'm not…"

"It must be hard—as a parent—to know that your child might have those thoughts and those insecurities."

"I don't."

"Reach out to your dad, Dylan. Take away the worry, okay?"

I watch her spin on her heels, her steps rushed as she walks through the door. I listen to those same steps move across the hallway, and finally, the front door open and close, shutting me out of her life and out of her world.

Riley

Dylan,
I realized something today as I let the memories of the forever you'd created for us rip my heart in two.

I was wrong.

There's no emotion greater than love.

No ache greater than longing.

No sound greater than you.

Fifty-One
Dylan

AN ENTIRE WEEK passes before I work up the courage to take her advice. I shower, dress, and do my best to look presentable. I call a cab to drive me the few minutes it takes to get to Dad's house.

IT'S HARD TO make eye contact with the people you hurt, especially when they love you as much as my family loves me. There was never a doubt in the loyalty and honor of the Banks men. Not until I went and changed all of that.

I disappointed them.

I disappointed myself.

I look up at my brother again, a man who's always been there for me, and then over at my dad as we sit around the kitchen table, my leg propped up on the seat Riley used to occupy.

From the corner of my eye, I see Sydney's arm move, her hand most likely going to Eric's leg under the table, showing her support.

I hurt her too.

I hurt everybody. Riley especially—but no amount of apologizing will ever make up for what I did to her.

Eric blows out a breath.

I switch my gaze back to him. After a thousand different words run through my mind—reasons, excuses, all of them useless, I decide on the truth. "Fuck man. I'm so fucking sorry."

"Quit cursing at the table," Dad says quietly.

Eric shrugs, not giving anything away. Then he leans forward, his forearms on the table. "Remember that time when you were in second grade and you fell off your bike and broke your arm?"

"Yeah…"

"Two days earlier I heard you tell Dad that you'd seen me smoking out in the yard when he was at work and I was supposed to be taking care of you. So, I saw you out on the sidewalk riding my old bike, happy as a pig in shit and I picked up a stick and threw that fucker right at your wheel. I told Dad you must've hit a rock. I convinced you of the same. So I guess this is payback."

Dad stands quickly. "We're family, son. End of discussion."

I'd created the chaos that brought me here and as easy as that, they offered me the calm to face reality again.

✧ ✧ ✧

JAKE'S CAR IS parked out front when Sydney drops me back at the house. He's standing at my door, back turned, hand raised as he knocks.

"What's up?" I ask, getting out of the car and hobbling up to him.

He lifts the giant plate of food in his hand. "My mom wanted me to drop this off." Then he sighs. "And I guess I just miss my friend. I've tried to give you time, like you said. But I don't know. I guess the worry won out and now I'm here, offering you food I bought at the diner to make it look like my mom made it just so I had an excuse to see you."

Without a word, I walk past him and open the front door, leaving it open as an invitation.

He stores the food in the fridge, along with the many others and sits in the living room with me.

"Lucy gave Cameron a black eye," he says, and I make a sound similar to a laugh but I can't be sure because it's been that fucking long.

"How?"

"Story goes she read a book—"

"It's always a fucking book."

"Right? So she read a book and told Cameron he needed to be more assertive and dominating. He said he wouldn't do it. She kept asking him to. And one night they were screwing and he told her, and I quote, '*to take it like the filthy whore she is*'. So yeah. Black eye."

I make that weird sound again, only this time, my shoulders shake with it. "They're fucking crazy."

"Yep," he says, and I glance over at him sitting on the couch opposite me, gazing up at the ceiling.

For a moment, I see the fifteen-year-old kid I met, the one who took in the new kid at school and quickly became my best friend, the only one who could read my actions when my words had failed me. "You ever feel stuck, Jake?" I ask, pushing away the memory from when I asked Riley the exact same question.

He lowers his gaze to mine. "What do you mean?"

"Like, sometimes I look out my window and see the world spinning around me, like time hasn't stopped and a life hasn't ended. I see people smiling, laughing, and I wonder how it is they can function and I'm just… stuck. I felt it when I came home on medical and I felt it after Dave died and I feel it now and I don't know why."

"Because you experienced near death twice and actual death once?" he says simply, sitting up higher in his chair. "I mean, when you think about it, time is just that… time. It's what life is made of. So time stops when a life ends."

Nothing in the entire world, besides Riley, has ever made more sense than Jake sitting in my living room right at this very moment.

He adds, "But that doesn't mean you don't fight to make time move again. If you want Dave's clock to keep ticking, find a way to make it happen."

"Like a legacy?"

Jake shrugs. "I did a little research… into your friend."

"You did?"

"He has three little brothers, right? They'd be missing him something fierce."

"Yeah, they would be."

"So."

"So?" I ask.

"So reach out to them if you think it'll help them. I'm almost positive it'll help you."

"What? You think I should write them a letter or something?"

He smiles and sits up higher. "Well you see, Grandpa Banks, there's this little thing called email. You can access it on something called the Internet."

Yeah. That weird sound is definitely a laugh. "I don't have a computer. It was Riley's."

Now it's Jake's turn to laugh. "Well you see, Grandpa Banks—" He dodges the cushion I throw at his head. "—there's this little thing called the Smartphone which has previously explained Internet."

"Fuck you."

We both pull out our phones at the same time. "So what do I do?" I ask.

"Well, this is tough. Riley ever get you to set up Facebook?"

I shake my head.

"Twitter?"

Another shake.

"Instagram?"

"Nope."

"Tumblr?"

"Now you're just making shit up."

He laughs again. "Swear it." He taps his phone and moves to sit next to me. "Let's start with the basics, Grandpa."

"Enough with the grandpa bullshit."

"Pops?"

"No."

"Gam?"

"No!"

"Fine. Gramps it is."

I look over his shoulder and watch him pull up an app. "Dave O'Brien, right?"

"Yep."

He types in: "Dave O'Brien USMC."

He's the first picture that pops up in the results. But it's not just him. It's us. We're standing next to each other, our smiles wide, head to toe in our combat uniform. I remember him getting Leroy to take the picture but I never actually saw it.

My chest tightens as I focus on his face, on his smile, and I remember the exact words he said after the picture was taken. "*This one's going right in the Banks spank bank.*"

"You okay?" Jake asks.

No. "Yeah."

"His profile's set to private, but we can see his friends." He types in "O'Brien" in another search window and *boom.* Two of his brothers are listed.

"Mikey—he's the oldest. I mean now he is..."

Jake nods, tapping more buttons and then hands me his phone. "You can write him a message but I have to go pick up my sister from the movies so if it's going to take you eighty years, *Gramps*, I'd rather you do a voice message."

"I can do voice messages?"

He nods. "Hold down that mic."

I do what he says. "Hey... uh... Mike. It's Dylan Banks. I'm using my friend's account. I don't have one. I was just seeing... um... checking up on you... I guess..."

Jake takes the phone from me, his thumbs flying across the screen and hitting send then switching it off and pocketing it all before I even realize I'm no longer holding the phone.

"I gave him your number and told him to text you. I gotta jet."

"How is Julie, anyway?"

He sighs, long and loud. "She's dating."

"What?" I ask, surprised.

He nods. "Yep. She's fourteen now."

"Shut up."

He keeps nodding. "I keep a bat in the back seat so the kid knows I'm not fucking around."

"So you don't like him?"

He scoffs. "I fucking hate him. He's a cocky little punk. Thinks he's God's gift to women."

"So she's dating Logan?"

His face drops. "That shit's not funny, man."

"If the shoe fits..."

"I'm going to fucking kill him," he says, rushing to the front door. I follow after him, laughing under my breath.

"Hey," he says, the door half open. "How'd you like the new workbench Riley got you?"

Fifty-Two
Dylan

I HADN'T BEEN in the garage since I'd been discharged from the hospital. I had no reason to. It was empty. No cars. No engine for me to work on. Besides, when it came to avoiding memories of Riley, the garage was as bad as the bedroom, if not worse. Maybe that's why it took an entire day and four hours of tossing and turning in bed, unable to find enough calm to sleep before I throw the covers off and make my way out there. I take a calming breath before opening the door and when I do, a million different emotions hit me at once.

Riley caught me on Pinterest once (shut up) looking at garage setups. I shut the screen quickly and told her I was just bored. Like most guys look at porn, I was looking at workbenches, dreaming that one day I'd have something similar.

Now the image that was on the screen is real and I'm fucking touching it.

I don't know when she did it. I don't know how Jake knew about it and I didn't. Right now, I don't know much of anything.

There's an empty jar in the middle of the bench, just like the ones she used to store her letters to Jeremy. I pick it up, my eyes squinting as I read the letters written in black marker: DYLAN.

I'm not exactly sure when I stopped breathing, but reading my name makes me start again. Only now, each breath is heavier and harder to get through.

I lean against the counter, moving the crutches aside so I can hold the jar in one hand phone in the other. A picture of her shows up on my screen as I fight a war in my head over whether to call her or not. Hearing her voice might just be my undoing.

Dylan: *I hadn't seen the garage untilxnow.*

Riley: *?*

Dylan: *Workbench.*

Riley: *Wow. I'd forgotten about it. I'm sorry.*

Dylan: *Why are you sorry?*

Riley: *You're not mad?*

Dylan: *Whyxwould I be mad?*

Riley: *I thought you'd be angry at me because I got rid of your old one.*

I read her text over and over, trying to figure out why the hell she would think that. Then I remember the smashed mirror in our bathroom, the times I'd yelled at her and used my anger to push her away, and it all makes sense.

Dylan: *Thank you, Riley.*

I stare at the screen, my hands gripping the phone tighter as I wait for her to respond. When enough time passes and I realize she has nothing left to say, I place the jar and the phone on the bench and stand in the middle of the room, my hands gripping the crutches as I circle slowly, getting lost in the memories created in this space.

My gaze catches on a stack of boxes in the corner of the room. All labeled Jeremy. I didn't stop her from bringing them with her when we moved in. And now they're here and she's not and it makes no sense. I make the decision to give them to Jake next time he comes by so he can give them back to her.

IT'S ONLY AFTER I've struggled—my leg aching and my chest burning—to move three of the boxes that I see more jars filled with letters stacked behind them. They're not Jeremy's, though. They have the same writing as the one on the bench, same black marker, same name.

I drop the box in my hand and stare at the jars. There are over twenty of them, all filled to the rim. I don't think twice. I grab two. Sit down on the cold concrete of the garage floor, and I do what I can to prepare myself for my heart's imminent destruction.

Dylan,
I love you.

I miss you.

Bryce, that vet from work, and Heidi are dating now. It's serious. Not sure why I wanted to tell you. I just did. I think there's a part of me that wonders if you worry whether she's happy. She is. At least, that's what they both tell me. And I'm happy for them.

Riley.

Dylan,
I love you.

I miss you.

So… don't be mad, but I brought a cat home from the shelter. (Sorry.) She was just so sad and cute and I couldn't help it. I named her Maple. Bacon and Maple. Get it? She was home two days before the Kline kids next door saw her and I guess they started giving her milk and food because they thought she was a stray. She does look like one. They named her—wait for it… Dog!

I spoke to Mrs. Kline about it and said I'd be happy to take her back but she said her kids would be devastated. Her kids had gotten super attached to her in the two days they'd had her. So, now I guess the neighbors have a cat. They're coming by tomorrow to look for a friend for Dog the cat. That's two cats I'm saving. I know it's nothing like what you do… but I kind of feel like a hero in a sense.

Riley.

Dylan,
I love you.

I miss you.

I went to your dad's house today for his birthday. It wasn't anything big—you know your dad—but Sydney and I made him a cake and got him presents. Did you ever buy your dad presents? And if you did, did you wrap them? Because swear he looked like a kid on Christmas morning when he unwrapped them. It was so cute, D. I wish you were there. Eric got him some fancy new version of that board game Battleship. I assume it means something to you guys because I swear he teared up a little. Sydney and I—well, we spent five hours at the mall trying to think of something for him and we came back with flannel shirts, socks and an old car calendar! I know, we suck, but your dad is the hardest person to buy things for. Mom was there too. She got him a beard grooming kit. I spent five hours at the mall and she came up with something that was actually useful to him.

But the best part of the night was when we brought out his cake. His smile got so wide. Then when we sat the cake in front of him, he looked up at me and did something amazing.

He offered me his wishes, babe.

I told him I couldn't, and that he should make the wish.

He took my hand, got up from his seat and made me sit down. Then he said, "I have everything I need right here. I have my family."

I know it's wrong to reveal your wishes, but I wished for you to come home to us. To all of us. So we can all be a family again.

I love you, Dylan.

I love you and I love your family.

I love that they accept me for everything I am and they care for and protect me and I just miss you.

I miss you so much, babe.

Forever yours,
Riley.

Dylan,
I love you.

I miss you.

I spent the day in bed with Bacon. I had this horrible dream last night and I guess I woke up and wasn't really up for functioning like a human. It was four in the afternoon when I got up to use the bathroom when I felt weak and got dizzy. I had to hold on to the sink in the bathroom to keep standing. I realized it was because I hadn't eaten all day. I still couldn't eat.

I think it's because I saw on the news last night that a life was lost out there, where you are. They didn't give names or which branch of military—something about respecting the families. It's dumb. Now all the other military families are out there wondering if it's their loved one.

Then when I finally got to sleep I had the worst nightmare ever. It's not like it was the first time I dreamed about it… me under water… my body weak, lungs and eyes burning, searching for the body… tasting the blood in my mouth. Only it wasn't Jeremy down there. It was you. Your face was white and your beautiful blue eyes stared back at me. I woke up in a cold sweat and ran straight to the bathroom and puked—which did nothing to take away the taste of blood in my mouth. I tried washing it out. It didn't work.

Most days I can be strong. Or at least strong enough to fake it. I didn't have the strength to fake it today.

You'll never read this.

I never want you to.

And I know that you're doing something important to you and I'm proud of you. Really, I am. Maybe I'm being a brat but I hate it, Dylan. I fucking hate it. I want you safe. I want you home. I want you in our bed. In our home. I want you in your truck. I want the horizon with you. I want everything with you and I can't have that if you don't fucking come home.

Riley.

✧ ✧ ✧

MY LEG ACHES, my lungs burn. Everything hurts. I don't know how I manage to keep standing long enough to knock, but the second the door opens, I lean against the frame releasing my grip on the crutches. They fall to the ground with a loud crash and my eyes drift shut as I force another round of air in my beaten lungs. "Dylan, what are you doing?" Holly says, her hands on my upper arms as soon as she opens the door.

"Riley," I breathe out, opening my eyes just long enough to look at her. "I need…" Breath. "…to see…" I try to swallow but my throat's too dry.

"Riley!"

Riley

I JUMP OUT of bed and run straight to the hall, my eyes darting and my heart beating out of my chest. I check left, check right. And then I stop. So do my frantic eyes and my erratic heart. "Dylan!" I run toward him, getting to him just in time to wrap my arms around his waist before he falls. "What are you doing?"

His breaths are sharp, loud, filling my ears with fear.

"Go next door and get Sydney!" I order Mom, helping Dylan into the house and onto the couch. His hand's on my wrist, and for as weak as he looks, his grip is strong. I look down at his hand, his knuckles are white.

"I need you, Riley," he whispers. Slowly, I peel his fingers from my wrist, allowing the blood to recirculate.

"I'm here." I sit on the couch, holding his face. His lids are hooded, his head heavy in my hands. "Do you need something?"

"You, Ry," he breathes out. "I need *you*."

Suddenly, the room fills with more bodies than the space can handle, I don't look at them. I look at Dylan. His eyes squeeze shut as he tries to swallow.

"Water?" I ask.

He nods.

I start to get up but he holds me to him. I look at Mom. "I'll get it," she says, and then she's gone.

Sydney's in front of him now, her fingers on his wrist. "Did you walk here, Dylan?" she asks, her voice calm and so out of place with the chaos in my head.

He nods again, weaker than the last.

"What the hell were you thinking?" Sydney asks. Same tone.

Dylan laces his fingers with mine, squeezing once, before rolling his head back on the cushion and looking up at the ceiling.

For a moment, everything is still. Silent. Only Sydney moves. She checks his pulse, gives him the water Mom brought him, and checks his temperature. He's sweating now, his chest heaving. His every movement, every breath is a struggle. He rolls his head to the side, his eyes on mine again. "I'm sorry," he whispers.

Inside, I break.

Outside, I smile. "Shh." I sit up on my knees, my arms around his head and I hold him to me, my chest soaking in the sweat across his forehead.

"Son," Mal says, speaking for the first time. "Let's go home, okay?"

"No!" I cry and hold him tighter. I look at Mom, pleading with my eyes. "He needs me! Mom, please!" All the emotions from the past few weeks finally catch up. I wanted him to *need* me. And now he's here. And I need him just as much.

Eric says, "Holly, we can take—"

"No!" I shout at everyone, one arm around Dylan's head and the other out in front of us.

Dylan's arms are around me now, his head still lowered, his breaths slowing. "It's okay," he whispers. "I shouldn't have come here."

"Mom," I cry, looking her in the eyes. I need her to see my plea, see the desperation we're both drowning in.

"I didn't take you away from him to keep you apart," Mom says, sitting on the other side of Dylan. "Not like this, sweetheart."

I look down at Sydney still kneeling in front of us. "He can stay with me, right? I can take care of him."

"He's overexerted himself. He needs to rest, Ry. Keep him hydrated and keep his leg elevated, okay?"

I nod quickly—my pulse resembling something like normal for the first time since Mom shouted my name, pulling me from the depths of my sleep. I had no idea it would end in this.

"Do you need anything, D?" Eric asks.

Dylan squeezes me in his arms, his head lifting just enough so he can look at me. "Riley. I just need Riley."

VOICES FADE FROM outside my bedroom door as everyone but my mother leaves. A moment later she knocks, not waiting for a response before popping her head into the room. I turn from Dylan lying in my bed, his hands behind his head, his gaze on the ceiling like it's somehow giving him answers to all the questions I'm positive are there. Not just in him, but in both of us. "Everything okay?" she asks, and I focus on Dylan's leg wrapped in a cast as I place a pillow beneath it.

"Everything's fine."

She steps in and hands me a glass. "Keep it on his nightstand in case—"

"I got it," I tell her.

She smiles. First at me. And then at Dylan. He doesn't notice.

"I'll check in in the morning."

"Thanks, Mom."

She smiles again then starts to leave the room.

"Holly," Dylan croaks, and her smile falters momentarily. "I'm real sorry, Ma'am. For everything."

HE FALLS ASLEEP right away, his arm around me, his hand settled on my waist when I turned into him. For hours, I lay awake, the endless questions swirling in my head. But the scariest one, the one I can't seem to shake… And I realize—just as my eyes drift shut—that I'm terrified of the circumstances that will lead me to the answer.

How long will this last?

Fifty-Three
Dylan

I WAKE UP, the sunlight filtering through the cracks of the blinds and for a moment, I forget where I am. It doesn't take long for me to find my bearings, because even though the room may be unfamiliar, the girl in my arms is the only thing I know.

I take a few minutes to soak in the events of last night and try to settle my emotions. I look down at Riley sleeping peacefully in my arms and I wonder how it is I spent the past few weeks, months, years, my entire goddamn life without her.

Slowly, I pull her off me, hoping not to wake her and sit on the edge of the bed. I look around her room again. Everything's changed—the pictures she had on the walls, the bookshelf, the desk, the nightstands which once held the speakers that led me to this room for the very first time. It's all changed. Everything but the corner of the room where cushions are scattered and jars are filled with letters.

She'd brought all her jars with her when we moved out so these are new.

There are no names on any of them to indicate which one of us she's been writing to and right now, I don't know which would hurt less.

I REACH FOR my crutches leaning against the nearby wall and grab the empty glass sitting on the nightstand. I struggle to hold both the glass and grip the crutch as I make my way to the bathroom. I make it two steps into the room before I lose my footing, dropping the glass. It shatters on the tiled floor, breaking into a hundred pieces.

"Dylan!" Riley shouts from the bed.

I turn swiftly, my hip crashing into the counter, my broken leg taking the weight and I fall, landing on my ass, my crutches giving out beneath me.

Riley runs toward me, stopping just outside the room, her gaze going right to the mirror and my heart drops.

The truth hits me, relentless, over and over again.

She's afraid.

She'll *always* be afraid.

With my hands in my hair, I drop my gaze to hide my shame.

"What's going on in here?" Holly shouts, walking into the bathroom. I look up just in time to see her look at the mirror first, then over at Riley, scanning over her entire body, looking for any damage I might have caused.

The walls close in and my stomach turns, my heart pounding in my eardrums. I gather whatever dignity I have left and look at both of them standing just outside the door, their eyes wide and filled with fear. I point to the shards of glass on the floor, shattered, just like all my hopes and determination to make everything right. "I dropped the glass," I tell them, my voice hoarse as I struggle to speak. "I shouldn't have tried to carry that and the crutches—"

"It's okay," Riley cuts in, moving around the glass and sitting next to me. "We'll clean it up."

"I'll get the broom," Holly says.

I wait for her to leave before looking at Riley, my voice low, my words meant only for her. "You looked at the mirror."

Her gaze falls. She doesn't speak.

"So did your mom," I tell her.

She exhales loudly.

"She thought I'd hurt you."

She stills.

"I'd never hurt you, Ry."

She takes the broom from Holly and sweeps up the glass, grateful to not have to respond.

"Are you going to work?" Holly asks her.

"Probably not," Riley says, focusing a little too much on clearing the mess I'd made.

"Okay. I'm going to try to clear my schedule for the afternoon. I'll be home early. I'd like to talk to both of you." Holly glances at me. "I'd prefer if you stayed here or if you need to leave, go over to Mal's. He's home just in case you need him. Sydney's coming by in an hour or so to check in on you."

"Okay," Riley answers.

Holly hasn't taken her eyes off me. "Okay, Dylan?"

I nod. "Yes, Ma'am."

✧ ✧ ✧

RILEY'S BY THE kitchen table, standing behind a chair she'd pulled out for me and fakes a smile when she sees me approaching. There's coffee, juice, sweet tea and water set out on the table. "I wasn't sure what you wanted," she says.

I take the offered seat and bring the coffee to my lips, watching her walk around me and to the other side of the table. She sits, looking down at her own coffee. "We need to talk," she murmurs.

"I know."

She looks up at me through her lashes. "Two minutes," she says, and my brows pinch in confusion.

A door opens, the sound of Holly's heels clicking across the hardwood floors gets louder with every step. "Will you guys be okay?" she asks, but I don't take my eyes off Riley.

She smiles. Fake again. And nods once. She stares at the spot her mother already vacated as I listen to the clicking of heels fade, the front door close, and then her car start and reverse out of the driveway. Riley must've been listening too, because it's not until a good minute later that she finally tears her gaze away from the blank space and focuses on me. She inhales deeply, taking another sip of her coffee. "So."

"So," I respond.

"So," she repeats.

I smirk. "What are you wearing?"

She smiles, then covers it quickly with her hand. "We can't do this, Dylan."

"Do what?" I ask, moving all four glasses out of my way and resting my elbows on the table. I lean forward, reaching for her hand.

She lets me take it. Just the tip of her fingers. Her nails are painted a bright blue. She's never had painted nails before. Or maybe she did.

Maybe I never noticed. I skim my thumb across the nail of her index finger, my mind lost, trying to remember.

"Dylan?"

"Yeah?"

She takes her hand away. "I feel like we should talk."

"About?" I say through a sigh, sitting back in my chair and looking down at the table.

"About what's happening. You. Me. Here. Now."

"Whatever you feel, whatever you want to say. I'm right here." I shrug. "Say it."

"I'm mad at you," she says quietly.

"I hurt you. You're allowed to be mad. I know that. And I can see you're afraid of me because of how I was. So is your mom. I get it."

"That's not—" She pauses to take a breath, her voice even softer when she adds, "That's not why."

"Then what?" I try to reach for her again, but she pulls back, hiding both her hands under the table.

"Dylan." She pauses. Swallows. Then continues. "You could've died."

"It was my job, Ry."

"No. Not that. Do you know what it was like for me seeing you in that car, not being able to get you out?"

I choke on a breath, realization setting in. "Fuck, Riley. I—"

"I thought you were dead! I thought it was happening all over again and I thought I was losing you, too. And in a way, I did." She looks up at me. "Right?"

I struggle to swallow. It's all I can do. "Ry…"

"And then I find out you'd been drinking that day. Not just drinking, but that you were drunk?"

"I wasn't—"

"How could you do that to me?"

I push my chair back and stand quickly, forgetting my broken leg.

"How could you get behind the wheel without a care for your life or mine and not think about me? How could you not think about me and how it would make me feel if I'd lost—" She breaks off on a sob, one that reaches the depths of my despair.

"Riley." I limp around the table and over to her, watching her head fall into her hands, releasing her anger along with her tears.

I place my hand on her shoulder. "I'm so sorry."

"I'm mad at you, Dylan," she says again, looking ahead. "I'm trying so hard not to be. But I am. I'm so mad at you."

"I know."

She stands up, pushing my hand off her shoulder. Then she looks up, her eyes the color of sadness.

I suck in a breath and hold it, a million emotions flooding me at once. "This was a mistake, Ry." I reach for my crutches across the table, get them situated and turn away from her.

One step.

That's as far as I get before her hands fist my shirt. "No, Dylan! You can't just run away. You can't run away from this. You can't fucking ignore it!"

I cringe, my shoulders tensing with the loudness of her voice. She releases me, just so she can walk around me. Standing in front of me, her sadness gone, replaced with anger and strength, she lifts her chin. "I did that, Dylan! I ignored what was happening to you, and to us, and look where it got us. I hated it. I hated that distance you created when all I wanted to be was enough."

"Riley—"

"And now you're about to do it again. You're about to push me away and—" She inhales deeply. "Why aren't I enough, Dylan?"

I drop the crutches, drop the bullshit pretenses and hold her face in my hands, forcing her to look at me. "Riley. I'm here because I need you. I'm here because you're the *only* thing I need. You're enough, babe. You're *everything*!"

I don't know how long we stand there, our breaths mingling, our eyes locked, our hearts beating, my hands on her face, hers circling my wrists before she narrows her eyes and lifts her chin with strength I'd once stolen from her. "Well?" she snaps.

"Well what?"

"Are you going to fucking kiss me because I have no problem throwing shit at you just because your leg's in a cast!"

"Fuck, I love you!"

I dip my head, watching her eyes drift shut before *knock knock knock*.

SYDNEY AND ERIC check in on me, so does Dad. For some reason, they refuse to leave. Meaning Riley and my moment in the kitchen is on pause. But that doesn't stop the build up, physical and emotional, of the things we want. The things we need.

She sits next to me, my hand on her leg, her eyebrows pinched. "B9," she says.

Dad grunts.

"Did I?" she squeals, her hands raised in victory.

Dad grunts again.

She points at him. "I sunk your battleship! Say it, Mal!" she says through a laugh.

"Yeah, Dad!" Eric chimes in, walking into the living room with sandwiches a foot high. "Say it!"

Another grunt. "Fine! You sunk my battleship."

Riley leans into me, her mouth pressed against my arm to muffle her cackle.

Dad drops his head and covers his eyes, but beneath his hands his beard shifts, revealing his smile. "You got me good, Riley."

Riley laughs harder.

The front door opens and Holly steps in, her eyes widening when she sees all of us taking up every space of her living room. Then she smiles. "Perfect. You're all here."

Eric does his best to tidy up the mess we'd made in her living room in the few hours she'd been gone but it doesn't seem to matter because she walks through the living room and into the kitchen. "Let's talk," she says, her voice firm.

Riley grasps my hand, helping me to stand, and like disobedient children, we file into the kitchen in a single line, Dad included, and each take a seat at the kitchen table.

Holly stands.

Dad grunts.

Eric chokes on a piece of ham.

Sydney sighs.

Riley won't let go of my hand under the table.

And me? Honestly? I'm fucking shitting myself.

"So," Holly says, pacing the small amount of space between the table and the kitchen counter. "I've had some time to think about things and firstly, I just need you all to know that my decision to take Riley home with me was not at all to separate the two of you long term. Do you understand?"

I look at Dad.

"Dylan?" Holly snaps, and I jump in my seat. "Do you understand?"

"Yes, Ma'am!"

Eric attempts to stifle his laugh. I glare at him. Fuck, I'd love to see him in this situation.

I squirm in my seat, my palms sweaty.

Holly sighs. "Good. Now that that's out of the way, we can discuss living arrangements."

I stare blankly at her.

"You are to stay here, at least until your leg is out of the cast. Even though I'm sure Eric, Mal and Syd visited you often, I never liked the idea of you living in that house alone. If something happened..." She shudders. "So?"

I look at Dad again. I don't know why I feel like he's somehow going to save me.

"Dylan!" she snaps.

I jump. *Again.* "Yes, Ma'am."

Eric chuckles. "D, you're twenty-four and still need a babysitter.

Sydney slaps his chest.

Dad grunts.

Holly says, "Eric, you're almost thirty, still live at home and still check the mail in nothing but your Spiderman underwear."

✧ ✧ ✧

IT'S RIDICULOUSLY HARD to imagine settling into a routine living in a house that's not yours, with two women... especially considering I've spent the majority of the past year with twelve cursing men who piss and shit in the open.

I feel like I'll be walking, or limping, or hobbling—whatever—on eggshells.

So I guess it's kind of a good thing that Holly invites my family to stay for dinner and even a few epic rounds of Battleship. It's a game Dad taught Eric and Eric taught me, and the only game Eric and I could really play together considering our age difference and his lack of imagination.

I'm assuming Battleship was played quite a bit while I was gone because a notebook that'd been used as a scorecard comes out and the games turn pretty serious. Even to the point where Eric goes over to their house and brings back a bright pink wooden contraption that sits between and around both boards—for extra secrecy, I guess. I'm not really sure what goes on for the four hours they play… but I do know one thing—our families are fucking crazy.

Riley stays by my side throughout all fifteen games, my hand on her leg and her side pressed against mine. We don't speak, at least not to each other, and when midnight comes around and we all call it a night, I finally get what I'd been craving for since the moment she ordered me to kiss her in the middle of her kitchen.

"Good night, Dylan," she says, lying in bed, resting her head on my shoulder and her arm on my chest. She leans up, kisses me once on the lips, and then smiles. "Batter up, rookie."

"Batter up?"

"You gotta earn that home run."

Two minutes later, she's out like a light.

And a few minutes after that, so am I.

Fifty-Four

Dylan

"Morning Dylan," Holly says from behind me. I drop the mug in my hand, coffee spilling, ceramic shattering on the floor.

"I'm sorry."

I blink hard, the images slowly fading. "No, it's my fault," I mutter, turning to her.

She's on the floor, a dish cloth in her hand as she picks up the pieces of the mug and starts wiping the blood off the floor. "Dylan?"

I can't take my eyes off the blood.

She stands quickly, reaching for me and I step back, my ass hitting the counter.

"Dylan?"

There's so much blood. "*I fucking failed, Dylan!*"

"Dylan!"

I gasp, choking on a breath as her hands find my shoulders, her face in my vision, her eyes like Riley's—back when she loved me. Before she feared me.

"Hi."

I drop my gaze. She can't see me. Not like this.

"Are you okay?"

Another blink. "Yes Ma'am."

"Why don't you sit?" she says, guiding me to a seat at the kitchen table. I look at the clock, the sounds of the seconds ticking and our heavy breaths the only thing I can hear.

I sit down, focusing on the grains in the timber of the table as she moves behind me, preparing another coffee. I flinch when she places it in front of me, her hand on my shoulder. "Do you need me to lift your leg?" she asks, her voice calm, just like her eyes.

"No, Ma'am."

She sits down next to me, cupping the mug in her hands. Smoke rises from the cup and my senses fill with the smell of gun powder. I blink hard again and rub my nose, doing what I can to fight the memories.

"I'm sorry for sneaking up on you like that."

"It's not…" I swallow loudly.

"Honey, can you please look at me?"

Slowly, I lift my gaze. She deserves that much.

Her hand reaches out again, soft and warm against my forearm. She glances at the hallway, and then at me, making sure Riley's not up yet. I already know what Holly's going to say. I can feel it. I can feel my life falling apart—feel Riley slipping out of my hands.

"I wanted to bring it up last night, but I didn't think it was necessary to speak about it in front of your dad and Eric."

I stare at her. Right into her eyes. And I can feel the calm start to take over. My breaths slow. My hands settle. "Okay."

"One of the other conditions for staying with us is that you speak to someone, Dylan."

I shake my head, my eyes leaving hers.

"Dylan? Please. I need you to look at me."

With a calming breath, I wipe my mouth with the back of my hand. Then I look up.

"It doesn't have to involve anyone else, Dylan. Just you and me," she says, nodding slowly. "Riley doesn't need to know. Your dad, the military—they don't need to either." She uses the hand not on mine to wipe her eyes, her eyes filling with tears. "I need you to do this for me." She pats her chest. "I'm a mother, sweetheart, and I worry about Riley." She glances at the doorway again. "I need to make sure she's safe."

I ball my fists, my eyes shutting tight and my heart racing again. "I would never hurt her."

"I know," she says quickly, leaning toward me. "I know that. But I've read about PTS—"

"Stop!" My eyes snap open, focused on hers. I expect fear. I see calm.

"Okay, sweetheart." She nods again. "Okay."

I take a few breaths, my head tilting, completely confused by the way she's looking at me. After a long moment of silence, I find my voice. "My friend Amanda…"

Holly smiles. "I know her."

"She's um… she's a psychology major."

"Okay," she breathes out, nodding faster. "That works for me."

Riley's bedroom door opens. Holly drops her gaze and removes her hand from my arm. Then she sits back in her chair. "Ms. Hudson?"

She looks up at me.

"I'm not going to lose her. Not again. She means too much to me."

✧ ✧ ✧

I WAIT UNTIL Riley and Holly have left for work before keeping my promise to Holly. I sit on the couch, my knees bouncing, my phone gripped tight in my hand.

Dylan: *How mucg do youxcharge a session?*

Amanda: *For you? One My Little Pony.*

I smile.

Dylan: *When?*

Amanda: *Where you at, Grandpa?*

Dylan: *Riley's.*

Amanda: *I'll be there in 30.*

"So I'm going to tell you how I think this session will go and then we can start, okay?" Amanda says, sitting on the couch opposite me.

"Okay?"

"After I finish with this speech, you're going to look away, and then sit there grunting at every one of my questions."

"What?" I ask.

"Yeah. You might just be the hardest client I'll ever have. You know, considering you actually have to talk to get anywhere."

"I talk."

"You talk!?" she shouts.

I roll my eyes.

"Ready?" she asks.

I shrug.

"So talk."

My eyes narrow. "Aren't you, like, supposed to ask me something?"

"I don't know why I'm here, though. So you have to start."

This was the dumbest idea ever. "How?"

She smiles, lifting her glasses higher on the bridge of her nose. "Why don't you tell me what you were doing, or thinking, when you decided to message me."

I nod and drop my gaze. "Riley's mom, Holly—"

"I know Holly well," she cuts in.

I nod again. "She said I had to speak to someone."

"Right," Amanda says, tapping on her iPad. "So you don't want to be here. You kind of have to. For Riley?"

Another nod. "Riley doesn't know, but if it means keeping her..."

"I get it."

I inhale deeply, looking up at the ceiling.

"So did something happen that made Holly ask you to see someone?"

Shrugging, I roll my head back and forth on the cushion. "I was remembering Dave. And thinking maybe I should write to him."

"Like Riley did with Jeremy?"

My eyes snap to hers. "She talk to you about Jeremy?"

"Not really. She mentioned that she wrote to him, but never really spoke about *him*. I only knew about it because we all went to the cliff."

I sit up, raising my eyebrows in question.

"Yeah," she says, waving her hand in the air. "You know, on the anniversary of Jeremy's death. We all went there..."

"You what?"

She rears back a little. "We went there because Jake thought she'd be there."

"And she was?"

"She didn't tell you?"

I shake my head. "So you were all there?"

"Not on the cliff," she tells me. "Not the first time anyway. It was only Jake then. We didn't want to pressure or overwhelm her to jump."

"She jumped?" I ask, clearly surprised.

Amanda nods. "A few times."

"Huh," is all I say, my mind too busy spinning with thoughts.

"So what would you have written?"

"Huh?"

"In the letter, Dylan. To Dave? What did you want to say?"

"I wanted to tell him that I hated him. *Again*."

"Again?"

"Long story," I mumble.

"It's valid."

"What is?"

"To hate him."

"It is?"

After typing something on her iPad, she looks up at me. "Of course it is."

"Why?"

She places the iPad on the cushion next to her. "All emotions are valid, Dylan. Regardless of whether you think it's right or wrong to feel them, they exist because they're real. I could list a number of reasons as to why I think it's okay to hate him. Or at least, to be mad at him. But that doesn't mean it's what *you* feel."

"List them," I snap. "Please." Because I need to know.

She inhales deeply, her eyes on mine. "He left you, D. I mean, that's basic right? When you think someone is going to be part of your life and then all of a sudden they're not, that hurts. And hurt can easily turn to hate. Because it's better than the alternative. He probably also made you feel guilty. Guilt can also turn to hate. Again. It's better than the alternative."

Even though I know the answer, still I ask, "Why would I feel guilty?"

"Because you feel like you should've known something was wrong. He was your friend. And now you're wondering if the signs were there or if you just chose to turn a blind eye to it. If you were too wrapped up in the joys of your life, you didn't see his."

I exhale loudly, causing her to smile.

She continues. "You probably hate him because you feel like you have to live your life a certain way now because of him. You try to justify your life based on his death and you feel like you have to go above and beyond to give value to his death."

"I don't feel like I *have* to."

She smiles wider. "But you want to?"

I nod.

"And, lastly, you're allowed to hate him simply because he's gone now. And there's nothing you can do to bring him back. And I think, out of all the reasons, that's probably the one that hits home the hardest." She pauses a beat. "You miss him?"

I look down at my hands and nod again. "Like crazy."

✧ ✧ ✧

"HOLY SHIT, BABE," Riley calls out, stepping into the house. "Did you fix the air conditioning?"

"Yep!" I remove the pipe from under the Riley's bathroom sink and move quickly to let the gunk of hair fall into the bucket.

"Where are you?"

"Bathroom!"

Her footsteps near, stopping just outside the doorway. "What are you doing?"

"Clearing your pipes."

She scoffs. "You wish."

I replace the pipe and start to screw it back on.

"You got bored, huh?" she asks, kneeling down next to me.

"A little." *Lie.* I was bored out of my fucking mind. There's not a lot you can do in a house that's not yours with a leg that doesn't work.

"You went home and got your tools, D?"

I finish my task and start to sit up, taking her offered hand half way. "I got Eric to get them for me when he got some other shit." I run my hands down my shorts. "Hi."

She smiles. "Hi."

"How was work?"

Shrugging, she says, "You had me looking at the clock, Banks."

I attempt to stand but she places a hand on my shoulders, keeping me down. "So…" She lifts a leg and straddles my lap and I'm instantly hard.

I bite down on my lip, my dirty hands itching to touch her.

"What have you been doing?"

"Missing you."

"Yeah?" she whispers, her hands on my neck, her eyes searching mine.

I nod.

She dips her head, her mouth finding my jaw. "I missed you too. All of you, babe."

"Ry."

"What?"

"Your mom's going to be home any minute."

Her lips move, hovering an inch in front of mine. "She's not home now."

Our mouths crash together, our kisses desperate. God I missed her. All of her. Her smell, her kiss, her taste. I use my hands to remember her, ignoring how dirty they are. I run them along her sides, down her waist and to her ass—forgetting where we are and what we're doing. I get lost. In her. In the memories of her and the lust building inside me. Her hips push down, pressing into me, a moan escaping her lips and landing on mine.

"Whoo!" Holly sings, shutting the front door. "Dylan fixed the air?"

Riley backs away quickly and stands to my side.

I cover my cock when Holly appears in the doorway of the bathroom. "What are you doing?" she asks, pizza boxes in her hand.

"Clearing Riley's pipes," I answer.

Riley chokes on air.

"The sink!" I rush out and point to the sink. "Not Riley—not her—this!"

Holly presses her lips together, nods once, and then leaves.

Riley shakes her head, her eyes filled with amusement. "You suck at talking, D."

"No shit."

I hear the front door shut. "I heard there was pizza!" Eric shouts.

Dad grunts.

Holly calls out, "Let's eat."

My phone rings on the bathroom counter and Riley reaches for it. She hands it to me, still standing above me, her legs toned and tanned beneath her skirt. "You going to answer?"

I kiss her leg. Just once. Then answer the call and bring the phone to my ear. "Hello?"

"Lance Corporal Banks?"

I instantly recognize the voice on the other end. "Yes, First Sergeant?"

"Conway and I are in town on a recruiter visit. Thought we'd come see you. We're at your house but no one's answering the door."

"I'm at my girlfriend's house, First Sergeant."

"I thought she lived with you?" he asks, his tone more casual.

I look over at Riley, her brow furrowed. "It's a long story."

"Can we come by, Banks? There's something we'd like to discuss."

"Yes, First sergeant."

"Send Conway the address. We'll be there soon."

I hang up and look down at my phone, knowing full well it's bullshit. There's no recruiter visit. They're here for me.

"What's that about?" Riley asks, helping me to stand.

I wash my hands, my eyes on her through the reflection of the mirror.

"They're coming by."

"Why?"

"To discuss the disciplinary action for my DUI."

Fifty-Five
Dylan

THEY SHOW UP fifteen minutes later to a waiting audience. I guess no one wanted to leave. Dad and Eric helped move the furniture in the living room so we could accommodate their visit.

Riley helps me to stand when First Sergeant Fulton and Conway enter the room. I shake hands, make the introductions and offer them a seat on the couch opposite us.

"How's the leg?" First Sergeant asks.

I tap it twice. "It's getting there."

He nods. "Listen," he says, holding the brim of his cap in his hands as he rests his elbows on his knees. "This wasn't a casual visit, Banks. I'm here to discuss—"

My throat clearing cuts him off. I glance at Dad quickly and then at Eric. There's no other reason for a First Sergeant to make the trip out to my home unless it's something dramatic. "I know why you're here," I tell him.

"So you've thought about it, Banks?"

My brow furrows.

He sighs, taking the folder that Conway hands him. "We got word of your DUI, Banks."

I nod, glancing at Dad again.

Riley takes my hand in hers.

First Sergeant continues. "You have four weeks left until your contract with the United States Marine Corps is up."

Everything inside me stills. Everything but my heart, racing, thumping hard in my chest.

He opens the folder in his hands, his eyes shifting from left to right. "You have four weeks of leave accumulated?"

My gaze drops. I know what's happening. And the thought of it turns my stomach to stone. "Yes."

"It's under recommendation from the Sergeant Major that you use your leave, Lance Corporal." He closes the folder and holds it above the coffee table between us. "We have all the paper work to begin the out process. Anything else we can get to you? I assume all your gear is still at the barracks rooms?"

I stare at him.

"You happy for Conway to go through your stuff and send you your personals?"

I look at Conway. He's looking down at his hands. He won't make eye contact. He's too goddamn nice.

In the corner of the room, Dad grunts.

And the walls—they start to close in. Like a cave, trapping me.

I look over at Dad and Eric. They won't look at me either. Shame can do that to people. I attempt to swallow but my mouth's dry. I reach for the glass of water on the table, my hands trembling.

"Banks," First Sergeant says. "Are you okay?"

No. "Yes." I ignore the water and take the folder from him before opening it on my lap.

"What's happening?" Riley says quietly.

"It's okay," I assure her.

"I'm sorry, First Sergeant Fulton Sir," Riley says, "What do you mean out process? What does that…" She takes a breath. "Dylan?"

I can feel her eyes burning a hole in the side of my head but my focus is on the page, the words blurred. I blink hard. It doesn't help.

"Mal?" Riley says, her panic evident. "What does it mean?"

Eric answers for him. "It means he's out."

"Out?" she says, on her feet now. "Out of what?"

"The military, Ry," Eric says, the disappointment in his words as evident as the panic in Riley's.

I try to take her hand but she shrugs out of it. "Ry, sit down."

"No!" she shouts. "You're forcing him out?"

"Don't Riley," Eric warns.

"With all due respect, First Sergeant, how fucking dare you come into my home and disrespect my boyfriend. The Marines mean everything to him. *Everything.* He took a fucking bullet serving this country. He earned a Purple Heart for this country!"

I stare down at my lap, all of the words blurred, but for Riley's which are clear as day.

"It should be his choice, Sir! If he wanted to leave, it should be his damn choice!"

"Riley," Conway says, speaking for the first time since he entered. "We're under orders to—"

"Fuck your orders!"

Holly gasps.

Riley's words are unrelenting. "Dylan watched his best friend take his life and for what?! For *fucking* what?! So he could be forced to give up something so important to him because he made a mistake! You know Dylan, Conway. You probably know him better than I do. You both do!"

I finally look up at her, her rage visible in the way her hands fist at her sides, the redness in her face, the anger boiling inside and releasing in her tears.

She looks at my dad. He won't say a word. She looks at Eric. He won't either. Then she looks at me. "It should've been your choice," she whispers. Then she stomps out of the room, slamming every door possible.

"She's feisty," First Sergeant tries to joke.

No one finds it funny.

"Banks, it's better this way. After what you witnessed with O'Brien—"

"Don't talk about him," I grind out.

First Sergeant inhales deeply. "There won't be any Military discipline for the DUI. Your record will remain clear if you ever decide to re-enlist."

Holly hands me a pen. "Here, sweetheart."

FIVE MINUTES LATER, everyone leaves. Holly stays. "You good?" she asks.

I nod.

"I'll give you some time."

An hour passes before my head is finally clear enough to face Riley. I get off the couch and make my way to her room. Riley's pacing the floor, her back turned, one hand balling and straightening, the other over her mouth.

"Ry."

She turns quickly. "I'm sorry," she rushes out, moving toward me.

"It's done, Ry."

"Dylan. I don't know what came over me. The way I spoke to them—"

"Ry!"

She swallows. Her eyes drifting shut. "I'm sorry, baby," she says, wrapping her arms around my waist.

"I'm tired."

"Okay."

She helps me to the bed and takes off my shoe. "Are you hungry? I'll heat up the pizza. We can eat in here."

"Please."

She leaves, returning a moment later with food and drink. After putting the drinks on the nightstand and sitting down next to me, she hands me a plate and sits hers on the bed next to her. "So," she says, her arms stretched, her grip on the edge of the mattress. "Did you want to talk about it? Um. With someone? It doesn't have to be me… or it can be… if you want to…"

I set my plate on the nightstand and turn to her. "Ry?"

Holly pops her head into the room. "Dylan, your dad's at the door."

My eyes drift shut, my heart racing again. Shame. It's all I can feel. Not mine. His.

Without a word, she closes the door. Though her voice is muffled, I can hear her. "He's fallen asleep, Mal," she says.

Riley's eyes snap to mine, sad and pleading.

"I promise, Riley. One day, we'll talk about this." I hold her face in my hands, kissing her once. "I'll tell you everything, okay? Just not now. Please."

"Okay."

"Okay? Just *okay*?"

Her hands circle my wrists, pulling them away from her. Then she inhales deeply, her words rushed when she says, "I've been wanting to tell you something for a while and I never found the right time to say it…"

"What's going on, Ry?" I ask, my heart dropping.

She releases my hands and shakes out hers. "I've never stopped loving you, Dylan. Through everything we went through there was never a time when I questioned how I felt about you. *Ever.* And I realized that I was wrong—when I felt like I wasn't enough… I was. I *am.* It's just that you weren't ready. The timing in each of our grievances weren't the same and if I had met you right after everything happened to me, there's no way I would've been ready to accept you. Just like you didn't accept me. You pushed me away, the same way I pushed Mom away and I understand it now. I think, in the end, we needed that pause—"

"Pause?" I whisper.

She lifts her chin, showing her strength. "We just needed this time apart to get back on the same page and now we're here."

"Riley…"

"First page. New book."

I exhale loudly, my fears leaving with my breath.

"Besides," she says, smiling now. "I promised you, right?"

"Promised me what?"

"Semper fidelis."

The words roll around in my head. Then I smile. "Always faithful."

She nods.

My shoulders relax. "I love you so much."

Smirking, she says, "So show me."

I kiss her. I can't not. Especially when she's looking at me the way she is.

My mouth covers hers, my hand on her waist. The force of the kiss has her moving back until she's lying on the bed, her hands in my hair as she smiles around my lips. She starts to giggle.

"What?" I ask, pulling away.

"I'm lying on the pizza."

I tug the fabric of her top. "You better take this off then."

Her head tilts. "You trying to get to second base, Banks?"

Awkwardly, I move until I'm sitting up on my elbow, looking down at her. "Actually, I'm trying to get to third. And maybe that'll be enough for you to let me limp to home base."

She sits up, chewing her bottom lip before removing her top, leaving her in her bra and her skirt. I swipe the plate off the bed, harder than intended, causing it to smash against the wall. A second later Holly's back.

"Mom," Riley squeals, covering her breasts.

I cover my hard-on.

"Sorry!" Holly squeaks, her hand over her eyes as she closes the door.

Riley gets up and locks the door. Then leans against it, facing me, her hands still on the knob. "So," she says.

I use my elbows to shift back on the bed until I'm sitting against the headboard, my legs out in front of me. "Come here, baby."

Slowly, she walks toward me, her hips moving from side to side. When she reaches the bed, she crawls toward me, her handful of breasts swinging beneath her. My eyes lock onto them, like a man deprived and I get flooded with memories of her. The smoothness of her skin against my finger tips, the taste of her on my lips… on my tongue. A groan emits from deep in my throat, getting louder when she straddles my lap, her hands on my shoulders, my hands on her back, moving higher until I find the clip of her bra. Her back arches when her breasts free from their confines, her gaze lowered. I keep my eyes on hers when I lower my lips, taking her nipple into my mouth. "God, I missed you," she whispers, her fingers digging into my nape as her hips push forward, rubbing on my cock. I flatten my tongue, licking up her nipple. I pull back, just enough for her to remove my shirt. Her fingers feel like fire as they land on my chest, her movements are slow, not at all desperate as they lower down to my shorts. She fingers the band, teasing me with her eyes and her tongue when she runs it across my lips. One hand on her back, I pull her into me, the other on the back of her head, tugging gently on her hair until her head tilts back. Her mouth parts, welcoming my assault on her lips, her tongue, her breaths, her sexy-as-fuck moan. She frees my cock, her hand circling it, stroking gently.

I run my hands up her legs, moving higher until my fingers find her panties. My thumbs stroke where her thighs connect.

Her strokes get faster while I move her panties aside, my finger entering her.

Her movements stop momentarily, her head throwing back. With two fingers inside her now, my thumb stroking her clit as her hips move back and forth, her wetness soaking my hand, I go for her breasts again, making sure to pay the same attention to each one.

She resumes her strokes, my hips jerking back and forth with her movements.

Then she moans again, her pussy tightening around me and I know she's close. So fucking close I can smell it. "Dylan," she whispers.

"Fuck, baby…"

Both hands around me now, she starts to move faster.

My hands ball in her hair, pulling her face to mine, using her mouth to drown out the grunt caused by my release. I free her quickly, her entire body covered in sweat as she moans my name, over and over, her hips moving grinding. Then she bites down on her lip, muffling her cry as she comes around my fingers.

"Holy shit, babe," she whispers, her forehead resting on my shoulder.

I stroke her hair, my lips to her ear. "Thank you, Ry."

She pants a few times, trying to settle her breaths. "For what?"

I wipe my brow on her shoulder. "For never giving up on me."

Fifty-Six
Dylan

MY EYES SNAP open, my body covered in a cold sweat. I try to breathe through the unbearable weight on my chest. I close my eyes again, trying to work out where I am.

I hear gun shots.

Smell them around me.

But the worst? The worst are the eyes I see.

The kid's.

Dave's.

And then Riley's.

All full of hope.

I roll my head to the side, my nostrils filling with the scent of Riley's shampoo. Blindly, I reach up, my fingers finding the mess of hair on her head. I move down her neck and follow her arm settled across my chest creating the weight I'd confused for pain.

My breaths slow, my mind doesn't.

As carefully as I can, I reach for my phone. 3:18 a.m.

Just as gently, I remove myself from beneath her and sit on the edge of the bed, my entire body tense. I rub my eyes, the dryness in my throat making it impossible to swallow. After retrieving my crutches, I hobble to the bathroom and drink water from the tap, then splash some on my face, trying to get my mind to catch up to my body—to make it wake up, move on, release it from its trap. I look over at Riley fast asleep, her body splayed across the entire bed.

Dave's in my mind, full combat gear, weapon to his chest, the sun beaming down on him making the freckles across his face extra dark. "*Banks,*" the fucker says, smiling at me. "*You're going to fuck it up, man.*"

I LEAVE RILEY to sleep and move out to the living room. I switch on the light and the TV, muting it as soon as it comes on. Then I hobble over to the couch and I sit.

I sit and I wait for the calm to hit me.

I don't know how long I'm there, watching but not really seeing anything on the screen when Holly whispers my name. I look at the doorway to the kitchen to see her standing, her arms crossed as she leans against the doorframe. "Did I scare you?" she asks.

I shake my head. "I'm sorry, did I wake you? It's hard to be quiet—" I point to the crutches. "—with them."

"No." She pushes off the frame and moves toward me, and then points to the spot next to me. "Can I sit?"

I nod, staring ahead.

After sitting down, she says, "I got up for a drink and saw the light on."

Moments pass, the silence building. Finally, I break. "How'd you know?"

"Know what, sweetheart?"

I turn to her slowly. "You handed me the pen."

She sighs. "I've been watching you, Dylan. I could tell you wanted out. You just didn't want to disappoint your family."

"How?"

Her lips thin to a line. "I see the way you look at your dad and Eric. Especially since the DUI. You think they're disappointed—"

"I always felt like my dad would be proud of me, no matter what I did, but the way he's looked at me since the DUI… I caused shame on him, on my family and on our name. They raised me to be honorable and strong and I'm neither of those things."

"Dylan," she whispers, her hand on my arm. "That's not true."

I keep looking ahead, keep waiting for the calm to hit me. It never does. My eyes shut, and just like that, my insanity kicks in. "I see him," I mumble.

"See who?"

"Dave O'Brien."

She sucks in a breath, then releases it slowly.

"It's like this movie playing in my mind, over and over. I see him hold his gun to his head, his finger curl, pulling the trigger. I hear the gun go off. Smell the gun powder. Feel my heart stop. See the blood everywhere. *Everywhere.* And I feel it, in my hands and on my clothes. I've tried to shake it, and since I've been here with Riley, they've slowed down. But they haven't stopped. And he was there…"

"Where, Dylan?"

"At the accident," I say, my voice breaking. I clear my throat. "I wasn't drunk, Ma'am. Dave—he was standing in front of the car, his head blown off. I swerved to miss him and I knew I was losing it so I made Riley get out of the car."

Her fingers are warm when they skim my cheek, wiping away tears I hadn't known were there. "Does anyone know?"

I shake my head.

"Your dad? Eric?"

"I'm a man, Ms. Hudson. And this makes me weak… I can't—" I choke on a sob, but push it down enough to add, "I've disgraced them enough. I can't admit this to them."

"What about Riley?"

"No."

"She'll understand—"

"No. And you can't tell her…" I wipe my cheeks. "You can't say a word."

"Dylan…"

"I'm supposed to be strong. She looks to me for strength. For glue. I need to be that for her… She can't know. You have to let me at least have that," I rush out. Pleading with a woman who owes me absolutely nothing to please, *please*, keep my secrets.

"Okay." She sniffs once. "So why tell me?"

I pause a moment, waiting for my heart to settle before turning to her, my eyes on hers—her tears clouding the pity. "Because you look at me like no one else does. No one *ever* has. You expect nothing of me but *me*, as a person. Not as a man of honor, or a man of strength." I blink. Tears fall. "You look at me like a mother would look at her son."

Riley

I COVER MY mouth to muffle my cry, my vision blurred from the tears flowing fast and free. Mom glances over Dylan's shoulder at me standing in the hallway, just like she did after he asked her how she knew he wanted out of the Marines. She wraps her arms around his neck, wiping her tears on his shoulder—shoulders that shake with the force of his cries—cries he's held in for so long.

I leave them in the living room and go back to bed, waiting for him to join me. Seconds, minutes, hours pass. The sun rises. The world awakes. And finally, Dylan walks in. I lay still, my eyes closed. The bed dips before I hear the clanking of his crutches. A moment later, I'm in his arms, his nose rubbing against mine. "Riley," he whispers.

"Mm?"

"I love you."

I open my eyes, lock them on his, clear and blue and everything I remember them to be, back when he still had control of the world around him… when his reality consisted of his purpose and of us and our love and nothing could get in the way of it. "I know."

Fifty-Seven
Riley

"DO WE EVEN know where the guys are going?" I ask, emptying the packet of corn chips in the bowl.

Heidi shrugs. "Who cares. I haven't had a slumber party in forever."

"Me neither," Mom says. She tries in vain to open the jar of salsa before giving up. "Dylan!"

"Yes, Ma'am," he calls out, and a second later he walks into the kitchen. He's been out of the cast for four days. "I love the way you say Ma'am," Lucy teases. *I think.* She fans her face, her eyes rolling back. "Say it again."

Dylan just smiles, shaking his head as he stops between me and Heidi. Mom hands him the jar. He loosens it with a pop before handing it back to her.

"At least your hands work," Heidi says, backhanding his stomach.

He feigns hurt.

"Oh, his hands work real good," I blurt out.

"Riley!" Mom squeals.

I cover my face to hide my embarrassment.

"So hot," Lucy mumbles.

"Gross," Heidi jokes.

Next to me, Dylan chuckles. I remove my hands and glare at him. Then throw a chip at his head. "What?" he laughs out. "I didn't do anything!"

He pulls out his phone after it beeps with a text.

I watch his lips curve to a smile as he reads it. "Your other girlfriend?" I ask.

"Wife, actually." He shows me the phone, a message from Mike O'Brien is on the screen with a picture of him and his brothers and his mom standing in front of a house. The caption reads "*Casa de O'Brien.*"

"They got the house?" I ask.

"Looks like it."

Dylan had been talking to Mike a bit lately on Facebook. Yes, Dylan got a Facebook. Apparently Dave's personals were sent to his family, so he and Dylan have been going through the stuff they received. They were waiting on the gratuity payment to come in so they could move out of their tiny apartment and far away from where Mr. O'Brien could find them and hurt them. In a way, I think it's kind of therapeutic for Dylan to speak to someone who knew Davey like he did, and not just the Marine version of him.

A car horn has Dylan pocketing his phone. "That's the guys."

"And Micky and Amanda!" Lucy says, clapping.

"What are you pretty girls planning on doing tonight?" he asks me.

"So hot," Lucy whispers.

I laugh. "Not much. Probably talking books."

"No!" Heidi stomps her foot. "Let's do girl stuff. Like… Oh my god! Makeovers!"

"We're not twelve," I tell her, the same time Mom says, "Yes!" She points to her. "I like your thinking, Heidi. I've been wanting to makeover Riley for years."

"Don't you change a thing about her," Dylan says, blocking me from their view.

Lucy sighs. "So hot."

He turns to me. "Walk me out?"

I take his hand and lead him to the bedroom, where he grabs his bag, and then out of the house, meeting Micky and Amanda on the driveway carrying sleeping bags.

If the guys get to go on a boys' night out to some cabin in the woods, why couldn't we have a girls' night in?

"HEY, RILEY," JAKE shouts, waving and grinning like an idiot as he pulls Cameron out of the trunk of his car. Logan and Jake are dressed in black, war paint smeared on their cheeks.

Cameron groans as he finds his feet, his hands tied behind his back, his mouth duct taped and his eyes blindfolded.

"What the hell?" I whisper.

"Quack quack!" Logan yells, ripping the tape from Cameron's mouth.

Cameron curses and starts kicking Logan's legs as soon as the blindfold is off him.

"Why are you quacking?" I yell walking down the path toward them.

"Hey Ry," Dylan says, stopping on the sidewalk. I turn around in time to see him reveal a jar of sugar from behind his back.

"What is that?"

He smiles. "I wanted to give you some sugar."

I take the jar off him. "Huh?"

Then his arms are around my waist, pulling me toward him. He smiles, right before he dips his head, his mouth warm and soft and wet against mine.

My body melts into his, one arm around his neck, the other too busy holding onto the jar. The force of his kiss has me bending backwards, gasping into his mouth. I smile against his lips as he slowly pulls away.

"Have a good night," he says, releasing me completely.

"Wait." I grab his hand. "Did you just tell me you wanted to give me some sugar and then kissed me?"

He laughs, his blue eyes bright against the evening sun. "Yes, Riley. I did."

"Such a grandpa joke."

"You love it." He starts to walk backward, his smile getting wider. "And you love me."

"I do."

"And I'm madly in love with you, Riley Hudson." He stops in his tracks, scans me from head to toe, before running back to me. His hands go to my face, cupping my cheeks and tilting my head up. "Hey, when I get back, maybe we can go away for the night? It'll be all romantic and stuff. Hearts, flowers, the works." He presses his lips to mine again. Just once.

I flatten my palms on his chest and look up at him. "I don't want hearts and flowers, Dylan."

"No?"

"I want your heart and soul."

"Well, you already own that." He smiles before turning around, leaving me standing in my front yard, my smile wide, my heart full and my future walking away from me.

I go to speak, but Cam beats me to it. "Hey everyone! Dylan's got a boner!"

✧ ✧ ✧

Dylan: *How's it going?*

Riley: *Good. You there yet?*

It's a dumb question. They only left a half hour ago. Still, it hasn't stopped me checking the phone, checking the time, waiting to see which one of us would crack first. Luckily, it was him. And lucky for me, his texting has gotten a lot better since he started talking more with Mikey.

Dylan: *Nope. Another hour or so.*

Riley: *Are you having fun?*

Dylan: *Not as much fun as I would with you.*

Riley: *You left me hanging, Banks.*

Dylan: *That was the plan. Keep you wanting more.*

Riley: *Your plan worked.*

Dylan: *Oh yeah?*

Riley: *Yep. Text me when you get there, okay? Be safe. The girls are yelling at me to get off the phone.*

Dylan: *Okay. I miss you.*

Riley: *Me too.*

Dylan: *I love you.*

Riley: *I love you, too.*

Dylan: *Riley?*

Riley: *Dylan?*

Dylan: *Nothing. I just love you.*

✧ ✧ ✧

Dylan: *We just got to the cabin.*

Riley: *Thanks for letting me know.*

Dylan: *You're welcome. Riley, you know I love the way you are, right?*

Riley: *Yes. Why?*

Dylan: *I just don't want you thinking you need to change the way you look. I think you're real pretty but if you want to do something then I don't mind. I was just kidding with what I said.*

Riley: *You own my heart, Banks.*

Dylan: *And the rest? I like that spot right behind your ear. The one that makes you squirm. And your ass too. And your tits.*

Riley: *Lol! You were doing so well! This taking it slow thing must be hard for you.*

Dylan: *I'm always hard for you.*

Riley: *I'll fix that when you get back. Maybe on that overnight trip you mentioned?*

Dylan: *I'll steal Jake's fucking car and come back right now. I'll book it online. You can do that, right?*

Riley: *Omg. Such a guy.*

Dylan: *I have to go set Logan's dick on fire. I'll call you later.*

Riley: *WHAT!*

I look up from my phone to see five sets of eyes watching me. We're sitting in a circle on the floor. I have no idea why. "What?" I ask, shrugging. "I miss him."

Amanda shakes her head. "It's one night, Ry."

"By the way, Dylan's about to set Logan's dick on fire."

"What?" Mom says, spitting her wine out of her mouth. She was going to make it an alcohol free night but I told her about the book clubs I'd hosted and the drinking that went on. I didn't have an issue with it. She shouldn't either. Besides, it's one night.

One night. Five friends. One mom. Pajamas. Food. Candy. And, apparently, one Drunk Lucy. "Ms. Hudson, if I ever have children and look like you at your age I'll be one happy fucking whore."

Kayla giggles. "Sorry, Ms. Hudson. Lucy curses like a sailor when she's drunk."

"Call me Holly…" Mom says, "…and bitch can say whatever the fuck she wants."

"Mom!"

"Let me be young and careless, Riley. Just one night." She pours another glass of wine. "Besides, you can't talk to me about being inappropriate, sweetheart. I'm in the bedroom next door and the walls are thin."

"Mom!"

"Oh yeah," Lucy says. "I bet you guys have been going at it like rabbits since his cast came off."

I shake my head. "No."

"Bullshit," Mom says. "I hear everything."

"We haven't had sex," I tell them, like I'm on the stand and pleading innocence.

Mom rolls her eyes. "No woman makes the noises you make on foreplay alone."

I scoff. "That's because you don't know Dylan."

"Gross," Mom says, her nose in the air.

"Seriously?" Amanda asks. "You guys haven't since…"

"Nope. We mess around and do other stuff but not sex."

"Why not?" Heidi says.

"Because we kind of rushed it at the beginning. I mean, we had sex before we were even together and—"

"You did?" Mom cuts in.

I smirk. "Right on that kitchen counter."

"Riley!" she squeals.

And we crack up laughing.

"So Dylan didn't want to wait at the start?" Heidi asks.

"Uh oh," Mikayla murmurs, chugging her wine like she's preparing for a showdown.

"No."

"Huh," Heidi says. "It took forever to get him to want to have sex with me."

I gag.

She laughs. "Sorry. It's just strange."

Lucy chimes in. "Dylan was a virgin when you guys were dating so…"

"You weren't a virgin?" I ask.

Heidi shakes her head.

I ask, "How many guys were you with before D?"

"One."

"Who?"

The girls look at Amanda.

"Gross," she says.

"So wait!" Mom throws her hand in the air. "Riley, you had sex on my counter?"

I nod.

Now she gags. "Gross." Then she looks at Heidi. "And you've slept with two of the boys in the group?"

Heidi raises her hand. "Yes, Ma'am. But Logan and I never really dated, we just… you know. Besides, now I'm dating a guy who asked Riley out."

Mom shakes her head and points between us. "And you're amicable?"

I shrug. "As long as she keeps her hands off D, I'm good."

"Wow." Mom's eyes widen. "Riley, you're a lot nicer than I am. If my boyfriend's ex-girlfriend was even around, let alone in the same room, I'd be ripping out her hair and slapping the shit out of her."

Lucy cackles. "You're a woman of my own heart, Holly."

"Right on," Mom says, high fiving her.

My phone sounds and the girls moan. "Leave it, Ry," Amanda pleads.

I laugh. "It's Skype, though. No one's messaged me on Skype since Dylan's been back."

I open the app, my breath catching when I see who it's from. "Dave?" I whisper.

"O'Brien?" Mom asks.

I nod slowly, focused on the screen. "He sent a video."

"How?" Lucy asks.

I read the message out loud. "Hey Riley. It's Mike. I just turned on Davey's phone and saw that he never sent this to you. Thought you'd like it."

"Play it," Mom says.

"Okay."

They gather around as I stare at the phone, wondering what it could possibly be. I'd spoken to Dave a little while he was there, but he'd never sent a video before.

"Hey, Banks," Dave says behind the camera.

Dylan's lying on a bed, his hands behind his head. It looks like they're in a tent but there doesn't seem to be anyone else in the room.

"What?" Dylan answers.

"What are you thinking about?

Dylan doesn't respond.

Dave laughs. "Stupid question. Riley, right?"

"Always Riley."

"You miss her?"

He moves one hand and rests it on his chest, never once looking over at Dave. "That's another stupid question."

"What do you miss most?"

For a long time, Dylan doesn't answer. Finally, "Are you comfortable, Dave?"

"What do you mean?"

"I mean, with who you are… around your family and friends. Are you comfortable?"

Dave chuckles. "Have you fucking met me, man? If I wasn't comfortable with myself, you think I'd be this much of an idiot? I don't give a fuck what people think. I am who I am."

"You are who you are," Dylan mumbles.

"So what's up? Why are you thinking about it?"

"I don't know," Dylan breathes out. "I was just thinking that I wasn't, you know? My entire life I don't think I really fit in anywhere. Even growing up I felt distant from my dad and brother… I think because of what happened to my mom. Not that I carried guilt because of it. I didn't blame myself for her death or anything but I kind of felt like they were privy to something that I wasn't. When I was a kid I found it hard to make friends, and when I did I still kind of felt like an outsider, you know? All through school, it was the same, until I changed high schools and it got a little better, but still. I was never really comfortable enough to be myself."

"I've never heard Dylan say so much," Lucy whispers and we all shush her.

"And then?" Dave asks.

Dylan shrugs. "And then I met Riley."

I gasp, my hand covering my mouth as my heart skips a beat. Mom places her hand on my shoulder, comforting me.

"Riley," Dave repeats, like my name has so much more meaning that just my name.

"I don't know, man," Dylan says, "I don't know if it's because I met her at my lowest point and she was accepting of that or..."

"Or what?"

Dylan exhales loudly, both hands on his chest now. "Sometimes she gives me these looks that terrify me."

"Like she's going to stab you in your sleep?" Dave asks.

Dylan laughs. "No. Like her world begins and ends with me and I'm scared that I'm going to do something one day and she won't look at me the same."

"Oh my god," I whisper, a sob caught in my throat.

"But... you're just being yourself around her, right? Like, who you really are," Dave says.

Dylan nods. "I guess."

"So why are you scared?"

"Because I never want that feeling to go away."

"How do you think you look at her?" Dave asks.

"I don't know," Dylan mumbles, deep in thought.

"Well, how do you hope she sees you?"

"I hope she knows I love her."

"Given."

Dylan sighs. "I hope she sees that she changed me, you know? That it wasn't just me who helped her get through struggles. I hope she knows that there isn't a single second I'm away from her when she's not on my mind. Even when I'm with her, I'm always thinking about her. I think about our future and everything we're still yet to do. I want her by my side for all of it. She's..." He chuckles lightly, "...she's so feisty and fierce and so damn cute. She gets this line on the bridge of her nose when she's mad and sometimes I purposely annoy her just so I can see that line because it's the way she was when I first met her, properly you know? And I like remembering that because I'm pretty sure I knew, even then, that there was something about her that I wouldn't be able to let go of. And I'm fucking lucky, Dave. I'm so fucking lucky that she felt the same because I don't know what I'd be doing right now if she wasn't at home waiting for me." Dylan pauses for a beat, a smile on his lips when he faces Dave. His eyebrows quirk when he sees the camera in his hand but he doesn't seem to care. "I'm in so fucking deep, man. And I love it. I love her. And I fucking miss her."

Dave's heavy breath distorts the speakers.

"You'll find her one day," Dylan says.

"Who?"

"Your Riley."

"I fucking hope so," Dave says through a chuckle. "You gonna marry her?"

"Isn't that the plan? I mean, at the base of any relationship, isn't that the end goal?"

"I guess."

"Hey," Dylan says, shifting to his side. "You gonna come to my wedding?"

"Fuck that, Banks. I'm going to be in your wedding."

Fifty-Eight
Dylan

LOGAN RETURNS TO the living room of the log cabin one of Cameron's clients had loaned us for the night, wearing a different pair of sweats and a scowl stronger than the whiskey we're drinking. "Fucking burned my nutsack, assholes!"

Jake holds his stomach, trying to ease the ache from laughing so hard.

"Your face was fucking priceless man," Cam says. "And the best part…" he breaks off in a fit of laughter. When he's calm enough, he adds, "We fucking lit it and you moaned Amanda's name!"

"I was confused!" Logan shouts, slumping down on the couch next to me. "It was so fucking warm, just like her mouth."

Jake shakes his head. "That's so wrong, dude."

I get up from my seat and walk over to the table where my bag holding my supplies is.

"How are things with Riley?" Jake asks.

I shrug. "It's going well. A little too well." I grab what I need and pocket it before turning around. "I fucked up pretty bad," I say, leaning back on the table. "I made a lot of mistakes… just waiting for it to catch up to me."

Cam shrugs. "We all make mistakes, dude. We all hurt the people we love. It makes us human."

I sit back down in my chair. "Not as bad as I have."

"Hello," Cam points to Logan, "*I ran away for the year under the pretense of saving lives.*"

"Fuck off," Logan says, but he's laughing.

"And me?" Cam points to himself. "Do I need to remind you of Slut-of-a-whore-gate? I fucking drew a picture of another girl, bro. I get stabby just thinking about it… and him." He points to Jake now, then scowls. "Fuck you, Mr. Perfect."

"Shut up," Jake snaps, then pauses a moment. "I got drunk and made out with a girl at a party on an away game once."

We stare at him. "Shut the fuck up," Logan says. We don't believe him. Not for a second.

"I just want to fit in," Jake whines.

"You'd cry if you so much as looked at another girl. Micky would be the one talking you off the ledge," Cam tells him, then looks over at me. "Truth? You messed up, Dylan. You had every right to. We deal with pain differently."

"Maybe." I shrug.

Cam yawns, loud and long and so damn perfect. "I'm fucking fading."

"Pussy," Jake says.

"Fuck you! Unlike the fucking rest of you fucking assholes, I fucking have a fucking job. I'm not just fucking cruising through the summer for the fuck of it. I've fucking been up since fucking five."

"Holy shit." Jake laughs. "Swear much?"

"Sorry. I'm always at work all professional and shit…" He loosens his tie. "…or Lucy's little brother is always at the cabin and I have to tone down the cursing and it just feels good to fucking swear sometimes."

I narrow my eyes at him. "You want to get it all out now because—"

"Fucking shit of an asshole motherfucking whore bastard son of a toe fucking titty whore!" He releases a breath, his eyes drifting shut. "So much better. Carry on."

Ten minutes later, he's fallen asleep in his chair, his glass of whiskey loose in his hand on the armrest. With his mouth open and his head tilted back, he snores quietly.

I smirk.

"Oh shit," Logan whispers.

I pull out the Ziploc bag from my pocket—the one containing a tampon that's been soaking in ketchup and tuna brine since I left the house.

"That's fucking disgusting," Jake says.

"You haven't even smelled it yet."

As silent as possible, the three of us get up and surround him. I open the bag, suppressing my chuckle when I see the guys cringe—their reaction to the smell. So fucking perfect.

I motion for them to hold down Cam's hand the second I drop it in his mouth and, because they know me and know me well, they both nod, ready.

I suck in a breath, hold it, then lift the tampon an inch above his mouth. Then I drop it.

"WHAFFUGGGG!" Cam screams, his eyes snapping open. He tries to move but his hands are held down and he subconsciously closes his mouth. Then gags, coughs and splutters until he spits it out. His legs are kicking wildly, trying to get me, and I can tell the boys' grip is weakening because they're laughing too hard. I hold my stance, my legs apart, my arms crossed. Then he looks down at what he'd just spat out. "Fuck you!" he shouts, legs kicking, arms attempting to get free. "What the fuck is that?"

Logan's lost it so much he can't hold him down. He drops to the floor, his hand wiping the tears from his eyes. Cam gets free, his arm raised.

I throw a hand up between us. "What's the third rule of mayhem?" I laugh out.

"Fuck you."

"No violence," Jake answers for him. "Mayhem is the only form of retaliation."

Cam stops in his tracks, his breaths harsh as they leave him. "You're going to pay, Banks."

"I'll be waiting, Gordon."

MY THIRD PLAN didn't really need any planning, but it does take a day or so to take shape. It's weak, I know. And to be honest, I didn't have the heart to do it myself. Jake's good people. Always has been. Didn't stop me from asking Cam to help me out. He was all for it. Besides, pink eye for days—totally worth it.

I SETTLE INTO bed, prepared to sleep with one eye open. I expect nothing less of my friends than retaliation. I grab my phone to send Ry a good night message, but there's already one there.

Riley: *I love you. I miss you. Come home to me, okay?*

I smile, remembering how all her letters to me started. Letters she doesn't know I've read.

Dylan: *You are my home, Ry.*

I go to switch off the phone but notice the Skype notification. Riley had downloaded and set it up for me when I came home on R&R. We've only ever used it when I was deployed. My eyes narrow as I click the icon, then widen when I see Dave's name. There's a bunch of images he's sent through along with a message.

Hey man. It's Mike. I just turned on Davey's phone and saw that he never sent these to you. Thought you'd like it.

I click on the first image—a screen shot of a Skype conversation Dave had with Riley.

Dave: *Hey beautiful.*

Riley: *How are you single, Dave?*

Dave: *Ikr. What girl doesn't love a strawberry blonde, scrawny kid with freckles and my mouth.*

Riley: *Lol. How's our boy doing?*

Dave: *We just had two units come in with their vehicles so he's out working. Poor bastard's out there earning his keep while I get to talk to his girl.*

Riley: *haha. Lucky me.*

Dave: *So what's going on?*

I move to the next image, my heart racing, eager for more.

Riley: *Not much. Had car trouble on the way home from work.*

Dave: *Wtf? Didn't D build you that car?*

Riley: *lol. Yes.*

Dave: *Ry. That dude is in charge of military transportation and you're telling me he couldn't fucking build you that piece of shit Honda engine?*

Riley: *Bahaha! No. It was my fault. Nothing to do with his work. Don't worry.*

Dave: *So what was it?*

Riley: *Oil.*

Dave: *Doesn't his dad work on your car?*

I quickly move to the next image, wondering how much they spoke and how he knew all this.

Riley: *Yeah. The check oil light was on… for I don't know how long… but I have a picture of D on my dash and it was blocking it so…*

Dave: *Oh man. He'd be pissed if I told him. Especially since you were probably alone, at night, stranded.*

Riley: *I called Mal right away and he was there within fifteen minutes. He made me sit in the car and lock all the doors until he got there. He was so mad at me. Lol. You know how D gets… that silent type mad.*

Dave: *Oh, I know the one.*

Riley: *Swear he looked so much like Dylan.*

Dave: *lol.*

Riley: *So yeah… goes without saying this stays between us.*

Dave: *Hand on my heart. Speaking of secrets…*

Riley: *:) I sent them one last Friday.*

Dave: *You are way too good to me.*

Riley: *You know I enjoy it.*

Dave: *Sure.*

Riley: *I do! I like going to the store and finding stuff to send your family. I had to send two boxes this time. I got Ricky this Minions doll but it was too big so he gets his own box.*

Dave: *He'd love that, Ry. Seriously. It's not often that kid gets something of his own. He's always had hand me downs.*

Riley: *That makes me so happy.*

Dave: *Swear, you just got me smiling so big.*

Riley: *Why not say it's from you then?*

Dave: *Because it's not from me. It's from…?*

Riley: *I signed the family one as Rosie and Ricky's one as Vanessa.*

Dave: *Nice!*

Riley: *I'm running out of different handwriting though. Hopefully they don't keep the letters.*

Dave: *Nah. Ma would keep them all.*

Riley: *I still don't get it, Dave. Why the different names and why from girls?*

Dave: *Keeps the dream alive.*

Riley: *How so?*

Dave: *My ma—she always worries about me. Not so much out here but more when I get home.*

Riley: *?*

Dave: *I guess she worries about how I'll be when I get back, you know? I mean mentally. She's always going on about how I should find a girl to take care of me. And since the perfect one is taken, I have to make them up.*

Riley: *She worries about that?*

Dave: *Don't you? About Dylan. Not me.*

Riley: *I try not to.*

Dave: *That's good, Ry. You keep the dream alive too. Besides, he has you to take care of him when he gets back.*

Riley: *I hope I'm enough.*

Dave: *Seriously, Ry?*

Riley: *What?*

Dave: *When I mentioned the perfect girl was taken, I was talking about you.*

Riley: *Shut up.*

Dave: *You take care of him, okay? Promise me.*

Riley: *You goof. I promise.*

Dave: *Sleep well, Ry. It's been real nice talking to you.*

Riley: *Until next time?*

I scroll down, my fingers as frantic as my heart while I look for the next image. There isn't one. I go back to the last and look for the date they spoke.

My breath catches.

My heart stops.

He planned it all.

He fucking knew.

He knew he was going to die that night.

And he knew what losing him would do to me.

Fifty-Nine
Dylan

"DUDE, YOU NEED me to drive?" Cam asks from the front passenger seat on the way home. "Why do you keep rubbing your eye?"

Jake pulls over on the side of the road. "It's fucking itchy as fuck." Then it dawns on him. "You fucking assholes! I have a reporter coming to the house tomorrow!"

He goes to punch Cam but Logan stops him. "No violence!"

Chuckling, I look out the window while Cam and Jake swap seats, wondering why it is there hasn't been any retaliation yet. Especially on me.

Fuck. I'm never going to sleep.

"Yo, Amanda just messaged me. She said to pick the girls up from your house, D," Logan says.

"Well, yeah. They stayed there last night didn't they?"

"No, I mean at *your* house."

"What are they doing there?" I ask.

Cam chuckles as he turns to me. "Mayhem, motherfucker."

Shit.

THERE'S NO SIGN of glitter from outside the house, which I guess is a good thing. And there's no loud *High School Musical* soundtrack blasting, either. Without the help of the boys, the girls aren't that creative. But then again, I did fuck the boys over. Individually, too. And that causes three times the panic that's currently flowing through me.

I stop a few feet away from the garage door leading to the yard, hoping that one of them will go through first. They don't. In fact, they stand behind me, arms crossed, legs spread, all scowling. "It's bad isn't it?" I ask.

Jake rubs his eye. "Fuck yeah, it is."

I huff out a breath, reach for the bike helmet hanging on the wall and put it on.

"That's not going to help you in this situation," Cameron says.

"How fucking bad is it?"

"Remember that time you tried to staple my nostrils shut? Think that. Only a thousand times worse."

"You sweating, Banks?" Logan asks.

I puff out my chest "No." Then I wipe the sweat off my brow.

"He's sweating, all right," Jake mumbles.

After a few deep breaths, I gain the courage I need to turn the knob and slowly push open the door. I walk out quickly; in case something falls from the roof. Nothing does. In fact, nothing happens at all. Or, maybe it's because my eyes are closed.

I ball my fists and open one eye first, then the other.

There's a sea of red, white and blue and a bunch of faceless other people who I'm sure I know but right now all I see, all I feel, is Riley standing in front of me. She's wearing red shorts, a plane white shirt under one of my blue flannel ones. She looks just like the picture I'd carried with me everywhere when I was deployed—the one I'd pull out when I needed a reminder of the reason I was there. Her hands are clasped together in front of her and she's smiling. "Happy homecoming, baby."

I take the stupid helmet off and cover the distance between us. "What?"

She lets me take both her hands before shrugging. "We never got a chance to celebrate you coming home… so…" She steps to the side, revealing everyone else.

My family, hers, the girls and all their parents.

"We didn't have much time to plan…" Riley tells me.

I switch my gaze back to her. "When did you—"

"This morning."

I reach up, my hands on her neck and my thumb stroking her cheek. "I love you, you know that?"

She smiles. "You better, Banks."

And then I kiss her, maybe a little too inappropriate considering

Holly groans, "Gross," and Lachlan, Lucy's little brother shouts, "That's yuck!" but I don't care.

A HALF HOUR later, I've greeted everyone here. Bryce, Heidi's boyfriend, Jake's mom, Cam's parents, Lucy's dad and a couple of her brothers and Logan's dad… who can't seem to take his eyes off Riley's mom.

I take a seat on the lawn chair next to him. "Dr. Matthews."

"Dylan." He nods, his eyes still on Holly. "It's good to have you home, Son."

"Thank you, Sir." I pause a beat, watching his reaction. "You see something you like?"

His eyes snap to mine. "Excuse me?"

Logan walks up, interrupting us. "He causing you any problems, Pops?" he asks, taking a seat on the other side of him.

"You want me to introduce you?" I ask, ignoring Logan.

Dr. Matthews eyes go wide and he sits up higher. "No!"

I smile.

"Introduce who?" Logan says, looking around.

"Riley's mom."

Logan nudges him. "Dad, you crushing on Ms. Hudson?" he says loud enough for Holly to hear. She faces us, ignoring the conversation she's currently having with Jake's mom. With narrowed eyes, she mouths, "Me?"

I nod and wave her over.

"Oh my God, why is she coming here?" Dr. Matthews mumbles, wiping his palms on his pants.

"Are you nervous?" Logan asks, eyeing his dad with amusement. "Holy shit, I've never seen you like this!"

We all stand when Holly closes the distance. "Did you say my name?" she asks me.

"Hey Holly, have you met Dr. Alan Matthews?"

She smiles and throws her hand out between them. "Doctor?"

I pat Alan's shoulder. "Have fun, kids."

"No!" he shouts.

Logan cackles. "Go easy on him, Ms. Hudson," he says, and we both walk away.

Logan runs to Amanda, no doubt to spy, and I walk over to Mr.

Preston, Lucy's dad, sitting around one of the tables with a couple of his sons, Cam and Lucy. I'd planned to go see him since I got out of the cast, but never had the time. He stands when I get to him. "Good to see you, Dylan!" he says, his handshake strong and his pat on my arm even stronger.

"Thank you, Sir. You too. Thanks for coming out."

"Ah, Lucy called this morning, told me what it was about—mentioned free food—so here I am."

I chuckle under my breath. "So I'd been meaning to come by and have a chat with you but…"

He tilts his head. "What's up?"

"You got any jobs going?"

His eyebrows shoot up. "You want to work construction?"

"I'll work anywhere, Sir. My leg's good. My shoulder's good. I don't have any real experience in construction but I'm good with my hands—"

"So hot," Lucy cuts in.

"I'm right here!" Cam yells.

Lucy laughs and takes his hand, kissing it gently. "I love you the mostest, baby."

"Shut up."

"Anyway…" I say while Mr. Preston shakes his head at them. "I'm back now and—" I point to Riley, "—I got a girl to take care of, you know? I understand if you don't have anything going at the moment but I'd appreciate it if you kept me in mind if anything does come up—"

"You come see me on site Monday. 7 a.m. Cameron will give you the location."

My eyes widen. "Really?"

"Of course!"

I shake his hand again. "Thank you, Sir. This means so much." I look over at Riley again, sitting with Dad and laughing at whatever he's telling her.

"Did your old man play football back in the day?" Mr. Preston asks.

I nod. "High school. Wide receiver for West High."

"I thought he looked familiar. I probably tackled him a few times."

"Oh yeah?" I smile, looking back at him. "He probably remembers it too, Sir. He's not the forgiving type."

"Watch the boys," Mr. Preston says over his shoulder. "Malvin Banks," he says, the name rolling off his tongue. "He was a hero back in the day."

"He's still my hero today, Sir."

Five minutes later, they're recalling their high school game days like it happened yesterday.

Riley takes my hand and walks us over to Eric while Sydney unfolds a napkin and hangs it off his collar.

"What's wrong with you?" I ask him.

He stuffs half a burger in his mouth. Sydney lifts the napkin revealing a streak of ketchup on his shirt.

Riley laughs.

"He's such a kid," Sydney says.

"Who's that talking to Dad?" Eric asks, his mouth full.

"Lucy's Dad. Apparently they played football against each other."

Eric swallows. "Naw. Our old man's making friends. They grow up so fast!"

"Sorry to interrupt," Mandy—Jake's mom—says, stopping in front of us. "I have to pick up Julie from her date—"

"I'll pick 'em up," Jake says, one arm around his mom's shoulders.

"No you won't, Jacob," Mandy snaps. "She told me you threatened her boyfriend's kneecaps with a baseball bat."

Jake lifts his chin. "Did not." *He totally did.*

Mandy rolls her eyes. "Dylan, I'm sorry to bother you with this but my car's making this noise…"

I stand. "What kind of noise?"

"This um…" Her face scrunches. "*Cluck cluck cluck.*"

Jake stifles his laugh. "How's that go again, Ma?"

"*Cluck cluck cluck.*"

I suppress my smile. "One more time?"

"*Cluck cluck cluck.*"

I nod slowly and rock on my heels. "Well, that's your problem, Ma'am. Your car's a chicken."

MANDY'S CAR IS an easy fix. I tell her I'll order the parts and drop by to replace it. By the time I get back in the yard, furniture has been rearranged and there's a cake on a table and a single chair behind it. "It's not my birthday," I tell Riley, coming up behind her.

She spins to me, her palms flat on my chest when she says, "There's no celebration without a cake."

She guides me to sit in front of what could possibly be known as the ugliest cake in the entire world. "This is um… nice," I tell her.

She giggles. "Lucy made it. Isn't it lovely?"

I look at Lucy and nod. "Thanks, Luce." Then I eye Cameron. *I get it now.* His eyes widen as he returns my nod. *I fucking told you.* Lucy's little brothers look at me, their eyes bigger than Cam's. *Don't fucking do it.*

"Where are the candles?" Riley asks.

"For what?"

She smiles. "Don't you want to make a wish?"

I shrug. "I guess."

"It's under the tray," Lucy tells her.

Riley lifts the tray and the next thing I know my eyes, nose and mouth are filled with cake and my ears filled with the cackling of everyone around me. I try not to curse because I know Lucy's brothers are watching. Next to me, Riley's laughing the loudest, and it's probably the only reason the rage dies down as fast as it does. "I'm sorry," she says through a giggle, wiping the cake from my eyes. I grunt, then grab her waist and pull her in for a sloppy kiss which isn't really a kiss but just an excuse to wipe my face all over hers. She squeals. People laugh harder. And I fall deeper.

"Okay," Amanda sings. "Here's the real one *I* made."

"Mine was better," Lucy laughs.

Riley reaches into the pocket of her shirt and pulls out a bunch of candles. I don't know how many are there but the heat they emit is enough to start making me sweat. After Riley wipes her face, and then mine, she motions to the cake. "Make your wish."

I pull her down to my lap. "You make the wish," I tell her, looking at everyone around me, finishing on Dad. "I got everything I need right here. I got my family."

Riley's eyes narrow at first, as if she's clicked that I've read her letters.

I won't tell her.

She won't ask.

Her gaze stays on mine for a long moment while silence fills the yard. Then her eyes drift shut, her chest rising with her intake of breath. Her cheeks puff with the force of her exhale and a second later, it's over.

Dad clears his throat and all eyes go to him. He raises the beer in his hand. "I uh, I wanted to make a toast to my son." He waves his hand toward me. "Dylan. Who, we all know. Obviously." He rubs the back of his neck while Riley squeezes mine. "I'm bad at this so I'll make it quick…" He looks down at his feet and takes a breath. Then rubs his eyes before looking back up. "I'm so damn proud of you, son. We all are. And I'm glad you're home safe and now I'm ramblin' so here," he says, reaching into his pocket and throwing something at me. I catch it. Ford keys.

"What's this?" I ask, looking from the keys to him.

"Well, you were deployed on your twenty-first birthday so it's a little late, but it's parked out front."

"You got me a car?" I almost shout.

"You got him a car?" Eric repeats. "Man, I was deployed on my twenty-first and all I got was a damn card with a giraffe on it!"

I practically push Riley off my lap. The guys laugh. "If this is a joke—"

"No joke. And a truck. Not a car. Go check it out!" Dad says.

Eric whines, "A *giraffe*! What did that even mean?"

DAD DIDN'T JUST get me any old truck. He got me my dream truck. The one I'd wanted when I'd turned sixteen but wasn't able to afford. A black 2005 Ford F150 dual cab.

"Holy shit." I open Riley's side first so she can get in and then run to the driver's side. I slip in the key, turn it and then I don't really know what happens but I'm pretty sure it's sexual considering everything that goes on in my pants.

I turn to Riley. "Did you know?"

She nods. "He's been looking since the accident."

"A giraffe!" Eric shouts.

"So?" Riley says. "Shall we?"

"Right now? What about—"

"My mom's going to help clean up. It'll be clear by the time we come home."

"Home?"

She nods again, scooting across the seat until she's next to me and my hand instantly goes to her leg. "*Our* home."

"And your mom's okay with us moving out?" I ask, glancing at Holly standing next to Dr. Matthews.

"Yeah. She supports us no matter what."

My smile matches hers. "So where to?" I put the car in gear.

"Where else?"

"Horizon, it is."

IT'S TWO IN the morning by the time we get home from the drive. And five in the morning when I find myself inhaling deeply, blinking at the reflection in the shattered mirror and wondering why… why the hell would he come to me now? After one of the best days of my life, why fucking haunt me now? It's been weeks since I've seen him. Not since I spent the entire night bleeding my heart out to Holly.

I thought it was over.

I was wrong.

His words replay in my head. "*I fucking failed, Dylan!*" Over and over.

"Babe?" Riley says, sitting up in the bed. "You okay?"

My shoulders tense. So does my jaw. "I'm fine."

Her hand skims across my side of the bed. She'll feel the sweat. It's impossible not to.

I sigh, looking back in the mirror before running the tap and splashing water on my face.

"Are you hot?" Riley asks, now walking toward me. "I can turn the air up." She grabs a face cloth and sits on the counter next to my arm, then runs it under the cold water.

Her eyes are tired, just like mine.

She wipes the cloth across my forehead, down my neck and onto my shoulders while I breathe through the visions.

"Did you have a bad dream?" she whispers, the towel on my chest now. "I'm sorry," she adds. "You don't have to tell me."

Behind the fatigue, I see the determination in her eyes, the need to make me better somehow.

And I remember the messages from Dave—her promise to take care of me. So I swallow my pride, and I give her what she needs. What she deserves. "Yeah, Ry. I did. And I can't get back to sleep now."

Her eyes widen in surprise. "Okay," she squeaks, sitting up higher. "Is there anything I can do? Do you want me to make you some… I don't know… warm milk or something? That used to help me when I had nightmares. I know it's not the same—"

I shift to the side, cutting her off, and place my hands on the counter either side of her. Tilting my head, I ask, "Warm milk?"

She nods quickly. Then, somehow, her eyes get even wider. "Oh, I know!" She raises her finger between us. "Wait here, okay?" She's smiling. I don't know why she's smiling but I love her smile and her need to resolve my pain makes me love her more.

She shoves my chest gently, moving me out the way. "Just wait," she rushes out, her bare legs moving quickly as she exits the room.

She takes the pillows from the bed, as well as all of the blankets and takes them somewhere out of my vision. Doors open. Doors close. Her feet shuffle across the floor moving around the house. And I wait in the bathroom like she told me to.

"Okay," she calls out. "You can come out now."

With heavy steps, I walk out of the bathroom and into the bedroom. She's sitting against the wall between both rooms, blankets and cushions surrounding her. She taps her lap, her smile soft when she says, "Lie down. Head here."

My grin is instant. So is the overwhelming calm that washes over me. I lie down on my back, my head on her lap, her hands in my hair as she continues to smile down at me. "Remember this?" she asks.

My eyes drift shut. "I'll never forget this."

"You said you liked it."

"I do."

"You almost fell asleep when I did it so I thought…"

"You take such good care of me, Ry," I tell her honestly.

"Really?"

"Swear."

Her smile widens.

"Tell me something, Riley."

"Something?"

"Anything. I love your voice. It's the thing I missed the most while I was deployed. I mean, besides your body. And your cooking."

She laughs quietly. "So Mom has a date with Dr. Matthews tomorrow. Or tonight, I should say."

"No shit?"

"Yep. She's really nervous."

"Believe me," I tell her. "He's worse. I'm surprised he had the balls to ask her."

"He didn't. She asked him."

"That's awesome."

"Oh! And apparently when we were gone Eric wouldn't shut up about you getting a truck and him getting a card so your dad called him out and told everyone that he started wetting the bed again when you were born. He kept thinking you would crawl into his room at night and stab him in his sleep."

I sit up slightly. "Shut up!"

She draws a cross on her chest. "Swear it. He used to call you Devil Baby."

"No way."

Riley nods. "So I was thinking we go over there and find a photo of you as a baby and make a cardboard mask that you can wear when you sneak into his room one night with a fake knife and just chant—" her voice deepens, "—Devil baby! Devil baby!"

I sit up completely, pushing her hands away. "Riley."

"What?" she asks, her hands mid air.

"How the fuck did I land you?"

She rolls her eyes. "You're kind of hot, Banks. That's all."

"That's all?"

She shrugs and pats her lap again.

I lie back down.

With a single finger, she starts to trace around all of my features, her eyes locked on mine. "You know when we did this the first time…" She runs her finger across my lips. "I noticed your smile."

I kiss her finger. "My smile?"

"Yeah. It tilts higher on the right than the left."

"It does?"

She nods.

I get more comfortable. "All I remember was wanting to kiss you.

Bad. *Really* fucking bad."

"I know. You asked me if I wanted you to," she says, her voice low.

"And you lied," I tell her.

She nods. "I was so scared."

"I know."

"I'm not scared of you anymore, Dylan."

Momentarily, I wonder if she means being with me or me in general. Then I realize I don't care. "No?"

"Not at all," she says, shaking her head. Then she smiles. "Hey Dylan?"

"Yeah?"

"Do you want me to kiss you right now?"

"Hudson. I want you to more than fucking kiss me right now."

She giggles. "Oh yeah?"

"You know what I saw when I came home tonight?"

She leans back, her brows bunched. "What?"

"You left the flat iron on."

Her mouth opens. Closes. Opens. Nothing comes out.

I arch an eyebrow. "You know what that means?"

She starts to undo the buttons of her shirt.

Ten minutes later, we're naked, rolling around on the floor surrounded by cushions. Our hands, our mouths, our tongues exploring every single inch of each other's bodies. A few minutes after that, she's on top of me, her hands flat on my stomach, her hips thrusting, moving me in and out of her. She's so warm, so wet, so damn perfect. Her back arches, her head tilted back causing her loose hair to tickle my thighs. "Dylan, I'm so fucking close," she whispers, her movements getting faster.

I sit up and flip us until she's beneath me, just like I know she likes. I start to move, pushing in and out of her while her nails scratch my back, her legs wrapped around mine and her back arching off the floor, her hips meeting mine. My mouth dips to her neck, kissing softly as I make my way up to her ear. Our bodies covered in sweat, moving as one.

"Oh fuck," she breathes. She's close, but not close enough. "Dylan."

I bite down on her ear and push into her.

"Fuck," she moans, her head falling back. I push off one hand, the other on her cheek. She moves her head to the side, taking my thumb in her mouth, her eyes on mine, filled with lust. "I fucking love being inside you," I tell her. She moans, her mouth opening just enough for me to remove my thumb and move it down her body. I thumb her clit, watching her eyes roll back. She moans louder. "Your pussy feels so fucking good, baby."

"Oh fuck!" She bites down on my shoulder, muffling her cry of pleasure. She comes around me, and a second a later, I join her.

"*You lucky fucking bastard,*" Dave says.

"I know," I mumble.

"Know what?" she breathes.

I settle my breaths enough to pull back. Leaning up on my forearm, I move the hair stuck to her brow so I can see her eyes. "How fucking lucky I am."

Sixty
Dylan

HERE'S THE THING about love, I've come to realize. It's just like time. The word, the term of endearment—it's the same for everyone. For friends, family, the person you intend to spend the rest of your life with—the "bones" of adoration are comparable. You do what you can to make the people you love happy… to make their wishes come true.

But what you do with that love—how you let it wrap itself around you and control your actions—that's what makes it unique.

And my actions will always, always, speak louder than my words.

✧ ✧ ✧

IT DIDN'T TAKE long for the guys to come up with a retaliation. A week after my homecoming party, I woke up for work at the construction site and like any other day, I walked into the garage. There, right on top of my truck, was a giant Play-Doh cock covered in glitter. Balls on the cab, shaft running down the bed and onto the ground, through the garage door and all the way down the driveway, ending on the road. If that hadn't been bad enough, they'd hooked up the hose somewhere inside the t-rex sized dick and had water coming out of the head and spilling out onto the road.

Well played, boys.

Well fucking played.

So, I had to come up with something better. Something bigger. Which was hard because I needed to make sure they'd all be at the same place at the same time.

That was the third item on the agenda for today.

The first was to get supplies.

The second would determine the third.

The second was also the most important moment of my life.

I GRASP RILEY'S hand as we walk with the pretense of heading home after the hardware store. I ordered what I pretended were my retaliation supplies and told them I'd pick them up another day. Truth is I didn't need any of it. I just needed a reason to get Riley out of the house. To this part of town. To this particular strip of shops.

I squeeze her hand tighter and lead her to the store with a glass door—the same glass door I'd walked through yesterday. She's too distracted on her phone, texting Sydney about the details of the next slumber party. Sydney is part of the plan for the second part of my agenda.

I open the door, heart racing, palms sweaty.

And then I stop in the middle of the store, waiting for Riley to come to.

When she must realize I've stopped, she looks up from her phone—first at me and then to our surroundings. Her eyes narrow. "What are we doing?"

She's clueless, just for a moment, before it hits her. And when it does, her eyes widen and her breath catches and even though I should probably feel the walls closing in and my breath leaving me, I feel none of it. I feel calm. The type of calm I can only find in her. "What are we doing?" she repeats, her voice softer.

"Just entertain me okay?"

"What…" Her hand loosens on her phone, causing it to fall on the ground. Neither of us bother to pick it up. Instead, I lead her to the glass display cabinet where the rings of the jewelry store are displayed. Right on cue, the clerk comes up behind the counter, her smile warm as she nods at me. Riley hasn't taken her eyes off mine—because just like the time I surprised her on her birthday, she thinks that seeing what we're doing will make it real and she's not ready.

I, on the other hand, have been ready since the night before I deployed.

I keep my eyes on Riley and speak to the clerk, "Do me a favor?"

"Sure," she responds calmly. She already knows what I'm about to ask.

"Can you pull out the rings and slowly run your finger over them?"

"Sure," she says again. Same calm from earlier. Riley though—she's everything but calm. Her chest rises and falls quickly, her mouth parted, her eyes—still locked on mine—filling with tears. *God, she's beautiful.*

"Take a look," I tell her.

She shakes her head, her teeth now clamped around her bottom lip.

"Please, Riley."

She takes a breath, and then another, before looking down at the rings.

I smile, her hand still in mine, my gaze focused on her.

"Okay," I order the clerk. "Start moving when you're ready."

I watch Riley's eyes move slowly from side to side, tears still falling and rolling down her cheeks. I don't wipe them away. I'm too focused on watching her—her lips as they tremble, her chest as it rises and falls, rises and falls. I watch her breaths leave her, loud but even, her eyes still moving. Then, suddenly, they freeze. Her eyes widen, her breath catches.

"Stop," I tell the clerk, watching Riley's shoulders tense, her gaze still locked on the rings. "Go back."

Riley gasps, her hand covering her mouth.

"That one," I say, not bothering to look at the ring yet. "Can we have that one?"

Slowly, Riley's eyes trail from the ring to me—tears flowing, lips shaking. "What are you doing, Dylan?"

I shrug.

From the corner of my eye, I see the clerk holding out the ring. Carefully, I take it from her and lift Riley's hand at the same time.

With shaky hands and bated breaths, I find the strength I need to tear my gaze away from Riley's and look down at the ring. It's gold with a single diamond in the center.

It's simple.

It's perfect.

Just like her.

Without a word, I get down on one knee and place the ring on her finger, hearing her sobs above me. Then I reach into my pocket, pull out a marker, uncap it with my teeth, and press the tip to her arm. I look up at her to see her already watching me. Not my hands, but my face—her own contorted with a held in cry. I take a mental picture of the moment right before we pass The Turning Point.

I sniff back my emotions and look down at her arm, my hands still shaking, making it almost impossible to write my intentions. I glance up at her, she hasn't taken her eyes off me.

Then I mark her with the words I'd been planning for months.

Marry me, Riley Hudson?

Riley

EVERY GIRL THINKS of this moment. The one where the man of your dreams is kneeling in front of you, declaring his love for eternity, hoping to share every single piece of his future as one.

Occasionally, you'll hear a song on the radio and think, "*That's my wedding song*" or you'll see images of dresses or rings online and go "*I'd want something like that.*"

Some even go as far as making stupid Pinterest boards about the perfect moment, the perfect day.

They plan their future, their kids, their house, their lives entwined for eternity.

But as Dylan kneels in front of me, his hands shaking along with his shoulders as he looks up, pleading with me for an answer to the question he's written on my arm—words I have yet to see—I don't think about the future.

I think about the past.

I think about what I've done in my life that deemed me so lucky that he's offering me his world. Forever.

I think about us—wondering how it is we got here.

I remember the day our paths collided—him in a fit of rage and me drowning in grief.

And I remember every single day since.

I look down at the boy I love—staring into his eyes—eyes locked on mine… eyes slowly losing confidence.

He's Here.

Now.

Forever.

And even though I've thought about this moment, dreamed about it, picked out the song and the dress and even created a hidden Pinterest board—nothing, and I mean nothing could've prepared me for the emotions that come with it.

The tears.

The surprise mixed with expectation.

But most of all the *love.*

The love as it wraps around me, suffocating me, drowning me in the best way possible and then forcing its way through my entire body and out my mouth in a single word: "Yes."

Sixty-One
Riley

MY MOM WAS there, in the store, standing behind me watching it all go down.

Obviously I'd been too wrapped up in the moment to realize it. It wasn't until she squealed that I finally turned around and came to.

After her gushing over the ring, and the proposal, Dylan offered to take us both out for lunch to celebrate. It was on the drive to the restaurant when Dylan told me that he had it all planned out.

Turns out Dylan had asked her permission one night when they'd both been up to get a water. Apparently, so Dylan says, she cried more than I did. In fact, she wouldn't stop crying. She told him about how much she loved me and him and us together, and that she couldn't be happier—more proud of the man I would one day marry.

Mom and I have a lot in common, it seems, because I love all those things too. About as much as I love her.

He'd gone to the store the day before and spoken to the clerk about his plans and paid for whatever ring I would've chosen. He did have a budget, he admitted, but the clerk was more than willing to change things around in the display to accommodate his needs.

"You were that certain?" I ask now, smiling over at him behind the steering wheel.

He glances at me quickly before returning to the road, his smile matching mine. "I've never been so sure of anything in my life, Riley Hudson."

I look down at the ring on my finger, then the words scrawled across my arm. An arm I plan on never washing. *Ever.*

When I tell him that, he pushes me away. "You're gross," he mumbles, but he's laughing.

So am I.

We pull into the parking lot of the restaurant he knows is my favorite and after stepping out, he opens my door and takes my hand. "My lady," he says, bowing his head while helping me out. "Wait. Can I say *my fiancée*? Lady doesn't seem to do you justice anymore."

I nod as I jump out. "I'll allow it."

"You'll allow it?" he asks sarcastically, leading me with his hand on the small of my back. "Riley, I hate to break it to you but I'm going to be your husband soon. Your allowance doesn't mean shit anymore. I say, you do," he jokes.

I don't have time to retort before we step through the entrance, the maître de nodding as she welcomes him. "We have you set up in the back room, Mr. Banks."

"Why do we have the back room?" I whisper, walking behind her as she leads us to room.

He dips his head, his voice a whisper against my ear. "Because fucking you in front of all these people would be probably frowned upon."

"Dylan!" I elbow his gut.

He winces in pain, right before a chuckle bubbles out him.

Then the door to the back room opens, and I freeze.

Just like everyone else in the room—Eric, Mal, Sydney, my mom and all our close friends. Even Heidi and Bryce are here.

"So?" Lucy asks, half standing.

Next to me, Dylan clears his throat, straightening his shoulders. "Family, friends, ladies and countrymen," he bellows.

I narrow my eyes at him. *What the hell's gotten into him?*

He curls his hand around my waist and adds, "I'd like you to meet my fiancée."

I'm not really sure what happens next. It's just a blur of flailing limbs as they all come charging toward me. Followed by shouts, cheers, handshakes and hugs, in between laughter and tears.

The girls reach for the ring on my hand.

The guys pat Dylan on the back.

And when the initial excitement fades, we sit and we eat.

We laugh some more, cry some more, and we love.

Boy, do we love.

I look over at Dylan, leaning back in his chair next to me, his smile wide and boyish and innocent as he looks around the table, finally landing on me. I shift to my side and hug his stomach. His arm goes around my shoulder, holding me to him as his chest rises with his slow intake of breath. "It's a good life, Riley Hudson," he murmurs, kissing the top of my head. "A damn good life."

I follow his gaze from earlier, watching our families, our friends—new and old—the people who played such a heavy hand in getting us here, by doing nothing more than existing and accepting and loving us, even when it could've been impossible to do so. I look over at Jake, who's already watching us, a slight smile on his face.

Then a loud sound comes from the door of our private room as five police officers step through, their gazes frantic as they search the space in front of them. I look up at Dylan, my heart racing, panic clear on my face.

He hasn't moved.

An officer stands in front of the others and after looking down at a piece of paper in his hand, lifts his head—his voice loud when he says, "We're looking for a Jake Andrews, Logan Matthews and Cameron Gordon."

"I'm Jake Andrews... officer sir..." Jake says, slowly standing up.

"What's going on?" Mikayla asks, standing with her boyfriend.

Logan and Cameron are on their feet—their fear and panic filled eyes wide and everywhere.

The officer clears his throat. "Arrest them, boys."

I look over at Dylan again.

He gets up and slams a fist on the table. "Wait one damn minute, good Sir. This is an outrage," he mocks, same deep voice from earlier.

"Oh, jeez," I whisper.

"What the fuck did you do, Cam?" Lucy shouts, fork gripped tight in her hand.

"Nothing, babe. Swear it." He's as loud as she is.

The cops walk behind the boys, taking their wrists behind their backs and handcuffing them.

The first cop speaks again. "You boys are under arrest for possession of illegal pornography."

"What!?" Amanda yells, standing in front of Logan now.

"Babe…" he shakes his head, his gaze on hers. "I don't know what the fuck—"

"Not only is it illegal," the cop with Logan cuts in. "It's also fucking weird, boys."

The officer with Jake shakes his head. "I mean pornography is one thing. Animals… ehhh… we've seen it before. But coming on figurines? Vegetables? Clown and monster porn? And don't even get me started on the inanimate objects! I mean, baseballs? Really?" he says, pointing at Jake. Then motions to Cameron. "And desks? What are you? A deskfucker?"

Slowly, Cameron's gaze moves to Dylan. "I fucking hate you," he says.

Dylan raises his hands in surrender. "I didn't do anything," he says through his smile.

"Take 'em away, boys," the lead cop announces. Then looks at Eric. "Thanks for the tip, Banks."

"You're going to pay," Logan warns, his eyes on Dylan.

They get led out of the room and restaurant, hands in cuffs while their girls scurry after them and the rest of us sit in silence, Heidi and Bryce included. The silence only lasts a moment before Dylan bursts out laughing, Heidi following soon after.

"You're so bad," I tell Dylan.

His grin gets wider. "Fight or die, Hudson."

"How did you even…"

He points at Eric. "Had my big brother call in some favors."

Eric chuckles, so similar to Dylan's. "You're going to be a Banks soon, Ry. You better get used to this."

"At least you left the girls out of it."

Dylan's smile drops.

"No." I shake my head. "What did you do?"

He shrugs and leans back in his chair. "You think the girls were innocent? Babe, it was a glitter cock! Besides, I didn't do anything. The waiters who put laxatives in their drinks and brought them out did all my work for me."

"Dylan!"

Heidi laughs louder.

I look over at her.

She shakes her head. "I'm just glad I wasn't part of it."

Dylan's smile is back in place. "Not yet…"

"But I had nothing to do with Operation Glitter Cock!" she shouts.

"But you knew about it, Heids," he says, sighing as leans forward. "And that's just as bad."

Bryce laughs next to her and when she turns to him, eyes narrowed, he simply shrugs and looks over at Dylan. "You need me to do anything, you let me know."

Heidi smacks his chest.

"So…" Mom says, sitting next to Logan's dad. "Is someone going to tell me what just happened?"

Dr. Matthews chuckles, shaking his head. "Mayhem, Holly. I really could've used you back when they were juniors and Logan came home with wax strips on his genitals."

Sixty-Two

Riley

DYLAN WALKS INTO the bedroom wearing his work pants, white tank, and blue flannel shirt—exactly the way he was when I fell in love with him. He stalks toward me slowly, his brow bunched. "What are you doing, baby?" he says, falling on the bed, his fingers linked behind his head.

I turn the laptop to him.

He cringes. "I'll be in the garage." He starts to get up but I stop him. He sighs. "Baby, I love you and I can't wait to marry you but swear if I see that Pinterest board one more time—"

My laugh cuts him off, I shut the laptop and throw it on the end of the bed. Bacon walks in, his head high looking for Dylan. Dylan lifts his head when he hears him and pats his chest twice. "Up bubba," he murmurs.

Bacon jumps on the bed and settles right on Dylan's chest, his head resting on his front legs.

I pat his fur and lie down with them, my head on Dylan's bicep.

"I was thinking," I mumble.

"Uh oh, this can't be good."

I lick his face.

He pushes me away. "Gross."

Bacon gets up on all fours and looks down at Dylan.

"Lick, Bacon!" I order.

"No!"

Bacon licks him.

Dylan picks him up and moves him between us. "You were thinking?" Dylan asks while we both pat Bacon.

I sigh. "I was just going to say that we've spent more of our relationship apart than we have together."

"You just worked that out now, Hudson?"

I look up at him. "Babe, we've never really discussed you re-enlisting so…"

"There's really nothing to discuss, Ry," he says. "Not for a while, anyway. My job's going okay. My family's here, so are my friends and my fiancée. Until I'm ready to give that up again, I'm staying put."

"But you might one day?"

He stares blankly at me. He won't promise me a thing.

I drop my gaze. "Well, now that we're getting married that means we can live on base, right? At least when you're not deployed, it won't be so bad."

"You've thought about it a bit, huh?"

"I have to, Dylan. If we have kids—"

"Oh, we're having kids, Hudson." He smiles wide, showing his perfect teeth. "Lots of them."

"You know, once we're officially married, you'll have to stop calling me Hudson."

"Nah. You'll always be Hudson to me," he says, leaning forward and kissing me once. "Forever the girl next door."

My phone rings and Sydney's face appears on the screen. I reject the call and throw my phone across the room.

Dylan quirks an eye brow and without taking his eyes off me, says, "Bacon. Bed."

Bacon jumps off our bed and moves to his in the kitchen. "What's going on? You guys fighting?"

"No. She probably wants to talk bridesmaid dresses. The girls can't agree between lavender, mauve and lilac."

Another blank stare.

"Purple."

He nods. "Right."

From across the room, my phone rings again. He waits until it stops before opening his mouth. Then his phone rings. Sighing, he reaches into his pocket and glances at it quickly. "It's your mom."

I roll my eyes. "She probably wants to discuss the venue."

"You want to take it?"

"Fuck no."

He chuckles as he throws his phone near mine. "So you're not enjoying the planning?"

I shake my head, resting my head on his chest. "It's so strange babe. It's not like I haven't thought about my wedding before. Every girl does, right? But it's been two months and I just don't think I care about any of it."

He starts stroking my hair. "You don't care about getting married?"

"No. It's the opposite. I just want to marry you, Dylan. I don't care about the dresses or the venues or the music. I feel like it's two separate things, you know? A marriage and wedding. The marriage is for us and the wedding is for everyone else."

His hands freeze mid movement. "So let's do that then."

"Do what?"

"Give them the wedding they want, and we'll have the marriage we want."

I sit up and look down at him. "How?"

Dylan

WE CHOOSE A date two weeks away. Some may think it's fast. But Riley and I—we're not really ones for waiting. Besides, when you think about it, we kind of did things backwards, right? We had sex, fell deep, got the house, got the dog, had a pause, then got engaged.

When I say it like that, our journey seems easy. It was far from easy. But that makes it all the sweeter that we ended up here—holding hands under a gazebo in a park Holly had chosen.

We keep it casual—invite only our close friends and tell them to wear whatever they want.

Sydney, Mikayla, Amanda, Lucy and Heidi show up in five different shades of purple, and the guys wear orange mankinis—something Holly isn't too pleased about but we did say to wear whatever they wanted. Besides, I'm not stupid. Retaliation had to occur, and what better day than the day of my wedding.

"Should I be nervous?" I ask Cameron, standing to my side between Logan and Jake.

"You're not nervous?"

"I'm more nervous about not being nervous."

"Why am I at the end of the line?" Eric whines. "I'm your damn brother!"

I smirk. "Because I'm a…"

"Don't!"

I lower my voice. "…Devil Baby."

"I fucking hate you!"

RILEY WALKS DOWN the aisle to a song all too familiar; track nine of the *High School Musical* soundtrack; "We're All in This Together."

If Holly was a cartoon character, she'd have smoke coming out of her ears. Dad wears a tux as he walks Riley down the petal scattered grass toward me. She stops in front of me, two dead flowers in an empty bottle of Boons Farm wine in her hand. She's barefoot, wearing a plain white summer dress. The very first dress I ever saw her in.

"You look beautiful," I tell her.

She smiles and curtsies and then runs her hand along my crisp white dress shirt. "And you're more handsome than I remember you."

"You saw me a half hour ago."

She smiles wider.

The "celebrant" says, "I now pronounce you husband and wife."

Holly squeals, "That's not—"

"I do," Riley and I say at the same time. We kiss without being told to and then duck the glitter thrown at us.

"Best wedding ever!" Lucy shouts, and we all cheer.

SO… MAYBE IT wasn't the wedding *everyone* wanted because Holly gives Riley and I an earful as soon as it's over. Riley and I take it like champs, holding hands, heads bowed, trying not to laugh.

Holly huffs. "At least behave at the reception," she says, then turns swiftly away from us and into the arms of Dr. Matthews. They'd been dating a while now. Apparently, it's pretty serious considering Logan told us he walked into the house unannounced one morning and witnessed way more than he needed to. According to the sounds Logan heard and the moans of "Oh, Doctor. Just like that!" Dr. Matthews is a goddamn boss.

Who'd have thought?

In my truck, Riley cackles the entire way to the reception lunch, one hand on my leg, the other on her stomach. "Mankinis!" she shouts.

"Retaliation." I shrug.

"Did you care?"

"Why would I?"

AFTER TWENTY MINUTES of driving around, per Holly's request, Riley navigates me to the address Holly had given us for the reception. We start getting confused when we hit an industrial area with nothing around but warehouses and factories.

"That's it," she says, glancing up from her phone and toward the large concrete building. The sign out front says "Banks Wedding" so I switch off the truck.

"What is this?" I ask.

She shrugs. "Mayhem?"

"From your mom?" I say incredulously.

"Yeah. You're right."

I face her. "You ready, Hudson?"

"Let's do this."

APART FROM THE seating areas and the table containing the buffet of catered food, the place is empty. Floor to ceiling concrete. More glitter gets thrown when we walk in, followed by a pie at my face—one that Riley licks off.

"Riley!" Holly squeals.

Riley rolls her eyes. "Oh Doctor!" she moans.

Holly's eyes bug out of her head.

I'll make it up to her, I promise myself. Maybe with a grandkid or ten.

WE SIT, WE eat, we laugh, and we love, surrounded by the people closest to us.

The wedding cake is comprised of individual cupcakes with single candles on them. And just like the time I gave her twenty wishes, she takes her time, her gaze lifting before each blow, thinking hard about every wish.

I remember watching her the first time and thinking she was amazing—that after everything she'd been through she still managed to have something to look forward to. But now I look at her—into her clear gray eyes and I see everything. *Everything*. Hopes, dreams, plans for our future. I take her hand and motion to the last candle. She smiles, right before her eyes drift shut. Her chest rises with her intake of breath, and she makes her wish. When she's done, she looks up at me. "I wished for you," she says.

"You already have me. Heart and soul, remember?"

She winks. "Yes, I do."

"So what do you think?" Holly says, her hands flipping through the air.

"It's a beautiful reception, Mom," Riley tells her.

Holly laughs, shaking her head. "You haven't worked it out yet?" she asks, spinning a slow circle.

I stand tall next to Riley, my hand on the small of her back and my ears and eyes taking in everything at once. I look for the guys and do a quick head count—just in case one of them is off creating some mayhem. They're all here. So are the girls. So are all the other guests.

"I'm confused," I mumble.

Logan laughs. "You look it, too."

I scowl.

Another pie in my face.

"Quit it with the fucking pies!" I snap, wiping my face.

Lucy chuckles as she high fives Jake. "Those pitching lessons came in handy!"

Dad grunts.

Silence fills the room.

He and Holly step toward us, almost in sync. I cover my face. "What's wrong with you?" Dad murmurs.

"Pie."

"No Pie," he says.

I drop my hands. "So?"

He lifts a set of keys, dangling them in front of me.

"Another car?" Eric yells. "*Giraffe*, Dad! I got a frickin' *giraffe*."

"Shut up," Dad yells over his shoulder. "It's not a car."

"We have a house," Riley says, and I look down at her. She looks as confused as I feel.

"It's not a house," Holly tells her.

"I'm so confused," I say again and duck the pie just in time.

"Dammit!" Mikayla huffs.

"It's the building," Holly says. "It's your wedding gift from Mal, Eric and I."

"The building?" Riley says, looking around.

"I'm so—"

"For your dang garage!" Dad yells, his patience fading. He takes a breath. "For you to open your own garage, son. Holly, Eric and I—we covered the first year's lease on the building and all the equipment and machines you need to get started."

"Oh my god," Riley whispers, taking the keys from him. She looks up at me, her eyes wide and her lips parted. "Babe."

I switch my gaze from her to Eric, now smiling like a mankini-wearing Cheshire cat.

"But I have a job," I mumble, because I don't know what else to say.

"*Had* a job," Lucy's dad's deep voice booms.

I look at him.

"Now you'll be contracted for maintenance on the forty-five trucks in my fleet."

"And all the trade-ins we get," Mark, Cameron's step dad, says.

Jake's dad laughs. "And every time my wife's car decides to be a chicken, we'll be taking it in."

Riley hands me the keys. "*Riley's House of Fixing Cars*! What a great name," she sings.

I shake my head, a little in disbelief and a little in *hell fucking no*.

"So what are you going to call it?" Holly asks.

Another fucking pie in my face.

I wipe my mouth, a smile forming as I look up at Jake—his arm around Mikayla's shoulders. He's the only one who knows that owning a garage was a dream of mine. And until today, that's all it was. An unreachable dream. He smiles wider, matching mine, and nods once. I look at my dad, standing in front of me, his eyes proud. Then I clear my throat. "Mayhem Motors."

I TAP DR. Matthews on the shoulder. "May I?" I ask him.

He nods, then kisses Holly on the cheek.

I take Holly's hand in mine and settle the other on her waist, bringing her closer to me. I'd never really been one for dancing, especially slow dancing, so our movements are more swaying from left to right than anything. She doesn't seem to mind. "I'm sorry," I say quietly, my mouth to her ear. I'm sure this wedding was not at all what Holly had in mind the night I asked for Riley's hand in marriage—the same night I bled my heart out to her and admitted to still seeing Dave. She's kept all my secrets. Always has. Always will.

She pulls back slightly, her hand on my chest as she looks up at me. "This is what you and Riley wanted?"

"Yes, Ma'am."

"If you're happy, then I'm happy. But I'm also not stupid, *son*," she says, smiling wider as the last word leaves her.

"I don't know what you mean, *Mom.*"

Her eyes instantly fill with tears, her head slowly shaking from side to side. Her smile falters, so do her movements. "I'm proud of you, Dylan."

"I know, Ma'am."

"You do?"

"You wouldn't trust me with your daughter if you didn't believe I was worthy of it. And I can't tell you how much that means to me." I reach up, wiping the tears flowing down her cheek. "I wanted to thank you."

"For what?"

"For many things. For looking at me the way you do. For getting me when no-one else did. For creating a girl so flawed and so perfect."

"Well," she says, rolling her eyes and sniffing back her sob. She makes light of the moment, because anything else would make her fall apart. "It wasn't easy. But like you told Riley. Sometimes you need to have nightmares to appreciate the dreams."

"You helped make both our dreams a reality, Ms. Hudson. Without you—"

"When?" she cuts in.

"When what?"

"When did you get married?"

My shoulders tense, just for a moment. "Two days ago."

Sixty-Three
Three days earlier
Riley

I KEEP MY eyes on Dylan while I strip out of my clothes.

He stands in front of me, already free of his, and steps forward, taking one of my hands in his, the other holding a glass jar with a single letter inside it. "You ready?"

I grip his hand tighter and inhale deeply, switching my gaze from his clear blue eyes—the same blue as the lake—to the edge of the cliff. "I don't know."

"We don't have to do this," he murmurs, his finger on my chin forcing me to look at him. "If you're not ready, we can wait… or we don't *ever* have to do this."

"I want to," I whisper, my eyes now trailing down his body, past his board shorts, to his bare feet. "I want to do this *with you*."

OUR STEPS ARE slow as we climb the cliff. He never lets go of my hand. I never let go of my fear. We stop at the top, at the clearing that brings back too many memories. I freeze, wiping the tears off my cheek. Dylan turns to me, his eyes instantly on mine. "Where is it?" he asks, and I point to the tree where Jeremy's plaque sits below.

He leads me over to it, only releasing my hand so he can squat down in front of it. "Your life is your legacy," he reads out loud. I kneel next to him, ignoring the pain from the rocks beneath my weight. "It makes sense." He looks at me. "*You* were his life… and now you're his legacy."

I sit on my heels and wonder why the hell we chose to do this. In theory, coming here seemed like the perfect idea. But now… "What's wrong?" Dylan asks, pulling me from my thoughts.

"It's dumb."

"So tell me anyway."

"I feel like I'm… I don't know… rubbing you in his face."

He chuckles lightly.

I slap his arm. "I told you it was dumb."

He scoots further away from me. "It's not dumb, Ry. I'm laughing because it's exactly how I thought you'd be."

My eyes widen. "Really?"

He nods, a sad smile pulling on his lips. "Remember what I told you, Ry. It doesn't have to be either/or with us."

"I know… but it's different now."

"Why?"

"Because I'm going to be your wife, Dylan. It *has* to be different."

He sighs before looking down at the jar in his hand. "You don't think I thought about all this before asking you to marry me? I know who you are, Ry. I know where your heart lies and I know that a piece of him will always be with you. It doesn't change my love for you, and unless you let it, it won't change the way you love me, either." He leans forward, his hand on my cheek and his lips on mine. When he pulls back, he smiles again. Not the same sad one he showed earlier, but a smile only I'm privy to. "Can you give us a minute? I need to have a man to man chat with the kid."

I hold my breath as I nod and stand up. Then I walk to the edge of the cliff, where I sit, my eyes on the horizon and my heart spread wide. Fragments of it lay in the bottom of the lake and the rest of it—the *majority* of it—is up here *with me.*

There are no words, no amount of unwritten letters to ever describe the emotions that built from the moment we drove up the winding road, to the moment we got out of the car and stripped out of our clothes—to this… the point in my life where I share everything with the two people who have shown me more than enough love to last a lifetime… no matter how short that life was or *will* become.

I DON'T KNOW how much time passes before Dylan's footsteps approach, the loose gravel crunching beneath his feet. "All done," he says, sitting next to me.

I look over at the tree, the plaque and the jar in front of it. "Did you say what you needed to?" I ask him.

Dylan nods, then he shifts until he's sitting behind me, his legs on either side and his arms around my waist. "Are you looking for something?"

It takes a long time for me to come up with a response. "Not looking so much as appreciating."

He kisses my shoulder. "Appreciating what, babe?"

I turn to him, a smile already in place. "My reality. Your calm." I motion to the horizon and place my hand on his chest. "It's all here."

WE SIT ON the cliff, waiting until the sun turns the sky an eerie orange before standing up, our hands locked as we take a few steps back. "You ready, Hudson?"

I nod. "I'm ready, Banks."

We run.

We jump.

We fall.

Deeper.

Harder.

In *love.*

Dylan

WE SPENT AN hour or so surrounded by the warmth of water, her arms and legs around me as we floated in the very place that created her grief and introduced her to heartache. I held her while she laughed, while she cried, and while she loved. And when it was time, she looked up at me, smiled her perfect smile, and said, "I'm ready." And I knew she was.

Really. Truly. *Ready.*

And me? I was ready the moment she said yes.

WE TOWEL DRY and don't bother getting dressed before we start the long drive through the night and into the early hours of the next morning, where we find a hotel, book separate rooms and spend the night apart. Because even though we may not be doing things the "right" way, there are still some traditions she wants to hold on to. And whatever Riley wants, Riley gets. Even if it means spending the entire night texting each other while she's in the next room.

Riley: *I miss you. Come baccccccck.*

Dylan: *You wanted this, remember. But hey… if you're lonely. You know where to find me.*

Riley: *Are you naked?*

Dylan: *Give me two seconds.*

Dylan: *Now I am.*

Riley: *LOL! You work fast.*

Dylan: *Are you coming?*

Riley: *No. I should stick to my plans. Sorry I made you get naked.*

Dylan: *I didn't get naked. I'm eating cake.*

Riley: *Why would you say that then?*

Dylan: *You think I don't know you, babe? You were never going to come in here.*

Riley: *You better be waiting for me tomorrow.*

Dylan: *You better show up.*

Riley: *I love you, Banks.*

Dylan: *I love you more, Hudson.*

Like so many nights in my past, I don't sleep. I can't. But this time—it's not because of the nightmares. It's because of the dreams. I lie awake, dreaming of our future and all the absolute possibilities. I picture her smiles, her laughs, her insecurities and her sadness—and I've never been so sure about anything in my entire life… I want to have all of her. I want to have it all.

I wait until the right time before I get dressed and stand tall in front of the full-length mirror in the corner of the room. It's been a long time since I'd worn my dress blues.

My eyes focus on the Purple Heart medal attached to my jacket. Until today, it'd sat in its box. I never looked at it long enough to study it. I didn't feel worthy of it. Today, I finally do.

✧ ✧ ✧

THE SUN BEATS down, the grass dry beneath my shoes. I stand tall, my head lowered, my trembling fingers causing my hat to shake in my hands. "You nervous, son?" the celebrant asks. He's old, but licensed, and the only one we contacted who was able to do what we wanted in the time we wanted it done.

"Yes. Sir," I tell him, switching my hat in my hands so I can rub my sweaty palms on my pants.

He smiles and nods, then looks around us, rocking on his heels. "Beautiful day out…" he murmurs, and I return his nod. "Not as beautiful as her, though." He points to my left, where Riley's stepping out of a town car, pulling out the train of her dress.

For a second, I regret our choice to make this moment private. It's not right that only myself and the man standing next to me are lucky enough to witness her looking as beautiful as she does. Her veil does nothing to hide the power of her smile when she spots us waiting for her. She thanks the driver, who closes the door after her.

She'd kept the dress a secret, not wanting me to see it until this moment. She picks the train of her dress off the ground and starts toward me. Every step closer, the air becomes harder to breathe through, until she's standing in front of me—her hair loose from its knot, running past her shoulders to the lace of the top of her dress. A string of tiny buttons run down the front, between her breasts down to her waist, where her dress flares out, the fabric spread a few feet behind her and nothing, *nothing*, has ever felt more right, more real, more raw than every single emotion coursing through me.

"Hi," she says through a shaky breath.

I place my hat under my arm and take one of her silk covered hands in mine, her other hand too busy gripping the glass jar. "Riley, you look…" I have no words to complete my thoughts.

"So do you," she says, her head tilted, her smile just for me.

"Are we ready?" the celebrant asks, and we both nod, not once taking our eyes off each other.

And just like all those times I've said goodbye to the people we love, the words he speaks are generic. The feelings are not.

We say "I do" and kiss for the first time as man and wife and a moment later, we're alone. Just me, Riley, and hundreds of fallen veterans, none more important than Davey O'Brien. She's the first to break our stare, looking down and between us at the white granite marker with his name on it. She squats down, her legs hidden behind her dress and places the jar next to his marker. She runs her glove-covered fingers over his name and whispers, "It's good to finally meet you in person."

I laugh, because any other reaction would be too overwhelming. I sit down next to her, my knees raised, my elbows resting on them. "You wanted to be *in* my wedding, so here we are." I take Riley's hand. "Davey O'Brien, I'd like you to meet my *wife,* Riley *Banks.*"

Epilogue

Jeremy,

Sometimes I think about what it'd be like to meet you. Not the kid version of you I met years ago, but the version of you now. Crazy, I know, considering where you are but I can't help it. I imagine walking into a bar or a party, holding Riley's hand and you being there. You stand taller when you see us—or in Riley's case—feel us, because you know as much as I do that it's her presence that has heads turning. Not her looks, or her voice, just her.

I wonder what you'd say to me, or what I would say to you—or if we'd even acknowledge each other. And then I picture Riley... what she'd be like. And I don't think I've ever seen anything as clear as I do her.

She'd be looking down at her feet, all awkward-like and she'd probably let go of my hand... not because she'd be embarrassed to be seen with me, but out of respect for you. And you'd smile at her. The same way I would.

And that's how I know that we'd get along—you and I—there wouldn't be any awkwardness between us because we have one thing in common and, at the end of the day, it's the only thing that matters.

We have Riley.

~

I want you to know that she's okay. For a long time, she wasn't. But she is now and I hope I had something to do with that.

She loved you. She'll continue to love you. And it's because of that, I'll continue to respect you. While she's laying in my arms at night, I'll keep my word to her... for you.

I told her once that I planned on loving her the way you did.

I hope that's enough.

I hope I do you justice, Jeremy.

And I hope I continue to do so—for as long as we both shall live.

This, I promise you.

– Dylan Banks.

✧ ✧ ✧

Dave,

I fell in like in a single text—when you told me to 'carry the fuck on.'

I fell in love when you asked me to take care of your mom's insecurities.

I fell in forever when you—a boy I loved—put his best friend and me <u>first</u>.

You were suffering, and no amount of times I wish upon a single candle that you'd come back, or that you'd have talked to someone—would change where you are now. But it changed the way I live my life. The way we both do.

Time and love is different. Love you can share; you can give to others. Love, in some cases, is even replaceable. Time is not. And I want to thank you for giving us yours. For being my anchor when I needed to be grounded and for being my calm when I had to hide my fear.

Your life was not for nothing, Dave. Every moment, every breath, every tick of the clock, Dylan and I grow as people, and as one. We live, we laugh, we love—not just with each other, but with everyone around us. You taught us that. You <u>gave</u> us that.

I love <u>our</u> boy. And I'll continue to love him. For better or for worse, even when death does us part.

This, I promise you.

Riley Banks.

The End

About the Author

Jay McLean is an avid reader, writer, and, most of all, procrastinator. She writes what she loves to read—books that can make her laugh, make her smile, make her hurt, and make her feel. She currently lives in a forever half-done home in Australia with her fiancé and her two sons.

Follow Jay on Instagram and Twitter @jaymcleanauthor. For more information, visit her blog at www.jaymcleanauthor.com.

84374888R00269

Made in the USA
Middletown, DE
19 August 2018